Praise for Martha Hall Kelly's debut novel,

LILAC GIRLS

"Brilliant . . . a powerful story for readers
everywhere . . . a firsthand glimpse into one
of history's most frightening memories."
—*San Francisco Book Review*

"A profound, unsettling, and thoroughly captivating
look at sisterhood through the dark lens of the
Holocaust . . . the best book I've read all year."
—JAMIE FORD, author of
Hotel on the Corner of Bitter and Sweet

"Harrowing . . . *Lilac* illuminates."
—*People*

"Spanning more than twenty years in the lives of three
women and based on real people and events, Kelly's debut
brings historical facts to startling life. . . . [A] gripping read
that lingers well after the book ends. Offer this to WWII
aficionados, biography fans, and book clubs."
—*Booklist*

"Called 'cinematic' and 'epic' by *Elle* jurors . . .
The lives of three vastly different women caught in the
crosshairs of World War II and its ensuing
fallout . . . are masterfully evoked."
—*Elle*

"*Lilac Girls* is *Gone With the Wind* for World War II. . . . This 473-page tale—centered on three women from separate worlds brought together by the infamous Ravensbrück concentration camp—is a book you cannot put down."

—*The Martha's Vineyard Times*

"The stories of three women intersect when one is sent to Ravensbrück, the notorious Nazi concentration camp for women. . . . A moving story about love and redemption."

—PopSugar

"*Lilac Girls* follows the intertwined threads of these women's lives. . . . Kasia and Herta's storylines are intimate and appalling, and will keep you transfixed."

—*Historical Novels Review*

"Martha Hall Kelly has recovered a great story about a warm-hearted, generous woman who should never should have been forgotten. Kelly fills her book with many details, a deep understanding of the terrible occupation imposed in Poland, and the unfair postwar situation created by what had been Poland's allies."

—*Cosmopolitan Review*

"A remarkable and compelling new novel . . . The author imbues all her women with souls we can recognize on some level; it is lyric but accessible writing of the highest quality. . . . One of the best reads of 2016."

—LIZ SMITH, New York Social Diary

"This is not a book one puts down easily. . . . Kelly's vivid descriptions and careful research will stun even the most informed reader. . . . *Lilac Girls* is truly an incredible novel. . . . Easily the most affecting book I have read about World War II and the Holocaust, and I recommend it to any reader."

—*Bookreporter*

"Spanning more than twenty years in the lives of three women and based on real people and events, Kelly's debut brings historical facts to startling life. . . . [A] gripping read that lingers well after the book ends. Offer this to WWII aficionados, biography fans, and book clubs."

—*Booklist*

LILAC GIRLS

Lilac Girls

A NOVEL

MARTHA HALL
KELLY

BALLANTINE BOOKS

NEW YORK

2017 Ballantine Books Trade Paperback Edition

Copyright © 2016 by Martha Hall Kelly

Reading group guide copyright © 2017 by Penguin Random House LLC

All rights reserved.

Published in the United States by Ballantine Books,
an imprint of Random House, a division of
Penguin Random House LLC, New York.

BALLANTINE and the HOUSE colophon are registered trademarks
of Penguin Random House LLC.

RANDOM HOUSE READER'S CIRCLE & Design is a registered trademark
of Penguin Random House LLC.

Originally published in hardcover in the United States by
Ballantine Books, an imprint of Random House,
a division of Penguin Random House LLC, in 2016.

Photos courtesy of the author.

ISBN 978-1-101-88308-2

Ebook ISBN 978-1-101-88306-8

Printed in the United States of America on acid-free paper

randomhousebooks.com

randomhousereaderscircle.com

16 18 19 17

Maps by Holly Hollon Designs
Book design by Barbara M. Bachman

To my husband, Michael,
who still makes my compact go *click*.

Part One

CHAPTER 1

Caroline

SEPTEMBER 1939

I F I'D KNOWN I WAS ABOUT TO MEET THE MAN WHO'D SHATTER me like bone china on terra-cotta, I would have slept in. Instead, I roused our florist, Mr. Sitwell, from his bed to make a boutonnière. My first consulate gala was no time to stand on ceremony.

I joined the riptide of the great unwashed moving up Fifth Avenue. Men in gray-felted fedoras pushed by me, the morning papers in their attachés bearing the last benign headlines of the decade. There was no storm gathering in the east that day, no portent of things to come. The only ominous sign from the direction of Europe was the scent of slack water wafting off the East River.

As I neared our building at the corner of Fifth Avenue and Forty-ninth Street, I felt Roger watching from the window above. He'd fired people for a lot less than being twenty minutes late, but the one time of year the New York elite opened their wallets and pretended they cared about France was no time for skimpy boutonnières.

I turned at the corner, the morning sun alive in the gold-leaf letters chiseled in the cornerstone: LA MAISON FRANÇAISE. The French Building, home to the French Consulate, stood side by side with the British Empire Building, facing Fifth Avenue, part of Rockefeller

Center, Junior Rockefeller's new complex of granite and limestone. Many foreign consulates kept offices there then, resulting in a great stew of international diplomacy.

"All the way to the back and face the front," said Cuddy, our elevator operator.

Mr. Rockefeller handpicked the elevator boys, screening for manners and good looks. Cuddy was heavy on the looks, though his hair was already salt-and-peppered, his body in a hurry to age.

Cuddy fixed his gaze on the illuminated numbers above the doors. "You got a crowd up there today, Miss Ferriday. Pia said there's two new boats in."

"Delightful," I said.

Cuddy brushed something off the sleeve of his navy-blue uniform jacket. "Another late one tonight?"

For the fastest elevators in the world, ours still took forever. "I'll be gone by five. Gala tonight."

I loved my job. Grandmother Woolsey had started the work tradition in our family, nursing soldiers on the battlefield at Gettysburg. But my volunteer post as head of family assistance for the French Consulate wasn't work really. Loving all things French was simply genetic for me. My father may have been half-Irish, but his heart belonged to France. Plus, Mother had inherited an apartment in Paris, where we spent every August, so I felt at home there.

The elevator stopped. Even through the closed doors, we could hear a terrific din of raised voices. A shiver ran through me.

"Third floor," Cuddy called out. "French Consulate. Watch your—"

Once the doors parted, the noise overpowered all polite speech. The hallway outside our reception area was packed so tightly with people one could scarcely step through. Both the *Normandie* and the *Ile de France*, two of France's premier ocean liners, had landed that morning in New York Harbor, packed with wealthy passengers fleeing the uncertainty in France. Once the all-clear horn signaled and they were free to disembark, the ships' elite streamed to the consulate to iron out visa problems and other sticky issues.

I squeezed into the smoky reception area, past ladies in Paris's newest day dresses who stood gossiping in a lovely cloud of Arpège, the sea spray still in their hair. The people in this group were accustomed to being shadowed by a butler with a crystal ashtray and a champagne flute. Bellboys in scarlet jackets from the *Normandie* went toe-to-toe with their black-jacketed counterparts from the *Ile de France*. I wedged one shoulder through the crowd, toward our secretary's desk at the back of the room, and my chiffon scarf snagged on the clasp of one ravishing creature's pearls. As I worked to extract it, the intercom buzzed unanswered.

Roger.

I pressed on through, felt a pat on my behind, and turned to see a midshipman flash a plaquey smile.

"Gardons nos mains pour nous-mêmes," I said. Let's keep our hands to ourselves.

The boy raised his arm above the crowd and dangled his *Normandie* stateroom key. At least he wasn't the over-sixty type I usually attracted.

I made it to our secretary's desk, where she sat, head down, typing.

"Bonjour, Pia."

Roger's cousin, a sloe-eyed boy of eighteen, was sitting on Pia's desk, legs crossed. He held his cigarette in the air as he picked through a box of chocolates, Pia's favorite breakfast. My inbox on her desk was already stacked with case folders.

"Vraiment? What is so good about it?" she said, not lifting her head.

Pia was much more than a secretary. We all wore many hats, and hers included signing in new clients and establishing a folder for each, typing up Roger's considerable correspondence, and deciphering the massive flood of daily Morse-code pulses that was the lifeblood of our office.

"Why is it so hot in here?" I said. "The phone is ringing, Pia."

She plucked a chocolate from the box. "It keeps doing that."

Pia attracted beaux as if she emitted a frequency only males could detect. She was attractive in a feral way, but I suspected her popularity was due in part to her tight sweaters.

"Can you take some of my cases today, Pia?"

"Roger says I can't leave this chair." She broke the shell of the chocolate's underside with her manicured thumb, stalking the strawberry crèmes. "He also wants to see you right away, but I think the woman on the sofa slept in the hallway last night." Pia flapped one half of a one-hundred-dollar bill at me. "And the fatty with the dogs says he'll give you the other half if you take him first." She nodded toward the well-fed older couple near my office door, each holding a brace of gray-muzzled dachshunds.

Like Pia's, my job description was wide-ranging. It included attending to the needs of French citizens here in New York—often families fallen on hard times—and overseeing my French Families Fund, a charity effort through which I sent comfort boxes to French orphans overseas. I'd just retired from an almost two-decade-long stint on Broadway, and this felt easy by comparison. It certainly involved less unpacking of trunks.

My boss, Roger Fortier, appeared in his office doorway.

"Caroline, I need you *now*. Bonnet's canceled."

"You can't be serious, Roger." The news came like a punch. I'd secured the French foreign minister as our gala keynote speaker months before.

"It's not easy being the French foreign minister right now," he called over his shoulder as he went back inside.

I stepped into my office and flipped through the Wheeldex on my desk. Was Mother's Buddhist-monk friend Ajahn Chah free that night?

"*Caroline*—" Roger called. I grabbed my Wheeldex and hurried to his office, avoiding the couple with the dachshunds, who were trying their best to look tragic.

"Why were you late this morning?" Roger asked. "Pia's been here for two hours already."

As consul general, Roger Fortier ruled from the corner suite with its commanding view of Rockefeller Plaza and the Promenade Cafe. Normally the famous skating rink occupied that sunken spot, but the rink was closed for the summer, the space now filled with café tables and tuxedoed waiters rushing about with aprons to their ankles. Beyond, Paul Manship's massive golden Prometheus fell to earth, holding his stolen fire aloft. Behind it, the RCA Building shot up seventy floors into the sapphire sky. Roger had a lot in common with the imposing male figure of Wisdom chiseled above the building's entrance. The furrowed brow. The beard. The angry eyes.

"I stopped for Bonnet's boutonnière—"

"Oh, that's worth keeping half of France waiting." Roger bit into a doughnut, and powdered sugar cascaded down his beard. Despite what might kindly be called a husky figure, he was never at a loss for female companions.

His desk was heaped with folders, security documents, and dossiers on missing French citizens. According to the *French Consulate Handbook*, his job was "to assist French nationals in New York, in the event of theft, serious illness, or arrest and with issues related to birth certificates, adoption, and lost or stolen documents; to plan visits of French officials and fellow diplomats; and to assist with political difficulties and natural disasters." The troubles in Europe provided plenty of work for us in all those categories, if you counted Hitler as a natural disaster.

"I have cases to get back to, Roger—"

He sent a manila folder skidding across the polished conference table. "Not only do we have no speaker; I was up half the night rewriting Bonnet's speech. Had to sidestep Roosevelt letting France buy American planes."

"France should be able to buy all the planes they want."

"We're raising money here, Caroline. It's not the time to annoy the isolationists. Especially the rich ones."

"They don't support France anyway."

"We don't need any more bad press. Is the U.S. too cozy with France? Will that push Germany and Russia closer? I can barely finish a third course without being interrupted by a reporter. And we can't mention the Rockefellers . . . Don't want another call from Junior. Guess that'll happen anyway now that Bonnet canceled."

"It's a disaster, Roger."

"May need to scrap the whole thing." Roger raked his long fingers through his hair, digging fresh trenches through the Brylcreem.

"Refund forty thousand dollars? What about the French Families Fund? I'm already operating on fumes. Plus, we've paid for ten pounds of Waldorf salad—"

"They call that salad?" Roger flipped through his contact cards, half of them illegible and littered with cross-outs. "It's *pathétique* . . . just chopped apples and celery. And those soggy *walnuts* . . ."

I scoured my Wheeldex in search of celebrity candidates. Mother and I knew Julia Marlowe, the famous actress, but she was touring Europe. "How about Peter Patout? Mother's people have used him."

"The architect?"

"Of the whole World's Fair. They have that seven-foot robot."

"Boring," he said, slapping his silver letter opener against his palm.

I flipped to the *L*'s. "How about Captain Lehude?"

"Of the *Normandie*? Are you serious? He's paid to be dull."

"You can't just discount every suggestion out of hand, Roger. How about Paul Rodierre? Betty says everyone's talking about him."

Roger pursed his lips, always a good sign. "The actor? I saw his show. He's good. Tall and attractive, if you go for that look. Fast metabolism, of course."

"At least we know he can memorize a script."

"He's a bit of a loose cannon. And married too, so don't get any ideas."

"I'm through with men, Roger," I said. At thirty-seven, I'd resigned myself to singledom.

"Not sure Rodierre'll do it. See who you can get, but make sure they stick to the script. No Roosevelt—"

"No Rockefellers," I finished.

Between cases, I called around to various last-minute possibilities, ending up with one option, Paul Rodierre. He was in New York appearing in an American musical revue at the Broadhurst Theatre, *The Streets of Paris*, Carmen Miranda's cyclonic Broadway debut.

I phoned the William Morris Agency and was told they'd check and call me back. Ten minutes later, M. Rodierre's agent told me the theater was dark that night and that, though his client did not own evening clothes, he was deeply honored by our request to host the gala that evening. He'd meet me at the Waldorf to discuss details. Our apartment on East Fiftieth Street was a stone's throw from the Waldorf, so I rushed there to change into Mother's black Chanel dress.

I found M. Rodierre seated at a café table in the Waldorf's Peacock Alley bar adjacent to the lobby as the two-ton bronze clock sounded its lovely Westminster Cathedral chime on the half hour. Gala guests in their finest filtered in, headed for the Grand Ballroom upstairs.

"M. Rodierre?" I said.

Roger was right about the attractive part. The first thing a person noticed about Paul Rodierre, after the initial jolt of his physical beauty, was the remarkable smile.

"How can I thank you for doing this so last minute, Monsieur?"

He unfolded himself from his chair, presenting a build better suited to rowing crew on the Charles than playing Broadway. He attempted to kiss my cheek, but I extended my hand to him, and he shook it. It was nice to meet a man my height.

"My pleasure," he said.

His attire was the issue: green trousers, an aubergine velvet sports jacket, brown suede shoes, and worst of all, a black shirt. Only priests and fascists wore black shirts. And gangsters, of course.

"Do you want to change?" I resisted the urge to tidy his hair, which was long enough to pull back with a rubber band. "Shave perhaps?" According to his agent, M. Rodierre was a guest at the hotel, so his razor sat just a few stories overhead.

"This is what I wear," he said with a shrug. Typical actor. Why hadn't I known better? The parade of guests en route to the ballroom was growing, the women stunning in their finery, every man in tails and patent leather oxfords or calf opera pumps.

"This is my first gala," I said. "The consulate's one night to raise money. It's white tie." Would he fit into Father's old tux? The inseam would be right, but it would be much too tight in the shoulders.

"Are you always this, well, energized, Miss Ferriday?"

"Well, here in New York, individuality is not always appreciated." I handed him the stapled sheets. "I'm sure you're eager to see the script."

He handed it back. "No, *merci.*"

I pushed it back into his hands. "But the consul general himself wrote it."

"Tell me again why I'm doing this?"

"It's to benefit displaced French citizens all year and my French Families Fund. We help orphans back in France whose parents have been lost for any number of reasons. With all the uncertainty abroad, we're one reliable source of clothes and food. Plus, the Rockefellers will be there tonight."

He paged through the speech. "They could write a check and avoid this whole thing."

"They're among our kindest donors, but please don't refer to them. Or President Roosevelt. Or the planes the U.S. sold France. Some of our guests tonight love France, of course, but would rather stay out of a war for now. Roger wants to avoid controversy."

"Dancing around things never feels authentic. The audience feels that."

"Can you just stick to the script, Monsieur?"

"Worrying can lead to heart failure, Miss Ferriday."

I pulled the pin from the lily of the valley. "Here—a boutonnière for the guest of honor."

"*Muguet?*" M. Rodierre said. "Where did you find that this time of year?"

"You can get anything in New York. Our florist forces it from pips."

I rested my palm against his lapel and dug the pin deep into the French velvet. Was that lovely fragrance from him or the flowers? Why didn't American men smell like this, of tuberose and wood musk and—

"You know lily of the valley is poisonous, right?" M. Rodierre said.

"So don't eat it. At least not until you've finished speaking. Or if the crowd turns on you."

He laughed, causing me to step back. Such a genuine laugh, something rarely found in polite society, especially where *my* jokes were concerned.

I escorted M. Rodierre backstage and stood awed by the enormity of the stage, twice the size of any I'd stood upon on Broadway. We looked out over the ballroom to the sea of tables lit by candlelight, like flowery ships in the darkness. Though dimmed, the Waterford crystal chandelier and its six satellites shimmered.

"This stage is enormous," I said. "Can you carry it?"

M. Rodierre turned to me. "I do this for a living, Miss Ferriday."

Fearing I'd only antagonize him further, I left M. Rodierre and the script backstage, trying to dismiss my brown-suede-shoe fixation. I hurried to the ballroom to see if Pia had executed my seating chart, more detailed and dangerous than a Luftwaffe flight plan. I saw she'd simply tossed several cards onto the six Rockefeller tables, so I rearranged them and took my place close to the stage between the kitchen and the head table. Three stories of red-draped boxes rose up around the vast room, each with its own dinner table. All seventeen hundred seats would be filled, a lot of unhappy people if all didn't go well.

The guests assembled and took their seats, an ocean of white ties, old mine diamonds, and enough rue du Faubourg Saint-Honoré gowns to clean out most of Paris's best shops. The girdles alone would ensure both Bergdorf and Goodman reached their third-quarter sales goals.

A row of journalists collected alongside me, pulling their pencils out from behind their ears. The headwaiter stood poised at my elbow, awaiting the cue to serve. Elsa Maxwell entered the room—gossipmonger, professional party hostess, and self-promoter *ne plus ultra*. Would she remove her gloves to write terrible things about this night in her column or just memorize the horror of it all?

The tables were almost full when Mrs. Cornelius Vanderbilt, known to Roger as "Her Grace," arrived, her four-story Cartier diamond necklace ablaze at her chest. I gave the signal to serve as Mrs. Vanderbilt's bottom made contact with her seat cushion, her white fox stole, complete with head and feet, draped over her chair back. The lights dimmed, and Roger lumbered to the spotlighted podium to heartfelt applause. I'd never been this nervous when I was the one onstage.

"*Mesdames et Messieurs,* Foreign Minister Bonnet sends his sincerest apologies, but he cannot be here tonight." The crowd buzzed, not sure how to react to disappointment. Did one ask for one's money refunded by mail? Call Washington?

Roger held up one hand. "But we have convinced another Frenchman to speak tonight. Though not appointed to a government role, he is a man cast in one of the best roles on Broadway."

The guests whispered to one another. There is nothing like a surprise, provided it's a good one.

"Please allow me to welcome M. Paul Rodierre."

M. Rodierre bypassed the podium and headed for center stage. What was he doing? The spotlight cast around the stage for a few moments, trying to locate him. Roger took his seat at the head table, next to Mrs. Vanderbilt. I stood nearby, but outside of strangling range.

"It's my great pleasure to be here tonight," M. Rodierre said, once the spotlight found him. "I am terribly sorry M. Bonnet could not make it."

Even sans microphone, M. Rodierre's voice filled the room. He practically glowed in the spotlight.

"I am a poor replacement for such a distinguished guest. I hope it wasn't trouble with his plane. I'm sure President Roosevelt will be happy to send him a new one if it was."

A swell of nervous laughter rolled around the room. I didn't have to look at the journalists to know they were scribbling. Roger, skilled in the art of the tête-à-tête, managed to speak with Mrs. Vanderbilt and send daggers my way at the same time.

"True, I cannot talk to you about politics," M. Rodierre continued.

"Thank God!" someone shouted from a back table. The crowd laughed again, louder this time.

"But I can talk to you about the America I know, a place that surprises me every day. A place where open-minded people embrace not only French theater and books and cinema and fashion but French people as well, despite our faults."

"Shit," said the reporter next to me to his broken pencil. I handed him mine.

"Every day I see people help others. Americans inspired by Mrs. Roosevelt, who reaches her hand across the Atlantic to help French children. Americans like Miss Caroline Ferriday, who works every day to help French families here in America and keeps French orphans clothed."

Roger and Mrs. Vanderbilt looked my way. The spotlight found me, standing at the wall, and the familiar light blinded me. Her

Grace clapped, and the crowd followed. I waved until the light, mercifully quickly, whipped back to the stage, leaving me in cool darkness. I didn't miss the Broadway stage really, but it was good to feel the warmth of the spotlight on my skin again.

"This is an America not afraid to sell planes to the people who stood beside them in the trenches of the Great War. An America not afraid to help keep Hitler from the streets of Paris. An America not afraid of standing shoulder to shoulder again with us if that terrible time does come . . ."

I watched, only able to look away for a few peeks at the crowd. They were engrossed and certainly not focused on his shoes. Half an hour passed in an instant, and I held my breath as M. Rodierre took his bow. The applause started small but rose in waves like a tremendous rainstorm pelting the roof. A teary-eyed Elsa Maxwell used a hotel napkin to dry her eyes, and by the time the audience rose to their feet and belted out "La Marseillaise," I was glad Bonnet didn't have to follow that performance. Even the staff sang, hands over their hearts.

As the lights came up, Roger looked relieved and greeted the crush of well-wishers that lingered near the head table. When the evening wound down, he left for the Rainbow Room with a gaggle of our best donors and a few Rockettes, the only women in New York who made me look short.

M. Rodierre touched my shoulder as we left the dining room. "I know a place over on the Hudson with great wine."

"I need to get home," I said, though I hadn't eaten a thing. Warm bread and buttery escargot came to mind, but it was never smart to be seen out alone with a married man. "Not tonight, Monsieur, but thank you." I could be home in minutes, to a cold apartment and the leftover Waldorf salad.

"You'll make me eat alone after our triumph?" M. Rodierre said.

Why not go? My set ate at only certain restaurants, which you could count on one hand, all within a four-block radius of the Waldorf, nowhere near the Hudson. What harm could one dinner do?

We took a cab to Le Grenier, a lovely bistro on the West Side. The French ocean liners sailed up the Hudson River and docked at Fifty-first Street, so some of New York's best little places popped up near there, like chanterelles after a good rain. Le Grenier lived in the shadow of the SS *Normandie,* in the attic of a former harbormaster's building. When we exited the cab, the great ship rose high above us, deck bright with spotlights, four floors of portholes aglow. A welder at her bow sent apricot sparks into the night sky as deckhands lowered a spotlight down her side to painters on a scaffold. She made me feel small standing there, below that great, black prow, her three red smokestacks, each bigger than any of the warehouse buildings that extended down the pier. Salt hung in the end-of-summer air as Atlantic seawater met Hudson River fresh.

The tables at Le Grenier were packed with a nice enough looking crowd, mostly middle-class types, including a reporter from the gala and what looked like ocean-liner passengers happy to be on terra firma. We chose a tight, shellacked wooden booth, built like something from the inside of a ship, where every inch counts. Le Grenier's maître d', M. Bernard, fawned over M. Rodierre, told him he'd seen *The Streets of Paris* three times, and shared in great detail the specifics of his own Hoboken Community Theater career.

M. Bernard turned to me. "And you, Mademoiselle. Haven't I seen you on the stage with Miss Helen Hayes?"

"An actress?" M. Rodierre said with a smile.

At close range, that smile was unsafe. I had to keep my wits about me, since Frenchmen were my Achilles' heel. In fact, if Achilles had been French, I probably would have carried him around until his tendon healed.

M. Bernard continued. "I thought the reviews were unfair—"

"We'll order," I said.

"One used the word 'stiffish,' I believe—"

"We'll have the escargot, Monsieur. Light on the cream, please—"

"And what was it the *Times* said about *Twelfth Night?* 'Miss Ferriday *sufficed* as Olivia'? Harsh, I thought—"

"—And no garlic. Undercook them, please, so they are not too tough."

"Would you like them to crawl to the table, Mademoiselle?" M. Bernard scratched down our order and headed for the kitchen.

M. Rodierre studied the champagne list, lingering over the details. "An actress, eh? I'd never have guessed." There was something appealing about his unkempt look, like a *potager* in need of weeding.

"The consulate suits me better. Mother's known Roger for years, and when he suggested I help him, I couldn't resist."

M. Bernard placed a basket of bread on our table, lingering a moment to gaze at M. Rodierre, as if memorizing him.

"Hope I'm not running off a boyfriend tonight," Paul said. He reached for the breadbasket as I did, and my hand brushed his, warm and soft. I darted my hand back to my lap.

"I'm too busy for all that. You know New York—parties and all. Exhausting, really."

"Never see you at Sardi's." He pulled apart the loaf, steam rising to the light.

"Oh, I work a lot."

"I have a feeling you don't work for the money."

"It's an unsalaried position, if that's what you mean, but that's not a question asked in polite society, Monsieur."

"Can we dispense with the 'Monsieur'? Makes me feel ancient."

"First names? We've only just met."

"It's 1939."

"Manhattan society is like a solar system with its own order. A single woman dining with a married man is enough to throw planets out of alignment."

"No one will see us here," Paul said, pointing out a champagne on the list to M. Bernard.

"Tell that to Miss Evelyn Shimmerhorn over there in the back booth."

"Are you ruined?" he said with a certain type of kindness seldom found in achingly beautiful men. Maybe the black shirt was a good choice for him after all.

"Evelyn won't talk. She's having a child, poorly timed, dear thing."

"Children. They complicate everything, don't they? No place for that in an actor's life."

Another selfish actor.

"How does your father earn your place in this solar system?"

Paul was asking a lot of questions for a new acquaintance.

"*Earned*, actually. He was in dry goods."

"Where?"

M. Bernard slid a silver bucket with handles like gypsy's earrings onto the table, the emerald-green throat of the champagne bottle lounging against one side.

"Partnered with James Harper Poor."

"Of Poor Brothers? Been to his house in East Hampton. He's not exactly poor. Do you visit France often?"

"Paris every year. Mother inherited an apartment . . . on rue Chauveau Lagarde."

M. Bernard eased the cork from the champagne with a satisfying sound, more thud than pop. He tipped the golden liquid into my glass, and the bubbles rose to the rim, almost overflowed, then settled at the perfect level. An expert pour.

"My wife, Rena, has a little shop near there called Les Jolies Choses. Have you seen it?"

I sipped my champagne, the bubbles teasing my lips.

Paul slid her picture from his wallet. Rena was younger than I had imagined and wore her dark hair in a china doll haircut. She was smiling, eyes open wide, as if sharing some delicious little secret. Rena was precious and perhaps my complete opposite. I imagined Rena's to be the type of chic little place that helped women put themselves together in that famous French way—nothing too coordinated, with just the right amount of wrong.

"No, I don't know it," I said. I handed the picture back. "She's lovely, though."

I finished the champagne in my glass.

Paul shrugged. "Too young for me, of course, but—" He looked at the photo a few moments as if seeing it for the first time, head tilted to one side, before slipping it back into his wallet. "We don't see much of each other."

I fluttered at the thought and then settled, weighted by the realization that even if Paul were available my forceful nature would root out and extinguish any spark of romance.

The radio in the kitchen blared scratchy Edith Piaf.

Paul lifted the bottle from the bucket and tipped more champagne into my glass. It effervesced, riotous bubbles tumbling over the glass's edge. I glanced at him. We both knew what that meant, of course. The tradition. Anyone who's spent any time at all in France knows it. Had he overpoured on purpose?

Without hesitation, Paul tapped his finger to the spilled champagne along the base of my glass, reached across to me, and dabbed the cool liquid behind my left ear. I almost jumped at his touch, then waited as he brushed my hair aside and touched behind my right ear, his finger lingering there a moment. He then anointed himself behind each ear, smiling.

Why did I suddenly feel warm all over?

"Does Rena ever visit?" I asked. I tried to rub a tea stain off my hand only to find it was an age spot. Delightful.

"Not yet. She has no interest in theater. Hasn't even come over here to see *The Streets of Paris* yet, but I don't know if I can stay. Hitler has everyone on edge back home."

Somewhere in the kitchen, two men argued. Where was our escargot? Had they sent to Perpignan for the snails?

"At least France has the Maginot Line," I said.

"The Maginot Line? Please. A concrete wall and some observation posts? That's only a gauntlet slap to Hitler."

"It's fifteen miles wide."

"Nothing will deter Hitler if he wants something," Paul said.

There was a full-blown ruckus in the kitchen. No wonder our entrée had not arrived. The cook, mercurial artiste no doubt, was having a fit about something.

M. Bernard emerged from the kitchen. The portholed kitchen door swung closed behind him, flapped open and shut a few times, and then stood still. He walked to the center of the dining room. Had he been crying?

"*Excusez-moi*, ladies and gentlemen."

Someone tapped a glass with a spoon, and the room quieted.

"I have just heard from a reliable source . . ." M. Bernard took a breath, his chest expanding like leather fireplace bellows. "We have it on good authority that . . ."

He paused, overcome for a moment, then went on.

"Adolf Hitler has invaded Poland."

"My God," Paul said.

We stared at each other as the room erupted with excited exchanges, a racket of speculation and dread. The reporter from the gala stood, tossed some crumpled dollars on the table, grabbed his fedora, and bounded out.

In the hubbub that followed his announcement, M. Bernard's final words were almost lost.

"May God help us all."

CHAPTER 2

Kasia

1939

IT REALLY WAS PIETRIK BAKOSKI'S IDEA TO GO UP TO THE BLUFF at Deer Meadow to see the refugees. Just want to set straight the record. Matka never did believe me about that.

Hitler had declared war on Poland on September 1, but his soldiers took their time getting to Lublin. I was glad, for I didn't want anything to change. Lublin was perfect as it was. We heard radio addresses from Berlin about new rules, and some bombs fell on the outskirts of town, but nothing else. The Germans concentrated on Warsaw, and as troops closed in there, refugees by the thousands fled down to us in Lublin. Families came in droves, traveling southeast one hundred miles, and slept in the potato fields below town.

Before the war, nothing exciting ever happened in Lublin, so we appreciated a good sunrise, sometimes more than a picture at the cinema. We'd reached the summit overlooking the meadow on the morning of September 8 just before dawn and could make out thousands of people below us in the fields, dreaming in the dark. I lay between my two best friends, Nadia Watroba and Pietrik Bakoski, watching it all from a flattened bowl of straw, still warm where a mother deer had slept with her fawns. The deer were gone by then—early risers. This they had in common with Hitler.

As dawn suddenly breached the horizon, the breath caught in my throat, the kind of gasp that can surprise you when you see something so beautiful it hurts, such as a baby anything or fresh cream running over oatmeal or Pietrik Bakoski's profile in dawn's first light. His profile, 98 percent perfect, was especially nice drenched in dawn, like something off a ten-*zlotych* coin. At that moment, Pietrik looked the way all boys do upon waking, before they've washed up: his hair, the color of fresh butter, matted on the side where he'd slept.

Nadia's profile was also almost perfect, as was to be expected of a girl with her delicate features. The only thing holding her back from 100 percent was the purple bruise on her forehead, a souvenir from the incident at school, less of a goose egg now, but still there. She was wearing the cashmere sweater she let me pet whenever I wished, the color of unripe cantaloupe.

It was hard to understand how such a sad situation could lead to the prettiest scene. The refugees had fashioned a most elaborate tent city out of bed linens and blankets. As the sun rose, like an x-ray it allowed us to see through the flowered sheets of one tent to the shadows of people inside, dressing to meet the day.

A mother in city clothes flapped open her sheet door and crept out, holding the hand of a child dressed in pajamas and felt boots. They poked the ground with sticks, digging for potatoes.

Lublin rose beyond them in the distance, like a fairy-tale city, scattered with old red-roofed pastel buildings as if a giant had shaken them in a cup and tossed them on the rolling hills. Farther west was where our little airport and a complex of factories once sat, but the Nazis had already bombed that. It was the first thing they hit, but at least no Germans had marched into town yet.

"Do you think the British will help us?" Nadia said. "The French?"

Pietrik scanned the horizon. "Maybe." He ripped grass from the ground and flung it in the air. "Good day for flying. They better hurry."

A string of spotted cows sashayed down the hill toward the tents to graze, bells tanging, led by kerchiefed milk women. One cow lifted her tail and scattered a troop of lumps behind her, which those following stepped around. Each woman carried a tall silver milk can against one shoulder.

I squinted to find our school, St. Monica's Catholic School for Girls, a tangerine flag swaying from its bell tower. It was a place with floors so polished we wore satin slippers inside. A place of rigorous lessons, daily mass, and strict teachers. Not that any of them had helped Nadia when she needed it most, except for Mrs. Mikelsky, our favorite math teacher, of course.

"Look," Nadia said. "The women are coming with the cows but no sheep. The sheep are always out by now."

Nadia noticed things. Though only two months older than me—already seventeen—she seemed more mature somehow. Pietrik looked past me at Nadia as if seeing her for the first time. All the boys liked her, with her perfect cartwheel, flawless Maureen O'Sullivan complexion, and thick blond braid. Maybe I was not as beautiful and a miserable athlete, but I was once voted Best Legs *and* Best Dancer in my *gimnazjum* class in an informal poll, a first, at our school anyway.

"You notice everything, Nadia," Pietrik said.

Nadia smiled at him. "Not really. Maybe we should go down there and help dig potatoes? You're good with a shovel, Pietrik."

She was flirting with him? A direct violation of my number-one rule: *Girlfriends first!* Pietrik pulled *my* wreath from the river on Midsummer Eve, gave me a silver cross necklace. Did traditions mean nothing anymore?

Maybe Pietrik was falling for her? It made sense. Earlier that month the Girl Guides had been selling dances with local boys for charity, and Pietrik's little sister Luiza told me Nadia bought *all ten* of Pietrik's dances. Then there was that awful dustup outside the school gates. Nadia and I were leaving school when street boys started throwing rocks at Nadia and calling her names because her grandfather was Jewish. Pietrik had been so quick to rescue her.

People throwing rocks at Jews was not something unusual to see, but it was unusual for it to happen to Nadia. I'd never known she was part Jewish before that. We attended Catholic school, and she'd memorized more prayers than I had. But everyone knew once our German teacher, Herr Speck, made us chart our ancestors and told the whole class.

I'd tried to pull Nadia away that day as the boys hurled rocks, but she'd stood firm. Mrs. Mikelsky, pregnant with her first child, had rushed out, wrapped her arms around Nadia, and shouted at the bullies to stop or she'd call the police. Mrs. Mikelsky was every girl's favorite teacher, our North Star, since we all wanted to be like her, beautiful and smart and funny. She defended her girls like a mother lion and gave us *krowki*, toffee candies, for perfect math tests, which I never failed to get.

Pietrik, who'd come to walk us home, chased the street boys away waving a shovel in the air but ended up with a little chip off his front tooth, which in no way damaged his smile and in fact only made it sweeter.

I was startled from my daydream by a peculiar sound, like the buzz of crickets all around us. It grew louder until the vibration soaked the ground beneath us.

Planes!

They zoomed over us, flying so low they turned the grass inside out, light bouncing off their silver bellies. Three abreast, they banked right, leaving an oily smell in their wake, and headed for the city, their gray shadows gliding across the fields below. I counted twelve altogether.

"They look like the planes from *King Kong*," I said.

"Those were *biplanes*, Kasia," Pietrik said. "Curtiss Helldivers. These are *German* dive bombers."

"Maybe they're Polish."

"They're not Polish. You can tell by the white crosses under the wings."

"Do they have bombs?" Nadia asked, more intrigued than afraid. She was never afraid.

"They already got the airport," Pietrik said. "What else can they bomb? We have no ammunition depot."

The planes circled the city and then flew west, one behind the other. The first dove with a terrible screech and dropped a bomb in the middle of town, right where Krakowskie Przedmieście, our main street, wound by the town's finest buildings.

Pietrik stood. "Jezu Chryste, no!"

A great thud shook the ground, and black and gray plumes rose from where the bomb had fallen. The planes circled the city again and this time dropped their bombs near Crown Court, our town hall. My sister Zuzanna, a brand-new doctor, volunteered at the clinic there some days. What about my mother? Please, God, take me directly to heaven if anything happens to my mother, I thought. Was Papa at the postal center?

The planes carouseled around the city and then flew toward us. We dove to the grass as they passed over us again, Pietrik on top of Nadia and me, so close I felt his heart beating through his shirt against my back.

Two planes circled back as if they'd forgotten something.

"We need to——" Pietrik began, but before we could move, both planes dove and flew closer to the ground, across the field below. In an instant, we heard their guns firing. They shot at the milk women. Some of the bullets hit the field and sent puffs of dust up, but others hit the women, sending them to the ground, their milk spilling onto the grass. A cow cried out as she fell, and the pup-pup-pup of bullets punched through the metal milk cans.

The refugees in the fields dropped their potatoes and scattered, but bullets found some as they ran. I ducked as the last two planes flew back over us, leaving the field below strewn with bodies of men and women and cows. The cows that could still run bucked about as if half-mad.

I tore down the hill, Nadia and Pietrik behind me, through the forest along pine-needled paths, toward home. Were my parents hurt? Zuzanna? With only two ambulances, she'd be at work all night.

We slowed at the potato field, for it was impossible not to stare. I walked a milk can's length away from a woman Zuzanna's age, potatoes scattered around her. She lay on her back across hoed rows of dirt, left hand across her chest, shoulder steeped in blood, face splattered with it too. A girl knelt next to her.

"Sister," the girl said, taking her hand, "you need to get up."

"Compress the wound with two hands," I told her, but she just looked at me.

A woman wearing a chenille robe came and knelt near them. She pulled a length of amber rubber from her black doctor's bag.

Nadia pulled me away. "Come. The planes might come back."

In the city, people were running everywhere, crying and yelling to one another, evacuating by bicycle, horse, truck, cart, and on foot.

As we neared my street, Pietrik took Nadia's hand. "You're almost home, Kasia. I'll take Nadia."

"What about me?" I called after them, but they were already off, down the cobblestones toward Nadia's mother's apartment.

Pietrik had made his choice.

I headed for the tunnel, which ran under the ancient Cracow Gate, a soaring brick tower with a bell-shaped spire, my favorite Lublin landmark, once the only entrance to the whole city. The bombs had cracked the tower down the side, but it was still standing.

My math teacher, Mrs. Mikelsky, and her husband, who lived close to me, cycled past, headed in the opposite direction. A very pregnant Mrs. Mikelsky turned as she rode.

"Your mother is frantic looking for you, Kasia," she said.

"Where are you going?" I called after them.

"To my sister's," Mr. Mikelsky shouted back.

"Get home to your mother!" Mrs. Mikelsky shouted over her shoulder.

They cycled on, disappeared into the crowd, and I continued toward home.

Please, God, let Matka be unhurt.

Once I arrived at our block, every cell in my body tingled with relief to see that our pink sliver of a building still stood. The house across the street had not been so lucky. It was razed to rubble, now just a mess of concrete, plaster walls, and twisted iron beds strewn across our road. I scrambled over the wreckage and, as I drew closer, saw one of Matka's curtains blow gently out the window in the breeze. That's when I realized every one of our windows had been blown out by the bombs, blackout paper and all.

There was no need to fetch the apartment key from behind the loose brick, for the door was wide open. I found Matka and Zuzanna in the kitchen near Matka's drawing table, gathering fallen paintbrushes scattered about the floor, the smell of spilled turpentine in the air. Psina, our pet chicken, followed behind them. Thank heavens Psina was not hurt, for she was more like our family dog than a hen.

"Where have you *been*?" Matka said, her face white as the drawing paper in her hand.

"Up at Deer Meadow," I said. "It was Pietrik's id—"

Zuzanna stood, holding a pile of glass shards in a cup, her white doctor's coat gray with ash. It had taken her six long years to earn that coat. Her suitcase stood next to the door. No doubt she'd been packing to go live at the hospital for her pediatric residency when the bombs had dropped.

"How could you be so stupid?" Zuzanna said.

"Where's Papa?" I said as the two came and brushed bits of concrete from my hair.

"He went out—" Matka began.

Zuzanna grabbed Matka's shoulders. "*Tell* her, Matka."

"He went looking for you," Matka said, about to dissolve into tears.

"He's probably at the postal center," Zuzanna said. "I'll go find him."

"Don't go," I said. "What if the planes come again?" An electric eel of fear punctured my chest. Those poor women lying in the field . . .

"I'm going," Zuzanna said. "I'll be back."

"Let me come too," I said. "They'll need me at the clinic."

"Why do you do such stupid things? Papa's gone because of you." Zuzanna slipped her sweater on and stepped toward the door. "They don't need you at the clinic. All you do is roll bandages anyway. Stay here."

"Don't go," Matka said, but Zuzanna rushed out, always strong, like Papa.

Matka went to the window and bent to pick up shards of glass but gave up because her hands were shaking so badly and came back to me. She smoothed my hair, kissed my forehead, and then held me tight, saying, *Ja cię kocham,* over and over like a skipping record.

I love you.

MATKA AND I SLEPT in her bed that night, both with one eye open, waiting for Papa and Zuzanna to walk in. Psina, more dog than fowl, slept at the foot of our bed, her head tucked beneath one downy wing. She woke with a squawk when Papa did come home, well before dawn. He stood in the bedroom doorway, his tweed jacket powdered with ash. Papa always had a sad face, like that of a bloodhound. Even in his baby pictures, those creases and folds of skin hung down. But that night the light from the kitchen cast a shadow on his face, making him look sadder still.

Matka sat up in bed. "Ade?" She threw back the blanket and ran to him, their silhouettes dark against the light from the kitchen. "Where's Zuzanna?"

"I haven't seen her," Papa said. "When I couldn't find Kasia, I went to the postal center and took my files outside to burn. Information the Germans will want. Names and addresses. Military lists. They've occupied the postal center in Warsaw and cut the telegraph line, so we're next."

"What happened to the staff?" Matka said.

Papa glanced in my direction and did not answer.

"Our best guess is German troops will be here in a week. Chances are they'll come here first."

"Here?" Matka gathered her housecoat around her neck.

"Looking for me. I may be useful to them." Papa smiled, but his eyes stayed dark. "They'll want to use the postal center for their communications."

No one knew the postal center like Papa. He'd run it for as long as I could remember. Did he know secrets? Papa was a patriot. He'd rather die than tell them anything.

"How do they even know where we live?"

Papa looked at Matka as if she were a child. "They've been planning this for years, Halina. If they take me, hopefully they'll need me enough to keep me alive. Give it two days. If you don't hear from me, take the girls and go south."

"The British will help us," Matka said. "The French—"

"No one is *coming*, my love. The mayor is evacuating, taking the police and fire brigade. For now we need to hide what we can."

Papa pulled Matka's jewelry box from the dresser and tossed it on the bed. "First, wash and dry any tin cans. We need to bury anything of value—"

"But we haven't done anything wrong, Ade. Germans are cultured people. Hitler has them under some kind of spell."

Matka's mother had been pure German, her father half-Polish. Even woken from sleep, she was beautiful. Soft but not fragile, a natural blonde.

Papa grabbed her by the arm. "Your cultured people want us gone so they can move in. Don't you see?"

Papa went about the apartment gathering our most valuable possessions in a metal box with a hinged lid: Matka's nursing certificate, their marriage license, a small ruby ring from Matka's family, and an envelope of family pictures.

"Get the bag of millet. We're burying that too."

Matka pulled the canvas bag from under the sink.

"They'll probably do a house-by-house search for Polish soldiers in hiding," Papa said, keeping his voice low. "They've broadcast new rules. Poland no longer exists as a country. No Polish will be spoken. All schools will close. There will be curfews. A pink pass is required to violate them, and we are not allowed weapons or ski boots or any food over our ration limit. Secretly possessing these things is punishable by—" Again Papa looked at me and stopped speaking. "They'll probably just take whatever they want."

Papa pulled his old silver revolver from the dresser drawer. Matka stepped back, away from it.

"Bury that, Ade," she said, her eyes wide.

"We may need it," Papa said.

Matka turned away from him. "Nothing good comes of a gun."

Papa hesitated and then placed the gun in the box. "Bury your Girl Guides uniform, Kasia. The Nazis are targeting scouts—they shot a pack of Boy Scouts in Gdansk."

A chill went through me. I knew not to argue with Papa and placed my prized possessions in tin cans: the wool scarf Pietrik once wore that still smelled like him, the new red corduroy shift dress Matka sewed for me, my Girl Guides uniform shirt and neckerchief, and a picture of Nadia and me riding a cow. Matka wrapped one of her sets of Kolinsky sable-hair paintbrushes, which had been her mother's, and added them to a can. Papa melted wax on the seams of the tin cans.

That night only stars lit our back garden, a patch of dirt surrounded by a few planks of wood held up only by the weeds around them. Papa stepped on the rusty shovel blade to push it into the ground. It cut through hard soil as if it were cake, and he dug a deep hole, like a baby's fresh grave.

We were almost done, but even in near darkness I could tell Matka had kept her engagement ring on her finger, the one her mother had passed on to her when Papa was too poor to buy her one. The ring was like an exquisite flower, with a big center diamond surrounded with deep blue sapphire petals. It glittered like a nervous firefly as Matka's hand moved in the darkness. "The diamond is cushion cut—from the seventeen hundreds when they cut stones to react to candlelight," Matka would say when people admired it. React it did, shimmering, almost alive.

"What about your ring?" Papa asked.

The firefly flew behind her back, protecting itself. "Not that," Matka said.

As children, when crossing the road, Zuzanna and I had always fought over who got to hold Matka's hand that wore that ring. The pretty hand.

"Haven't we buried enough?" I said. "We'll be caught out here."

Standing there arguing in the dark would only attract attention.

"Suit yourself, Halina," Papa said. He flung shovelfuls of dirt into the hole to cover our treasures. I pushed earth into the hole with my hands to make things go faster, and Papa tamped it down smooth. He then counted his steps back to the building so he'd remember where we buried our treasure.

Twelve steps to the door.

ZUZANNA FINALLY CAME HOME with terrible tales of the doctors and nurses working all night to save the wounded. Word was many were still alive trapped under rubble. We lived in fear of hearing the sound of Germans at our front door, our ears to the radio in the kitchen, hoping for the best news but hearing the worst. Poland defended herself, sustaining great losses, but in the end could not match Germany's modern armored divisions and airpower.

I woke Sunday, September 17, to Matka telling Papa what she'd heard on the radio. The Russians had also attacked Poland, from the east. Was there no end to the countries attacking us?

I found my parents in the kitchen peering out the front window. It was a crisp fall morning, a light breeze blowing in through Matka's curtains. As I drew closer to the window, I saw Jewish men in black suits clearing the rubble from in front of our house.

Matka wrapped her arms around me, and once the road was cleared, we watched a parade of German soldiers roll in, like new tenants in a boardinghouse with their mountains of luggage. First came trucks, then soldiers on foot, then more soldiers standing tall and haughty in their tanks. At least Zuzanna did not see this sad sight, for she was already at the hospital that morning.

Matka heated water for Papa's tea as he watched it all. I did my best to keep us all quiet as could be. Maybe if we were silent, they would not bother us? To calm myself I counted the birds crocheted on Matka's curtains. One lark. Two swallows. One magpie. Wasn't the magpie a sign of imminent death? The rumble of a truck grew louder.

I breathed deep to quell the panic inside me. What was coming?

"Out, out!" a man shouted. The terrible clatter of hobnail boots on cobblestones. There were lots of them.

"Stay away from the window, Kasia," Papa said, stepping back himself. He said it in such an offhand way I knew he was scared.

"Should we hide?" Matka whispered. She turned her ring around and closed her hand so the stones hid in her palm.

Papa walked toward the door, and I busied myself with prayer. We heard a good bit of yelling and orders, and soon the truck drove away.

"I think they're leaving," I whispered to Matka.

I jumped as a rap came at our door, and then a man's voice. *"Open up!"*

Matka froze in place and Papa opened the door.

"Adalbert Kuzmerick?" said an SS man, who strode in all puffed up and pleased with himself.

He was two hands taller than Papa, so tall his hat almost hit the top of the door when he entered. He and his underling were dressed in full Sonderdienst uniform, with the black boots and the hat with the horrible skull emblem with two gaping holes for eyes. As he passed, I smelled clove gum on him. He looked well fed too, his chin held so high I could see the blood through a little piece of white paper stuck on his Adam's apple where he'd cut himself shaving. They even bled Nazi red.

"Yes," Papa said, calm as could be.

"Director of the postal center communications?"

Papa nodded.

Two more guards grabbed Papa by the arms and pulled him out without even time for him to look back at us. I tried to follow, but the tall one blocked my way with his nightstick.

Matka ran to the window, eyes wild. "Where are you taking him?"

Suddenly I was cold all over. It was getting harder to breathe.

Another SS man, skinny and shorter than the first, stepped in with a canvas bread bag across his chest.

"Where does your husband keep his work papers?" asked the tall one.

"Not here," Matka said. "Can't you tell me where they're taking him?"

Matka stood, fingers locked at her chest, as the skinny one went about the house opening drawers and stuffing whatever papers we had into his bag.

"Shortwave radio?" the tall one said.

Matka shook her head. "No."

My stomach hurt as I watched the skinny guard fling our cabinet doors wide and toss what little food we had into his bag.

"All provisions are the property of the Reich," the tall one said. "You will be issued ration cards."

Tinned peas, two potatoes, and a sad little cabbage went into the skinny one's bag. Then he grabbed a rolled paper bag that held the last of Matka's coffee.

She reached for it.

"Oh, please—may we keep the coffee? It's all we have."

The tall one turned and looked at Matka for a long second. "Leave it," he said, and his underling tossed it onto the counter.

The men stepped through our three little bedrooms and pulled drawers from bureaus, dumping socks and underclothes on the floor.

"Weapons?" said the tall one as the other searched closets. "Any other food?"

"No," Matka said. I'd never seen her lie before.

He stepped closer to her. "You may have heard that withholding that which is due the Reich is punishable by death."

"I understand," Matka said. "If I could just visit my husband . . ."

We followed the men out to the back garden. The yard, fenced on all sides, suddenly seemed smaller with the SS men standing there. It all looked normal, but the ground where we'd buried our things the week before was still beaten quite flat. It was so obvious something was buried there. I counted the guard's steps as he walked into the yard. *Five . . . six . . . seven . . .* Could they see my knees shaking?

Our chicken, Psina, moved closer to our buried treasure spot, scratching near it, looking for bugs. My God, the shovel was there, leaning against the back of the house, dirt still clinging to the blade. Would they take us to Lublin Castle or just shoot us in the yard and leave us for Papa to find?

"Do you think I'm stupid?" the tall guard said, walking toward the spot.

Eight . . . nine . . .

My respiration shut off.

"Of course not," Matka said.

"Get the shovel," said the tall guard to his underling. "You really thought you'd get away with this?"

"No, please," Matka said. She held on to the St. Mary medal she wore on a chain around her neck. "I am from Osnabrück, actually. You know it?"

The taller guard took the shovel. "Of course I know it. Who hasn't been to the Christmas market there? Have you registered as Volksdeutsche?"

Volksdeutsche was the German term for ethnic Germans living in countries other than Germany. The Nazis pressured Polish citizens with German heritage like Matka to register as Volksdeutsche. Once registered, they got extra food, better jobs, and property confiscated from Jews and non-German Poles. Matka would never accept Volksdeutsche status, since that showed allegiance to Germany, but this put her at risk, because she was going against the Reich.

"No, but I am mostly German. My father was only part Polish."

Psina scratched the soil around the smooth spot and pecked something there.

"If you were German, you'd not be breaking rules, would you? Withholding what is due the Reich?"

Matka touched his arm. "It is hard dealing with all of this. Can you not understand? Imagine your own family."

"My own family would have handed what they had to the Reich."

The SS man took the shovel and continued toward the spot.

Ten... eleven...

"I'm so terribly sorry," Matka said, following him.

The man ignored Matka and took one more step.

Twelve.

How far would he dig before he hit the box?

"Please, give us another chance," Matka said. "The rules are so new."

The guard turned, leaned on the shovel, and gave Matka a thorough looking over. He smiled, and I could see his teeth clearly, like little chewing gum tablets.

He leaned closer to her and lowered his voice. "Maybe you know the rule about curfew?"

"Yes," Matka said, a tiny crease between her brows. She shifted in her shoes.

"That is a rule you can break." The SS man took Matka's medal between his thumb and forefinger and rubbed it, watching her the whole time.

"One needs a pink pass to violate curfew," Matka said.

"I have them here in my pocket." He dropped the medal and put his hand over his heart.

"I don't understand," Matka said.

"I think you do."

"Are you saying you will let this go if I come visit you?"

"If that is what you heard—"

"The Germans I know are cultured people. I can't imagine you would ask a mother of two to do that."

The man cocked his head to one side, bit his lip, and picked up the shovel. "I am sorry you feel that way."

"Wait," Matka said.

The man lifted the shovel into the air above his head.

"My God, no!" Matka cried. She reached for his arm, but it was too late. Once the shovel was in the air, there was no stopping it.

CHAPTER 3

Herta

1939

AT MIDNIGHT, FATHER AND I WALKED SIX BLOCKS FROM OUR basement apartment to a nicer part of Düsseldorf, to the white stone townhomes where servants swept the streets and pinched back geraniums in window boxes. It was late September, but the air was warm still, "Führer-weather" they called it, since it permitted Hitler success in his campaigns. It had certainly worked with Poland.

I climbed the steps to the double doors, inset with filigreed, white-painted ironwork over frosted glass. I pressed the silver button. Was Katz even home? There was a faint glow behind the frosted glass, but the gas lanterns to either side of the door were not lit. Father waited on the street in the darkness, arms hugging his midsection.

I was twenty-five that year when Father's symptoms grew bad enough for him to seek out his favorite old Jewish treater of the sick, a man named Katz. We were not allowed to call Jews doctors. The term "treaters of the sick" was preferred. Nor were Aryans allowed to frequent non-Aryan doctors, but my father seldom followed the rules.

The doorbell chimed somewhere deep in the house. I'd never set foot in a Jew's house before and was in no hurry to do so, but Father insisted I accompany him. I wanted to spend as little time there as possible.

A brighter light appeared behind the frosted glass, and a dark shape moved toward me. The door to my right opened a crack to reveal a former medical school classmate of mine, one of the many Jewish students no longer welcome at the university. He was fully dressed, tucking his shirt into his pants.

"What do you want this time of night?" he said.

Behind him Katz descended the stairs, steps soundless on thick carpet, the train of his midnight-blue dressing gown fanned out behind him. He hesitated, hunched like a crone, eyes wide. Expecting the Gestapo?

Father hobbled up the front steps and stood next to me. "Excuse me, Herr Doktor," he said, one hand on the doorjamb. "I am sorry to bother you, but the pain is unbearable."

Once Katz recognized Father, he smiled and ushered us in. As we passed, the former medical student looked at me with narrowed eyes.

Katz led us into his paneled study, three times the size of our apartment, the walls lined with shelves of leather-bound books. It had a spiral staircase, which led up to the second level, to a railed balcony lined with more bookshelves. Katz turned a knob on the wall, and the crystal chandelier above us, hung with a thousand icicle pendants, came to life.

Katz eased Father down into a chair that looked like a king's throne. I ran the tips of my fingers along the chair's arm, across the red damask woven with threads of gold, smooth and cool.

"It's no bother at all," Katz said. "I was just reading. My bag, please, and a glass of water for Herr Oberheuser," he said over his shoulder to the former medical student. The young man pressed his lips together in a hard line and left the room.

"How long has the pain been like this?" Katz asked.

I'd never known many Jews, but had read many accounts of them in schoolbooks and in *Der Stürmer*. Grasping and controlling.

Cornering the market on law and medical jobs. But Katz seemed almost happy to see Father—strange, since we'd intruded on him at such an hour. This was a man happy in his work.

"Since dinner," Father said, hugging his belly.

I was almost done with medical school at the time and could have counseled my father, but he insisted on seeing Katz.

I studied the room as Katz examined him. The black-and-white marble fireplace, the grand piano. The books on the shelves looked oiled and dusted, each one worth more than I made in a year, trimming roasts for *Onkel* Heinz part-time at his butcher shop. There was no doubt a well-used volume of Freud among them. Several lamps stood about the room throwing down pools of light even when no one was using them. If only Mutti could have seen that wastefulness.

Katz fingered the sides of Father's neck. As he turned Father's hand to take his pulse, the light caught a fat letter *K* monogrammed in silver thread on Katz's dressing-gown sleeve.

"Working at the Horschaft factory may be causing this," he said to Father. "I would stop working there immediately."

Father winced, his skin sallow. "But we can't live without that job."

"Well, at least work in a ventilated area."

The former medical student returned with a crystal glass of water and set it on the table next to us. Could he not bring himself to hand it to Father? Little did he know Father was on his side. If he hadn't been so sick, Father would have hidden a whole tramcar of those people in our back bedroom.

Katz shook a pill from a bottle into Father's hand and then smiled. "No charge."

Was that how they did it? Got you hooked, then charged more later? Our schoolbooks outlined the various strategies Jews used to undermine hardworking Germans. They were taking over the medical world. My professors said they were stingy with their research results and barely shared findings outside their own circles.

While Father took his pill, I browsed the titles on the bookshelf: *Clinical Surgery. Stages in Embryo Development in Humans and Vertebrates.* Whole shelves of green leather tomes with titles such as *Atlas of the Outer Eye Diseases* and *Atlas of Syphilis and Venereal Diseases.*

"You like to read?" Katz asked.

"Herta graduates soon from medical school," Father said. "On an accelerated track. She's interested in surgery." I excelled in the few surgery classes I was allowed to take, but being a woman, under national socialism, I was not allowed to specialize in surgery.

"Ah, the surgeon," Katz said, smiling. "King of doctors, or at least the surgeons think so." He pulled one of the green books from the shelf. "*Atlas of General Surgery.* Have you read it?"

I said nothing as he pushed the book toward me. It seemed some Jews shared.

"Once you learn everything in here, bring it back, and I'll give you another," he said.

I did not touch it. What would people say, me taking the book of a Jew?

"You are too generous, Herr Doktor," Father said.

"I insist," Katz said, still holding the book out.

It looked heavy, the leather cover soft, embossed in gold. Could I borrow such a thing? I wanted it. Not so much to read it. I *had* textbooks. Ugly and secondhand, other people's notes scratched in their margins, breadcrumbs in their gutters. This book was a beautiful thing. It would be nice to be seen with it, to walk into class and drop it casually on my desk. Mutti would rage at Father for allowing me to take it, but that alone was worth it.

I took the book from Katz and turned away.

"She's speechless," Father said. "And a fast reader. She'll return it soon."

———

IT WAS A USEFUL BOOK, in some ways more detailed than our medical school textbooks. In less than one week, I read from "Inflammation and Repair of Tissue" through "Cancer of the Lymphatic System." The text and color plates provided additional insight into my father's condition. Epithelioma. Sarcoma. Radium treatments.

Once I made it through the last chapter of Katz's book, "Amputations and Prosthesis," and practiced two new surgical knots described there, I walked to the Jew's house to return it, hoping for another.

When I arrived, the front doors were wide open, and the SS were carrying cardboard boxes of books, Katz's black medical bag, and a white wicker baby carriage, its wheels spinning in midair, to the curb. Someone was plunking out a German folk tune on Katz's piano.

I held the book tight to my chest and left for home. Katz would not be coming back for it. Everyone knew of these arrests. Most of the time they happened in the night. It was sad to see someone's possessions taken in such a way, but the Jews had been warned. They knew the Führer's requirements. This was unfortunate, but not new, and it was for the good of Germany.

Less than a week later I spied a new family with five sons and a daughter carrying suitcases and a birdcage into that house.

MY MOTHER WAS HAPPY to work in her brother Heinz's meat market, across the bridge in Oberkassel, a wealthy part of town, and she had gotten me a job there too. It was a small shop, but Heinz filled every inch with meat. He hung hams and long ribs of pork outside along the front of the store like socks on a clothesline and displayed whole hogs spread-eagled, bellies slit wide, glistening entrails scooped and saved.

At first I blanched at the sight, but as a medical student interested in surgery, I gradually grew to see beauty in the most unlikely places. The startling ivory of a splayed rib cage. A calf's severed head, peaceful as if asleep, a fringe of lashes black against the damp fur.

"I make good use of every part of an animal," Heinz often said. "Everything but the squeal." He boiled pig parts on the stove all day until the windows fogged and the shop somehow smelled both putrid and sweet as only a butcher shop can.

As greater numbers of Jews left the city, we became one of the few quality meat shops left, and business improved daily. One afternoon Heinz passed along news benefiting the customers lined up two deep at the front counter.

"You have to get over there to the *platz*, ladies. They are selling everything from the warehouses. I heard Frau Brandt found a sable coat there with a silk lining. Hurry, now."

No one said they were selling items taken from the Jews, but we all knew.

"How awful they took people's things away like that," said *Tante* Ilsa, Heinz's wife, who avoided the shop as much as she could. When she did come, she brought me a jar of her strawberry marmalade, which I'd once complimented. Ilsa kept her coat wrapped tight around her even though it was summer and stayed only two minutes. "It's a sin to pick through someone's things as if they're dead."

Tante Ilsa paid for most of my medical school costs. A kind praying mantis of a woman, tall and gentle with a head too small for her body, she'd been left a great deal of money by her mother and used it sparingly, no matter how *Onkel* Heinz brayed.

Heinz smiled, causing his piggy eyes to disappear into the folds of his fat face. "Oh, don't worry, Ilsa. They probably *are* dead by now," he said.

The patrons turned away, but I knew he was right. If Ilsa was not careful, her own considerable belongings would end up there alongside the Jews'. The gold cross around her neck was no protection. Did Ilsa know what Heinz did in the refrigerated room? Perhaps on an instinctual level, the way a calf knows to become restless on slaughter day.

"You shed a tear when the Jew Krystel's shop closed, Ilsa. My own wife a Jew friend, shopping at the competition. That is loyalty, *nicht?*"

"He has those baby hens I like."

"*Had*, Ilsa. It doesn't help my business when this gets around. Soon you'll be on the *Pranger-Liste*."

I held my tongue, but I'd already seen *Tante* Ilsa's name on the *Pranger-Liste*, the public list of German women who shopped at Jewish stores, posted about the town, a black stripe running diagonally across it.

"You don't see Krystel's wife in *here*," Heinz said. "Thank God. And no more Frau Zates, either. Wants a cabbage but will only pay for a half. Who buys half a cabbage? I cut it, and who buys the other half? No one, that's who."

"Why should she buy whole when she needs only half?" Ilsa asked.

"*Mein Gott*, she does it on purpose. Can't you see?"

"Keep your thumb off the scale, or you'll have *no* customers, Heinz."

Mutti and I left Heinz and Ilsa to bicker and walked along to the sale at the *platz*. It was rare Mutti had any time to shop, since she was up at five-thirty each day to do mending before she cleaned houses or worked in the shop. Thanks to the Führer's economic miracle, she was working fewer afternoon hours but still seemed just as tired at day's end. She took my hand as we crossed the street, and I felt her rough skin. I could barely look at her dishpan hands, red and peeling from cleaning toilets and dishes. No amount of lanolin cream could heal them.

People gathered in the square to watch as Wehrmacht soldiers threw household items into great piles and displayed finer items on tables. My pulse quickened as I approached the heaps, sorted according to use and gender. Shoes and handbags. Crates of costume jewelry. Coats and dresses. Not all the finest styles, but with a little hunting, one could find the best labels for next to nothing. That elevated Mutti's mood, and she started a pile for us.

"Look, Chanel," I said, holding out a red hat.

"No hats," Mutti said. "You want lice? And why cover your hair, your best asset?"

I tossed the hat back on the pile, pleased with the compliment. Though my shoulder-length hair was not white blond, many would have considered it honey gold in the right light, a good thing, since every German girl wanted blond hair, and the use of peroxide was discouraged.

We passed a mound of canvases and framed pictures. A painting of two men embracing lay on top, the canvas spiked through on a spear from a sculpture below.

"My God, Jew art," Mutti said. "Can't they just hang a calendar on the wall like the rest of us?"

On his way home from the pharmacy, Father joined us there by the piles. The creases on his face looked deeper that day. A rough night on the sofa.

I lifted a scrapbook from a table and flipped through the pages, past black-and-white photographs of someone's beach vacation.

"This is undignified," Father said. "You two call yourselves Christians?"

Of course he disapproved. Why had he even stopped to speak with us? I tossed the scrapbook on our pile.

"Anton, can you not relax a bit?" Mutti said.

I pulled a painting, one of two of grazing cows, out from under a crush of framed canvases. It was well done, perhaps even a masterwork. Traditional German art. Just what the Propaganda Ministry found suitable, and something every cultured woman should own.

"What do you think, Mutti?"

Mutti pointed at the cows and laughed. "Oh, it's you, *Kleine Kuh.*"

Kleine Kuh was Mutti's nickname for me. Little heifer. As a child she'd had a brown cow that I reminded her of. I had long ago dealt with not being as dainty and blond as my mother, but the name still rankled.

"Don't call Herta that," Father said. "No girl should be called a cow."

It was good to have Father's support, even if he was a lawbreaker who listened to foreign broadcasts and read every foreign newspaper he could lay hands on. I took the two paintings and set them in our pile.

"Where have the owners of all this gone?" I asked, though I had a general idea.

"To the KZ, I suppose," Mutti said. "It's their own fault. They could have stepped aside. Gone to England. They don't work; that is the problem."

"Jews have jobs," Father said.

"*Ja,* of *course,* but what jobs? Lawyers? That is not really work. They own the factories, but do they *do* the work? No. I'd rather do ten jobs than work for them."

Mutti pulled a dressing gown from the pile and held it up. "Would this fit you, Anton?" Father and I didn't have to see the silver *K* on the sleeve to know who the former owner was.

"No, thank you," he said, and Mutti walked off, scouting the piles.

"Are you sure, Father?" I took the dressing gown and held it out to him. "It's a nice one."

He took a step back. "What has happened to you, Herta? Where is my girl with the tender heart, always first to take up the collection can for the neediest? Katz was a man you could have learned from."

"I haven't changed." It was obvious he didn't support or even like me much, but did he have to broadcast this?

"Katz was compassionate. A doctor without love is like a mechanic."

"Of course I'm compassionate. Do you know what it's like to be able to change a person's life just with these hands?"

"You'll never be a surgeon with Hitler around. Can't you see that? Your generation is so pigheaded."

Much as I hated to admit it, he was right about the surgeon part. As one of a handful of women in my medical school, I'd been lucky to be able to study dermatology, never mind surgery, and had received only basic surgical training.

"We all must sacrifice, but Germany's changing thanks to my generation. Such poverty yours left us with."

"Hitler will be the death of all of us, just taking what he wants—"

"*Quiet*, Father," I said. How dangerous for him to respond in such a way in public. He even told jokes about Party leaders. "Hitler is our hope. In no time, he's gotten rid of the slums. And he *must* take. Germany can't thrive without room to expand. No one will just give back the land we've lost."

Many parents had grown wary of confronting their children for fear of being denounced by them, but not my father.

"He's killing Germany to feed his own vanity."

"This war will be over within weeks. You'll see," I said.

He turned with a dismissive wave.

"Go straight home and rest before afternoon coffee, Father."

He walked away, barely avoiding a passing tram. Father would need a nap. The cancer was having a party in his body. Could Katz have helped him live? It was no good wasting time with such thoughts. I busied myself searching the piles for medical books.

Mutti hurried to me. "I found rose-scented soap . . . and a toaster."

"Don't you worry about Father, Mutti? He's going to be denounced. I can feel it."

Though my parents were both products of German blood and could trace their pure German ancestry back to 1750, my father could not hide his lack of enthusiasm for the Party. He still put his traditional striped German flag in our front window next to Mutti's new red Party one, though Mutti was always moving his to a side window. No one noticed it in the sea of swastikaed flags hung outside every building, but it was only a matter of time before someone turned him in.

"*Ja, feind hirt mitt, Herta,*" Mutti said. The enemy is listening.

She pulled me closer. "Don't worry about that, *Kleine Kuh.* Focus on work."

"I'm allowed only dermatology——"

Mutti pressed her fingers into my forearm. "Stop it. You'll be working with the best and brightest soon. You can go all the way."

"Someone needs to rein Father in."

Mutti turned away. "What will people say if we have these things in our home?" she said, shaking her head at the toaster in her hand.

We paid for the items we'd chosen: the toaster, the scrapbook, the paintings, and a mink stole with the glass-eyed heads still attached, a luxury item Mutti was willing to risk lice for. The soldiers threw in a doctor's framed diploma Mutti said she'd use to display her Aryan blood certificate and some canvas running shoes for me. All for only ten marks. We seldom had bread to toast, and Mutti could not afford to go anywhere she could wear such a mink, but the smile on her face made it all worthwhile.

I WAS HAPPY TO HAVE those new running shoes for a sleepaway trip I was chaperoning the next week at Camp Blossom, a camp situated in a pine forest half a day's train ride north of Düsseldorf. It was run by the Belief and Beauty Society, which was affiliated with the BDM, the Bund Deutscher Mädel or the League of German Girls, the female wing of the Nazi Party youth movement. The Belief and Beauty Society was for older girls only, to prepare them for domestic life and motherhood. This sleepaway trip was intended to transition the younger ones into the organization, and my job as unit leader was to look after the girls in my cabin—not an easy job.

Unit leaders received day assignments, and I was sent to the craft hut, a blatant mismatch, since I considered painting amateurish watercolors and weaving gimp lanyards a complete waste of time. Plus, my considerable talents lay outside the art world. With my extensive medical training, I should have been running the camp health clinic, but one serves where one is needed. At least the hut looked out over the lake, which reflected the reds and oranges of the trees surrounding it.

Pippi, another girl assigned to work the craft hut, joined me there one afternoon. I'd known Pippi since we'd both joined BDM, and though she was a few years younger than I, we were good friends, well on our way to being best friends, something every other girl seemed to have. Pippi and I had done everything in BDM together. Earned our badges and leadership cords. Taken turns carrying the flag in at meetings. At the camp we shared meals and even tidied up the worktables in the craft hut together.

"Let's hurry," I said. "It's about to rain."

Pippi took the scissors from the tables and plunked them into the metal cans around the room. She was terribly slow about it.

She nodded out the window. "Look who's waiting."

At the edge of the woods, two boys stood, one blond, one darkhaired, next to a rowboat pulled up onshore, a deep rut in the sand behind it. I recognized them, unit leaders from the adjacent boys' camp, dressed in camp uniform khaki shirts and shorts. They were part of the boat crew. Handsome boys, of course. No camper of low racial value was allowed at any German youth camp, so everyone was attractive, guaranteed to be racially pure. There'd been no need to measure our heads and noses with calipers and craniometers. We'd all submitted pure genetic histories.

They fiddled with the boat's oarlocks, taking glances back at the craft hut.

"You know what those boys want, Pippi."

Pippi checked her face in the mirror above the sink. Next to it a poster fixed to the wall with tacks read: REMEMBER YOU ARE GERMAN! KEEP YOUR BLOOD PURE!

"So what? I just want to try it. It's fun."

"Fun? We can't finish a relay race here without couples heading for the woods." What fun was a race if no one won?

At Camp Blossom, the staff were encouraged to look the other way if Aryan couples paired off. If a pregnancy resulted, the mother was sent to a luxurious SS spa-clinic, and the birth of a healthy child was celebrated, no matter if the mother was married. All this focus on children was understandable, of course, since the future of Germany depended on populating our country. But with my sights set on becoming a physician, I could not afford a pregnancy. I slid a pair of scissors from one of the metal cans and secreted them in my shorts pocket.

Pippi's eyes widened. "Ever done it yourself?" she asked in a casual voice.

"It hurts, you know. And no matter what they say, if you have a baby, you'll be sent out of the BDM, shipped off to Wernigerode. The middle of nowhere."

Pippi pulled a stack of postcards from her shorts pocket. They featured views of Die Mutter-hauser des Lebensborns, a stately chalet. One showed a nurse tending to a ruffled bassinet on a tree-lined terrace under the SS flag.

"They say it's like being on holiday—the best of everything. Meat. Real butter—"

"Maybe, but the father will not be involved. Once the child is born, they take it away to be raised by strangers."

"You throw a wet blanket on everything, Herta," she said, fanning herself with the cards.

Once the boys finished fiddling with the boat, they stood, hands in pockets. I tried to stall, waiting for them to leave, but eventually we had to go.

Side by side, Pippi and I started down the path to our cabin. We turned, saw the boys following us, quickening their pace, and Pippi bit her lip into a smile.

"Hurry," I said, pulling Pippi by the arm.

The boys picked up speed and Pippi and I took off toward the woods. I left the path and crashed through low brush and briers while Pippi, an accomplished sprinter, lagged behind. As I ran, the sting of the scissors' point stabbed my leg. Why did this make me feel so oddly alive?

I ran around to the far side of an abandoned cabin next to a rushing stream and crouched on the mossy bank. Catching my breath, I set my scissors down and examined the wound on my thigh. It was a surface wound but had produced a startling amount of blood. Despite the sound of the rushing water, I heard the boys nab Pippi.

"You run so fast," she said, laughing. The three clambered into the cabin, and I brushed away the jealousy I felt. What would it be like to kiss such a good-looking boy? Did I need to tell my supervisor if Pippi succumbed?

"What a good kisser you are," I heard Pippi say.

I heard the creak of the bedsprings, more giggling from Pippi, and then moans from one boy. Where was the other one? Watching?

Pippi put up embarrassingly little resistance, and I heard them breathing hard and loud. How could she?

"You can't keep your clothes on," one boy said.

"It's so dirty in here," Pippi said.

I crouched there motionless, for any move would reveal my position. Pippi seemed to be enjoying it all, but then she had a change of heart.

"No, please," she said. "I need to get back—"

"It's not fair to get this far—"

"You're *hurting* me," she cried. "Herta!"

Friends help each other, but I'd warned her. Why hadn't she listened? Her lack of discipline was a weakness.

"Help!" Pippi cried. "Someone, please—"

Aiding her would only endanger me, but I couldn't leave her in that situation. I took up the scissors, cold and heavy, and stole to the rotted cabin steps in the almost darkness.

The screen door lay on the ground, off its hinges, so the doorway provided a good view. There were many rusted metal beds in there standing on end, and Pippi lay on the only horizontal one. It had collapsed, the mattress ticking stained and torn. One of the boys was lying on top of her, his ass blue-white in the dark room, smooth and hard and pumping as she cried. The second boy, the dark-haired one, stood at the head of the bed pinning Pippi's shoulders.

I stepped over gaps from missing floorboards into the cabin.

"Stop it," I said.

The second boy lit up when he saw me, perhaps hoping for a chance himself. I brandished the scissors, a dull silver in the dark room.

"She's serious," said the dark-haired boy. He released Pippi's shoulders.

The blond one slammed himself into Pippi with renewed vigor at the prospect of her backing out.

I stepped closer. "Get off her," I said.

"Let's *go*," said the dark-haired boy.

The blond pulled himself off Pippi, grabbed his shorts from the floor, and left with his friend, both avoiding my scissors. Pippi just cried there on the mattress. I untied the bandanna from my neck and placed it on the bed.

"You can use this to clean yourself," I said.

I left her and walked outside to make sure the boys were gone. Satisfied they were not coming back, I walked to the stream. I raised the scissors and felt for a handful of my long hair, pulled it taut, and cut. Every muscle relaxed with that release, and I continued, feeling for any stray lock, until my hair was cropped to less than a thumb's length all around. I tossed my hair into the river and watched it travel downstream, sliding over rocks, off into the darkness.

I helped Pippi back to our cabin. With much crying, she thanked me for rescuing her and admitted she should have followed my advice. She promised to write once she got home to Cologne.

Pippi's parents retrieved her the next day, not at all happy, if their abrupt manner was any indication. I watched her leave, as she waved through the rear window of her parents' car, my one friend gone.

For the rest of my stay, I kept my scissors close, but in the end my self-cut hair did the trick, and boys let me be. When the sleepaway trip concluded, half of my cabin went home fingers crossed, hoping to have a baby, while I left camp happily without a fertilized egg.

CHAPTER 4

Caroline

1939

ONCE HITLER INVADED POLAND, MILD FOREBODING TURNED to genuine panic at every New York consulate, and all hell broke loose at our office. To make things worse, Washington tightened visa restrictions, and it became almost impossible to enter the United States from Europe. France limited its visas as well. By November, people desperate to be at the head of the line braved the cold and slept the night under the stars in sleeping bags beneath my office window. Once we opened in the morning, the line of French citizens desperate to get home often snaked out from our reception area into the hallway.

My bosom friend Betty Merchant chose a gray, late November day to stop by with her donation. I heard her arrive and issue orders to Pia for hot tea that would never come. Betty forged her way into my office, dressed in an indigo bouclé Schiaparelli suit and a hat adorned with indigo and scarlet feathers, a folded newspaper under one arm. In one hand she carried an old wedding present from a New Jersey couple, a three-foot-high money tree made of sixty one-hundred-dollar bills folded into little paper fans on a wooden base. In the other she balanced a tower of nested shoe boxes.

Betty set the money tree on my blotter. "I brought this for your French babies. That should buy some tinned milk."

It was good to see Betty, but I was behind schedule, and case folders were stacking up. In the French tradition, our office was closed for lunch from twelve-thirty to three, and I'd allocated that time to eat canned tuna at my desk and regroup for the afternoon onslaught.

"Thank you, Betty. Good to see you, but—"

"And shoe boxes, as promised. I only brought the French ones so those babies would feel at home." Betty's shoe habit provided the vessels for the comfort boxes I sent abroad, and I knew there'd be a steady stream to come.

Betty closed my office door. "I'm closing this on account of Miss Big Ears out there."

"Pia?"

"She listens to everything, you know. Desperate to know where we're lunching, of course."

"I'm swamped and not hungry either, I'm afraid."

"You can't sneak in a bite? There's nothing like a martini to stir up a lazy appetite."

"How can I take lunch with that crowd waiting? I just had a couple from Lyon who haven't heard from their daughter back in France since June. Both sobbing."

"Honestly, Caroline. You're a volunteer and you can't even take *lunch*."

"These people need me."

"That elevator boy of yours—Cuddy?—maybe I'll take *him* to '21.' There's something about a man in uniform."

Betty looked in her compact mirror, checking herself for imperfections. Finding none, she shrugged, disappointed. Betty was often compared to Rita Hayworth, for she was blessed with an abundant head of hair and curves that once caused an elderly fellow in a wheelchair to stand and walk for the first time in years. She wasn't always the prettiest girl in the room, but it was hard to take your eyes off her, like a train accident or a dancing bear.

"You need a break, Caroline. Why not be my bridge partner?"

"I can't, Betty. Things are crazy here. With Hitler throwing his weight around, half of France is trying to get out, and the other half is desperate to get back in. I have sixty comfort packages to assemble. You're welcome to help."

"I do love the French. Seems you do as well. Saw that new boyfriend of yours yesterday, on his way to the theater."

A few snowflakes fell outside the window. Was it snowing at our house up in Connecticut?

"He's not my boyfriend." Unfortunately, too true, though I saw Paul often that fall and early winter. He would stop by the consulate before rehearsal, and we'd share a brown-bag lunch up on the French Building's roof garden, no matter the weather.

"You seem to find time for *him*. Mother told me she saw you step across to Sardi's. 'Tête-à-tête at lunch with a tall European.' Her words. The whole town is talking about it, C. Seems *he's* become your best friend now." Betty lobbed a folded newspaper onto my desk. "There's a blurb about you two in the *Post*. Did you know he was voted World's Most Handsome Man by *Physical Culture* magazine?"

I wasn't surprised but was somehow flattered by that. Who even voted for those things?

"One lunch," I said. "Really. Giving him notes on his show——"

Betty leaned across my desk. "You deserve a lover, Caroline, but keep it quiet, darling. Does it have to be a theater person? And one so, well, public? I know you're still smarting from David. If I'd known my brother was——"

"That's over, Betty."

"I can run interference for you, but once a reputation's tarnished, there's no polishing it. Evelyn Shimmerhorn is enormous. Can't leave the house."

"Would you leave Evelyn alone? I don't care what people think."

"You'll care when you're not called up for get-togethers. Why not let me fix you up? Honestly, David may be my brother, but he has his faults, God knows. You're better off without him, but don't rebound with some *Frenchman* just to spite him. Every man has a silhouette, you know, of the woman he'll end up with. We just need to find a suitable man with yours in mind."

"You must have better things to think about, Betty."

Betty had been my biggest supporter since our first day at then-coed Chapin, when a boy in French class called me *le girafon* and she ground the heel of her white kid boot into his foot.

"If it were up to me, I'd have you and Paul both stark naked atop the Chrysler Building, but I'm trying to protect you, dear."

To my great relief, Betty said she had to run. I followed her to the reception area, where she took the money tree and dropped it on Pia's desk.

"I hope you don't expect me to deposit this," Pia said, leaning back in her chair, Gauloise in hand.

"Won't you be a sight on Fifth Avenue? By the way, do you own a bra, Pia dear?"

"The word is *brassiere*."

Betty tossed a dollar on Pia's desk. "Take this, and buy yourself one. They're cheaper in the children's department."

As Betty left the reception room, Paul bounded off the elevator, brown bag in hand, and held the door for her. Betty just gave me her best "I told you so" look and headed on her way.

Paul had come that day to iron out his visa issues with Roger, and I elbowed in on the meeting. I wanted to show my support for Paul, for it would surely convince Roger to help him stay. Roger had installed a Murphy bed in his office, and he'd left it down, the bed linens balled atop it like used tissues. It had not been productive sleep.

"I need to get Rena out of France," Paul said.

Roger pulled an electric razor from a drawer and set it on the blotter. "We can try. The U.S. visa is a hot item. You saw the line. Even French citizens with U.S. visas are stuck in France. So few boats."

"Rena's father is Jewish," Paul said. "Will that complicate things?"

I went to the Murphy bed and unballed the linens.

"Since Washington changed immigration quotas in '24, everything's harder now," Roger said.

"She'd settle for a tourist visa."

Roger slammed his desk drawer closed. "Would you get away from that bed, Caroline? Everyone in that line out there would settle for a tourist visa, Paul. Rena needs two sponsors."

"I can be one," I said, plumping Roger's pillow. Was that lipstick? Rockette red.

"Thank you, Caroline," Paul said with a smile.

"Shouldn't you be helping Pia out front, Caroline?" Roger said.

I tucked the blanket edge under the mattress.

"Has Rena booked passage?" Roger asked.

"Yes, but without a visa, her ticket expired. She'll rebook once she has the new visa."

Roger turned on his razor and applied it to his cheeks, cleaning up stray hairs. Left to its own devices, that beard would have swallowed his face whole. "I'm not making any promises. More visa restrictions are due any day."

"More?" I asked.

"You know it's not my decision," Roger said.

I lifted the Murphy bed up and into its wall closet.

"Can't we expedite things? This doesn't seem fair. Paul is a prominent French citizen, an ambassador to the world—"

"I'm at the mercy of the U.S. State Department, Caroline. A case of champagne only gets you so far."

"I may go back to France for a visit," Paul said.

"Go back, and you're back for good," Roger said.

I stepped to Paul's chair. "Why not wait until spring?"

"It will be a very different situation by spring," Roger said. "I would go now, Paul, if you're serious."

Paul sat up straighter.

"Of course I'm serious."

Was he? I'd given him the reentry forms and he'd lost them, twice. Not that I wanted him to leave.

"Then you need to apply," Roger said.

"I can fill out the forms for you," I said.

Paul reached over and squeezed my hand.

"You must be eager to see your wife," Roger said.

"Of course," Paul said.

Roger stood. "It's up to you, but if you're in your room at the Waldorf when Hitler decides to move on France, you won't be going back."

The meeting was over. Paul stood too.

"Caroline, can you stay behind for a minute?" Roger asked.

Paul made his way to the door.

"See you upstairs," he said and left for the roof garden.

Roger closed his door. "I hope you know what you're getting yourself into here."

"I've sponsored ten applicants—"

"You know what I mean. With Paul."

"It's nothing," I said. *Stay calm.* . . . A tired Roger was trouble.

"Paul would be gone by now if not for you. I see what's happening."

"That's unfair, Roger."

"Is it? He has a family, Caroline. Isn't it odd he's in no hurry to get back?" Roger picked up Paul's folder and paged through it.

"His new show—"

"Is more important than his *wife*?"

"I think they're somewhat, well . . . estranged."

"Here we go." Roger tossed the folder onto his desk. "Pia says you two spend lunch up on the roof garden."

"No need to overreact, Roger." I stepped toward the door. Little did Roger know, Paul and I had crisscrossed Manhattan together many times over. Eaten chop suey and rice cakes on MacDougal Street in Greenwich Village. Strolled the Japanese garden in Prospect Park.

"Look, Caroline, I know you're probably lonely—"

"No need to be insulting. I'm just trying to help. It isn't right he and Rena should suffer like this. Look at all Paul's done to help France."

"Please. You want me to get Rena out so he can stay. Then what? Three's a crowd, Caroline, and guess who'll be left out? He needs to do his duty as a French citizen and go home."

"We have to do what's right, Roger."

"*We* don't have to do anything. Be careful what you wish for, Caroline."

I hurried back to my office, sidestepping a stray *pétanque* ball. Would Paul still be waiting?

Roger's words hung in the air. Maybe I was attracted to Paul. I hoped Betty was right about men and their silhouettes. Did Paul like mine? There were worse things in life.

WE WERE TERRIBLY BUSY at the consulate, but Mother insisted I volunteer at the thé dansant she and her friends arranged at the Plaza. If you've never attended one, a thé dansant is a relic of a bygone age, a casual afternoon gathering at which light sandwiches are served and dancing is encouraged.

There were a million places I'd rather have been that day, but Mother's thé dansant was to benefit her White Russians, those former members of the Russian aristocracy, now exiled, who had supported the tsar in the Russian Civil War. Helping these former aristocrats had been Mother's pet cause for years, and I felt obligated to help.

She'd booked the Plaza's neorococo Grand Ballroom, one of the most beautiful rooms in New York with its mirrored walls and crystal chandeliers, and commissioned a Russian balalaika orchestra to provide the music. Six of the tsar's former court musicians, in white tie, sat ramrod straight on risers at one side of the ballroom. Each held his triangular three-stringed balalaika on his knee, waiting for Mother's cue. Though these world-class musicians had been reduced to playing at thé dansants, they seemed happy for the work. The assisting hostesses, committee members Mother had strong-armed and a few of my Junior League friends, went about the room setting up in traditional Russian dress. She'd even convinced a sullen Pia to join our ranks.

I told no one outside of my fellow hostesses that I volunteered at these gatherings, for it was humiliating beyond belief to be seen in Russian dress. As an actress I'd happily worn every species of costume imaginable, but this one was too much, for it included the *sarafan,* an elongating black trapeze-like dress embroidered with bright red and green stripes and a puff-sleeved white blouse adorned with crewelwork flowers. Mother also insisted we all wear the particularly embarrassing *kokoshnik,* the high headdress embroidered in gold and silver, set with semi-precious stones, and festooned with long strings of river pearls. As if I weren't tall enough already, the headdress made me resemble an only slightly shorter Empire State Building draped in pearls.

Mother slid an empty Russian gilt-and-enamel donation bowl onto the front table and then placed one hand on my embroidered sleeve. This sent a lovely wave of perfume my way, the one her friend Prince Matchabelli, a displaced Georgian nationalist himself, had made just for her, with her favorite lilac, sandalwood, and rose notes. He and his actress-wife, Princess Norina, sent Mother every one of their fragrances, resulting in a colorful city of cross-topped crown bottles atop her dressing table.

"There will be low turnout," Mother said. "I feel it."

Though I was reluctant to tell Mother, low attendance was inevitable, for Americans had become increasingly isolationist. The poll numbers showed that our country, still smarting from huge casualties in the First World War and from the Great Depression, was opposed to being swept into the new conflict. New Yorkers were in no mood for thé dansants that benefited anyone outside our forty-eight states.

"With the war on in Europe, your White Russians are no longer a priority, Mother."

Mother smiled. "Yes, think of all the poor displaced Europeans." She looked at charitable opportunities in the way some eyed a plate of pastries.

Our cook Serge stepped across the ballroom, a pleated toque on his head, his chef's jacket dusted with flour. He cradled a silver bowl of *tvorog* in his arms, a Russian peasant dish of farmer's cheese infused with blackberry syrup. Born Vladimir Sergeyevich Yevtushenkov, Serge was descended from some sort of Russian nobility, which Mother had always been vague about. Having Serge live with us was like having a heavily accented, much younger brother who spent every waking hour thinking up new things to flambé for Mother and me.

Serge's appearance caused Pia to approach, like a crocodile sliding into the water, crystal punch cup in hand. "That looks delicious, Serge."

Serge blushed and wiped his hands on his apron. Lanky, sandy-haired Serge could have wooed any girl he wanted in New York City, but he'd been born with a crippling shyness that kept him in the kitchen, happily salamandering his crème brûlée.

"Maybe booking the Grand Ballroom was a mistake, Mother," I said.

The chances of filling over four thousand square feet with merrymakers were slim. I stole a piece of Mother's *khachapuri*, buttery bread cut in triangles. "But you advertised it in the *Times*. People will come."

Mother's orchestra played a passionate version of the Russian folk song "The Ancient Linden Tree," incompatible with any modern-day dance step.

Mother gripped my elbow and pulled me aside. "We're selling Russian tea and cigarettes, but leave them alone. Pia says you've been smoking them with your French friend."

"He's not—"

"Your social life is your affair, but we need to make a profit."

"I know you don't approve of Paul, but we're just friends."

"I'm not your minister, Caroline, but we both know how theater people are. Especially married actors away from home. But you're a thirty-five-year-old woman—"

"Thirty-seven."

"You don't need my approval. But if you ask me, one or two from the orchestra might make suitable beaux." Mother tipped her head in the direction of the band. "Once the toast of Russian aristocracy."

"There isn't one under sixty."

"The picky bird goes hungry, dear."

Mother wandered off to drum up donations, and I finished readying the room. I was on a ladder adjusting a spotlight to shine on the orchestra, well aware that being up so high only increased my conspicuousness, when Paul appeared at the ballroom door. He stepped straight to the ladder.

"Roger told me I could find you here."

The grand room suited Paul, the cream-colored walls with gold accents a fine contrast to his dark good looks. I felt a wave of *la douleur*, one of the many French words that do not translate into English well, which means "the pain of wanting someone you cannot have."

"Delightful," I said, climbing down the ladder steps, pearls swaying. Could he not at least suppress the smile?

"I'm on my way to the theater, but I need your signature for Rena's visa application. If this is a bad time—"

"Of course not."

Mother approached us, and the orchestra picked up their tempo.

"Mother, may I introduce Paul Rodierre?"

"Lovely to meet you," Mother said. "You're in *The Streets of Paris*, I hear."

Paul gave Mother one of his best smiles. "Just one of a hundred."

Mother seemed immune to him. To the untrained eye, she appeared perfectly cordial, but after years of watching her in society, I could detect the chill.

"If you'll excuse me, I need to see about refreshing the *khachapuri.* Someone seems to be eating it all."

Paul turned to face Mother. "*Khachapuri?* My favorite."

"It's for the paying guests, I'm afraid," Mother said. "Not that there will be many of those tonight."

Paul bowed a little bow in Mother's direction, so formal with her. "If you ladies will excuse me, I must be going." He smiled at me and exited the way he came. So soon?

"Good job, Mother, alienating our one guest."

"The French can be so sensitive."

"You can't expect people to stay here. New Yorkers would rather die than eat *tvorog*, and it does help to offer alcohol, you know."

"Next time we'll sell weenies and beans. If it were up to you, we'd all be out at a bump supper, a jug of corn whiskey on the table."

I turned my attention to hanging Mother's pine garlands above the doorways, assisted by a sulky Pia. As we worked I mentally addressed the long list of things I was behind on. Reports for Roger. My comfort packages. Why was Mother so stubborn? She had to adapt to the twentieth century. I felt someone's gaze on me and turned to see one of the more elderly members of the orchestra, balalaika in hand, wink at me.

An hour later even Mother conceded defeat. Our only potential customers had been Plaza guests, a couple from Chicago who'd wandered in by mistake and left quickly, as if they'd happened upon a nudist colony.

"Well, this was a bust," Mother said.

I pulled a garland down from the wall.

"I told you—"

I didn't finish the sentence, for such a clatter grew in the hallway outside the ballroom we could scarcely hear each other. The doors were flung wide, and a crowd streamed in—every sort of person you can imagine, from up and down the social ladder, all heavily rouged and dressed in 1920s French attire. Women in low-belted sweater sets, their hair finger-waved. Some wore dropped waist dresses and Louise Brooks bobs. Gorgeous creatures in satin tea gowns embroidered with beads and rhinestones, their hair Eton cropped and slick à la Josephine Baker. The men wore vintage suits and bowler hats. A slew of black-tuxedoed musicians brought up the rear, violins and saxophones in hand. Mother looked ready to shoot through the roof with happiness as she waved the musicians over to join the orchestra.

"We have *khachapuri*, everyone," she announced. "Leave your coats with dear Pia."

In the wake of it all, Paul strode in.

"My goodness, what's all this?" Paul said, squeezing past two women carrying a drum set, cloche hats pulled down over their eyes. I recognized them, of course.

"I think you know, Paul. How did you get the whole show here?"

"You know theater people. They were already dressed for a party. Carmen has a migraine, so no matinee today. We're free until curtain call at six."

The Streets of Paris pit band mixed well with Mother's Russian orchestra friends and found "Love Is Here to Stay" their musical bridge across the nations. Once the dancers recognized the song, they took to the dance floor, women foxtrotting and swing dancing with women, men with men.

Mother rushed to us, straightening her headdress as she walked.

"It's a nice-looking group, isn't it? I knew we'd eventually draw a crowd."

"Mother, Paul did all this. They're from his show. The whole cast."

Mother blinked, momentarily nonplussed, and then turned to Paul. "Well, the American Central Committee for Russian Relief thanks you, Mr. Rodierre."

"Is there any way those thanks might include a dance? I've never danced to Gershwin played on balalaika."

"Well, we mustn't deprive you of the opportunity," Mother said.

Once word leaked that the famous Paul Rodierre was at the thé dansant, the whole hotel came by, and Serge had to replenish the *tvorog* three times. Soon I managed to lose my headdress, and everyone was having a grand time, including Mother's orchestra friends, who'd brought some Russian vodka to liven up the iced tea.

By the time Paul left, his pockets were pregnant with Russian cigarettes pressed upon him by Mother, and the donation bowl for the American Central Committee for Russian Relief was overflowing.

Mother stopped near me to catch her breath between dances. "Feel free to collect as many French friends as you like, darling. I do miss theater people, don't you, dear? Such a refreshing change of pace."

Paul waved goodbye to me as he left, a job well done, off to deliver the cast back to the theater for curtain call. His kindness could not have found a more grateful object than Mother. She hadn't danced like that since Father died. How could I not be immensely thankful to him?

Betty was right. He really was my best friend.

CHAPTER 5

Kasia

1939

MATKA SCREAMED AS THE SS MAN BROUGHT THE SHOVEL down on Psina. After one dreadful squawk she lay quiet, the only sound the scratching of her still-running feet against the hard ground. A few butterscotch feathers hammocked in the air.

"That's how we did it back home," said the SS man. He threw down the shovel, picked poor Psina up by her limp neck, and tossed her to the skinny guard. I tried not to look at her legs, still scratching at the air.

"I'll let this go," the SS man said to Matka. He wiped his hands on a handkerchief. "But remember, withholding food from the Reich is a serious offense. You're lucky to get a warning."

"Of course," Matka said, one hand on her throat.

"Psina," I blurted out. Hot tears burned my eyes.

"Listen," said the skinny guard, holding Psina upside down, avoiding her talons. " 'Psina' means 'doggie' in Polish. They call a chicken a dog. Stupid Poles."

The men took Psina and stomped out, tracking soil on our floors.

My whole body trembled. "You let them kill her, Matka."

"Would you rather die for a chicken?" Matka said, but she had tears in her eyes, too.

We hurried to the kitchen and watched through the front window as the men left in their truck. Thank God my sister had not seen all that.

Zuzanna returned the next day, having spent the night at the hospital. Her mentor and hospital director Dr. Skala, famous for his cleft palate repair work, had been arrested, and she'd been ordered to leave the ward and told Poles were unfit to hold important positions. I'd never seen her so shaken, wild and angry at having been forced to leave her patients, who were mostly children. Later we learned that as far back as 1936 Nazis had been putting lists together of Poles they suspected of being anti-German and even marking targets like hospitals with giant X's that their pilots could see from the air. No wonder it was so easy for them to take those they wanted.

Papa returned as well after three days of interrogation by the Gestapo. He'd not been beaten, but he was ordered to work early each morning and spent long hours at the postal center. We were relieved he was alive, but he told us how hard it was to watch the Nazis open packages and letters from the post boxes of Polish citizens and just take what they wanted. They scattered sawdust on the floor after hours to make sure he and his staff did not visit the postal center at night when it was unattended.

Soon it seemed every Nazi in Germany rolled in. Our German neighbors went to the streets and hailed the arrivals with salutes and flowers while we stayed inside. Russian troops stayed east of us, advancing only as far as the Bug River.

After that, we were like flies stuck in honey, alive but not really living. We were lucky the Nazis reassigned Zuzanna to the Lublin Ambulance Corps, since they rounded up all the other doctors at the hospital, male and female, and took them away. They issued her papers complete with her photo and stamped with a dozen black Nazi eagles. These papers allowed her to be out at any time, even after curfew. Every morning that we woke up in our own beds we were grateful. So many of our Polish friends disappeared in the night with no explanation.

One day to keep warm I sat on my bed wrapped in a quilt and took a quiz in an old *Photoplay* magazine, my favorite indoor sport. A student in Pietrik's clandestine economics class had paid him in American magazines and I memorized every word in them. The quiz said you would feel a *click* like the sound of a compact closing if you were in love, and I felt that click every time I saw Pietrik. Our interests matched perfectly (a rare thing according to the quiz).

Pietrik stopped by that day. It was good to see him. I didn't care what we talked about. I just wanted to keep him there any way I could.

"How long can you stay?"

I cut a picture of Carole Lombard from the magazine. She was surrounded by white poinsettias, somewhere in Los Angeles. It was hard to remain casual when I could feel the compact going *click*.

Pietrik came and sat near me on the bed. The springs sagged under his weight.

"Not long. I came to ask a favor. It's about Nadia." He looked tired and had not shaved in days. "She had to go away for a while."

"What happened?" I said, suddenly cold all over.

"I can't say."

"But—"

"It's not safe for you to know. But trust me, people are working to change things."

It was obvious to me he was working with the underground. Though he didn't say as much, he must have been among the first to join after the Nazis invaded. I had noticed mysterious late-night meetings. Day-long absences with no explanation. He didn't wear the big black boots some boys in the underground did, making them sitting ducks for the Germans, but he was in deep.

I hoped it was not so obvious to the SS. Most of us boycotted German orders and sabotaged what we could, but the Home Army, the Armia Krajowa or AK, was serious. Though at the beginning it was not yet officially called AK, it represented the Polish government-in-exile in London. Our exiled government broadcast warnings to us through the BBC and the Polish radio station Swit and all of Lublin's seventeen underground newspapers.

"If you want to help, you can do me a big favor, Kasia."

"Anything."

"When Nadia and her mother left, they had to leave Felka behind. The Nazis are doing terrible things to the cats and dogs owned by Jews. Can you go and get her?"

"Where is Nadia? Can I see her?"

I didn't care anymore if she and Pietrik were in love. I just wanted them both to be safe.

"I can only tell you the Nazis almost arrested them, and they escaped just in time."

"For being Jewish? She's Catholic."

"Yes, but her grandfather was Jewish, so that puts her at risk. Nadia has to stay away for a while. She'll be fine, but right now Felka's not." He held my arm. "Will you help? Bring her here?"

"Of course."

"Also, Nadia's mother left something in her nightstand, and she needs to put it in a safe place. A yellow envelope tucked inside the phone book."

"I don't know, Pietrik. Nadia's mother always locks up."

"The back door is open. You need to take that phone book with the envelope inside it. I hate to involve you because you're precious to me, but I have no one else."

Were those tears in his eyes?

"Yes, you know I'll help."

I was precious to him? He took my hand, turned it over, and kissed my palm. I thought I might melt right there, through the floorboards and into the basement. For a moment, I forgot all the bad things going on.

"Bring the phone book with the envelope to 12 Lipowa Street tomorrow morning just after ten. Ring the bell. Someone will ask you who it is. You say, '*Iwona.*'"

"Is that my code name?" *Iwona* meant yew tree. I wanted a sexier code name like Grazyna, which means beautiful.

"Yes, that's your code name. Wiola will buzz you in. Just give her the book, and tell her it's for Konrad Zegota. Then leave as you came, and cut through Park Ludowy before you head home."

Later, when I replayed the scene in my head, I wasn't sure if he'd really said, "You're precious to me." But maybe the *Photoplay* love quiz was right after all.

THE NEXT MORNING I departed for Nadia's house, a fine apartment on the first floor of a two-story building, a five-minute walk from our place. I wanted to do a good job on my first mission for Pietrik.

On the way I stopped at the stone wall next to her house where we left secret notes and our favorite books for each other. I pulled our special square stone out, smooth, edges rounded from so many years of ins and outs. The last book I'd left was still there, Kornel Makuszynski's *Satan from the Seventh Grade,* our favorite book we'd passed back and forth so many times. Would she have a chance to take it? I left it and slid the stone back in place.

I continued on without the least bit of nerves, until I came to Nadia's house, that is. Once I saw her orange door, my knees became quaky. *Deep breath in. Deep breath out.*

I stepped around back to the little fenced-in yard, peeked through the slats, and saw Felka curled up on the back step. I could clearly see her ribs, even through her thick fur. Nadia's yard was even smaller than ours, a sickly rosebush and a rusted child's wagon the only ornaments.

I had a time of it getting over the fence and then walked slowly to Felka. Was she waiting for Nadia? I stroked her chest, and at my touch she tried to wag her tail, though she could barely lift her head. She was warm, but her breath was coming in shallow pants. Poor girl was starving.

I stepped over Felka, swung the back door open, and crept into the kitchen.

From the looks of the apple kugel on the table, it had been at least a week since Nadia and her mother left. The milk in their glasses was thick, and the flies had found the plums. I walked through the kitchen to Nadia's bedroom. Her bed was made, as always.

I stole through the rest of the house and into Nadia's mother's bedroom. In this room there was little sign of departure, hasty or otherwise. A white-painted iron bed, covered in a down duvet, took up most of the room, and a crocheted blanket lay at the foot. There was a depression in the down where a suitcase had been, and a Polish copy of *Gone with the Wind* waited on the bedside table. Two tapestries showing country scenes, a small crucifix, and a calendar hung on the wall. The calendar showed a smart-looking woman standing in front of a locomotive, a bunch of yellow flowers in her arms, with GERMANY WANTS TO SEE YOU printed across the top. It also featured the name of Mrs. Watroba's travel agency: WATROBA TRAVEL. LET US TAKE YOU THERE.

I opened the bedside table drawer, found the phone book, and paged through it to find the fat envelope. It was sealed, with the word *Zegota* written on the front in a spidery hand, the color of money faintly visible through the paper. I took the book, pulled the blanket from the foot of the bed, and retraced my steps back through the kitchen, where I grabbed a loaf of shiny, braided egg bread from the table. It was rock hard, but any bread was precious.

I reached the backyard and struggled Felka into the wagon. She barely made a peep, poor girl. I set the phone book next to her, smoothed the blanket over it all, and trundled off toward Lipowa Street, taking side streets to avoid Nazi guards. When we were almost there, we picked up speed, and the wagon bounced over the cobblestones.

"What have we here?"

An SS brownshirt stepped out of an alley and startled me no end.

I saw a girl from my *gimnazjum* class standing behind him, but she retreated into the shadows. I almost fell over, my knees jellied so.

"Just heading home," I said in German. Thank goodness I knew German, since all conversation in the Polish language had been banned.

"Ah, German, are we?" He lifted the blanket with his nightstick.

"No, Polish."

The officer ignored me and walked around for a closer look at the wagon.

"What is this? A dead dog?"

I could barely hear him. My heart was thumping so loud in my ears. "Just sick. I hope it's not catching."

The guard dropped the blanket. "Move along," he said. "Get that sick animal home." He disappeared back into the alley.

By the time I arrived at the office on Lipowa Street, I was soaked through with sweat. It was a busy road. I left Felka covered in the wagon and walked up the steps, legs shaking like the aspic on Matka's gaster carp. I was finally, officially a *spy*. At just sixteen years old, an enemy of the Nazis. There was such power in that! I stood a bit taller and rang the bell. What was the code name of the one who would accept the package?

Wiola.

"Who is it?" came a voice from inside.

"It is Iwona," I said.

I looked back at the street, cars and horse-drawn wagons driving on their way, people on the sidewalks. *Hurry,* Wiola. I could be spotted by the SS there with my telephone book for all the world to see.

The door buzzed, I entered and closed the door behind me.

I recognized the girl with the code name Wiola, Janina Grabowski, from my former Girl Guide troop. She held all ten fingers splayed, each tipped with wet ruby lacquer.

"Sorry I didn't answer the door straightaway," she said.

I held out the telephone book. "Wiola, this is for Konrad Zegota."

Janina was a good sort, with hair dyed flame red and a farm-girl build, but not my first choice for a partner when risking my life. She didn't have one serious Girl Guide proficiency badge in first aid or orienteering, and everyone knew she'd gotten her art badge for doing makeup.

Janina took the book between her palms.

"Thank you, *Iwona.*"

The office was in a converted apartment building with tall windows that overlooked the street, covered only with transparent white drapes. It was furnished with one metal desk, an old typewriter atop it; two easy chairs; and a dusty table scattered with outdated Polish fashion magazines. Someone had placed a glass bowl on the table, inside it one goldfish. The goldfish, suspended in place with his fins beating, stared at me, mouth agape in a surprised *O.* Even he could tell this office was a fake.

Janina flopped the telephone book onto the desk. A smile teased at her face until she burst out with a loud laugh.

"You can't expect me to keep a straight face, Kasia. *Iwona.* This is all so funny."

The name Pietrik had given her, Wiola, meant violet flower, not a fitting name for her, since she was a tall girl with wrists thick as table legs.

"Keep your voice down. Who knows who's nearby watching?"

The overhead lights were so bright. Were we lit up for every Nazi to see?

"The only Nazis that've come anywhere *near* here followed Anna Sadowski when she was carrying grenades in her bra. Flirted with her the whole way. Some girls get fun jobs." Janina stepped closer. "Stay for cards?"

Cards?

"There's money in that book. Shouldn't you hide it? Do you want to get us shot?"

"Come on, stay. I'll do your hair."

"I need to get home before dark."

She clutched her hands to her chest. "An updo?"

Janina worked part-time at the best hair salon in Lublin.

"Pietrik told me to leave right away."

"Are you two sweethearts?"

"I have to go—"

"Everyone says he likes you . . ."

I hurried to the door. "Don't listen to rumors."

Janina picked a magazine from the table, and slid herself up onto the desk. "So you're not interested in *any* rumors?"

I turned.

"Even rumors about, say . . . Nadia Watroba?"

I stepped toward the desk.

"What do you know?"

Janina thrust her chin in the air. "Oh, now you'll stay."

"She's my best friend."

"Oh, really?" Janina said, flipping through the magazine.

"Would you stop? Her dog is outside waiting, very sick—"

She slapped her magazine closed. "Not *Felka?*"

Nadia's Felka was a famous dog.

"Yes, Felka. So tell me now."

"Well, I only know a little . . ."

"Janina, if you don't tell me—"

"Okay. Okay. All I know is that Pietrik—well, I *think* it was Pietrik—took Nadia and her mother to a safe apartment."

"Close by?"

"In Lublin, yes. But that's all I know."

"*Nothing* else?"

"Just that I heard she's somewhere right under the Nazis' noses."

Dazed, I thanked Janina, walked back down the front steps, and started for home, through the park as Pietrik had told me. Nadia really was safe! My whole body relaxed as I pulled the wagon quicker to get Felka home and fed. Nadia was with her mother and still in Lublin! There was much I could do for her—care for Felka, keep working for the underground.

After all, my first mission had gone well even if Janina hadn't taken it seriously. Was I now part of the resistance? I'd delivered *money.* I would take the oath tomorrow and make it official.

Halfway home, the skies opened, flooding the cobblestone streets, soaking Felka and me through.

"You were lucky once," my wet shoes said with each step. "Don't make a habit of it."

CHAPTER 6

Herta

1939–1940

I TOOK THE TRAIN HOME FROM CAMP BLOSSOM, HAPPY TO LEAVE, my thoughts fixed on finding a job as a physician. I wore my BDM uniform, but before long regretted this. It would have been restful to watch the thick forests fly by outside the train window, assembling a mental checklist of possible clinics to visit. But I did not get a moment of solitude, for every passenger stopped to display admiration for my uniform.

"May I touch your eagle please, Fräulein?" a young boy asked.

He stood at my train seat, posture good, arms by his sides, rocking slightly as the train swayed. His mother stood behind him, two fingers to her lips, eyes wide, as if meeting the Führer. Yes, it was somewhat burdensome to represent the BDM, but flattering as well, since great respect was shown to those of us in that uniform. As young people, we had such power.

"You may," I said.

Water came to my eyes as he stroked the gold thread with the touch of a butterfly.

Nothing grips the heart like an unspoiled German child.

It was understandable my uniform caused a fuss, since most Germans had never seen the full complement of BDM badges on a woman. While the all-male Hitler Youth had patches and pins for every activity, down to potting plants, BDM achievement badges were limited in number and hard-won. On my navy-blue leader's jacket, I wore the Red Cross patch, the silver proficiency clasp for nursing, and the first aid and physical fitness badges.

But it was the eagle indicating the highest level of leadership, the golden bird worn over my heart, his bullioned wings fanned out, which attracted the most attention. Mutti had cried with pride the day I first wore it home. She'd been more impressed with that than my diploma from medical school, accelerated on account of the war.

Once home, I tried to find my first job as a doctor, but even though I'd graduated second in my class, practices were reluctant to hire a woman doctor. It seemed the Party rhetoric about a woman's rightful place being at home raising children had taken root and many patients requested a male physician. Since, as a female university student, I'd been required to take needlework classes, I took in sewing work for extra money.

I finally found a part-time post at the Skin Clinic of Düsseldorf, which paid a small fee for each patient I treated. It was a dull job, the highlight of most days lancing a boil. Would I forget the few surgical techniques I'd learned in medical school? A surgeon must operate consistently to stay proficient.

Our economy had improved markedly by then, which only reduced the number of patients seeking skin treatment. Even dishpan hands, once the bread and butter of dermatology, were not a problem for most German housewives anymore. Polish laborers provided by the Reich, imported from the east, took care of the scullery work.

As a result, my earnings soon dropped to almost nothing. Father's condition went from serious to critical, and Mutti had to stay home with him. I barely sustained all three of us. In no time I became the only starving doctor in Düsseldorf, so I continued to work part time at *Onkel* Heinz's butcher shop.

After the stillness of the Camp Blossom woods and the quiet clinic, the bustle of the crowds coming to the shop for their meat, the anxious *Hausfrauen* in their ironed housedresses jostling to the counter, like a polite herd of cattle themselves, was a welcome variation. There I could escape my troubles and just tear great sheets of white paper from the roll and practice surgical knots as I wrapped packages in striped twine.

I came to work as usual one Sunday, when the shop was closed to the public. That was the day Heinz had me work there alone, so no one could see what I made for him.

His special project.

"Hurry up," Heinz said.

He pressed himself against the butcher-block table, which sagged from the blows of his cleaver and his father's before him. His bulge was plain even under his butcher's apron, which was stiff with dried calf's blood. How did I get myself in such a fix? Years of being too afraid to say anything; that is how.

Heinz watched as I stood at the worktable and chose the tautest lamb intestine. The waiting was the best and worst part for Heinz. I turned the tissue inside out, macerated it in bleach, and removed the mucous membrane, careful to leave the peritoneal and muscular coats. *Onkel* Heinz urged me on, but I took my time, since any tear or pinprick could spell disaster.

"I'm going as fast as I can," I said. It was best to stall, for once I finished, the worst part came, and the whole process began again.

Bad thoughts stung me as I worked. Why wasn't I home researching new jobs? It was my own fault I was stuck there, trapped by Heinz, fearing he would reveal our secret. I should have told on him years before, but *Tante* Ilsa would never have paid for my schooling if she'd known. What would Mutti say? I could never tell her, of course. Even sick as he was, Father would murder *Onkel* Heinz if he knew. This was the price I paid for my education. Heinz said I'd brought it on myself, a young woman alone there with him.

Heinz moved next to me and lifted my skirt. I felt the familiar creep of his calloused fingers onto my thigh.

"Why does it take you so long?" Heinz asked. I smelled that sweet wine he liked on his breath.

I pushed his hand away. "Things take time."

Heinz was not exactly the cream of the master race. With an IQ somewhere between borderline deficient and mildly retarded, he was easily put off by any excuse more than two words long. I patted the delicate tissue dry, measured, and cut. Heinz was red in the face by the time I rolled it down, smooth and clear as a silk stocking.

I didn't have to be told to go to the meat locker with the tin bucket of lard. There was a curious comfort in the sameness of it. I pulled the string attached to the bare bulb to illuminate the space and braced myself against the cold wooden shelf behind me. Even with the flour sack across my face, I knew what was coming. The sweet flour smell cut his odor of beef blood, cigars, and bleach. *Don't cry.* Crying only angered Heinz and made it take longer. He inched my handiwork over himself, dipped one paw into the lard, ran it down the membrane, and began.

I reviewed the bones of the hand.

One: the scaphoid bone, derived from the Greek skaphos, *which means boat.*

Folds of fat hung from Heinz's abdomen like a hairy apron and flapped against me with each thrust. With his irregular breathing coming faster, it would not be long.

Two: the lunate bone, shaped like a crescent moon.

I had long ago stopped wishing for a sudden heart attack. Years of fatty roasts must have provided him with arterial plaque buildup two fingers thick, but he managed to stay alive nonetheless.

Three: the triquetrum bone. Four: the round pisiform bone, named for the Latin for pea.

Heinz could not contain himself and began his usual moaning and so on, his breath a cold fog on my neck. His hands shook as he gripped the shelf, his thick butcher's wrists supporting his weight.

Without warning, the refrigerator door opened, and the flour sack slipped from my face. Ilsa stood in the doorway, holding the door open with one hand, a jar of marmalade in the other. She must have heard Heinz groaning like a stuck pig.

"Shut that door, woman," Heinz said, pants puddled at his ankles, face purple.

Was that disgust on her face or just weariness? She placed the marmalade on the refrigerator shelf, turned, and left.

The locker door chunked shut behind her, and Heinz went back about his work.

ONE SLOW DAY AT the skin clinic, I sat at my desk after finishing with my last patient, a rotund four-year-old thumb-sucker. I'd sent his mother home with some antiseptic cream for a rash. How would I make a living doing this? I was much better suited to the tranquility of a university position, but a teacher's salary would not support my family much better.

I picked up *The Journal of Medicine* and noticed a classified ad for a *doctor needed at a reeducation camp for women, 90 km north of Berlin, near the resort town of Fürstenberg on Lake Schwedt.* There were many such camps at the time, mostly for the work-shy and minor criminals. The idea of a change of scenery was appealing. A resort town? I would miss Mutti but wouldn't miss Heinz.

The only other thing I knew about the camp was that Fritz Fischer, my former medical school classmate, worked there, but it had a pleasant-sounding name.

Ravensbrück.

CHAPTER 7

Caroline

DECEMBER 1939

CHRISTMAS EVE DAY, PAUL AND I MADE IT OVER TO THE FIFTH Avenue Skating Pond in Central Park. I loved to skate, having learned on Bird Pond near our house in Connecticut, but rarely practiced, since I avoided most activities that made me look taller than necessary. Plus, I'd never had anyone to skate with before. Betty would have rather swallowed live bees than be seen on skates. I vowed to take full advantage of Paul's time in New York.

It was perfect skating weather that day, clear and sharp with a stiff wind, which overnight had made the ice smooth as the finish on a billiard ball. As a result, the flag atop Belvedere Castle was up, the red sphere on a white field every skater coveted. Word that the ice was ready passed from doorman to doorman along Fifth Avenue, and the pond became thick with skaters as a result.

The first tier of skaters was already there when Paul and I arrived. The men, near professionals, performed their genuflections and whirligig spins, icicles on their beards and noses. Then the ladies arrived, two or three at a time, their heavy coats like sails blowing them across the ice. With a little practice, Paul proved to be a serviceable skater, and arms linked, we glided throughout the network of adjoining ponds. My old self never would have skated in such a public place, but I tackled the ice with vigor, and we soon found a nice rhythm together. Suddenly I felt like trying every sort of new thing.

We sailed under arched bridges to Beethoven's *Moonlight Sonata* and Waldteufel's *The Skaters' Waltz*, which couldn't have sounded lovelier, even transmitted through the skate shack's tinny speakers.

The ice grew more crowded, so we skated back toward the shack, the scent of warm chestnuts in the air. We were about to sit and change out of our skates when I heard my name.

"Caroline. Over here."

It was David Stockwell. He skated to us and stopped with a sharp edge and a smile, posing like something out of a Brooks Brothers advertisement, drawing his jacket back with one gloved fist. How could David act as if nothing had ever happened between us, as if up and marrying an acquaintance after stringing me along for ten years was completely natural?

"Hey, who's this guy, Caroline?" David said.

Was that a flash of jealousy? David did seem small by comparison. Would he think Paul and I were romantically engaged? Slim chance of that. Paul was keeping his distance and gave off only friend signals, not even standing close to me. What if he did show David I was his? Thinking about that made me wish it were true.

Paul extended his hand. "Paul Rodierre."

David shook it. "David Stockwell. I've known Caroline since—"

"We really must be going," I said.

"Sally is over there lacing up. She'd hate to miss you."

I'd had advance warning about Sally from Betty, of course. Her new sister-in-law was a petite girl whom Mrs. Stockwell had showered with a haute couture wedding trousseau the cost of which could have fed half of New York for a year. I gave David my best "we really can't stay" look.

He turned to Paul. "I'm with the State Department. Working to keep us out of the war. Heard about your speech at the gala. Seems you're working to get us into it."

"Just telling the truth," Paul said.

"It was our most successful event ever," I said.

Paul skated closer to me and linked my arm in his. "Yes, darling, overwhelming, wasn't it?"

Darling?

David blinked, taken aback.

I moved closer to Paul. "Deafening applause. And the *donations.* Everyone's behind France now."

Sally Stockwell skated toward us through the crowd. It was hard to ignore the *smallness* of her, maybe five feet two inches tall. She was done up in full skating costume, boiled wool A-line skating skirt, a snug little quilted Tyrolean jacket, and white fur of some kind at the top of her skates. The yarn tassle on the knitted cap she wore, tied under her pretty chin, swayed as she neared.

"You must be Caroline," Sally said. She stretched a white angora-mittened hand out to me, and I shook it.

Sally was more Olivia de Havilland than Bette Davis and impossible to dislike, with a disarming honesty that made even the most trivial conversation awkward.

"David's told me everything about you. 'Caroline helps French babies. Caroline and I starred in our first play together—' "

"I was Caroline's first leading man," David said. "Played Sebastian to her Olivia."

Paul smiled. "They share a kiss, don't they? How were the reviews?"

"Lukewarm," I said.

Sally skated closer. "Sometimes I think you and David should have married."

"So good to see you both," I said. "Sorry to run off, but we have to be going."

"Yes, spending the whole day together, aren't we, sweetheart?" Paul said.

He was laying it on thick. That would activate the gossip mill, but I didn't care. It felt good to be loved, if only for show.

We said our goodbyes and waved to Sally and David as they merged into the flow of skating couples. How lovely it was of Paul to pretend to be my beau. He was not mine to flaunt, of course, but it was still nice to have someone in my life to show off, especially to David Stockwell, who'd so thoroughly trampled my ego.

After skating, Paul went back to the Waldorf to change, and I decorated the fat blue spruce Mother's bosom friend Mr. Gardener had brought down from the country and made coq au vin. Serge had sent down a winter vegetable soup from Connecticut, loaded with sugar parsnips, fat carrots, and gorgeous sweet fennel, for our first course.

That night the snow, which had hit Connecticut earlier, made it to Manhattan with a vengeance, leaving Mother stranded with Serge up at our country house. Paul arrived at my door with snow-flakes in his hair and on the shoulders of his overcoat. His face was cold against mine as he leaned in to kiss me on each cheek. He'd gone heavy on the Sumare, once one of my father's favorite scents. I'd peeked in Paul's medicine cabinet at the Waldorf when I used his bathroom and seen the bottle there beside the blue jar of Noxzema.

Paul held a bottle of Burgundy and a nosegay of crimson glory roses wrapped in white paper. I would need to keep my wits about me and watch my wine intake. I was relieved he'd dressed up, in his aubergine jacket, for I was wearing a dress and silk stockings.

He slid the bottle, heavy and cold, into my hands.

"*Joyeux Noël.* It's the last of the case my cousin sent from his vineyard. Hope you don't mind, but I left your number with the Waldorf operator in case I need to be reached."

"Of course not. Worried about Rena?"

"Always, but it's just a precaution. I spoke with her this morning and gave her the visa update. Roger says he'll know in a few days."

Rena. It was as if she stood there with us.

Paul stepped into the living room. "You could land an airplane in here. Just us tonight?"

"They can't get out of the driveway up in Connecticut."

"So I'm your only amusement? Such pressure."

After dinner, I left the dishes in the sink and sat on the lumpy horsehair sofa, sharing a bottle of Father's cognac with Paul. That sofa had belonged to Mother's mother, whom we called Mother Woolsey. She'd gotten it to deter Mother's beaux from lingering.

It grew chilly once the fire reduced to embers, for we kept the heat low in the apartment. Paul heaved a birch log onto the grate, and the blaze went full tilt, licking the firebox, so hot I could feel it on my face.

I kicked off my shoes and tucked my legs up under me.

"Someone's been drinking the cognac," I said, holding the bottle to the firelight.

"Maybe it is just the angel's share," Paul said. "That's what they call the part that evaporates from the cognac cellars."

He stabbed at the log with the iron poker, face somber in the firelight. Why were men so serious about fires?

Paul came back to the sofa. "I feel like everything's ahead of me when I'm here like this. Like a child."

"Somewhere in a corner of our hearts, we are always twenty," I said. How many times had Mother said that?

Paul tipped a slosh of cognac into his glass. "Your old boyfriend is a beautiful man."

"He'd agree, no doubt." I held my glass out for more cognac.

Paul hesitated.

"Man, being reasonable, must get drunk," I said. Why was I quoting Byron? It made me sound two million years old.

"The best of life is but intoxication," Paul said, as he poured cognac into my glass.

He knew Byron?

"How come you never ask me about Rena?" Paul said.

"Why would I?" That was the last thing I wanted to talk about.

"Oh, I don't know. Thought you might be curious how I can stay away so long."

"The show, of course," I said. The amber in my glass glowed in the firelight.

"We don't have much of a marriage now."

"Paul. Such a cliché." Why could I not stop talking to men like a schoolmarm? I deserved to end up alone, sent out on an ice floe as the Eskimos do with their elders.

"Rena's so young. A lot of fun—you'd like her, I'm sure—but we could never sit here like this and talk about life."

"What does she like to do?" I said.

The fire popped and whined as it consumed a drop of pitch.

"Dancing, parties. She's a child in many ways. We got married very soon after we met. It was great fun at first, and the bedroom time was incredible, but soon she grew restless. I've heard she's had some attractive boyfriends."

Incredible bedroom time? Heavenly, no doubt. I flicked a bit of lint off my sleeve.

"By the way, in this country, men don't talk about their bedroom exploits."

"In this country, men have none to speak of," Paul said. "They get married, and their exploits shrivel up and fall off. Rena is a wonderful girl, but according to her, we are just incompatible. Believe me, I've tried."

He fiddled with the fire some more and came back, this time sitting closer to me on the sofa. For such a virile man, he had a lovely mouth.

"Is anyone compatible anymore?" I said. "My parents are the only couple I've ever thought were truly in sync."

"How did your father die?"

"I've never talked about it before. I was eleven, and back then one didn't discuss such things."

"Was he a good father?"

"On weekends he came up from the city to Connecticut. He exchanged his starched collar and waistcoat for khakis and pitched to us, endlessly, at the baseball field Mother had made at the far end of our property."

"Was he often sick?"

"Never. But the spring of 1914, one day he was sequestered in his bedroom here, out of the blue. Only Dr. Forbes and Mother were allowed in. By the time I was sent to relatives with my valise packed, I knew something was terribly wrong. The maids stopped talking when I came into the room, and Mother's face had a hunted look I'd never seen on her before."

"I'm so sorry, Caroline." Paul held my hand in his warm and soft one and then released it.

"Five days later I was allowed to come home, but no one would look me in the eye. As always, I got my best information hiding in the dumbwaiter just off the kitchen, peeking through a crack. We had four Irish maids living in at the time. The eldest, Julia Smith, filled her coworkers in on the big event as she shelled peas at the kitchen table. I still remember every word. Julia said, 'I knew Mr. Ferriday wouldn't go down without a fight.'

"Mary Moran, a skinny new girl, was pushing a dirty gray squid of a mop back and forth across the black and white tiles. She said, 'Pneumonia's the most wretched way to die. Like drowning, only slower. Were you in the room? Better not have touched him.'

"Then Julia said, 'One minute he was laughing like a lunatic, and the next he was clawing at his chest saying it was too hot and crying for Dr. Forbes to "Open a window, for God's sake." Then he started asking for his daughter, Caroline, and it just about broke my heart. Mrs. Ferriday kept saying, "Henry, darling, don't leave me," but he must have already died, because Dr. Forbes stuck his head out the door and told me, "Run get the undertaker."'

"Lily Clifford, the youngest of the four, chimed in: 'Just caught a glimpse of Mrs. Ferriday, arms around him there on the bed, saying, "I can't live without you, Henry," sounding so sad and lonely I wanted to cry myself.'

"That evening, Mother told me the news. I just stared at Father's humidor, wondering what would happen to his cigars now that he was gone. Mother and I never spoke much of Father's death and she never cried in front of me or anyone else after that day."

"What a terrible thing, Caroline," Paul said. "You were so young."

"I'm sorry to ruin our festive mood."

"That's a heavy burden for a child."

"Let's talk about happier things."

"You have a kind heart, Caroline," Paul said, as he reached over and tucked a lock of hair behind my ear. I almost jumped, his touch a jolt of warmth.

"Enough death and dying," I said. "What else can we talk about?"

We both stared into the fire for a while, listening to the logs crack and pop.

Paul turned to me. "Well, I do have a confession to make."

"Don't good Catholics do that with a priest?"

He ran one finger down my stockinged foot. "It's just that, well, I can't be trusted around silk stockings."

Did he understand the power he had in his fingertip?

"I'm afraid I was scarred for life by a school friend."

I sat up straighter. "Maybe I'd better not know."

"He had boxes of old photos under his bed."

"Nature shots?"

"Well, in a way, yes. Mostly of women in silk stockings. Little else." Paul swirled the amber in his snifter. "I've never been the same. It's something about the seams. After I saw Marlene Dietrich in *The Blue Angel* sing 'Naughty Lola,' I had to wait until everyone else left the theater before I could stand up."

"Marlene wore sheer black stockings in that."

"Can we not talk about it? It still gets me a bit, well, overstimulated."

"You brought it up."

"Guess I've always been drawn to strong women," Paul said.

"Have Mother introduce you to Eleanor Roosevelt."

Paul smiled and placed his snifter on the floor. "You're unique, you know, Caroline. Something about you makes me want to bare my soul." He looked at me, silent for a moment. "I get attached, you know. You may not be able to get rid of me."

"Like a barnacle," I said.

He smiled and leaned closer to me. "Yes, whatever that is."

I stood, smoothing my dress. We needed to change gears before things became complicated.

"Wait here," I said. "I have something for you. Nothing elaborate."

"So mysterious, Caroline. Much like Marlene."

I went to my bedroom. Was this a mistake? Did male and female friends give each other gifts? He had nothing for me, after all. I brought out the silver-papered package I'd wrapped and rewrapped to give it a casual appearance and handed it to Paul.

"What is this?" he said. Was the pink in his cheeks from embarrassment or the cognac?

"It's nothing," I said and sat down next to him.

He slid his hand under the paper to break the cellophane tape.

"Really, it's just a friend gift," I said. "Betty and I give each other gifts all the time. Just casual."

He pulled back the folded ends and sat with the paper open on his lap, staring down at the folded rectangle, the color of aged claret, apparently struck mute.

"It was Father's," I said. "He had dozens of them. Never wore them, of course. Maybe if he had—"

Paul lifted the scarf, merino wool backed in silk, and held it, working the fabric with his fingers.

"I don't know what to say," he said.

My mouth went dry. Had I been too forward with such a personal gift?

"Won't your mother object?"

"She would have dispensed with all Father's things by now if I'd let her."

"Maybe it is hard for her to see them now, with him gone."

"She almost gave his vicuña coat to an underdressed delivery boy."

He lifted one end of the scarf and slowly wound it around his neck, head bent. "This is too beautiful, Caroline." He finished and opened his hands, palms up. "Well?"

He looked like one of the boys about to go out sledding on Bird Pond up in Bethlehem, high color in his cheeks. What would it be like to kiss him? Would we both regret it, seeing as he had a wife, incompatible or not, who would soon be waking up in France waiting for his call?

Of course.

I stood, a bit light-headed.

"Would you like to see them? Father's clothes, I mean."

I led Paul down the hallway to Father's room. Mother and Father had kept separate bedrooms, as was the custom then. The desk lamp in the corner sent shadows up the wall. The maids still dusted the room, washed the organza curtains each spring, and laundered the Greek key linens, as if Father were expected back any day, ready to shout, "Hi-ho!" and throw his leather valise on the bed. A small sofa sat in the bay window alcove, slipcovered in relaxed, faded chintz that lost its waxy sheen long ago. I opened the door to Father's closet, releasing a wave of Vicks VapoRub and tobacco-scented air, and clicked on the light.

"Oh, Caroline," Paul said.

Father's double-hung closet was almost as he'd left it, with rows of khaki, brown wool, and white flannel trousers folded over hangers; all manner of jackets, from belted Norfolks and worsted serge to a one-button cutaway. Legions of two-tone shoes and one pair of patent leather dress slippers, stuffed with tissue paper, lined up on the floor. Foulard ties shared rack space with belts, hung by their brass buckles. Mother's black bunting from the funeral lay in a heap on the top shelf. Not that I'd been at Saint Thomas Church that day, being only eleven. *The New York Times* had said, *The Woolsey women locked arms that day in the front pew.* I pulled on one belt and slipped the suede-lined sealskin leather through my fingers.

"He was very neat," Paul said.

"Not really. Mother kept him together."

Paul lifted a gray fedora, stuffed tight with yellowed tissue paper, from the top shelf. He turned it in his hands, like a scientist examining a rare meteorite, and put it back. He seemed somber all at once. Why had I spoiled the mood?

"Father was color-blind, you see," I said.

Paul just looked at me. If only I could stop blathering.

"And to make matters worse, he refused to be dressed by a valet."

Paul made no attempt to stop me, just watched with a look I couldn't place. Pity for a poor spinster who missed her dead father?

"Father insisted on dressing himself. So Mother bought him only basic colors. Browns and navys." I clicked off the closet light. "Before that, you should have *seen* his outfits."

As I closed the closet door, I felt tears coming but held them back.

"One morning at breakfast, he appeared in a yellow jacket, purple tie, burnt-orange trousers, and red socks. Mother almost choked, she laughed so hard."

I turned my face to the closet door, forehead against the cool paint. "I'm sorry, Paul. I'll get myself together."

Paul took my shoulders and turned me to face him and then pulled me close. He smoothed back my hair, and his lips found my cheek. They lingered in the little dip there under my eye and then traveled across my face. He took the long way to my mouth, and once there, tasted of coq au vin and French cigarettes.

Paul unwound the scarf from his neck and released a wave of Sumare.

Pine. Leather. Musk.

We made our way to the sofa as icy snow pelted the windows above us like sand in a hurricane. My heart skipped a beat as his hand brushed the inside of my thigh on the way to release a stocking. He sent two fingers into the silk and drew it down. I unbuttoned the top button of his shirt. Then another. I slipped my hands inside his open shirt, down his sides, smooth as the inside of a conch shell.

"I think maybe you had more than the angel's share of the cognac," Paul said in my ear.

He unfastened the top button of my dress. In the low light, his face was especially beautiful, so serious. We were really doing this . . . I pushed away thoughts of him with Rena.

The second and third buttons went, so slowly.

He pulled my dress down off my shoulder and kissed my bare skin. "I can't believe how beautiful you are," he said, working his lips down to my chest, in no hurry at all.

"Perhaps a bed would be a good idea."

I could only nod. My canopy bed with the pink satin bedspread? That bed had never seen anything like Paul Rodierre.

We zigzagged to my bedroom, leaving my underthings along the way.

"Arms up," Paul said once we made it to the bed.

I raised my arms as if ready to dive, and he slipped my slip and dress up and off in one motion. He slid out of his jacket and brought me to him. My fingers shook as I felt for his belt. He kissed me as I pulled the end free from the buckle and slid the whole thing through the loops. The zipper purred down. He stepped out of his pants and brought us both to the bed. We fell onto smooth satin, the slats surprised by the sudden weight.

"Are you still wearing your socks?" I said.

He kissed the base of my throat.

"What is that sound?" Paul asked, working his way downward.

"What?" I propped myself up on one elbow. "Is someone here?"

He pulled me back down, lips close to my ear. "It's nothing." His sandpapery chin grazed my cheek in a good way. "Don't worry about it."

It was lovely having Paul in my bed, all to myself. I sank deeper into the pink satin as he rolled on top of me and kissed my mouth, now urgently.

I heard the sound this time. Someone knocking. How had someone gotten past the doorman? I froze, as Paul's lips traveled downward.

"Someone's here," I said, shaking in the darkness.

CHAPTER 8

Kasia

1940–1941

WHAT YOU MUST UNDERSTAND IS HOW SOCIAL THE POLISH underground was for a young person. After the Germans invaded and deemed Girl Guides and Scouts criminal organizations, we just continued clandestinely and became known as the Szare Szeregi, or Gray Ranks. We answered to the Polish government-in-exile in London, and most of the Girl Guides joined. This group was my only source of companionship, since Zuzanna worked long hours at the Lublin Ambulance Corps and was never home. Plus, it was a good way to vent our frustration at being occupied by the Germans.

We'd had excellent first aid training in Girl Guides, but in the Gray Ranks, we continued educating ourselves and attended secret medical courses. The older girls fought alongside the boys or worked as nurses and seamstresses and managed orphanages. Some even helped free people from German prisons, blow up bridges, and steal German military plans.

We younger girls in my seven-person squad saved Polish books from being destroyed by German soldiers and taught secret classes. We trained as decoders and delivered fake identity cards and messages. We did our part to sabotage the Nazis, rearranging street signs to make sure the SS got lost. At night we connected to German broadcast speakers in the streets and played the Polish national anthem. The more we got away with, the more we wanted it, as if it were a drug. We had to be careful, though, since not only had the Nazis chosen Lublin as their Polish headquarters, but all across Poland, German spies had started identifying our former Girl Guide leaders and arresting them.

Plus, *lapanka* were occurring more frequently. A *lapanka* was something Matka lived in fear of for us—a sudden, wild manhunt executed by the SS. No longer did the authorities wait for the cover of night. They took their prey, random Polish citizens, in daylight in the most unexpected places: Churches. Train stations. Ration lines. Anyone unlucky enough to be caught was seized and taken to a confinement center. Most were sent to Germany to be worked to death. Aryan-looking Polish children were at risk too. They started disappearing in great numbers from the cities. One day a whole train of them was rounded up and taken. The German guards shot the mothers as they ran after the train. In the country, if too few laborers reported, whole villages were burned.

Though Pietrik wouldn't speak of it, his father, a captain in our Polish army, had been arrested along with his fellow officers, leaving Pietrik the only man in his house. Before the war every man who'd graduated from university had been required to join the military as a reserve officer, so it was easy for the authorities to eliminate our most educated by arresting all members of the Polish Officers Corps. At least Pietrik had not been conscripted into the army when the war broke out.

I begged Pietrik for more important assignments, like those the older girls got, but as our group commander, he was full of excuses.

"Tell me I'm not good at missions," I told Pietrik one afternoon at our apartment. "Look what a good job I did with Nadia's house."

Pietrik helped me wash the few paintbrushes Matka had not buried. She'd placed them under a floorboard so she could still paint at night. They were not just any brushes, but Kolinsky sable-hair watercolor brushes, and washing them was a task of honor Matka trusted me with. She inherited those Stradivariuses of the brush world from her mother, and each was worth a fortune. They came tucked in a red-flannel roll, each one with its own narrow sleeve to live in, each made of Russian weasel hair, from the male weasels only, three times more precious per pound than gold.

"I have nothing for you, Kasia," Pietrik said. "Things are quiet now."

For a boy with such large hands, he was gentle with the brushes. He dipped one in the soapsuds and ran his fingers gently over the nickel ferrule and down the sable tip.

"If I spend another day in this house, I'll go mad."

Pietrik set his brush next to mine on the dishrag. "You know the rules. You're not old enough. Read a book."

"I'm capable of more——"

"No, Kasia."

"Nothing feels better than fighting them, Pietrik. Send me anywhere. It doesn't have to be big."

"If you were ever caught, being a beautiful young girl is no defense against them. They'll shoot a pretty one as soon as any other."

Beautiful? Me? Pretty?

"If you don't assign me, I'll go work for the Free Press. I heard they need runners."

"You are safer with me."

"There you go."

Finally, progress!

Pietrik turned to me, serious.

"Well, there is one thing. A complicated assignment, so you have to *listen*."

"In the ghetto?" I asked.

He nodded.

Right away I was afraid but didn't dare show it. One frightened look, and that would be the end of my assignments.

"You need to go to Z's Pharmacy." He paused. "No, on second thought, you're not doing this."

"Who is better? I used to have chocolate ice cream at Zaufanym's with Nadia. Mr. Z goes to our church."

Though it was in the ghetto, there was no rule against Christians buying at Z's. All sorts of people shopped there, even the SS, since the pharmacist and owner, known as Mr. Z to most, was practically a doctor and somehow stocked every remedy, even with the war on.

"Can you be there at exactly two tomorrow?"

"Have I ever been late?"

"The patrol shift changes then, so you'll have exactly five minutes when there will be no guards who will stop you. Avoid the blackshirts as best you can. They've added patrols."

"Got it," I said with a smile, though all the blood in my body seemed to stop running. I had the feeling in my stomach that said, "Think twice about this," but I shooed it away.

"Enter, and go straight to the door at the back of the shop," Pietrik said.

"To the basement?"

"Yes. Take the stairs down." Pietrik took my hand and looked into my eyes. "Once you make contact, stay five minutes only. You'll be accepting an important package, Kasia. Do you understand?"

I nodded. Doing my best to keep a calm voice, I asked, "Might anything explode?"

"No, but speak to no one as you leave. Come back to your regular shift at the theater. Your cover story is you are buying aspirin."

Pietrik was so serious as he gave me my instructions. A cover story. It was a real mission, and though my hands shook, I would execute it perfectly. Five minutes was a world of time just to pick up some things.

I BARELY SLEPT THAT NIGHT, a running loop of all that could go wrong playing in my head. The ghetto. Just being in the wrong place could get one arrested. Every day one heard of neighbors and friends taken to Gestapo headquarters, "Under the Clock," the innocent-looking office building with cells in the basement, or worse, to Lublin Castle, where prisoners were shot in the courtyard.

I set out for Z's Pharmacy the next afternoon with shaky legs. It was a gray day, the wind pushing heavy clouds about the sky. No need to be afraid. That was what got you caught. Nazis could smell the fear.

I was halfway to Grodzka Gate, the official entrance to the ghetto, when I saw something that stopped me in my tracks. It was Matka coming out of Deutsche Haus, the restaurant where every German in town ate. The one with the extra big FÜR POLEN VERBO- TEN! sign on the door. The SS men especially loved the place, since they knew the food was safe to eat and practically free, and they knew they didn't have to eat sitting next to any Polish person. Rumor was the place was full of cigarette smoke and the portions were so large much went uneaten, but no one I knew had been in- side, or so I thought. At least not to live to tell of it, for this was the rule. No Poles allowed. Just the week before, our greengrocer had been caught in the kitchen, there to deliver potatoes, and was ar- rested. He never came back.

These arrests were becoming common events. That morning I'd read in Zuzanna's underground newspaper that in just three months of war, fifty thousand Polish citizens had been rounded up and mur- dered, about seven thousand of them Jews. Most were town leaders—lawyers, professors, and religious leaders, anyone who broke rules or opposed the occupying forces. The Nazis saw the Catholic Church as a dangerous enemy, and there was a long list of priests arrested. Citizens were often wrongly accused of crimes and sent away or executed in public squares, the shots waking us at night.

So once I saw Matka come out of Deutsche Haus clutching a brown package no bigger than a small loaf of bread at her chest, I had to know what she was doing there. It was lunchtime, and peo- ple packed the sidewalks, heads down against the wind. She walked in the opposite direction from me, toward home.

I pushed through the crowd to reach her. "Matka!" I called.

Matka turned and, once she saw me, looked like the icy hand of a spirit had touched her. "Kasia. You're not at the theater? I'm bringing your sandwich later."

"I took late shift today." I had worked as ticket girl at the movie theater near our flat since Zuzanna bequeathed the job to me.

We sidestepped a water-ration line that wound down the block.

"You were at Deutsche Haus? No Poles are allowed in there."

"They consider me German."

I felt a little sick just thinking about her in that place. It was true about the cigarettes! I could smell them on her.

"How could you?"

"Don't be hysterical, Kasia. I was just dropping—"

We both stepped off the sidewalk and let a German couple promenade by us, per regulations.

"Dropping what?"

She clenched the paper bag tighter and squeezed out a fragrant scent—dark and exotic—of palm trees and sunburned Brazil. Coffee.

"You can tell me, Matka." I breathed deep to dispel the panic. "Is that a new eau de toilette?"

She stepped back up onto the sidewalk and picked up her pace. "Leave it alone, Kasia."

I'd seen the new silk stockings in her bottom drawer, puddled under folded shirts, limp as shedded snakeskins. The realization wound around me. "You can't just ignore it. You must go to confession."

She stopped again and drew me close, voice low.

"Bless me, Father, for I have had coffee with an SS man? Lennart is—"

I laughed. "*Lennart?* The name Lennart means brave, Matka. Lennart the *Brave* killed our Psina with a *shovel.*"

The sun broke through the clouds, and the barest smudge of

black in the hollow of her cheek caught the light, iridescent. Char-
coal.

"You've been sketching them." *Deep breath in . . .*

She pulled me to her. "Quiet, Kasia. They like my work, and it
gets me close—"

"It's dangerous."

"You think I like it? It's all for Papa. They would have *shot* him,
Kasia."

"If I had a husband like Papa I'd rather die than be unfaithful to
him."

She walked on, pushing through the crowd, and I followed,
knocked about by people rushing in every direction.

"How could you understand?" she said.

I pulled at her jacket sleeve.

She brushed my hand away.

"They call it race defilement, Matka. A Pole and a German. Together."

She spun to face me.

"Would you be *quiet?* What is wrong with you?" Her breath
smelled of coffee and pear *chrusciki.*

I was beyond crying. How could she be so reckless?

"They'll take us all. Papa too."

"Get to work," she said with a cross look. She rushed away across
the street and narrowly missed being hit by a couple in a fancy open
car, who honked and yelled something in German. She made it to
the curb and turned. Feeling badly she'd been cross with me?

"I'll bring your sandwich to the theater," she called to me, one
hand next to her mouth. "I'll drop it off early!"

When I didn't answer, she clutched her coffee to her chest and
walked along, swallowed up by the crowd.

I stood there trembling. Whom could I tell? Not Papa. He would
kill Lennart the Brave, and we'd all be shot. I glanced back to
Deutsche Haus and saw Lennart walk down the steps with three

others, digging a toothpick in between his teeth. How could Matka meet with such a man?

I brought my thoughts back to the mission. What was our Girl Guide motto? "Be aware!" It was important to stay focused so I could execute Pietrik's mission without a hitch. I would tell Zuzanna later. She would help Matka regain her senses.

I continued on toward the ghetto, passed through Grodzka Gate, and made it down to Zaufanym's Pharmacy in record time. That was easy enough. I'd been to Z's Pharmacy millions of times with Nadia, but this time as I walked down the cobblestone road, I couldn't shake the impression I was descending into Dante's Inferno.

Once, Old Town had been the most active shopping district in Lublin; it was always a fun day with Nadia going to see the shops and feast on Hanukkah doughnuts, warm and sprinkled with powdered sugar, the wagons on the street piled high with turnips and potatoes. Groups of children played in the streets, and black-hatted shopkeepers in their bell-sleeved gabardines stood out front and talked to customers, their doors flung wide to display their wares: Shoes and slippers. Rakes and pitchforks. Cages of squawking hens and ducks.

Back then, at the massive Chewra Nosim Synagogue on Lubartowska Street, men with white-and-black prayer shawls over their shoulders came and went. We would see many leaving for home from the men's bathhouse, the steamy air felt all the way down the street.

But since the Germans came, crossing into the ghetto, one felt a terrible, sad mood. Lublin Castle, which loomed over the area, had been requisitioned by the Nazis as their main prison, and it peered into the twisting cobblestone streets below, streets no longer full of shoppers and children playing. The Nazis had taken most of the younger men away for a construction project, clearing land to build what they said was a new labor camp called Majdanek on the outskirts of Lublin, south of the city. As a result, many of the shops

were shuttered, and the few peddlers who opened their doors offered little. SS men patrolled here and there and the teenagers of
working age who hadn't been marched off to work for the Nazis
stood in groups with a worried air. I saw women crowded around a
tray of meat scraps on the ground, and a young boy was selling
white armbands he kept on his arm, each stenciled with a Star of
David. The synagogue was boarded up, signs in German nailed to
the doors, and the baths stood quiet, no longer breathing steam into
the air.

I was relieved to make it to the pharmacy. It was one of the few
places open, and it was lively there that afternoon. Word was Mr. Z
bribed every Nazi he could to stay in business, since he was the only
non-Jewish shop owner in the ghetto.

Through the plate-glass window at the front of the shop, I spied
tables of men in black hats, busy about their chess games. Mr. Z
stood at the wood counter that ran the length of the pharmacy, assisting a couple with a remedy.

I turned the smooth crystal knob. The door creaked as it opened,
and a few of the men looked up from their games. They followed
me with their eyes as I entered, some with quizzical looks. Though
I knew Mr. Zaufanym a little from church, he did not acknowledge
me when I walked in. As I skirted the tables, I caught bits of conversations, most in Yiddish, a few in Polish. Once I made it to the door
along the rear wall of the place, I took the doorknob in my hand
and turned it, but it would not budge. Was it locked? I tried it again,
my palm slippery on the metal. Still no luck. Should I abandon the
mission?

I swiveled to face Mr. Z. He excused himself and started toward
me.

Just then, a Nazi brownshirt, one of Hitler's everyday enforcers,
gun strap across his chest, cupped two hands to the front window
and peered inside. He was looking at me! Even some of the men at
the tables noticed and sat up straighter, watching it all. I repeated
this oath in my head: *I shall serve with the Gray Ranks, safeguard*

the secrets of the organization, obey orders, and not hesitate to sacrifice my life.

The "sacrifice my life" part was becoming all too real.

Mr. Z came to me and led me back to the counter. I barely made it there, my legs wobbled so.

"You need aspirin?" he said.

"Yes. I have a terrible headache."

Once the brownshirt moved along, Mr. Z took me to the door. He jiggled the knob and let me through in a most natural way.

I made it to the bottom of the steps, rapped my knuckles on the wood door, and stood beneath the bare lightbulb. A chill ran through me. Maybe I would tell Pietrik this was my last mission.

"Who is it?" came a woman's voice.

"Iwona," I said.

The door opened.

"They send me a child?" the woman said from the shadows. I entered, and she closed the door behind me.

A child? I was eighteen after all and often told I looked older.

"I'm here for the aspirin. I only have five minutes."

The woman stared at me for a long moment, as one looks at the last piece of fish at the market, and then walked to an adjacent room. I stepped farther into the basement. It was twice the size of our apartment and black paper covered the windows, so it was dark. The smell of mildew and dirty socks down there was strong, but it was well furnished, with a long sofa, a kitchen table and chairs with a bright blue-and-red lamp hung above, and a sink on the far wall. Long silver drips plopped from the sink faucet, and the thuds of footsteps and chairs scraping the floor came from above. Where was the woman?

She came back shortly with a thick package. I tucked it in my rucksack and peeped at my watch. I was finished in less than one minute even with Mrs. Slowpoke taking such a long time. That's when I noticed the girl on the sofa. She sat in shadow, her head bowed.

"Who is that?" I asked.

"None of your affair. You should go."

I stepped closer.

"Have you hurt her?"

"Of course not. Anna is going to live with a Catholic family. Her parents think she will be safer there."

"Dressed in such a way?" The girl wore a dark coat over a hand-knit sweater, black boots, and stockings, and her hair was tucked up under a black-and-red plaid scarf tied like a turban, puffed up on top. I was an expert on how Catholic girls dressed, of course, being one myself and, thanks to Matka, the first at mass every Sunday. That girl wouldn't get far in those clothes.

"No Catholic girl would dress like that," I said.

I turned to go.

"Would you take a moment and tell her what to wear?" the woman said.

"I don't know——" I began. This woman was now nice to me when she needed something? I had problems of my own: carrying secret packages through the streets.

"It would mean a lot to her," said the woman. "She's all alone."

"I suppose so," I said.

I stepped closer to the girl and sat on the sofa beside her.

"I'm Kasia." I put my hand over hers, which was even colder than mine. "Anna, what a beautiful name. Did you know it means 'favored by God'?"

"Hannah is my real name," she said without even a look at me.

"If you are going to live with a Catholic family, first of all, you must give up your scarf."

Hannah hesitated and looked at me with stormy eyes. It was all I could do not to stomp back up the stairs and leave her.

Slowly, she pulled off the scarf, and her dark hair dropped down around her shoulders.

"Good. Now, it's best not to wear black stockings or boots. Here, switch with me."

The girl did not move.

"I can't do this," she said.

"Hannah—"

"Three minutes left," said the woman, standing at the door.

"You need to hurry," I said.

"I've changed my mind," Hannah said.

I stood and brushed my skirt. "Fine then. I'm leaving."

"My boyfriend says I am dead to him for doing this."

I sat back down. Boyfriends could be such trouble!

"You can't base everything on a boy."

"He hates me anyway, now. Says I am abandoning my parents."

"Your parents want this, and your boyfriend will see it's best."

The woman stepped toward us. "Finish up, now."

"They are only taking away the men," Hannah said. "Maybe I am better off staying home—"

"It's better to live with a new family than be sent off to work somewhere. Go through with the plan, and you can get food to them—"

"Impossible."

"People do it all the time. For now, you *must* cheer up. No sad eyes. The SS look for that."

She wiped her face and sat up straighter. A start! She was a pretty girl with a sprinkling of freckles across the bridge of her nose.

"Take my shoes. Quickly now."

"Two minutes," the woman said from the door.

"Oh, I couldn't," Hannah said.

"You *must.* Your boots are a dead giveaway. Switch with me."

What if I was stopped? I had authentic papers, and Papa would help me no matter what. Hannah pulled down her dark hose and traded them for my white anklets. I took her boots—just a bit smaller than my shoes.

"There. Now turn around." Fast as I could, I braided her dark hair in one fat plait down her back. "Unmarried Catholic girls wear one braid. Do you know the Lord's Prayer?"

She nodded.

"Good. Learn the Polish national anthem too. They're asking for that more now. And remember, if someone offers you vodka, no sipping. Take it in one gulp, or refuse it altogether."

"It's time," the woman said.

I admired my handiwork.

A white Bible lay on the table. "That is a pretty Bible." I handed it to her. "Just make sure you crack the binding. Make it seem used. And in church, genuflect like this, right knee to the floor, and make the sign of the cross"—I demonstrated—"so. No—the right hand. Yes. Just follow the others. And don't chew the host. Let it melt in your mouth."

She took hold of my arm. "Will I have to eat pork?"

"Just say you were sick once from it and can't stand the sight—"

"Thank you," Hannah said. "I have nothing to give you."

"Iwona, please," the woman said.

"Don't worry about it. And above all, don't fret. Your Polish is good as anyone's. One last thing." I unlatched my silver cross necklace and fastened it around her neck.

The girl looked down at her chest.

"This may be hard for you to wear, but every Catholic girl has one."

Pietrik would understand.

I went to the door and stopped for one last look. Hannah stood, Bible in hand, looking much like any Catholic girl on her way to Sunday mass.

"It has been over five minutes," the woman said. "Perhaps you should wait until dark?"

"I'll be fine," I said. Pietrik would be waiting.

I headed back upstairs, through the pharmacy, and out to the street. It felt good to be out in the fresh air, my job well done. That is my last assignment for a while, I thought as I headed for the cinema. A peek at my watch told me I would be early for my shift. My boss would be happy. All I wanted was to get there safely. Pietrik would be there if I needed help.

I made good progress, but before I was even out of Old Town, I felt someone following me. I bent to tie Hannah's boot, the paper package crinkling in my sack, and glanced behind me. There was the brownshirt who'd seen me at Z's, busy dispersing a group of young people. Had he seen me go into the basement? I shook off the bad thoughts and ran on.

I made it to the theater, five minutes early for my shift. The theater marquee read THE ETERNAL JEW. Once the theater had been requisitioned by the Nazis, all films were sent from Nazi headquarters, Under the Clock, and no Poles were allowed in, but just from the name we knew this film was Nazi propaganda. The line at the ticket booth was already forming, the German customers queued up, that expectant look of theatergoers on their faces. A new thing the Nazis had forced upon us was patriotic music, played via loudspeaker outside the theater. A loop of the "Horst Wessel Song," the Nazi Party anthem, a dirge-like march, complete with trumpets, resounded across the cobblestone square all night long, even through the movie!

"The flag on high!" sang the German choir. "The ranks tightly closed! The SA marches with quiet, steady step."

I slipped through the ticket booth door and caught my breath. It was a small room, barely the size of a small bathroom, and featured a paper-shaded ticket window and one high stool. Had anyone followed me? I flipped on the lights and touched the cashbox, cold and smooth, to calm myself. I would need to keep my wits about me, sort the money, and keep the window shade pulled down for now.

Where was Matka? She was due with the cheese sandwich she'd promised. As a former nurse, she'd been pressed into service in the Old Town Hospital. Why was she late this one time when I was starving? The smell of the German candy bars made me crazy with hunger.

I moved the shade aside and peeked out the ticket booth window. An electric jolt ran through me. Was it possible? The brownshirt who'd seen me at Z's stood talking with two older *Hausfrauen* in the ticket line.

How glad I was to see Pietrik burst into the ticket booth and take his usual seat on the floor at my feet, under the window, back to the wall. His cheeks, flushed pink, made his eyes seem extra blue. Luiza, his little sister, was close behind. She slid her back down the wall to sit next to him. She was almost the complete opposite of Pietrik: While he had light eyes, hers were dark. He was serious. She laughed a lot. At fifteen, she was half his size.

"How did your trip to Z's go?" he asked.

I sat high on the ticket taker's stool and arranged my skirt to make the best presentation of my legs. "Well enough, with one loose end—"

He sent me a quick glance, a warning not to speak of it in front of Luiza.

"I'm searching for my greatest talent," Luiza said. "What do you think it is, Kasia?"

Why did Luiza have to bring up the silliest subjects at such a time? I pulled the shade aside and checked the line out front. The brownshirt was still there, now in an animated conversation with two men. About me?

"I don't know, Luiza," I said. "You're a good baker . . ."

"That's something anyone can do. I want something unique."

I looked outside again. Something was not right. Don't be paranoid, I thought as I sorted the money and ran through my mental list:

Candy price cards set? Check.

Cashbox sorted? Check.

Now that our movie audience was mostly German, I needed to be extra organized, for my boss would hear a terrible ticking off of complaints about my smallest slipup.

Zuzanna came into the booth and shut the door behind her.

"Kasia, why are you so white?"

"Did you see a brownshirt out there?"

She tossed her bag in the corner. "That's a fine hello. I've been in the country doctoring the sick in exchange for the eggs for your breakfast, dear sister."

I pulled the shade aside, and there he was. He had moved on to speak with a young woman in line.

"I think he followed me. From Z's. Leave. Now." I turned to Pietrik. "You and Luiza too. If they find you here with me, they'll take us all."

Zuzanna laughed. "Last time I heard, there was no law saying Z's is off-limits. Though there's a law about everything else these days . . ."

I checked the line outside again. The woman nodded and raised a finger in the direction of the ticket booth door. My whole body went cold.

"He's asking them about me," I said, a giant drain sucking me down. "They're telling him I'm here."

My heart contracted with what I saw next: Matka, at the far end of the line, shouldering her way through the crowd toward us, basket in hand.

Zuzanna pulled the shade from my hand. "Keep looking guilty and you *will* be in trouble."

I could barely breathe.

Don't come, Matka. Turn back now, before it's too late.

CHAPTER 9

Herta

1940

FRITZ WAS LATE PICKING ME UP AT FÜRSTENBERG STATION, a fine way for me to start my first day as a camp doctor at Ravensbrück. Would he recognize me? This was doubtful. At university, he'd always had some pretty nursing student on his arm.

The compact train station was built in the Bavarian style, and I had ample time to admire it, left standing on the platform for five minutes. Would I receive important assignments? Make good friends? It was warm for fall, and my wool dress irritated my skin. I couldn't wait to slip into a lighter dress and a cool, smooth lab coat.

Fritz finally came along in a Kübelwagen-82, top down, a green bathtub for four, the Ravensbrück utility vehicle. He stopped, one arm slung over the passenger seatback.

"You're late," I said. "I meet the commandant at quarter past ten."

He came to the platform and took my bag. "No handshake, Herta? I've gone a whole year without seeing you."

He remembered me.

I stole a glance at him as we drove. He still had the good looks every female at the university had noted. Tall, with well-behaved black hair and Prussian blue eyes. Refined features that reflected his aristocratic parentage. He looked tired, though, especially around the eyes. How stressful could it be to work at a women's re-education camp?

The wind in my short hair felt good as we set off down Fritz-Reuter-Strasse, through the small town of Fürstenberg, where sod-roofed cottages flanked the street. Very old Germany. Like a scene from a Black Forest box.

"Sometimes Himmler stays here in Fürstenberg when he's in town, which is *often*. He sold the Reich the land on which they built Ravensbrück, you know. Made a fortune. Can you see the camp over there across Lake Schwedt? It's brand-new— Are you crying, Herta?"

"Just the wind in my eyes," I said, though he was perceptive. It was hard not to become emotional driving through Fürstenberg, for I'd visited a similar town with my parents as a child, for fishing. This was the essence of Germany, so beautiful and unspoiled. What we were fighting for.

"What time is it, Fritz?" I said, drying my eyes. Just what I needed, the commandant pegging me as a crier. "I can't be late."

Fritz accelerated and raised his voice over the engine. "Koegel is not a bad sort. He owned a souvenir shop in Munich before this."

A dust cloud followed the Kübelwagen as we raced down the road, along the lake toward camp. As we rounded the bend, I looked back across the lake and admired the distant silhouette of the town of Fürstenberg where we'd just come from, with its tall church spire.

"You'll have your pick of the doctors here," Fritz said. "Dr. Rosenthal loves blondes."

"I am not blond," I said, though I was happy he thought so. My mood improved riding with Fritz, about to embark on a new adventure.

"Close enough. A clean German girl is a rare thing here. They've had their fill of Slavs."

"I love my men with syphilis."

"Just doing my part to repopulate Germany," Fritz said with a smile.

"Is this how you woo the girls?"

He cast a glance at me and lingered a second too long, betraying his carefree tone. How lucky I was to be one of the few female doctors under Hitler. It put me in a whole different class. Fritz Fischer would never flirt like this with a Düsseldorf *Hausfrau.* Maybe I'd grow my hair long again. No doubt he would be impressed once I became the most accomplished doctor there.

We sped by a crew of gaunt women in striped dresses, in the advanced stages of muscular atrophy, leaning their full weight against the metal harness of a massive concrete roller like sick oxen. A female guard in a gray wool uniform restrained a lunging Alsatian. Fritz waved to the guard and she scowled as we passed.

"They love me here," Fritz said.

"Looks like it," I said.

We stopped in a cloud of dust at the brick administration building, the first thing one saw of the camp, at the end of the road. I exited the *Wagen,* brushed the dust off my dress, and examined the surroundings. My first impression was of quality. The lawn grew lush and green, and red flowers rose up along the base of the building. To the left, high on a ridge overlooking the camp, sat four leader houses built in *Heimatschutzstil,* homeland-preserving style, with natural stone columns and half-timbered balconies. A mix of Nordic and German styles, pleasing to the eye. This was a place of superior value—high-class, one might even call it.

"Up on the ridge, the one overlooking the camp is the commandant's house," Fritz said.

If not for the glimpse of high stone walls topped with barbed wire behind the administration building, one might have mistaken the camp for a convalescent home, not a reeducation camp for prisoners. I was determined to like Commandant Koegel. Those of superior rank can always tell if a subordinate does not like them, and this can be fatal to a career.

Just inside the camp gates, a caged aviary, which held monkeys and parrots and other exotic birds, stood off to the side of the road, the only incongruous element. Animals reduce stress, certainly, but what was the purpose of such a collection?

"You waiting for the butler, Herta?" Fritz called to me from the doorway.

A secretary ushered me across parqueted floors, upstairs and into the commandant's office, where Koegel sat at his desk, under a rectangular mirror, which reflected the man-sized potted plant in the corner. It was hard not to be intimidated by the grandeur of his office. The wall-to-wall carpeting, the expensive-looking draperies, and the chandelier. He even had his own porcelain sink. All at once I wished I'd shined my shoes.

Koegel stood, and we exchanged the German salute.

"You're late, Dr. Oberheuser," he said.

The Black Forest clock on his wall chimed the half hour. Dirndled and lederhosened dancers twirled out of their arched doorways to "Der fröhliche Wanderer," celebrating my tardiness.

"Dr. Fischer——" I began.

"Do you always blame others for your mistakes?"

"I am sorry to be late, Herr Commandant."

He folded his arms across his chest. "How was your trip?" He was a fleshy sort, something I ordinarily dislike in a person, but I forced a smile.

Koegel's second-floor view offered a wide expanse of the camp and overlooked a vast yard where women prisoners stood at attention, five abreast. A road bisected the camp, covered with black slag, which glittered in the sun. Neat rows of barracks stood perpendicular to this road and extended into the distance. How nice to see immature linden trees, the hallowed "tree of lovers" in German folklore, planted at regular intervals along the road.

"It was a comfortable trip, Commandant," I said, doing my best to lose my Rhineland accent. "Thank you for the first-class ticket."

"Comfort is important to you?" Koegel asked.

The commandant was a stern man with stumpy legs and a sour disposition. Perhaps his unpleasant demeanor was due in part to his regulation brown shirt collar and tie, so tight they squeezed the adipose tissue up around his neck, making it look like a lardy muffler. The friction had produced a bumper crop of skin tags, which hung flaccid along the edges of his collar. He wore a cluster of medals at his chest. At least he was a patriot.

"Not really, Commandant. I——"

"I am afraid there has been a mix-up," he said with a wave of his hand. "We cannot accommodate you here."

"But I received a letter from Berlin——"

"You will be the only woman doctor here. That presents problems."

"I didn't think——"

"This is a *work* camp, Doctor. No fancy beauty salons, no coffee klatches. How will men feel about you eating in the officers' canteen? One woman among so many men spells trouble."

I felt the salary floating away as he spoke. Would Fritz take me to the next train back to Berlin? Mutti would have to work full-time again.

"I am used to living simply, Herr Commandant."

I released my clenched fists and saw I'd dug my fingernails into my palms. They left a row of little red smiles, mocking me. I deserved this. When would I learn not to be overconfident? "I assure you I will be fine in any living situation. The Führer himself says simple living is best."

Koegel took in my short haircut. Was he weakening?

"They sent me a dermatologist? That is no use to us here."

"And infectious diseases, Commandant." He mulled that over, one hand on his belly.

"I see," he said. He turned to the window and surveyed the camp. "Well, we do sensitive work here, Doctor."

As he spoke, the sound of a whip drew my attention to the square below. A female guard lashed one of several prisoners gathered there with a horsewhip.

"We require complete confidentiality here, Doctor. Are you willing to sign a statement? You can confide in no one. Not even your mother or girlfriends."

Nothing to worry about there. I had no girlfriends.

"Any breach of security, and you'll face your family's imprisonment and a possible death penalty for you."

"I keep to myself, Herr Commandant."

"This work is, well, not for the squeamish. Our medical setup is adequate at best—in a terrible state."

Koegel ignored the spectacle below his window. As the prisoner fell to the ground, her hands folded across the top of her head, the guard intensified the punishment. A second guard held back a leashed Alsatian as it sprang forward, teeth bared.

"Well, it would make Berlin happy," Koegel said.

"What will my role in reeducation be, Herr Commandant?"

The guard in the courtyard kicked the woman in the midsection with her boot, the woman's screams hard to ignore. This was a violent form of reeducation.

"You are joining an elite group. You'll work with some of the best doctors in Germany to accommodate the medical needs of the camp staff and their families and of the women who have been resettled here to do the Führer's work. Dr. Gebhardt has several projects as well."

In the courtyard, the guard rewound her whip and two prisoners dragged their bloodied companion off as the rest stood at attention. "After your three-month training period, a resignation will not be accepted under any circumstances."

"I understand, Commandant."

Koegel walked back to his desk. "You will share a house with Dorothea Binz, our head of female security personnel. Our hair salon is not fancy but quite good. Right downstairs. The Bible girls operate it. Jehovah's Witnesses. They've dedicated themselves to making my life a living hell, but you can trust them with scissors."

"I will keep it in mind, Herr Commandant," I said and excused myself with a German salute.

I left Koegel's office happy he'd relented but unsure I wanted to stay at Ravensbrück. A vague unsettled feeling came over me. What if I just got back on the train for home? I could work three jobs if I had to.

I WAS ASTOUNDED TO SEE my room in the newly built high-ranking wardresses' cottage just steps from the entry gate. It was bigger than our whole apartment at home, outfitted with a shared bath complete with shower *and* tub, a comfortable bed with white eiderdown, and a vanity table. I wore no makeup, per regulations, but the table would make a nice desk. Best of all, the cottage was centrally heated. Such clean, elegant quarters with my own balcony. Mutti would just shake her head in wonder to see me in such a place.

I walked into the main camp for lunch, through the personnel entrance, and found the officers' dining hall. The noise level was high, for the small building was packed with SS doctors and guards, including many of the fifty SS doctors assigned to Ravensbrück, all male and all enjoying a lunch of pork roast, buttered potatoes, and various cuts of beef. I hoped to become acquainted with the top-flight doctors Koegel had promised. Though I was in no hurry, the male-female physician ratio was a promising forty-nine to one.

As I stepped closer to the table where Fritz held court, groups of men stopped their conversations and stared as I passed. I was used to being among men from medical school, but *one* woman colleague would have been nice. I found Fritz and his three companions sitting, bellies extended, sharing what seemed like postcoital cigarettes.

"Ah, Herta," Fritz said. "Care for lunch?" He motioned to a plate piled with fatty pork chops, and I stemmed a wave of nausea.

"I am vegetarian," I said.

The man next to him stifled a laugh.

Fritz stood. "Where are my manners? Let me introduce you. At the end of the table there, we have Dr. Martin Hellinger, toast of the SS dental world."

Dr. Hellinger was a beetle-browed fellow, with wire-rimmed glasses and an endomorphic body type whose blood sugar had apparently dipped so low he could barely acknowledge me. He penciled in answers to a crossword puzzle from a newspaper.

"Next, Dr. Adolf Winkelmann, visiting from Auschwitz."

Winkelmann sat in his chair as if poured there. He was rotund, with skin like wormholed wood.

"And this is the famous Rolf Rosenthal," Fritz said, indicating the weaselly, dark-haired fellow sprawled out in the chair at his left. "Former navy surgeon and our gynecological wunderkind." Rosenthal leaned forward into his cigarette and looked at me as a cow merchant considers a purchase.

The slam of a screen door caused the doctors to turn, and the blond guard I'd seen from Koegel's window stepped into the dining hall. She was taller than she'd appeared from above. Finally, a fellow female.

She ambled over to our table, her steps heavy on the wooden floor, riding crop tucked in one boot, cap off, hair rolled up off her forehead per the fashion of the time. Though a young woman, nineteen years old or so, her complexion already hosted a colony of sunspots and freckles. Perhaps the result of farm labor?

Fritz draped one arm over the back of his chair.

"If it isn't the lovely Fräulein Binz. Pride of the Ravensbrück charm school."

Fritz did not stand to greet her and the other doctors shifted in their chairs as if suffering a cold wind.

"Hello, Fritz," Binz said.

"Don't you know you're not allowed in the officers' canteen without permission?" Fritz said. He lit a cigarette with a gold lighter, his hands white and almost incandescent, as if dipped in milk. Hands you might expect to see on a famous pianist. Hands that had never touched a spade.

"Koegel wants me to get your medical staff and my girls together."

"Not another picnic," Rosenthal said.

"He suggested a dance . . ." Binz said.

A dance? A great fan of dancing, I was interested in that.

Rosenthal groaned.

"Only if Koegel throws in a case of French claret," Fritz said. "And only if you staff it with some attractive Poles. Those Bible girls barely speak."

"And only bring the *Aufseherinnen* under one hundred kilos," Rosenthal said.

"You will come, Fritz?" Binz lit a cigarette.

Fritz waved one hand in my direction. "Binz, say hello to your new roommate. Dr. Herta Oberheuser, may I present Dorothea Binz, head of the punishment bunker. Also trains most of the *Aufseherinnen* for the entire Reich right here."

"Woman doctor?" Binz said. She sucked her cigarette and looked me over. "That's a new one. Happy to meet you, Doctor. Good luck with this group."

She addressed me informally, using the word *du* instead of *Sie,* which struck me as inappropriate, but no one else noted this.

"Thank you, Fräulein Binz," I said, walking her to the canteen door.

"Never thank an *Aufseherin,* Doctor," Fritz said. "Bad precedent."

Binz let the door slam behind her and strode out onto the *platz.* She discarded her cigarette, not even half-smoked, flicking it onto the cobblestones with her thumb and forefinger. It was clear Binz was not the friend I was seeking.

After lunch, I walked with Fritz and Dr. Hellinger toward the utility block, where new prisoners were processed. On the way I saw every *Häftling* in uniform wore a colorful triangle on her sleeve, just below her number.

"What do the colored badges mean, Fritz?" I asked.

"Green triangle is a convicted criminal—mostly from Berlin, rough sorts, though some are here for breaking insignificant rules. Many *Blockovas* wear this. Purple is Bible girl—Jehovah's Witness. All they have to do is sign a paper saying they put Hitler above all else, and they can walk free, but they won't—crazy. Red triangle is political prisoner. Mostly Poles. Black is asocials: Prostitutes. Alcoholics. Pacifists. The letter sewn inside the triangle indicates nationality. Jews get two triangles put together to make a star. Himmler's idea."

We walked to the utility block, along a line of naked women waiting outside. The women all appeared to be Slavs of some sort, of all ages and body types. Some were visibly pregnant. When they saw the male doctors, some shrieked, and all tried to cover themselves.

"These women need clothes, Fritz," I said.

Once inside, we stood in a quiet corner to talk. "Here's how we do our selections," Fritz said. "First, Hellinger looks for and records all silver or gold fillings and bridgework. Then we choose those least fit to work. If those two things line up, the prisoner is chosen. A prisoner too sick to work with a mouthful of metal goes on this list. We tell them anything but the truth."

"And the truth is?" I asked.

"Express bus to heaven, either the gas van or Evipan. Gasoline if we run out. After that, Hellinger extracts the Reich's payment. We'll do Evipan today."

I hugged my waist. "I thought the prisoners needed to work."

"Old ladies can't pull a concrete roller, Herta."

"Few of them are that old and the ones that are can be put to work knitting. And the pregnant ones need to be off their feet."

"It's German law. No child can be born at a camp. And a certain percentage needs special handling. Otherwise this place will be too crowded, and I don't know about you, but I'm not crazy about typhus. And besides, some of them are Jews."

The reeducation-camp label was a front. How could I have been so naïve? My nausea returned.

"I need to go to my room and unpack," I said.

"You were fine with the cadaver lab at school."

"They weren't breathing, Fritz. I'd rather not be involved."

"Rather not? You won't be here long with that attitude."

"I'm just not comfortable with all this. It's so, well, personal."

The thought of administering a lethal injection was too abhorrent to dwell on. Would we inject into the arm? Lethal injections were barbaric and bound to be psychologically damaging for those administering them.

I touched Fritz's hand. "But cyanide is quick and quiet. Mixed with orange juice—"

"You think I like this?" Fritz asked, drawing me closer. "You do what you have to here. The alternative for them is *Vernichtung durch Arbeit.*"

Death by labor. Planned starvation.

"It's orders. Direct from Himmler. They all get just enough calories to keep them alive to work for three months. Slow extermination."

"I can't . . ."

He shrugged. "They'll die anyway. Just don't think about it."

Fritz approached the line of naked women and clapped his hands, and they huddled together like horses in a barn.

"Good day, ladies. Any of you who are over fifty years old, have a temperature above forty degrees, or are pregnant, step to the side, and we'll make sure you get a rest, after your typhus inoculations. I can only take sixty-five, so step up now."

The women talked among themselves, some translating Fritz's instructions into other languages, and soon volunteers emerged.

"Here, this is my mother," said one young woman as she prodded an older woman forward. "She has been coughing so hard she cannot work."

"Of course," Fritz said.

One obviously pregnant, dark-skinned girl with brown, heavily lashed eyes like those of a dairy cow came forward and smiled at Fritz, her arms crossed, resting on her swollen belly. In minutes Fritz had his sixty-five candidates, and he instructed a guard to accompany them to the *Revier.* At least they went along calmly.

"Since when is there a vaccine for typhus?" I asked, keeping my voice low, in case some of the prisoners understood German.

"Of course it doesn't exist. On average sick *Häftlings* only live fourteen days, so we're simply hastening the process. It's far more humane than other methods."

Fritz led us to my new workplace, the *Revier,* the prisoner medical clinic, housed in a low-slung block identical to the rest. The front reception area opened onto a large room filled with cots and bunk beds, crowded with patients, some lying on the bare floor, some in advanced stages of disease. One *Häftling* hosted such an abundance of adult lice, her short hair was white with them, and she had scratched great patches of her skin raw. Not a quality operation.

A young prisoner-nurse named Gerda Quernheim greeted us. Gerda, a pretty, chestnut-haired girl from Düsseldorf, had attended the School of Midwifery there. She was an excellent nurse, but even Gerda couldn't handle the *Revier.*

Fritz led us down the hall, past a large meat locker, not unlike Heinz's.

"What is this?" I asked, touching the door, cold and damp with condensation. I brushed away a flash of *Onkel* Heinz's face.

"Cold storage," Fritz said. "Gebhardt's."

Fritz led me to a back room, painted a soothing, pale green, two stools and a tall lab table the only furniture. The light caught the silver barrel of a syringe, one of three laid out on the table, certainly not sterile. A gray rubber apron hung on a wall hook swayed with the breeze as we entered. The windows in that part of the building were painted white, like cloudy cataract eyes. It felt claustrophobic, as if we were snowed in.

"Why are these windows painted over?" I asked.

"Gebhardt is a freak for privacy," Fritz said.

"Honestly, Fritz, I am tired from the train today."

"Take half a pethidine if you have to," Fritz said, his brow creased. "Would you rather take last call? Shooting-wall duty."

"*Shooting* wall?" I said. "Perhaps this is better."

"*Much* tidier. The first is the hardest; trust me. Like jumping in a cold lake."

Two *Aufseherinnen* brought in the first prisoner from Fritz's selection, a surprisingly spry older woman wearing only wooden clogs and a blanket over her shoulders. She tried to speak to Fritz in Polish through a jumble of confused teeth.

Fritz smiled. "Yes, yes, come in. We're just preparing the inoculations."

He tied on the rubber apron.

"Kill them with kindness," Fritz said. "Makes it easier for all."

The *Aufseherinnen* led the old woman to the stool. Over my shoulder I watched Gerda load a 20-cc hypodermic syringe, drawing enough yellowish-pink Evipan into the barrel to kill an ox.

"We painted this room pale green since it soothes patients," Fritz said.

The *Aufseherinnen* removed the blanket, wrapped a towel around the woman's face, and held her left arm out as if preparing for a venous injection.

"Injections were not my forte in medical school," I said.

One of the *Aufseherinnen* pressed her knee into the old woman's back to thrust her chest forward.

Fritz pressed the heavy syringe into my palm.

"Look, you are doing them a favor," Fritz said. "Think of them as sick dogs needing to be put down. Do this well, and they won't suffer."

The woman must have seen the needle, for she began to fight the guards and flailed her freed arm. That would be all I needed—Fritz telling Koegel I couldn't handle a syringe.

I backed away, a milky drop at the tip of the needle. "I'll try it tomorrow."

"Here," Fritz said, wrapping his arms around me from behind. "We'll do it together."

He covered my hand that was holding the syringe with his and placed the fingers of my other hand on the woman's skin, above the rib cage. The guards used her arms like a straitjacket, and Fritz slid my fingers down the torso, to the fifth rib space.

"Close your eyes," Fritz said. "Feel it? Just below the left breast."

I pressed my fingers deep into the warm, crepey skin.

"Yes," I said.

"Good. Almost done."

Fritz placed his thumb over mine on the plunger, guided my hand to the spot, then helped me plunge the needle in. I felt the pop as it punctured the rib space.

"Stay with me now," Fritz said, his lips soft against my ear. "Breathe."

Fritz pressed our thumbs against the smooth knob with steady force, sending the Evipan straight to the heart. The woman reared back, but the guards held her in place.

"Steady, now," Fritz said, his mouth close to my ear. "Just fourteen seconds. Count backward."

"Fourteen, thirteen, twelve . . ."

I opened my eyes and saw the towel fall from the woman's face, her lower lip pulled down in a hideous grimace.

"Eleven, ten, nine . . ."

The woman struggled, and I took deep breaths to fight a wave of nausea.

"Eight, seven, six . . ."

She reared up as if in cardiac distress, then fell limp and unresponsive.

Fritz released me.

"She was a quick one," he said. "You're drenched."

One of the *Aufseherinnen* dragged the old woman off to the side of the room. Gerda left to fetch the next subject.

"Gerda is Rosenthal's girlfriend," Fritz said, as he made notes on a clipboard. "He did a termination on her. Keeps it in a jar in Gebhardt's refrigerator. She picks pet *Häftlings* to treat with a warm bath, complete with flowers. Combs their hair and tells them sweet stories before she brings them here."

I walked toward the door for air. "How do you do this, Fritz? It's so—"

"It's no glamour job, but if you leave, there will be a replacement here tomorrow. We handle a certain quota every month. Orders from Berlin. It can't be helped."

"Of course it can be helped. We can refuse to do it."

Fritz refilled the syringe. "Good luck with Koegel on that one."

"Well, I can't do this." How could I have ended up in such a place?

Hellinger entered the room with his leather roll of tools. I tried not to listen as he removed the woman's dental metals. He stamped the cheek with a star to mark her as completed.

"You'll be fine, Herta," Fritz said. "Once you get used to it."

"I'm not staying. I didn't go to medical school to do this—"

"That's what I said too," said Hellinger, with a laugh. He tucked the cotton sack of gold into his coat pocket.

"Me too," Fritz said. "And then, before I knew it, three months passed. After that, you're here to stay, so make up your mind soon."

There was no question. I would be gone by sunrise.

CHAPTER 10

Caroline

1939–1940

IN THE DARKNESS OF THE BEDROOM I FELT FOR MY CLOTHES. I found my slip and slid into it, then felt Paul's velvet jacket and threw it on, the satin lining cool on my bare arms. Who was pounding on the apartment door?

"Stay here, Paul. I'll see who it is."

He lay back against my pink satin pillow, his Cheshire Cat smile white in the semidarkness, fingers locked behind his head. This was funny? What if it was Mother? What would I tell her? The world's handsomest man is in my bed, half naked? But Mother had her own key. Maybe she'd left it behind?

I inched down the hall. Who would create such a racket? I passed the dark living room. In the fireplace, orange embers still glowed.

"Caroline," came a voice through the door. "I need to see you."

David Stockwell.

I stepped closer and put one hand to the painted door. David pounded, and it vibrated under my fingers.

"What are you doing here, David?" I said through the door.

"Open up," he said. "It's important." Even through five inches of oak, I could tell he'd been drinking.

"I'm not dressed—"

"I need to talk to you, Caroline. It'll only take a minute."

"Come back tomorrow, David."

"It's about your mother. I need to speak with you, most urgently."

I'd been through David's "most urgent" situations before, but I couldn't take the chance.

I flipped on the hall light and opened the door to find David, in rumpled white tie, leaning against the doorjamb. He pushed by me, into the vestibule, his gait unsteady. I pulled Paul's jacket tighter about me to hide my underdressed state.

"It's about *time*," David said. "My God, Caroline, what are you wearing?"

"How did you get past the doorman?"

David took me by the shoulders. "Please don't be mad at me, Caroline. You smell so good."

I tried to push him away. "David, stop. What's wrong with my mother?"

He pulled me close and kissed my neck. "I miss you, C. I've made a terrible—"

"You reek, David."

I tried to pull away but not before Paul appeared behind me, dressed in his undershorts and a shirt he'd hastily thrown on. Even in the harsh overhead light, Paul was lovely: the open shirt, my lipstick smeared down the placket.

"You need help, Caroline?" Paul asked.

David, drunk as he was, lifted his head at the sound of Paul's voice.

"Who's *this*?" David said, as if confronting an apparition.

"Paul Rodierre. You met him today in the park."

"Oh." David straightened. "How would your mother feel about—"

I took him by the arm. "You need to leave, David."

He groped for my hand. "Come with me, C. Even Mother misses you."

This was doubtful. Even after knowing me for years, Mrs. Stockwell still referred to me as "the actress."

"Don't call me C, David. And you're married. Remember? 'The wedding of the decade' the papers called it?"

He looked at Paul as if he'd forgotten he was there. "God, man, put some clothes on." David leaned into me, his blue eyes pink-rimmed. "Caroline, you can't possibly think he's good for you—"

"You have no say in my life, David. You gave that up on one knee in front of everyone at the Badminton Club. Did you have to propose at Father's club? He got your father in there."

Paul walked back to the bedroom. With any luck he was going back to the bed.

"It's a meaningful place to us. Sally and I won mixed doubles there."

News of Sally and David's triumphant badminton win had been all over *The Sun* and trumpeted by the likes of Jinx Whitney, my Chapin nemesis. I'd never liked the Badminton Club, even when Father was alive. Any club with a shuttlecock in its crest cannot be taken seriously.

Paul came back to us in the vestibule, this time buttoned up and wearing pants.

"Maybe you two can finish this another time?" He slipped his overcoat on.

"You're leaving?" I said, trying not to sound desperate.

"David needs to be shown out, and I have early rehearsal tomorrow." He leaned to me and kissed one cheek. I breathed him in as he kissed the other and murmured in my ear, "Aubergine is your color."

Paul pulled our impromptu guest out the door and downstairs as David protested, using his full repertoire of curse words. It was certainly painful to watch Paul go. He'd left my virtue intact, but was it the last chance for me? At least it hadn't been Mother at the door.

I MADE IT THROUGH the holiday season, spending more time than was probably healthy with Paul. We listened to a lot of jazz up in Harlem, side by side in a halo of candlelight. He'd taken on a roommate, a member of the *Streets of Paris* supporting cast, and Mother was back in New York, so it was near impossible to find private time. I saw his play seven times, watching the company of one hundred go through their paces. In addition to playing a lead role, Paul sang and danced in the show, demonstrating great range. What could he not do? The poster for the show boasted the cast included 50 PARISIAN BEAUTIES. With all that female companionship available, it was a mystery why Paul chose to spend his free time with me.

THINGS GREW ALMOST UNBEARABLY tense at the consulate that spring of 1940, and I practically lived at the office. As Hitler invaded Denmark and Norway on April 9, sending a new wave of panic through the consulate, the world braced for the worst.

One chilly late April day, Paul asked me to meet him at the observation deck atop the RCA Building after work. He said he wanted to ask me something. What was it? I'd already offered to sign as Rena's visa sponsor, so that wasn't it. The thought teased me all day. We often met up there to look at the stars through the telescope, but I had a feeling he wanted to talk about something other than Ursa Minor. He'd hinted we should costar in something. Maybe a one-act play? Something off-Broadway? I would consider it, of course.

I made it up to the deck early as usual, and waited.

A trio of nurses huddled in yellow Adirondack chairs, which ran down the middle of the deck, then snapped pictures of one another in front of the sign that read A PROOF OF YOUR VISIT. BE PHOTOGRAPHED ON THE RCA OBSERVATION ROOF. Only an elbow-high iron railing separated us from the edge, so all of Manhattan lay below us, the East River to our east, and Central Park to our north, like a lumpy brown Sarouk rug someone had unfurled down the middle of Manhattan. To our south, the Empire State Building rose up, and to the west the Fiftieth Street docks jutted into the Hudson, lined with ships waiting their turn to sail. Below us, a message painted in white stood out, bright in the deepening gloam, against Macy's dark roof: MACY'S. IT'S SMART TO BE THRIFTY.

Paul arrived, a bouquet of *muguet* in hand.

"These are early but I hope you don't mind."

Of course he referred to the French tradition of giving loved ones lily-of-the-valley on May 1. I closed my hand around the emerald stems and inhaled the sweetness.

"Hopefully next May first we'll be together in Paris," he said.

I slid the bouquet under the décolletage of my dress, the stems cold against my chest. "Well, New York is lovely on May Day—"

I stopped. How had I not noticed? He was more formally dressed than usual, a red silk handkerchief in the pocket of his navy-blue jacket. He was leaving?

"You're looking chic," I said. "You've broken out the white flannels. Some people dress that way to travel."

It was too late to beg him to stay. Why had I not spoken up sooner?

Paul pointed to the harbor. "I'm taking the *Gripsholm.* Seventhirty call."

Tears pricked at my eyes. "A Swedish ship?"

"Hitching a ride with the International Red Cross, thanks to Roger. Göteborg and then on to France. Would have told you sooner, but just found out myself."

"You can't go now, what with all the U-boats and X-craft out there? Surely it isn't safe. You'll be sitting ducks on the water. And what about Rena's visa?"

"Roger says it may be another month before I find out."

"Maybe if Roger calls Washington . . ."

"There will be no last-minute miracle, C. Things are just getting worse."

"But I need you to stay. Does that not count for something?"

"I'm trying to do the right thing here, Caroline. It isn't easy."

"Maybe wait and see how things progress?"

"Roger says he'll keep trying. It'll be easier to work on it from there, but I have to go. Half of Rena's family has already left Paris."

I leaned my cheek against his coat. "You still love her—"

"That's not what this is about, Caroline. I'd stay here with you if I could, but how can I sit in my suite at the Waldorf while all hell's breaking loose at home? You wouldn't do it."

Was he really going? Surely it was all a joke. He would laugh, and we'd go to the Automat for pie.

As the sun retreated, the temperature fell, and Paul wrapped his arms around me, his heat was all I needed to stay warm. Even from seventy stories up, we could pick out the individual ships docked at Fiftieth Street. The *Normandie* still in place. The *Ile de France*. Only the *Gripsholm* was ready to sail, flying her Swedish flag. The wind drew the gauzy smoke from her stacks up the river.

I looked east. The mid-Atlantic would be the most dangerous part of their journey, where there was the largest gap in air coverage. Even that early in the war, German U-boats had already sunk several Allied ships in the Atlantic in order to keep supplies from reaching England. I pictured the German submarines waiting there, suspended midwater, like barracuda.

Paul held my hands in his. "But what I wanted to ask you is, will you come to Paris once this blows over?"

I pulled away. "Oh, I don't know, Paul."

My mind flashed to us at Les Deux Magots on Saint-Germain des Prés, at a café table under the green awning watching Paris go by. A *café viennois* for him, a *café crème* for me. As the sun retreated, some Hennessy. Maybe champagne and a raspberry tart as we plotted his theatrical career. Our one-act.

"What would Rena say?"

He smiled. "Rena would applaud it. Might join us there with one of her beaux."

The wind whipped my cheeks and sent my hair into a tornado around us. He kissed me. "Promise me you'll come? My biggest regret is leaving you with your moral high ground intact." He smiled and slid his hands around my waist. "This must be rectified."

"Yes, of course. But only if you write me letters. Long, newsy ones telling every minute of your day."

"I am the worst writer, but I will do my best." He kissed me, his lips warm on mine. I lost all sense of time and space, suspended there at the top of the world until Paul released me, leaving me dizzy, unmoored.

"Walk me out?"

"I'll stay here," I said.

Just go. Don't make this any harder.

He walked to the deck door, turned, and left with a wave.

I don't know how long I stayed, leaning on the railing watching the sun set. I imagined Paul in a taxi arriving at the great ship. Would he be annoyed that people asked for his autograph? Only if they didn't. Did Swedish people even know Paul? There would be no one-act for us. Not anytime soon.

"We're closing up," the roof guard called from the door.

He joined me at the railing. "Where'd ya fella go, miss?"

"Home to France," I said.

"*France,* eh? Hope he makes it okay."

We both looked toward the Atlantic.

"Me too," I said.

THE MORNING OF MAY 10 was like any other. I could hear our reception area was full by ten, and I readied for the onslaught by neatening up my desk drawers—anything not to think about Paul.

"More postcards from your pen pals," Pia said. She lobbed a stack of mail onto my desk. "And stop filching my cigarettes."

It was a lovely May day, but even the tender breeze that rustled the elms outside my window couldn't cheer me that Monday morning. The prettiest days were the hardest without Paul to share them. I fanned through the mail, hoping for a letter from him. Of course the chances of a letter from Paul being included in that pile were slim, for mail delivery by transatlantic passage took at least one week each way, but I stalked the mail like a scent hound on a fox, nevertheless.

"You read my mail?" I said.

"That's a *postcard*, Caroline. Half the world has read it, if they care about some French orphanage."

I flipped through the postcards. Château de Chaumont. Château Masgelier. Villa La Chesnaie. All once-stately French mansions converted to orphan asylums. They returned confirmation cards upon receipt of the aid packages I sent. I hoped a sweet soap, a pair of clean socks, a candy, and a piece or two of Mother's lovely handsewn clothes, all wrapped in neat brown paper, would raise a child's spirits.

I stood and pinned the cards to my bulletin board. It was already crammed with pictures of French children. One of a dark-haired angel holding a sign that read, MERCI BEAUCOUP, CAROLINE! Another of children posed in plein air art class, one child at an easel, the rest on campstools, assembled by age, pretending to read their books under a linden tree.

I assumed that photo was snapped by the lovely sounding Mme Bertillion, director of Saint-Philippe in Meudon, an orphanage southwest of Paris. I'd become friendly with Mme Bertillion by mail and waited eagerly for her letters, filled with charming anecdotes about the children and how much they appreciated my packages. There was a new letter from her in this batch of mail, and I pinned up the enclosed crayon drawing of Saint-Philippe, the imposing stone façade colored goldenrod yellow, smoke swirling out of the chimney like the icing on a Hostess Cupcake.

What would it be like to adopt one of these children? A boy? Girl? Our place up in Connecticut, which we called The Hay, was absolute heaven for children. Mother maintained my playhouse, still there in the meadow, complete with woodstove. Adopting a child would give me someone to pass it all down to. Great-grandmother Woolsey's loving cup. Our lovely duck-footed table. Mother's silver. But I put it out of my mind, for I would never raise a child alone. I knew too well the difficulties of growing up without a father, that aching hole Mother had tried too hard to fill. Feigning sick every father-daughter day at school. Being reduced to tears at the sight of fathers and daughters holding hands on the street. The gnaw of regret that I hadn't said goodbye.

At the bottom of the pile, I found a letter, written on onionskin airmail stationery in a lovely hand. The postmark read ROUEN. Paul.

As well as I knew Paul, how had I never seen his handwriting before? It suited him.

Dear Caroline,

I decided to write right away, since, as you say, waiting is not your strong suit. So much is happening here. Rouen has been remarkably sane about this Phoney War, but many have already left, including our neighbors who wheeled their grandmother away with them down our street in a baby carriage last night. The rest of us now are just hoping for the best. I am in talks to commit to a new play in Paris. *All's Well That Ends Well,* can you believe it? Shakespeare. I like to think it is your good influence on me.

Rena may have to close her shop. There is little fabric and notions to be had, but she will be fine. Her father has taken to smoking sunflower leaves, for there is no tobacco to be found.

I hope this counts as a newsy letter, for I have to go now to make the embassy bag. Do put a good word in with Roger for our visa situation. I think of you often, there at work. Make sure you don't let Roger bully you. Remember, he needs you.

With much love and
until next time,
Paul

p.s. I dreamed last night I watched you on stage, here in Paris, in a very steamy version of *A Midsummer Night's Dream*, and you played an angel. Could this say something about your acting career? About my missing you? My dreams always come true.

Paul had made it home to Rouen, past the U-boats. At least he was safe.

For a gregarious man, he wrote a succinct letter, but it was better than none at all. A new play? Perhaps things would blow over in France. Maybe the French producers knew more about the situation than we did half a world away. And the dream! He really did miss me.

I found an April 23 copy of *Le Petit Parisien*, one of the many French newspapers Roger had delivered by bag, somewhat outdated but precious nevertheless. The lead headline read: THE REICH IN SCANDINAVIA! BRITISH TROOPS FIGHT ON LAND AND SEA. CONSIDERABLE SUCCESS IN THE WAR IN NORWAY DESPITE LARGE DIFFICULTIES. My mood lightened at reading that good news. Maybe the United States would continue to avoid the war, but the Brits were holding fast, despite horrific Luftwaffe bombing. Maybe France would escape Hitler after all.

I scanned the theater page. Any ads for Paul's new venture? I found no Shakespeare but did see a small ad for Rena's shop, a simple black square, bordered with a row of pearls: *Les Jolies Choses. Lingerie et sous-vêtements pour la femme de discernement.* Lingerie and undergarments for the discerning woman?

Roger came to my doorway, tie askew, a Rorschach-test coffee stain on his shirt.

"Bad news, C. Hitler has just attacked France, Luxembourg, the Netherlands, and Belgium all at once. It is just hitting the news now. I'm afraid things are going to get bumpy."

I hurled myself after him and watched him pace about his office.

"My God, Roger. Have you called Paris?"

The oscillating fan in the window cooled one side of the room and then the next. The red ribbon someone had tied to it flapped like a little Nazi flag.

"The phones are out," Roger said. "All we can do is wait."

I'd never seen Roger afraid before.

"What about the Maginot Line?"

"Seems Hitler went around it, over it, under it. He came right across Belgium."

"What will Roosevelt do?"

"Nothing, probably. Has no choice but to recognize whatever government represents France."

Pia came to Roger's door, encryption headphones around her neck. "I tried to call my father in Paris, and I can't get through. I have to go home."

"You can't go anywhere right now, Pia," Roger said.

"I can't stay here."

"Don't be ridiculous, Pia," I said. "You can't just *leave*."

Pia stood, arms limp at her sides, heaving great sobs. I wrapped my arms around her. "It will all be fine, dear," I said. To my immense surprise, she returned my embrace.

ON JUNE 14, 1940, the Germans took Paris, and eight days later France surrendered.

Pia and I stood in Roger's office and listened to radio reports of Nazis marching past the Arc de Triomphe. France was split into two zones, the northern zone occupied by German Wehrmacht soldiers, known as the *zone occupée*, and the so-called free zone in the south. Marshal Philippe Pétain headed up the new French Republic, called the Vichy regime, in the southern free zone, which most considered a Nazi puppet state.

"What will happen to our office here?" Pia asked.

"I don't know," Roger said. "We'll sit tight for now. Do the best we can for our people here. Can't get any calls through."

"Can the Brits help?"

"Already have," Roger said. "They just shared reports of German dive-bomber activity in the English Channel." We were lucky that Roger was close to what Pia called his "British spy friends," our neighbors in the International and British Buildings of Rockefeller Center, who were especially generous with their classified information.

Roger's personal line rang, and Pia picked it up. "Roger Fortier's office. Oh yes. Yes, she is. Hold the line."

Pia held the phone out to me. "It's Paul."

"How did he get through?" Roger asked.

I grabbed the phone. "Paul?" I could barely breathe.

"I have only a minute," Paul said.

Paul.

His voice was so clear, as if from the next room. I pressed one finger to my free ear. Was it really him?

"*Caroline*. It's so good to hear your voice."

"My God, Paul. We just heard. How did you get a call through?"

"My friend here at the embassy let me phone. You can't imagine how crazy things are now. It's just a matter of time before Hitler's here."

"I can ask Roger to rush the visas."

"I don't know, Caroline. This place is practically shut down."

"What else do you need?"

"I must be quick. I just want you——" I heard a series of clicks on the line. "Caroline? You there?"

"Paul—I'm here."

"Caroline?"

"Don't leave me, Paul."

The line went dead.

I listened to the vibration of the dial tone for a moment and then placed the receiver back in the cradle. We all stood there waiting for the phone to ring again. Roger and Pia just stared at me, hands at their sides. I'd seen those looks before. Pity. Like when Father died.

"I'll patch him through if he gets a free line again," Pia said.

I started back to my office, followed by a terrible feeling that would be the last time I would ever speak to Paul.

CHAPTER 11

Kasia

1940–1941

BEFORE I COULD EVEN ANSWER ZUZANNA, THE TICKET BOOTH door burst off its hinges, and three SS blackshirts jumped over it into the booth. One grabbed Pietrik off the floor, and the other dragged me by the arms out of the booth, the coins from the cashbox flying everywhere.

"We were just visiting," Pietrik said. "This is my girlfriend. There's been a misunderstanding!"

Girlfriend? The guards said nothing, just dragged us on. I scanned the crowd for Matka. Where was she?

"Please, I have money," Pietrik said.

The SS guard clubbed him across the cheek. Pietrik! His beautiful face.

The SS men pulled us past the crowd, and the people in line stared and whispered to one another. I turned and saw the SS man who had followed me, close behind holding Zuzanna and Luiza, each by one arm.

Matka broke through the ticket line and ran after us. The look on her face scared me as much as anything. I'd only seen that look once before, on the wild-eyed face of a horse hit by a carriage and dying in the street. She clutched the little basket with my sandwich in it close to her chest.

"Go home, Matka," I called.

"No. Please, you have the wrong people," she said to the guards.

"*Kriminelle*," one woman in line said.

"They've done *nothing*," Matka said, appealing to the crowd, her wild horse eyes wide. "This is my daughter. I am a nurse at the clinic."

She went on like that, then came running after us, begging the men to release us until one of them said, "If she wants to come so badly, let her join them," and grabbed Matka as well. He snatched her basket and threw it to one of the German women waiting in the ticket line.

"But who will sell us tickets?" a Fräulein in line asked the officers.

"Who needs tickets?" he said. "Just go in. It's free tonight."

The Germans hesitated, confused, and stood where they were as the SS dragged us off into the dark, the trumpets of the "Horst Wessel Song" blaring into the night air.

THEY SEPARATED MEN FROM women at Lublin Castle and the next day trucked a load of us to the rail station. Many around us shoved letters and bribes at the guards. Matka handed a letter to one of them.

"Please, I am German. Can you get this to *Oberscharführer* Lennart Fleischer?" She handed the man some money, and he stuffed both that and the letter in his pocket without even looking at them. They had no time for such things and simply pushed us along. Fleischer was Lennart the Brave's last name? It means butcher. This was fitting.

They shoved Matka, Zuzanna, Luiza, and me and at least one hundred other women into what was once the dining car of a train, now with all the tables removed, and locked the door. Metal bars stood affixed to the windows and a tin bucket for our sanitary needs sat in the corner.

I recognized a few girls from my old Girl Guide troop, including a dazed Janina Grabowski. Had the Gestapo come for her at Lipowa Street? My heart sank when I saw Mrs. Mikelsky was there too, baby daughter in her arms. They'd been arrested when the Gestapo caught Mr. Mikelsky distributing underground newspapers. Their child was almost two years old by then, aptly named Jagoda, for she did look like a blond little berry.

After a few hours, we stopped in Warsaw, but soon started moving again and picked up speed. Not one of us in that car wept. We were mostly silent, the shame of it all so heavy to bear.

I made my way to the window as night fell and watched through the iron bars as we passed moonlit fields and dark forests. There was something disturbing about those trees, so close to one another.

While Mrs. Mikelsky slept, Luiza and I busied ourselves taking turns holding Jagoda. Small for her age, the baby wore only thin cotton pajamas, so we held her close, but even with that task to distract us, Luiza was soon in a state.

"What will my mother do without me?" she said. "I always help her bake."

"Don't worry. You'll be home before long. This is all temporary."

"What about Pietrik?" Luiza said. "Is he on this train?"

The car lurched right, and the excrement in our toilet bucket spilled over the top, onto two women sitting on the floor, causing them to cry out and jump up.

"How should I know?" I said. "Keep your voice down. People are sleeping."

"Will they let us write letters?"

"Of course, Luiza. We will probably go to work somewhere. Picking beets or something."

"Will they lock us up?" Luiza asked.

"I don't know, Lou. You'll see. It won't be so bad."

Mrs. Mikelsky came to take the baby, and the train rocked like a terrible cradle, lulling most of my fellow travelers to fitful sleep. Luiza rested against me near the window while Matka slept with

Zuzanna in a corner on the floor. The two looked beautiful lying there, Zuzanna resting her head on Matka's shoulder like a baby, her long legs curled up beneath her.

Luiza traded places with Zuzanna and fell asleep at last and as we sped toward Germany, my own demons crawled out to visit. How could I have gotten us all arrested? It was one thing to suffer myself on account of my own stupidity and quite another to bring everyone I loved down with me. Why had I gone to the theater? My lack of thinking had ruined us all. Would there be a trial? They surely would release the others once they realized they'd done nothing. Only I would be detained.

Had Pietrik already been shot? They did it in the castle courtyard, we all knew. I trembled all over. Where was Papa? We needed to get off that train right away if we were to have any hope at all. I reached up to the window and unlatched the sash. Though it was night, the shapes of spruce trees sped by. The air was growing colder as we went farther west.

"It's time for you to rest," Zuzanna said.

"We have to get out of here."

"Get a hold of yourself, Kasia."

"I can't stay here," I said, the anxiety mounting. "Why can't I breathe?" Something compressed my neck, squeezing.

"Stop it," Zuzanna said. "You'll scare Luiza. She's already bad enough."

I doubled over at the waist. "I'm dying."

Zuzanna turned my wrist and fixed the pads of her fingers in a row along the inside of it. "Your pulse is elevated. You are having a panic episode. Breathe. Big breath in. Deep breath out."

I filled my lungs as best I could.

"Look at me, Kasia. Breathe again. Don't stop. This may take ten minutes to pass." Having a sister who knew everything about medicine came in handy. It took almost exactly ten minutes for the episode to abate.

Hours later we passed through Poznan and then veered off

northwest. The morning light showed the leaves on the trees, redder and more orange the farther we went. I dozed, cheek against the cool iron bars, and woke once the train slowed.

Luiza and others came to stand next to me at the window.

"What is happening?" she asked.

The whistle screamed, long and high, as the train slid into a station.

Matka pushed through the women and stood with me. "What do you see?"

I held her hand. "Sign says Fürstenberg-Mecklenburg."

There were women on the platform, blond giantesses wearing hooded black capes over their gray uniforms. One threw a cigarette down and squashed it with her boot. A few held dark Alsatians at their sides. The dogs seemed to anticipate our arrival, watching the train cars go by much as a pet waits for its owner. Had they done this before?

"Germany," a woman behind me said, craning her neck to see.

Luiza cried out. The train whistle screamed a second time, and my breath again started coming hard.

Matka held my hand tighter. "Must be a labor camp."

"I can see a church steeple," I said. The thought of the Germans of that town sitting in church on Sundays with their hymnals was comforting.

"God-fearing people," said someone.

"Fürstenberg?" said Mrs. Mikelsky. "I know it. This is a resort town!"

"As long as we work hard, we will be fine," Matka said.

I curled my hands around the iron window bars to steady myself as the train lurched to a stop. "At least they know the commandments," I said.

None of us knew how wrong we were that morning as we stepped out of that train and fell headlong into hell.

CHAPTER 12

Caroline

1941

As spring approached, the situation in France grew more desperate. Every morning by ten, the consulate reception area was already jammed and my schedule full. The Nazis stomping all over Paris had thrown those French citizens stranded in New York into the depths of despair and, often, dire financial circumstances, something we were powerless to assuage. Under strict orders from Roger not to offer my own funds, I could provide chocolate bars and a shoulder to cry on but little else.

One morning I set one of Betty's shoe boxes on my desk and began assembling an orphan package. There'd been no new word from Paul. I tried to stay occupied to stop the dark thoughts, anything to tamp down the ache in my chest.

"You've got a full schedule," Pia said, as she dropped a pile of folders on my desk. "First up, your high-society friends who don't take no for an answer."

"That doesn't narrow it down, Pia."

"I don't know. Pris-something and her mother."

It was Priscilla Huff, a leggy blonde who had been a year behind me at Chapin. Flawless in a blue Mainbocher suit, she was uncharacteristically friendly. Electra Huff, an only slightly less trim version of her daughter, followed and shut the door behind her.

"What a chic little office you have here, Caroline dear," Mrs. Huff said.

"I'd like to adopt a French child, Caroline," Priscilla said, as if ordering Chateaubriand at the Stork Club. "I'll even take twins."

"There's a waiting list for the few children waiting for adoption, Priscilla, but Pia can help you with the paperwork. You'll just need your husband's signature."

"How is Roger Fortier?" Mrs. Huff asked. "Such a lovely man, your boss."

"Well, that's the thing, Caroline," Priscilla said. "I'm not married."

"*Yet,*" Mrs. Huff said, browsing the silver frames on the mantel. "There are two offers pending."

I set a clean pair of oatmeal-colored socks into the shoe box. Two offers pending? What was she, a two-acre parcel in Palm Beach with privacy hedge?

"It takes two parents to adopt, Priscilla."

"Mother's French is excellent. I'm *plus que* fluent as well."

Priscilla had the French language requirement down. She'd beaten me in the French essay contest every year. The fact that their cook prepared an elaborate *bûche de Noël* for the class each Christmas didn't hurt, since our French teacher, Miss Bengoyan, the sole judge, had a well-known sweet tooth. Why did I want a cigarette so badly?

"I understand, Priscilla, but I don't make the rules. These children come from tragic circumstances, as you can imagine. Even two parents can have a difficult time."

"So you send packages to orphaned children but turn down a perfectly good home? I can offer a child the best of everything."

Maybe. Until the next bright, shiny object came along.

"I'm sorry, Priscilla. But I have several appointments this morning." I walked to my file cabinet.

"Word is, *you* are adopting," Priscilla said.

"You hear many things these days," I said.

"Seems some can go around the regulations," Mrs. Huff said, adjusting one glove.

"I lost my father when I was eleven years old, Mrs. Huff. Growing up fatherless is a terrible thing. I wouldn't do that to a child."

"More terrible than no parents at all?" Priscilla said.

I shut the file drawer. "It is a moot point, I'm afraid. There just are not that many French children to adopt."

Priscilla pouted, and I stifled the urge to throttle her.

"I thought there were ships of orphans arriving daily," she said.

"No, very few, actually. After the *City of Benares*—"

"City of *what*?" asked Priscilla.

Mrs. Huff reached for her bag. "Well, if it's money you need. I heard you and your mother had to pull out of the Meadow Club . . ."

I sat back down in my desk chair. "We sold our Southampton house, Mrs. Huff, and we summer in Connecticut now, so we've no need for the club, and no, you can't just buy a *child*, Priscilla. If you read a newspaper now and then, you'd know the *City of Benares* was a British passenger ship, carrying one hundred English children sent by their parents to Canada to escape the London bombings. En route from Liverpool to Halifax, Nova Scotia—"

Mrs. Huff placed two hands on my desk and leaned in. "We're interested in a *French* child, Caroline."

"Four days into the journey, the children, ages four to fifteen, were in their pajamas, ready for bed . . ." I felt the tears coming.

Priscilla folded her arms across her chest. "What does this have to do with adopting a French—"

"A German submarine sank the ship, Priscilla. Seventy-seven of the hundred children on board drowned. As a result, all child evacuation programs have been brought to an abrupt halt for now. So I'm terribly sorry that you ladies won't be buying a child today. And now

I must ask you to leave immediately. I'm very busy at the moment, in case you didn't notice the packed reception area."

Priscilla checked her stocking seams. "No need to get snippy, Caroline. We're only trying to help."

Pia knocked, entered in the nick of time, and showed the Huffs out, just missing Roger, who came to stand in my doorway.

"You'll be happy to know I've granted you a higher security clearance, Caroline."

I opened my drawer and arranged a row of new Hershey's bars, hoping Roger wouldn't notice my shaking hands. "Whatever for?"

"We've known for a while there are transit camps all over the free zone. They've been herding in foreigners. Jews mostly, but not exclusively. Now there are reports of transports out to camps in Poland and other places. I was wondering if you could take it on."

I swiveled to face Roger. "Take on what, exactly?"

"We need to figure out where they're going. Who. How many. What they've been arrested for. I'm tired of telling people I don't know what's happened to their families."

"Of course I'll do it, Roger."

I would have access to classified information, a ringside seat to the events in Europe. No more having to wait for *The New York Times* to get the news. Maybe some new intelligence would surface about Paul.

"It's hard to ask this of you with no paycheck in return."

"Don't worry about it, Roger. Mother and I are fine." Truth was, Father had left us comfortable, but we still had to watch our pennies. We had a few income trickles, and a few assets we could sell. And there was always the silver.

When we closed for lunch that afternoon, I ran downstairs to the Librairie de France bookstore just off the Channel Gardens, borrowed every atlas they had, went back to my office, and lunged into a whole new world of classified information. British reconnaissance photos. Confidential documents. Pia dumped files on my desk, and I lost myself in research about the camps. Transit camps in the free zone. Gurs. Le Vernet. Argelès-sur-Mer. Agde. Des Milles. The surveillance photos were disturbing, detailed, and voyeuristic, like peering into someone's backyard.

I organized the camps into folders and soon discovered a whole new classification in addition to transit camps.

Concentration camps.

I taped a map to my office wall and peppered it with pins as we were notified of new camps. Roger fed me the lists, and I kept track. Soon Austria, Poland, and France were dotted with red pins, as if sick with scarlet fever.

Months went by without another letter from Paul. With the Nazis running roughshod over France, it was hard not to imagine the worst. Roger passed on news from abroad. At first the French had adopted a wait-and-see attitude about the Germans. As Nazi officers requisitioned the best restaurant tables, Parisians did their best to simply ignore them. Paris had been occupied before, after all. They seemed to be hoping it would all go away.

Never particularly good at taking a hint, the Nazis started requisitioning the best charcuterie and wine for themselves and announced their plan to relocate Paris's entire fashion industry to Hamburg. After all this, and once the Nazis started rounding up French citizens with no warning, we received reports that said small resistance groups had started to crystallize here and there in Paris and distribute anti-German leaflets, laying the groundwork for an effective intelligence network. Less than a week after we received these first reports, there was a sharp increase in reports of underground activity all over France.

I HAD MY ORPHAN WORK to keep me busy, and Mother was a tireless partner for the cause. One evening I pulled everything out of the guest-room closets at the apartment searching for garments we could dissect and transform into orphan clothes, while Mother stitched together the few decent pieces of material we had.

The guest room was a curious combination of Mother and Father, for it had once been his study and retained a masculine air with its striped wallpaper and ebonized partners desk, but had later become Mother's sewing room and bore the remnants of her projects: tissue-thin amber dress patterns flung about; padded Wolf dress forms of assorted sizes, unfortunately growing less wasp-waisted over the years.

I hauled out Mother's rummage sale bags and our winter woolens, scrounging for soft scraps of material. I've never shown aptitude for sewing, and it's just as well since it's ruinous to good posture, but Mother was a brilliant seamstress. She sat at her sewing machine, head bent over the old black Singer, her hair white in the lamp's arc of light. Once Father died, her dun-colored hair had turned the color of Epsom salts almost overnight. She had cut it short, started wearing mostly riding clothes, and put her rouge away. She'd always loved her horses and was more comfortable with a currycomb than a silver one, but it was sad to see such a beautiful woman give up on herself.

We listened to war news on the radio as we worked.

April 19, 1941. While Belfast, Northern Ireland, sweeps up after a heavy Luftwaffe raid, London has suffered one of the heaviest air raids of the war to date. As German troops advance into Greece, Greek Prime Minister Alexandros Koryzis takes his own life, and the British evacuate Greece.

"Oh, do turn it off, Caroline. There's so little hopeful news."

"At least we've stuck a toe in the war."

Though still officially a neutral nation, the United States had finally begun sea patrols in the North Atlantic.

"To think of Hitler running about what's left of the Parthenon," Mother said. "Where will it stop?"

I slipped a seam ripper into the tin sand pail Mother used as a catchall for bobbins and scissors and felt metal meet grit. There was still sand at the bottom of it, from the beach at Mother's family's Gin Lane cottage in Southampton. Such a lovely beach. I could see Mother and Father there—she in black bathing costume, he in suit and tie, wrestling with his newspaper in the wind, the salt air pricking at my lungs. At night, in the chiaroscuro of the vast living room, I would pretend to read, one cheek to the cool linen sofa, and watch them play gin rummy, laughing and drinking each other in.

"Let's go out to Southampton, Mother. A change of pace will do us good." We had sold the Gin Lane cottage by then, but Betty still kept a house there.

"Oh no, it's full of New Yorkers now."

"You're a New Yorker, Mother."

"Let's not bicker, dear." She avoided the beach. It brought back memories of Father for her too.

"I suppose we can't leave now anyway. The orphanages will be desperate for warm clothes once the weather turns colder."

"You can still post your comfort boxes through the mail?"

"The Germans encourage people to send help for the orphans and even to those in transit camps. Keeps costs down for them."

"How kind of the Boche." Mother used the French word *Boche*, meaning "square-headed," when referring to the Germans, her small act of defiance.

I turned to the bed and gathered an armful of Father's woolen jackets.

She pulled the sleeve of one toward her. "We can cut those down—"

"We're not cutting up Father's things, Mother. And besides, we need fabrics that children can wear next to their skin."

I pulled the jackets away from her.

"It has been over twenty years since he died, Caroline. Camel hair is moth candy."

"I've been having Father's jackets cut down for myself, actually."

Father's jackets fit me well after alterations. They were made with the best two-ply cashmere, vicuña, or herringbone, each leather button a work of art. The pockets were lined with satin so thick putting a hand in one felt like dipping it in water. Plus, wearing Father's jackets kept a piece of him near me. Sometimes when I was standing on a street corner waiting for a light to change, I found crumbles of cigar tobacco in a deep crease or an old peppermint in cloudy cellophane in a hidden pocket.

"You can't keep every old thing of his, Caroline."

"It saves money, Mother."

"We're not in the poorhouse yet. The way you talk you'd have us all lashed together singing 'Nearer My God to Thee.' We always make do."

"Maybe we should cut back on staff."

After Father died, Mother collected mouths to feed the way some people collect spoons or Chinese export porcelain. It wasn't unusual to find some poor soul from a hobo den living in the guest room, propped up with a goose-down sham reading *The Grapes of Wrath*, cordial glass of sherry in hand.

"It's not as if we keep liveried footmen, dear. If you're talking about Serge, he's family. Plus, he's the best French chef in this city and doesn't drink like most."

"And Mr. Gardener?" I said.

That question needed no answer. Our gardener, oddly enough called Mr. Gardener, was practically family as well. With his kind eyes and skin brown and smooth as a horse chestnut seed, he'd been by our side since we planted our garden up in Bethlehem just before Father died. It was rumored his people had come to Connecticut from North Carolina by way of the Underground Railroad through a stop once located in the old Bird Tavern just across the street from The Hay. In addition to having a genius for cultivating antique roses, Mr. Gardener would have taken a bullet for Mother and she for him. He would be with us forever.

"And a few day maids don't break the bank," Mother said. "If you want to pinch pennies, have the consulate pay shipping for your orphan boxes."

"Roger's been splitting the cost with me, but I won't have much to send this time. There isn't a scrap of wearable material to be bought."

"Why not arrange a benefit performance? You may enjoy being onstage again, dear, and you still have the costumes."

The *costumes*. Yards of material, disintegrating in an old trunk, of no use to anyone, perfect for every sort of children's clothing.

"Mother, you're a genius."

I ran to my bedroom and dragged the trunk from the closet. It still wore the souvenir stickers from every city I'd played in. Boston. Chicago. Detroit. Pittsburgh. I hauled it back to the guest room, winded. I had to stop stealing Pia's cigarettes.

Mother straightened up in her sewing chair as I entered. "Oh, no, no. Don't do it, Caroline."

I threw open the lid of the trunk and released a lovely scent of cedar, aging silk, and stage makeup.

"It's brilliant, Mother."

"How *can* you, dear?"

We'd collected props and costumes from all over, a nineteenth-century silk bodice here, a silk and bone Tiffany fan there, but Mother had sewn most of the costumes I'd worn onstage, from *Twelfth Night* at Chapin to *Victoria Regina* on Broadway. I wasn't allowed to keep every ensemble, but I still had my high school costumes, and Mother often sewed a backup of the Broadway ensembles. She used the best velvets and the richest, most vivid silks and soft cottons. She finished each with mother-of-pearl buttons she made from mussel shells she'd scavenged from the beach at Southampton. A button once put on by Mother was put on forever.

"*Merchant of Venice*," I said, pulling out a periwinkle blue velvet jacket and pants, both lined in mustard silk. "Two toddler shirts right there. What can we do with the lining?"

Mother withered. "Underpants?"

"Genius, dear." I held up a coral pink satin gown, the bodice embroidered with seed pearls. "*Twelfth Night.*"

"Are you not the least bit nostalgic?"

"Not at all, Mother, and if you resist, I'll cut them myself."

She grabbed the dress from me. "Certainly not, Caroline."

I pulled out another velvet dress the color of Amontillado sherry, a white faux ermine pelerine, and a scarlet silk robe.

"All's Well That Ends Well," I said, holding up the dress. Had my waist ever been that small? "We can get six nightshirts from the robe, two coats from the dress. The fur will line mittens."

We worked into the night. I ripped seams and cut, the teeth of my pinking shears biting through velvets and satins.

"Any news about your friend Paul?" Mother asked.

"Not a word. Not even getting French newspapers at the office anymore."

Though Mother was on a need-to-know basis about my relationship with Paul, she somehow understood how important he'd become to me. With all the developments in France, she seemed almost as concerned about him as I was.

"His wife has a dress shop?"

"Lingerie shop, actually. Called Les Jolies Choses."

"Lingerie?" Mother said, as if I'd told her Rena juggled flaming hatchets.

"Yes, Mother. Brassieres and—"

"I know what *lingerie* is, Caroline."

"Don't judge, Mother, please."

"Well, even if Paul comes out of this war in one piece, there's no accounting for men."

"I just want to hear from him, Mother."

Mother ripped the seam of a lavender satin lining. "And the French, you know how that goes. Friendships with married men are quite common there, but—"

"All I want is another letter, Mother."

"You'll see. This war will blow over, and he'll be knocking at your door. The Germans probably have him someplace special. He's somewhat famous, after all."

I hadn't considered that. Would the Nazis treat Paul specially given his celebrity?

By morning, we had stacked the guest bed with an exquisite assortment of children's wear. Soft coats and trousers. Jumpers and hats.

I lugged it all to work and left it on Pia's desk, though she was nowhere to be found.

WEEKS LATER, I HAD three generations of the LeBlanc family camped out in my office and taking turns bathing via the consulate ladies' room sink when suddenly, Roger rushed to my door and swung into my office, one hand on the doorjamb, face the color of his dove-gray shirt. My stomach lurched. His bad news face. The knit brow. Mouth set in a tight line. As long as he didn't close the door, I would be fine.

He ran his fingers through his hair. "Caroline——"

"Just tell me, Roger."

"I have some news."

I held on to my wooden file cabinet. "Just do it——"

"It is bad, I'm afraid, C."

"Should I sit?" I said.

"I would imagine so," Roger said as he closed the door.

CHAPTER 13

Kasia

1941

THE TRAIN DOORS OPENED, AND WE STOOD AS IF FROZEN THERE inside the car.

"*Out, out!*" the woman guards on the platform shouted. They poked and swatted us with their sticks and leather truncheons. If you've never been hit with a leather truncheon, it stings like you cannot believe. I'd never been struck with anything before, and that sting was a terrible shock, but the dogs were the worst part, snapping and barking at us, close enough for me to feel their warm breath on my legs.

"You stink like pigs," one guard said. "Poles. Of course, covered in shit."

This made me madder than anything. They give us one small bucket to use and then complain that we smell?

We marched at a quick pace through Fürstenberg in that Sunday's first light, five abreast, Matka on my one side, Mrs. Mikelsky and baby Jagoda on the other. I glanced back and saw Zuzanna and Luiza one row behind, their eyes glassy with that special kind of terror we would grow used to. Fürstenberg seemed like a medieval village out of a storybook, the buildings with sod roofs and window boxes overflowing with red petunias, windows shuttered up tight.

Were the Germans still asleep in warm beds? Dressing for church? Someone was awake, for the scent of toast and fresh coffee was in the air. A second-story shutter opened a crack and then closed.

Those who could not keep up had a time of it, for the guards beat the slowest, and the dogs nipped at their legs. Matka and I held Mrs. Mikelsky to keep her from stumbling. She massaged her baby's feet, blue from the cold, kneading them like bread dough as we hurried along.

They rushed us along a cobblestone road by the banks of a lake.

"What a pretty lake," Luiza said behind us. "Will there be swimming?"

None of us answered. What would they do with us? This was Germany, after all. As a child, a trip to Germany had always been entertaining, as long as one did not have to stay too long. With most things you knew what to expect. Like when you went to the circus for the first time, you had some idea. Not with this.

Soon we saw an enormous brick building at the end of the road. It was only September, but the trees turned early that far north, orange and flame-red among the pines. Even the salvia planted along the foundation of that brick building was Nazi red.

As we marched closer, German patriotic music blared in the distance, and the smell of cooking potatoes filled the air, which sent my stomach growling.

"It's a KZ," the woman behind me said to no one in particular. *"Konzentrationslager."*

I'd never heard that word. Nor did I know what a concentration camp was, but the sound of the word sent ice water down my spine.

We approached the high, smooth walls that surrounded the camp and stepped through green metal gates, to an open plaza surrounded by low wooden buildings. Even through the music, I could hear the wire atop the wall buzz with high voltage.

A wide road cut through the middle of camp, officially called Lagerstrasse or Camp Road, but which we soon came to call Beauty Road.

That road really was beautiful. It started at the vast cobblestone plaza known as the *platz* and ran straight back through camp, covered in black, shiny sand and chunks of black slag that glinted in the sun. A honey-sweet scent caught my nose and drew my attention to the trees, which lined the road as far as the eye could see. Linden trees. What a comfort it was to see this, the favorite tree of the Virgin Mary. The linden is revered in Poland, and it's bad luck to cut one down. In front of each block was planted a cheerful little garden of flowers, and at each block window hung a wooden flower box, planted with geraniums. How bad could such a neatly kept place be? Oddest of all, an ornate silver cage stood at the beginning of Beauty Road, filled with exotic animals—yellow-winged parrots, two brown spider monkeys who swung about the cage playing like children, and a peacock with an emerald-green head who fanned out his feathers. The peacock shrieked, and a shiver went through me.

Matka gathered us close, as we took it all in. Across the *platz*, rows of women in striped dresses stood at attention, five to a row, not one looking in our direction. A female guard pulled a revolver from the holster at her hip and asked the guard next to her a question about it. Matka spied the gun and quickly looked away.

A girl in a striped dress passed near me.

"Polish?" she said, her voice almost drowned out by the music.

"Yes," I said. "All of us."

The spider monkeys stopped playing and watched us, fingers fisted around the cage bars.

"They will take any food you have, so eat it up quickly," she said and walked away to line up.

"Give us everything you have—you won't need it," said an older woman passing by, her hand out as she walked the length of the column.

We clutched our coats around us tighter. Why would we give up the few things we had? I glanced at Matka. She reached out, and her hand trembled as she squeezed mine. I wanted only a bed for sleep and something to end my terrible thirst.

The guards herded us into the utility block: two big open rooms with low ceilings and a shower room off to one side. A tall blond guard we later learned was named Binz stood at the door, as frantic and exercised as Hitler himself.

"*Hurry, hurry!*" she cried, as she stung my bottom with her crop.

I came to a desk, and a woman sitting behind it in a striped dress took down my name. In German she told me to empty my pockets, and she dumped the few possessions I had—a handkerchief, my watch, some aspirin, the last vestiges of normal life—into a yellow envelope and placed it with the others in a file box. Next I was ordered to strip while a prisoner-guard watched.

"Move along!" she said once I was naked.

I saw Matka, behind me, stop next at the table. They wanted her ring, but she was having trouble twisting it off of her finger.

"Her finger is swollen," said a woman doctor standing nearby, tall and blond in her white doctor's smock. Binz lifted Matka's hand, spat on the ring, and tried to work it off. Matka turned her head.

"Try petroleum jelly," the woman doctor said.

Binz spat on the ring again and finally twisted it off. The woman behind the desk dropped it into a yellow envelope and placed it in the file box.

Matka's ring was gone. How could they just *take* a person's things with no feeling at all?

I saw Janina Grabowski, far ahead of me in line, wrestling with a guard and crying out. She was undergoing the hairdresser's exam. A second guard came to assist the first and held Janina by the shoulders.

"Stop, no—please," she said as they tried to cut her hair off.

A guard pushed me along, and I lost Matka, who was swallowed up in the crush of women. I tried to cover my nakedness as a prisoner with a green triangle on the shoulder of her striped jacket pushed me to a stool. Once I felt a toothpick touch my scalp, I knew I was about to follow Janina's fate, and my heart tried to escape my chest, it thumped so.

The scissors were cold against the back of my neck, and the woman swore in German as she hacked through my braid. Was I to blame for my thick hair? She threw the braid onto a pile of hair so high it reached the windowsill and then, as if in payment for making her work harder, shaved my head roughly. I shook all over as every click of the trimmers sent hunks of hair sliding down my bare shoulders. She pushed me off the stool, and I felt my head—smooth, with just tufts of hair here and there. Thank God Pietrik wasn't there to see that. How cold it was without hair!

A prisoner with a purple triangle—a Bible girl, I later learned—pushed me back onto a table used to examine gynecological parts. She held my legs apart while a second prisoner shaved me with a straight razor, leaving me cut and scraped.

When that was finished, they sent me on to the woman doctor, who said, "On the table," and took a cold silver instrument, put it in me, and opened me up, all without even toweling it off! She spread me out for all the world to see and jabbed her rubber-gloved fingers inside me and felt around. She was not at all horrified by her job and might just as well have been washing a dish. She acted with no regard for the fact that I was young and she was violating me in a way that could never be undone.

I had little time to mourn my lost virginity, for guards lined us up naked, five across, in the shower room. A shower attendant in white coveralls hit the women in front of us with a truncheon, leaving red welts on their backsides, as they ran to the showerheads. I stayed near Mrs. Mikelsky and braced for the sting of the rubber. She held baby Jagoda close to her, shivering so badly it was as if cold water were already running over her. A prisoner with a green badge on her sleeve came to Mrs. Mikelsky, put two hands around the baby's skinny, naked body, and pulled. Mrs. Mikelsky held Jagoda tight.

"Give it to me," the prisoner-guard said.

Mrs. Mikelsky only held tighter.

"She's a good baby," I said to the guard.

The guard pulled harder at the child. Would they tear her in two?

"It can't be helped," the guard said. "Don't make a scene."

The baby cried out, which caught the attention of the nasty head wardress, Dorothea Binz, who came, almost at a run, from the front of the building, a second guard close behind. The name Dorothea means "God's gift," and a name could not have been more wrong for a person.

Binz came to a stop next to Mrs. Mikelsky and pointed her leather crop at little blond Jagoda.

"Is the father German?"

Mrs. Mikelsky glanced at me, her brow creased.

"No, Polish," she said.

"Just take it," Binz said with a wave of her crop.

The guard who had come with Binz held Mrs. Mikelsky from behind while the first guard pried Jagoda from her mother's arms.

"I made a mistake," Mrs. Mikelsky said. "Yes, actually the father is German . . ." She glanced at me.

"From Berlin," I said. "A real patriot."

The green badge held naked Jagoda to her shoulder and looked at Binz.

"Just *take* it," Binz said with a jerk of her head.

The guard hiked the baby higher on her shoulder and walked back through the incoming crowd.

Mrs. Mikelsky crumpled to the floor like a burning piece of paper as she watched her baby be taken away. "No, please, where are you taking her?"

Binz poked her crop into Mrs. Mikelsky's ribs and pushed her toward the showers.

I folded my arms across my naked chest and stepped closer to Binz.

"That child will die without her mother," I said.

Binz turned to me, her expression bringing to mind a bubbling teapot.

"There is no greater cruelty," I said.

Binz raised her crop to me.

"You Poles . . ."

I closed my eyes, bracing myself, waiting for the sting of the leather. Where would the blows land?

Suddenly I felt arms slide around me. Matka, her naked body smooth on mine.

"Please, Madame Wardress," she said in her prettiest German. "She is out of her head to speak to you this way. How sorry we are—"

Was it my mother's German that caused Binz to take a step back? Her gentle way?

"You tell her to keep her mouth shut," Binz said, shaking her crop in my direction. She retreated through the crowd.

The guards shoved me dazed into a shower, my tears for poor Mrs. Mikelsky mixing with the sting of cold shower water.

THEY RELEASED US FROM quarantine two weeks later, with only our uniform shift and blouse, enormous wooden clogs, a toothbrush, a thin jacket, gray bloomers, a tin bowl and spoon, and a piece of soap we were told had to last two months. Two months? Surely we'd be home by then!

Our new home, Block 32, was much larger than the quarantine block. Women, some in their uniform gray shirts and striped dresses, some naked from the shower, ran about dressing, squaring up their straw mattresses, and tucking in their blue and white checked sheets. There was a small washroom in the block with three showerheads and three long sinks, each filled by means of a spout. Women sat with no modesty atop a platform drilled with holes to send nature's offerings to the putrid ground below.

The block smelled like a chicken coop, rotten beets, and five hundred unwashed feet. All of the girls in the block spoke Polish, and most wore the red triangle of political prisoners. If there was any good thing about the camp, it was that so many of the prisoners were Polish—almost half—most there, like us, for what the Nazis called political crimes. After Poles, the next largest group was German women arrested for violating one of Hitler's many rules or for criminal activity such as murder or theft.

"Square your bed!" shouted Roza, the *Blockova*, a German woman with sleepy eyes. She was from Berlin and not much older than my mother. Later I learned she'd been arrested for sticking her tongue out at a German officer.

"Attend your mess kit!"

We quickly learned that survival at Ravensbrück revolved around one's tin bowl, cup, and spoon and the ability to safeguard them. If one looked away for a moment, they might disappear, never to return. As a result we kept our kits tucked in the chests of our uniforms or, if one was lucky enough to acquire a piece of twine or string, made that into a belt and wore them strung on it at the waist.

Luiza and Matka chose a top bunk, what the prisoners called the coconut palms, since it was high up. It was very close to the ceiling, so they could barely sit up, and in the winter icicles hung from above it, but it was more private up there. Zuzanna and I slept just opposite.

I had to push down my jealousy at Luiza sleeping with my mother. I got Zuzanna, who shifted all night in her sleep, mumbling doctor talk. When she woke me up, I would spend the night fretting in the darkness, paralyzed with guilty thoughts. How could I have been so reckless to have gotten us all sent to this terrible place? To make things worse, the block was never quiet, always filled with the sounds of shrill voices of women tortured by nightmares or the itch of lice, night-shift workers returning home, sleepless women exchanging recipes, and calls for a basin for the sick who could not get to the washroom in time.

I did find moments to be alone with Matka, though. That night I crawled into the bunk with her before dinner.

"I am so sorry I got you here, Matka. If you hadn't brought that sandwich, if I hadn't—"

"Don't think that way," she said. "In here, you have to concentrate all you have on being smarter than the Germans. I'm glad I'm here with you girls. This will all be fine." She kissed my forehead.

"But your ring—I hate them for taking it."

"It's just a thing, Kasia. Don't waste your energy on the hate. That will kill you sure as anything. Focus on keeping your strength. You're resourceful. Find a way to outsmart them."

Blockova Roza strode in. She had a kind face but did not smile as she made announcements.

"Work call is at eight A.M. Those without work assignments, report to the labor office next to the block where you were processed. That is where you will pick up your badge and number."

"She speaks only in German?" I whispered to Matka. "What about the girls who don't understand?"

"Say a prayer of thanks for Herr Speck's German class. It may save your life."

She was right. I was lucky I spoke German, since all announcements were made in that language, no exceptions. The non-German speakers had a terrible disadvantage, since ignorance was no excuse for disregarding rules.

THE NEXT MORNING THE SIREN startled us awake. I'd just dozed off, dreaming about swimming with Pietrik in Lublin, when the lights in our block came on at 3:30 A.M. The worst part was that siren, a screech so loud and piercing it was as if it were from the bowels of hell. With this siren, Roza and her *Stubova* assistants came through the rows of beds. One *Stubova* banged on a tin pan, and one poked at sleepers with the leg of a stool, and Roza splashed ladles of water from a bucket onto sleeping women's faces.

"Get up! Hurry! Everyone up!" they called.

This was a special kind of torture.

Matka, Zuzanna, Luiza, and I made our way to the dining hall, the long room next to our sleeping quarters, and squeezed onto a bench at the end. Breakfast was the same as it had been in quarantine, lukewarm yellowish soup that was more like turnip water and a small piece of bread that tasted like sawdust. The soup hit my stomach and almost came back up.

Roza read a list of new assignments.

Matka was assigned to the bookbindery, one of the highly sought-after inside positions. It was much harder to work a prisoner to death when she was sitting at a desk.

Luiza became an assistant to the Bible girls who processed Angora rabbit fur. The Angora rabbits lived at the far end of the camp in specially heated cages and were fed tender lettuce from the commandant's greenhouse. Their fur was periodically shaved and sent to the tailor's workshop, a massive complex of eight interconnected warehouses where prisoners assembled German army uniforms.

Zuzanna, who did not reveal she was a medical doctor, ended up sorting the booty piles—the mounds of Hitler's stolen plunder that came by train.

I was assigned as an Available, a good and bad thing. Good since we lined up every day and, if not chosen to work, had that day to lie in the bunk. But bad since, if chosen, we were assigned some of the worst jobs, like latrine cleaner or road crew worker. Being assigned to the road crew and used like an animal to pull a heavy concrete roller could kill a person in one day.

OUR FIRST CHRISTMAS AT RAVENSBRÜCK was especially bad, for many of us had been certain we'd be home by then. Matka, Zuzanna, Luiza, and I had only been there for three months, but it felt like three years. We had received a few letters from Papa by then. They were written in German, per regulations, and mostly struck through with black marker, leaving only a few words and his last line, *Your loving Papa.* We wrote letters too, on single-paged camp stationery, limited by the censors to writing about the weather and vague positive thoughts.

As the days grew shorter, Zuzanna warned us to keep our spirits up, for sadness was often a more potent killer than disease. Some just gave up, stopped eating, and died.

Christmas morning started with a pane of glass shattering in the cold. The air rushed in, waking us all. Did this devil wind prying us from our beds on Christ's day mean bad things for us?

Every prisoner in camp shuffled out onto the *platz,* for *Appell,* a massive, group roll call. We then lined up ten abreast in the darkness next to the *Revier,* the only sound the stomping of hundreds of clogs echoing around the *platz* as we tried to ward off the cold. How I wished for a warm coat! The searchlights arced overhead. Surely *Appell* would be short and uneventful because of Christmas. Didn't Germans celebrate Christ's birth? Maybe Binz would take Christmas off? I tried not to look at the pile of bodies, stacked like firewood next to the linen shop, covered in a light dusting of snow. There the bodies waited for the man from town with his morgue car to come and slide each into one of his paper bags with frilly ends and drive them off.

A young guard in training named Irma Grese, Binz's star protégé, hurried down the rows counting us and marking numbers down on her clipboard. She stopped now and then to enjoy a cigarette, standing there wrapped in her thick black cloak. While Grese and Binz were like truant teenaged best friends, both blond and beautiful, there was no mistaking one for the other. Binz was tall with slightly coarser features and wore her hair in an Olympia roll, teased and rolled up from her forehead. Grese was petite and moviestar pretty, with almond-shaped blue eyes and naturally pink lips. Under her uniform cap, she wore her hair pulled back into two shining ringlets, like rolls of golden coins, one down each side of her neck. Unfortunately for us, Irma had no talent for numbers. Often her hasty head counts failed to match Binz's, leading to three- and four-hour *Appells*.

The sun breached the horizon, sending golden rays over the *platz*, and a collective moan of happiness went up in the crowd.

"Quiet!" shouted Irma.

Despite our best efforts to hang back and stand in the warmer, soft middle of the crowd, all five of us in our little camp family had ended up in the front row that morning. It was a dangerous place to be, since prisoners on the outer edges were more vulnerable, open to attacks from bored and sometimes volatile guards and their dogs. I stood next to Matka, Luiza on her other side. Mrs. Mikelsky, whom we'd all watched decline quickly after losing her baby, stood between Zuzanna and me. Zuzanna had diagnosed my teacher with dysentery and severe depression, a bad combination.

It had been snowing off and on since early November. To help the time go by, I watched the birds shake snow from their wings, and was jealous of them for being able to come and go as they pleased. A bitter wind was slashing off the lake that morning, so we'd helped Mrs. Mikelsky slip two sheets of smuggled newspaper down the front of her thin cotton jacket for insulation. When Irma was not looking, we turned our backs and rubbed up against one another, trying to stay warm. The guards had erected a tall fir in a sturdy wooden base as a Christmas tree at the end of Beauty Road, and it swayed in the wind.

Mrs. Mikelsky swayed as well, and I held her arm to steady her. Even through her cotton coat, I felt the bone of her elbow sharp against my palm. Was I already that emaciated too? Mrs. Mikelsky leaned into me, and the newspaper crinkled and peeped out over the neck of her shift.

I tucked the paper down, out of sight. "You have to stand straight," I said.

"I'm sorry, Kasia."

"Count in your head. That helps."

"Quiet," Zuzanna said to me across Mrs. Mikelsky's back. "Binz is coming."

A wave of dread washed through the crowd as Binz rode through the camp gates and across the *platz* on her blue bicycle. Had she overslept, warm in her bed with her married boyfriend, Edmund? At least he wasn't there that morning, kissing her as a prisoner was whipped, their favorite pastime.

As Binz rode, she strained against the wind, one hand on a handlebar, the other on her dog's leash, her black wool cape fanned out behind her. She reached the *Revier*, leaned her bicycle against the wall, and navigated the cobblestones with her farm-girl stride, dog by her side, straining at its collar. As Binz walked, she waved her crop in the air like a child with a toy. It was a new crop, made of black leather, from the end of which sprouted a long braid of cellophane.

Binz's dog was named Adelige, which means "aristocratic lady," and she was the most magnificent and most terrifying Alsatian of them all, black and tan with a thick shawl of fur around her chest, the type you could imagine a fine coat being made from. The dog responded to a series of commands, which Binz communicated by way of a green metal clicker.

Binz walked straight to Mrs. Mikelsky and jabbed her out of line with the crop.

"You. Out."

I tried to follow, but Matka held me back.

"What were you talking about?" Binz asked, dog at her hip.

"Nothing, Madame Wardress," Mrs. Mikelsky said.

Irma stepped to Binz's side. "The tally is complete, Madame Wardress."

Binz didn't answer, her gaze trained on Mrs. Mikelsky.

"My baby Jagoda——" Mrs. Mikelsky began.

"You have no baby. You have nothing. You are only a number."

Was Binz showing off for Irma?

Mrs. Mikelsky held one hand out to Binz. "She's a good baby—"

Binz reached for the newspaper under Mrs. Mikelsky's shift and yanked it out in one motion.

"Where did you get this?" Binz asked.

Irma slid her clipboard under her arm and lit another cigarette.

Mrs. Mikelsky stood taller. "I don't know. I have nothing. I am only a number."

Even from five paces away, I could see Binz's whole body tremble. "You're right," she said, then drew back her arm and sent her crop across Mrs. Mikelsky's cheek.

The cellophane slashed Mrs. Mikelsky's cheekbone, and after a quick look at Irma, Binz bent at the waist and unleashed her dog. Adelige sat motionless at first, then at the chirp of Binz's clicker lunged at Mrs. Mikelsky, ears pinned back, teeth bared. The dog clamped her mouth around Mrs. Mikelsky's hand, shook it side to side, and pulled my teacher to her knees. The dog's growls echoed around the square as she lunged and bit the neckline of Mrs. Mikelsky's shift and brought her down onto the snow.

Matka took my hand in hers.

Mrs. Mikelsky rolled to her side and tried to sit but the dog clamped her jaws around her throat and shook its head back and forth.

I held back the urge to retch as the dog dragged Mrs. Mikelsky away from us, like a wolf with a freshly killed deer, leaving a cherry stain along the snow.

The chirp of Binz's metal clicker echoed about the *platz*.

"Adelige, release!" Binz called out.

The dog sat back on her haunches and panted, her golden eyes trained on Binz.

"Seven seven seven six!" Binz shouted.

Irma tossed away her cigarette and let it lie there on the snow, a lazy blue spiral rising from it, as she wrote on her clipboard.

The dog trotted to Binz, tail between her legs, and left Mrs. Mikelsky lying motionless.

Binz turned and waved me out of line. I stepped one pace out.

"Your friend?"

I nodded.

"Yes? How so?"

"My math teacher, Madame Wardress." Tears blurred my sight, but I held them back. Tears only inflamed Binz.

Irma touched her fingers to her pretty mouth and smiled. "Polish math."

Binz tossed me a violet grease pen.

"Write it," she said.

We'd all witnessed the process. Binz wanted me to write the number on Mrs. Mikelsky's chest, the final indignity for every dead or dying prisoner. My heart hammered as I stepped along the dark cherry trail Adelige had left in the snow to where my teacher lay. I found Mrs. Mikelsky on her back, the flesh at her throat ripped to the bone, and there was blood smeared across her bare chest as if painted there. Her face was turned toward me, eyes partially open, the gash across her cheekbone like a gaping smile.

"Write it," Binz said.

With my jacket sleeve, I wiped the blood from Mrs. Mikelsky's chest and wrote in grease pen, *7776*.

"Remove that piece," Binz said.

She wanted the body dragged to the pile beside the linen shop.

I took hold of both of Mrs. Mikelsky's wrists and dragged her, still warm, across the snow, exhaling the white fog of my breath like a plow horse. The horror of it. The hate grew black in my chest. How could I live without revenge?

By the time I reached the stack of bodies, snow covered and shoulder high, my face was wet with tears. I tucked Mrs. Mikelsky along the side of the pile with great care, as if she were sleeping there. Our lioness. Our hope. Our North Star.

"Poles," Irma said to Binz as I walked by her, back to lineup. "Why do they even try to teach them math?"

"True," said Binz with a laugh.

I stopped and turned to Irma.

"At least I can count," I said.

This time I didn't have to wait for the sting of Binz's crop.

CHAPTER 14

Herta

1941

I STAYED AT RAVENSBRÜCK.

Once I received word my father had died and Mutti would need rehabilitative care for her back, my salary became more important.

It was lonely there with only male doctors for company, so I kept to my office when Fritz was not available and worked on my scrapbooks. I pasted in a photo that Fritz had asked a waiter to snap of us lunching in Fürstenberg, matchbooks, and other souvenirs. So many newspaper clippings. German infantry had just invaded the Soviet Union with great success, so there were many positive articles to save.

I wrote back and told Mutti how hard I was working to get the *Revier* cleaned up and running efficiently. How I expected the commandant would notice my hard work if I somehow brought a sense of order to that place.

On my way back to my cottage one night after my daily duties concluded, I noticed a light on in the bookbindery and stopped, hoping to find someone there to talk with. Binz sat on a low stool, back straight, in full uniform, her chin high. A prisoner with a red badge sat in a chair nearby sketching her. It was a Pole I'd seen in processing, the one with the ring Binz had spat on to pull off. There was a pale band of white skin on her finger where the ring had once been.

Binz waved me into the room, a compact space devoted to the production of the Reich's educational materials. Stacks of pamphlets and books sat on a long table along one wall. "Come in, Doctor. I'm just having my portrait drawn."

"Please be still, Madame Overseer," said the prisoner. "I can't draw if you are talking."

A prisoner giving Binz orders? Even stranger, Binz was obeying them.

"Halina here is our resident master artist," Binz said. "You should see the portrait Koegel commissioned. You'd swear the medals are real."

The prisoner stopped sketching. "Should I come back another time, Madame Overseer?"

Anyone would notice that the bookbindery, once a mess of paper, ink, and supplies, had become vastly more organized.

"Commissioned?" I said to the prisoner. "How are you paid?"

"In bread, Madame Doctor," she said.

"She gives it away to the other Poles," said Binz. "Crazy in the head."

It was soothing, almost hypnotic, to watch her sketch, the pencil tapping out rough little lines on the paper.

"You are Polish? Your German is good."

"Fooled me too," Binz said.

"My mother was German," the prisoner said as she sketched, her eyes trained on Binz. "Grew up on an estate not far from Osnabrück."

"And your father?"

"Born in Cologne, where his mother was raised. His father was Polish."

"So you are group three on the Deutsche Volksliste," Binz said. The German People's List categorized Poles into four categories. Group three consisted of persons of mostly German stock who had become Polonized.

"As close to German as you can get," I said.

"If you say so, Madame Doctor."

I smiled. "If a chicken lays an egg in a pigsty, does that make the chick a piglet?"

"No, Madame Doctor."

I walked behind the prisoner and watched her finish the shading on Binz's chin. The portrait was remarkable. It captured Binz's strength and complex personality along with her likeness.

"I'm giving this portrait to Edmund for his birthday," Binz said. "I wanted a nude version, but she isn't good at those."

Halina colored slightly but kept her eyes focused on her pad.

"You should commission a portrait, Doctor," Binz said. "Your mother would like it."

Would my mother care about a portrait of me now that Father had died and she was busy with her new life?

Binz smiled. "All it will cost you is bread."

The prisoner put down her pencil.

"I really should get back for *Appell*."

"Halina, I'll fix it with your *Blockova*," Binz said. "Sit down, Doctor. What else are you doing tonight?"

Binz walked around the prisoner to look at the finished product and clapped her hands together like a delighted child.

"I'm giving this to Edmund tonight. Make sure you turn the light out, and Halina, I'll tell your *Blockova* you'll be in by nine. I will send a white loaf tomorrow for this."

I took Binz's place on the stool. Halina turned to a fresh piece of paper and began sketching, taking a peek at me now and then.

"Why were you sent here?" I asked.

"I don't know, Madame Doctor."

"How can you not know? You were arrested?"

"My daughters were arrested, and I tried to keep them from taking them."

"Arrested for what?"

"I don't know."

Probably the underground.

"What did you do when you went to Osnabrück?"

"We visited my grandparents' country house," said the prisoner in excellent German. "He was a judge. My grandmother was Judi Schneider."

"The painter? The Führer collects her paintings." The prisoner had the same talent the Führer admired so much in her grandmother. "And where in Poland are you from?"

"Lublin, Madame Doctor."

"There is a well-known medical school there," I said.

"Yes, I completed my nursing certificate there."

"You are a nurse?" How nice it would be to have someone cultured and bright to talk medicine with.

"Yes. *Was*. I illustrated children's books before . . ."

"We could use you in the *Revier*."

"I haven't been a practicing nurse in ten years, Madame Doctor."

"Nonsense. I will have Binz reassign you immediately. What block did you end up in?"

"Thirty-two, Madame Doctor."

"You will be a *Lagerprominent* and move to Block One."

"Please, I would like to stay—"

"The *Revier* prisoner staff lives in Block One. You will not only be treating prisoners but the SS staff and their families. You will find clean bed linens in Block One and not a single louse."

"Yes, Madame Doctor. Could my daughters come with me?"

She said this nonchalantly, as if she did not care. This was out of the question, of course. Block One was reserved for Class I workers only.

"Maybe later. The food is fresh, and you receive double rations." I didn't mention that the food in the elite barracks did not contain the drug they put in the regular soup to kill the prisoners' sex drive and cease menses.

After two more sessions, Halina completed my portrait, covered it with translucent white paper, and left it for me in my office. I lifted the paper and was taken aback. The level of detail was astonishing. No one had captured me so perfectly before, a woman doctor of the Reich in my lab coat, strong and focused. Mutti would frame it.

It took a few days to get Halina transferred from the bookbindery to the *Revier.* The infirmary was technically not an SS operation but an offshoot, so bureaucratic matters took extra time.

Jowly, square-jawed Nurse Marschall was the only one not happy with the arrangement. She lumbered to my office, where she squawked like a goose the day we moved her out of her seat at the *Revier* front desk and replaced her with Halina. I transferred Nurse Marschall to a perfectly good office in the rear of the building, a former supply closet.

From the first hour Halina took charge, the *Revier* improved. The patients responded to her efficient manner, no doubt a result of her German ancestry. By the end of the day, most beds were emptied, the work-shy back at work, and the entire building disinfected. There was no need to babysit Halina, since her decision-making skills were almost equal to mine, and this allowed me to tackle my backlog of paperwork. Finally I had a partner I could rely on. The commandant would surely notice the change in no time.

LATER THAT MONTH, Binz came up with a plan she considered brilliant.

For weeks the male staff had planned a trip to Berlin to coincide with Commandant Koegel's absence while he was in Bonn. It was to be a "special mission," which they thought was secret. But the female staff knew the details of this mission, thanks to several of Binz's *Aufseherinnen* who regularly slept with the male guards. It was to be a trip to Salon Kitty, a high-class brothel in a wealthy part of Berlin. Fritz, home visiting his mother in Cologne, had escaped the trip, but almost all the other male staff members emptied out of the camp into buses and motored off, looking like naughty schoolboys on holiday.

This left the following people in charge of the camp: Binz and her *Aufseherinnen*, three older male SS tower guards who patrolled the wall, one poor gate guard who had drawn the short straw, and me.

"I hope there is no escape attempt while you are gone," I had said to Adolf Winkelmann as he prepared to leave.

"It has all been approved, Dr. Oberheuser. You are the ranking officer in charge tonight. Extra *postenkette* have been arranged as a precaution." I was glad for the extra tower guards, expert marksmen all, but they were not allowed to leave their posts.

Winkelmann shuffled off toward the bus as several of our esteemed colleagues called out the windows, threatening to leave him behind.

In their absence, Binz suggested a party at one of the *Aufseherinnen*'s houses, a snug chalet-like home at the far end of the staff compound, outside the camp walls. They'd planned the celebration with great pains. There was to be a drinking relay, dancing, and card games. They had even had some Polish *Häftlings* snip their famous paper cuttings from scarlet tissue paper and then strung them like garlands about the house.

I decided to forgo this party and stay at my office with Halina to finish some work. This was not a hardship, because for the first time since I'd come to camp, I had an intelligent friend, someone whose company I enjoyed, instead of just Binz, who told filthy stories. Not only had Halina cleaned up the *Revier* and reduced by three quarters the number of patients awaiting treatment; she also still completed important projects for the commandant in the bookbindery. She showed me the books she was assembling for Himmler himself. They chronicled the Angora rabbit fur operation at each camp, complete with detailed photos. Ravensbrück's was one of the best fur producers, with twice the number of cages as Dachau. Halina bound the books by hand, wrapping each cover with soft angora fabric.

"You have so much paperwork, Madame Doctor," Halina said. "How can I help?"

How quick she was with that, my favorite phrase. What a pleasure to spend time with a competent prisoner who was not *afraid* of me. Halina had no hunted-animal look, none of that contagious terror that sent me looking at the clouds or at a beetle in the yard. At anything but them.

"Address the envelopes, and I will insert the cards," I said.

We mailed condolence cards, also known as comfort cards, to the families of prisoners who died at the camp by any number of means. Those chosen as special-handling cases and terminated. Those shot trying to escape. Those who died by natural causes. In my terrible doctor handwriting, I wrote, *Body cannot be inspected due to hygienic considerations* on most cards in case the family wanted to view the body. It was a ridiculous charade and added at least ten extra hours of work to my already busy week, but the commandant required it for appearances' sake. Halina addressed envelopes whenever she had a spare moment, until her piles far outnumbered my completed cards.

"It must be hard for a family to receive such a note," Halina said, addressing an envelope in her flowing script. Had tears come to her eyes?

With the condolence card was included an official form so the family could apply for that prisoner's ashes. Four pounds of generic ashes were sent per female prisoner, in a tin canister, if a request was approved. At least I was not responsible for coordinating all that.

"We can take a break from this," I said.

Halina sat up straighter. "Oh no, Madame Doctor, I'm fine. But I do have a favor to ask of you. Please tell me if—"

"Yes? Get on with it." Halina had been a great help to me. Didn't I owe it to her to at least listen to her request?

She pulled a letter from her pocket. "I wonder if you could post this. Just a letter to my friend." It appeared to be written on camp stationery.

"Post it yourself. You're allowed."

Halina rested one hand on the sleeve of my lab coat. There was a piece of blue string knotted on her ring finger. "But the censors cut them to pieces, take out even remarks about the weather or one's digestion."

I took the letter from her. It was addressed to Herr Lennart Fleischer at a Lublin address.

What harm was there in sending such a letter? After all, Halina had been valuable to the Reich. There was plenty harm in it, though. If I was caught, the punishment could be severe. I would be reprimanded at best.

"I will think about it," I said and slipped it in my desk drawer.

Halina bent her head back over her task.

"Thank you, Madame Doctor."

From my office in the *Revier*, I could hear music and laughter coming from Binz's party at the staff quarters at the far end of the camp in the woods. I chafed at the thought that almost every man in the camp had to leave before I was considered highest in rank.

Less than one hour into the evening, Halina and I were making excellent progress when a great bang was heard and the vibration from it shook the ground. Halina and I just looked at each other and then went about our work. Had it been a car backfiring? Loud noises were not uncommon at the camp and were often amplified by the lake.

Seconds later, Binz and others could be heard shouting from the direction of the party.

"Dr. Oberheuser, come! Irma has been hurt."

Halina and I looked at each other, struck dumb.

In such situations, the instinct of a medical professional takes over. Halina stood and ran out. I followed close behind. We came to the main camp gate and could hear a great many cries from the direction of the house in the distant wood.

"Open the gate," I said to the guard.

"But——" His gaze went to Halina. No prisoner was allowed to leave through that gate unless accompanied by an *Aufseherin*.

"Do it. You know I outrank you." Why does a woman's voice so often not command the respect it deserves?

After more stalling, the guard finally opened the gate.

Halina hesitated.

"Come," I said. I needed an assistant, but would I be reprimanded for this?

Halina hurried with me toward the house, the sound of her heavy clogs muffled as we ran from cobblestone road to the soft pine needles of the woods. Abundant moonlight allowed us to see the house at the end of the pine grove, all light extinguished within.

Binz came running from the direction of the house. "The kitchen collapsed, and Irma's down," Binz called.

Irma Grese was one of Binz's most fervent disciples and, some argued, more severe in her punishments than Binz. What would the commandant say?

Halina and I ran toward the house and Binz followed. "For God's sake, Binz. How did this happen?" I asked.

"The gas stove——she lit her cigarette there, and the damned thing just went up. I told her not to smoke——"

Halina and I entered the house and found Irma unresponsive on the living room floor. The electricity had been knocked out by the blast, and the room smelled of gas. The kitchen wall behind the stove had been blown clear off, and above the stove a mangled piece of metal swayed, making a strangely human groaning sound. Even the wall calendar near us was knocked askew.

Halina and I knelt beside Irma. Even in the near darkness, I could see her accelerated breathing. Shock. Blood soaked the shoulder of her dress.

"Someone get a blanket," I said.

"And a candle," Binz said.

"There is still gas in the air," Halina said. "Get a battery-powered flashlight. A good strong one."

Binz paused a second. Take orders from a prisoner?

"A flashlight," Binz called over her shoulder.

I tried to apply direct pressure to Irma's shoulder but it was difficult to see in the darkness. The metallic smell of human blood was unmistakable, though. In seconds, I felt the rug become wet, turning into a sticky pool.

"Need to move her back to the *Revier*," I said.

"She won't make it," Halina said. "Have to work here."

Was she mad? "We have nothing . . ."

Binz's guards huddled around us, quiet. Halina hesitated a long moment. Reluctant to save the life of an *Aufseherin*? She then reached over and ripped the sleeve off Irma's dress.

Binz lunged toward Halina. "What is she *doing*?"

I held Binz back.

"Exposing the wound," I said.

This not only gave us access to the injury but also revealed the source of the bleeding. One of Binz's girls came with a strong light, and we saw the extent of the damage—loss of consciousness, multiple contusions, second-degree burns, and cyanosis—clammy blue skin—a symptom of shock. But the most immediate problem was the source of the blood loss, a gash the size of a deck of playing cards in her upper arm, perhaps inflicted by a piece of projectile iron from the stove. The wound was so deep the bone was clearly visible. I held my fingers to Irma's wrist but could barely find a pulse. These injuries were not compatible with life.

Halina slipped her uniform shift over her head, leaving her in only gray undershorts and wooden clogs in the cold night. She kicked off her clogs and ripped her uniform into long strips two inches wide. It was hard not to marvel at Halina's decisiveness as she went about this task. The exertion brought color to her cheek, and her eyes shone in the light. This was the work she was meant to do.

Until then I'd not realized how underweight Halina had become.

Even on Block One rations she had become wasted, especially about the hips and thighs. But her skin was unblemished and creamy white, the color of fresh milk. She practically glowed in the low light.

"We have to get to the *Revier*," Binz said.

I joined Halina and we ripped strips of cotton. She wrapped the cloth strips two inches above the injury and tied them with a perfect overhand knot.

"First a tourniquet," I said to Binz.

I walked to the calendar on the wall and pulled the wooden dowel from it. I handed it to Halina, and she tied two cloth strips to the stick to make a torsion device. I helped her twist the stick until the material was tight and the bleeding stopped.

Soon the patient was responsive, and we made a blanket sling, onto which four *Aufseherinnen* lifted Irma, and hurried back to camp. I ordered an *Aufseherin* to fetch a blanket and arranged it across Halina's shoulders, for she was trembling after that performance.

Halina and I followed Binz and her girls out the door of the house as they carried Irma back to the *Revier*. I considered follow-up care. We'd start an intravenous drip . . .

Halina paused there in the darkness. What was she doing?

She looked out toward the lake, which shimmered in the moonlight as if diamonds were scattered there.

"What is it?" I asked.

Was she in shock too?

"Halina. There's much to be done."

Then the thought occurred to me—she was considering escape! Could it be? A prisoner clothed only in a blanket and undershorts would not get far. Only three escapes had been attempted at Ravensbrück, and two had ended badly for those *Häftlings*, who were brought back to camp, made to wear a placard with the words HURRAH, HURRAH, I'M BACK AGAIN! on it, tortured, and then shot at the wall.

That was all I needed—an escape on my watch.

"Come *along*," I said.

Halina stood still, her blond hair bright in the moonlight, face hidden in the shadows. In the quiet, I heard the lapping of the lake waves on the shore.

"*Now*," I said. "That patient needs follow-up care."

Halina barely moved in the darkness.

An arc of light from the tower swept the yard and moved on to the lake. They were looking for us.

"You've done a great service to the Reich tonight, Halina. You'll be rewarded. I'm sure of it. Come along now."

The dogs in the kennel barked. How long before we would be reported missing and the dogs would be released?

Still Halina did not move. Were the guards watching us from the towers?

She inhaled deeply, then exhaled, and the fog of her breath rose like a specter, lit by the moon.

"I just wanted to look at the camp from here," she said in a faraway voice.

Why had I let her come out of those gates?

Halina inhaled once more. "It's been so long since I've breathed free air. The lake. It's so . . ."

"Hurry, now," I said.

Quite slowly she joined me, and we walked back to the *Revier,* the sound of her wooden clogs loud on the road, my coat soaked through with perspiration.

Not until the gate closed behind us did I allow myself to breathe fully once again.

WORD OF THAT EVENING'S events spread quickly the next day. Once the commandant returned and the men rolled back in from their brothel trip, the commandant personally told me how much he appreciated my quick thinking and said he'd write to Himmler of my ingenuity and bravery in saving one of the Reich's best workers. The whole camp lauded my efforts, except Nurse Marschall, of course, who remained cold and tight-lipped when the subject came up, jealous a Pole had assisted me.

LATER THAT WEEK Halina and I sat finishing up some paperwork, side by side at my desk. By then we barely had to speak; we knew each other's rhythms and routines so well around the office. Her *Blockova* had given her permission to stay past lights out, so I knew we would have a chance to visit. That morning I had been to the *Bekleidung* building, known to all as the booty piles, the Reich's great assemblage of goods confiscated from Hitler's conquered nations. These materials—clothing, silver, dishes, and the like—were well sorted, and I quickly found many helpful things, including a warm sweater for Halina and a phonograph with a limited selection of recordings. I had a green badge set it up in my office, cranked it, and played some music with the volume low.

A Bible girl brought us bread and cheese from the officer's dining hall, more for Halina than me, and I put a record on the phonograph, "Foxtrot from Warsaw."

"I love this song," Halina said.

I turned the volume down. No need for the whole *Revier* to hear me playing a Polish song.

Halina swayed slightly to the music as she addressed her envelopes. "I learned the foxtrot to this song."

"Can you teach me?" I asked. What was the harm? Everyone at the camp knew this step but me. There had been no time for these things in medical school.

Halina shook her head. "Oh, I don't think—"

I stood. "I insist."

Halina rose quite slowly. "Madame Doctor, I'm not the best teacher."

I smiled. "Hurry, before the song is done."

She reached one hand to my back and took my hand with the other.

"The hold is up," Halina said, "like other ballroom dances."

We took two steps forward and then one to the side in time to the music. Halina had sold herself short. She was an excellent teacher.

"Slow, slow, quick, quick. Do you see?"

It was not a difficult dance. Right away I mastered it. Halina kept me turning about the small office, the two of us perfectly in sync. Soon we both were laughing at how ridiculously well we danced together. I hadn't laughed like that since coming to the camp.

We stopped, out of breath. I brushed a lock of hair back off Halina's forehead.

Halina turned, and I felt her stiffen. I turned as well and found Nurse Marschall in the doorway, a supply requisition form in hand. Neither of us had heard the door open.

I tried to catch my breath. "What *is* it, Marschall?"

Halina lifted the needle from the record.

"I have a supply order," Marschall said. "I was going to leave it on your desk, but I see you are busy." Her eyes flashed to Halina. "Plus, you left the apothecary closet open."

"I'll take care of it. I am busy, if you don't mind."

Nurse Marschall handed me the form and withdrew, but not without sending Halina a penetrating look.

Once Marschall left and shut the door as quietly as she'd opened it, Halina and I looked at each other. Something intangible had been let out of a box, something dangerous, and there was no going back.

"She needs to learn to knock," I said.

Halina stared at me, her face drained of color. "She seems unhappy, Madame Doctor."

"The barking dog never bites," I said with a shrug. "She's useless."

If only I'd known the price of underestimating Nurse Marschall.

CHAPTER 15

Caroline

1941

I GRIPPED THE EDGE OF MY FILE CABINET DRAWER. "WHAT IS it, Roger?"

"I just heard, Caroline. They found Paul's and Rena's names on an arrest roster."

Paul arrested?

"Thank you for not telling me in front of Pia." I kept the tears at bay, but my manila files swam in a blur. "Any word on Rena's father? He lived with them in Rouen."

"Not yet. I check the sheets every hour. You know, of course, we'll do whatever it takes to track them."

"At least we know they're alive, right? On what charges were they arrested?"

"Wish I knew. Our London intelligence is spotty. No destinations listed, either. There's more, C. Three million German troops have begun marching into Russia."

"What about the nonaggression pact?" Hitler was a lying mad-man, but every new reversal came as a fresh slap.

"Hitler ignored it, C. The Bear is not happy."

Roger loved referring to the Soviets as "the Bear." It did seem an apt name.

"Hitler's taking whatever he wants. This doesn't bode well for us."

He didn't have to say it. Before long, Hitler would own half the world. Would England be the next to go?

"I'm sorry about all this, C."

Roger seemed genuinely sad. Perhaps he regretted not acting on Rena's behalf.

I barely functioned that day, numb with what-ifs.

What if Paul had stayed here, safe in New York? What if I'd pushed Roger more to wrangle Rena a visa?

To complicate the day, I received a call informing me that Betty Stockwell Merchant had delivered a seven-pound baby boy she named Walter, after her father. Though work was busy, I snuck away at lunch to visit her at the hospital. I was desperate to see the baby, though I'd been stuffing down jealousy since I'd heard the news, along with a few jelly doughnuts. I hoped a change of venue would clear my head. It would be nice to share my concerns about Paul with Betty.

I bought Betty's favorite parrot tulips on the way to the hospital, not that she needed more flowers. Her suite at St. Luke's looked like Whirlaway's stables at the Kentucky Derby, flowers in great sprays, a horseshoe of roses, and carnations on an easel with a sash across it reading CONGRATULATIONS! In a vase, two dozen roses dyed baby blue hung their heads in shame.

"Thank you for the tulips, Caroline," Betty said. She lay propped up with down pillows in her custom hospital bed, lovely in a pink satin bed jacket and matching turban. "You always know what I like."

A nurse came in with the baby, her crepe soles silent on the tile. Seeing him pushed my troubles to the background.

"Go ahead and hold him," Betty said with a wave in our direction. The baby settled in, warm against me, swaddled tight. His fists were balled under his chin, his face prizefighter swollen. Little Walter would have to be pugnacious to survive parents who got along best when in separate time zones.

"I know it sounds ungrateful, Caroline, but I'm not ready for a baby," Betty said. She held a hankie to one tear duct.

"How can you say that, dear?"

"I told Phil I didn't want a child this soon, but he didn't listen. And after all I've done for him. I wore golf shoes for that man."

"You'll be a wonderful mother."

"The service is excellent here, Caroline," Betty said, brightening. "Better than the Plaza; I'm telling you. They were bringing the baby in at all hours, and I had to tell them to keep him in the nursery. They specialize in infants."

"What a beautiful baby," I said.

I stroked his fist, petal soft.

Walter stretched in my arms, and his eyelids fluttered in a baby dream. I felt the familiar ache and the tears welling up. Not now.

"Now we just need to get you a husband and a baby, Caroline. In that order."

"I'm done with all that," I said.

"Have you started borrowing your mother's underwear yet? No, right? Then you're not done."

The nurse came and took Walter, as if Betty had pressed the call button under her dining table for the maid. I held on to him until the last second before handing him to the nurse. My arms felt cold and empty as I watched them go.

"Roger told me today that Paul and Rena were arrested," I said.

"Oh no, Caroline. I'm so sorry, dear. Do you know where they were taken?"

I stepped to the window, arms folded across my chest.

"No one knows. To a Paris jail or some transit camp probably. I don't know what to do."

Outside the window, down in the park, a boy tried to fly a kite, but its bottom bumped along, refusing to lift. The tail is too heavy, I thought. Just take off the tail.

"How terribly painful for you, darling," Betty said.

"I can't work."

"I'm having a luau party when I go home. Help me plan it. Or you could be my bridge partner for the Vanderbilts' party. I'm playing with Pru, but she'll gladly step aside."

"I can't think about parties, Betty. I need to find out where they've taken Paul."

"Let it *go*, C. It's all terribly sad, but you'll never have a normal life with Paul Rodierre."

"Who's to say what's normal?"

"Why do you always take the hard way? You and David could have—"

"David left *me*."

"He would have married you if you'd been around more. A ten-city theater tour doesn't strengthen a relationship. Men like to be the center of your world. Now that you're more settled, you need to hurry up and get married and have children. A woman's eggs disintegrate, you know."

Just the mention of eggs floating inside me, fragile and microscopic, made me wince.

"That's ridiculous, Betty."

"Tell that to your ovaries. There are eligible men all over New York, and you're chasing one in a French jail."

"I have to get back to work. Would it kill you to be sympathetic? We're talking about people's lives."

"I'm sorry you don't want to hear it, but he's not quite our class, dear."

"Our class? My father made his own way in life."

"After his parents sent him to St. *Paul's*."

"With all due respect to your brother, being pampered by one's parents fails to build character."

"That coming from a woman who was dressed by maids until

she was sixteen. Oh, let's be practical about all this, Caroline. It's not too late, you know . . ."

"To what? Save my reputation? Marry someone I can't stand just to have a luau partner? You may have the baby and the husband, but I want to be happy, Betty."

Betty picked at the satin hem of her blanket. "Fine, but don't cry to me when this ends badly."

I turned and left, wondering how I could have such a friend who didn't give a fig for my true happiness. I didn't need Betty. I had Mother. That would have to do for now.

There was no earthly way I would give up on Paul.

LATER THAT WEEK, Roger told me the consulate could no longer help me fund the comfort packages I sent to France. The postcards and letters kept coming from the French orphanages, requesting help in the nicest possible way. How could I turn them down? I didn't dare ask Mother for money from her household account. Since Father had died, she'd been on a short leash. For a while, I hoped for a miracle, but then realized where I needed to go.

Snyder and Goodrich Antiques.

Years before, Mother had actually hinted we might consign some of the less used silver and donate the proceeds to charity. I wasn't surprised, for she'd inherited Mother Woolsey's inclination toward charity along with her sterling. She never measured our worth in troy ounces, so I knew we wouldn't miss a few oyster forks that hadn't been touched since the Civil War.

I'd never part with the dinner forks, of course.

The Snyder and Goodrich Antiques Shop was just far enough downtown to be discreet, located next to a thriving little shop that sold realistic hairpieces. Everyone acted differently once they ended up at Snyder and Goodrich, selling their family heirlooms to support a rummy uncle or an overdue tax bill. Betty's second cousin, whose husband went to jail for tax evasion, swallowed a bottle of pills the day her wedding china went down to Snyder and Goodrich. She recovered, but her reputation never did.

Those with buckets of money to spare didn't care a fig about appearances. After spring cleaning, they'd send a liveried chauffeur or uniformed housemaid down to S&G with the items to be disposed of. A dingy Hamadan carpet. Limoges finger bowls.

Mother never kept a chauffeur for the city, and our few maids left on staff were up at The Hay, so one morning I took a roll of oyster forks from the pyramid of rolled Pacific cloth bundles in the silver closet at the apartment and delivered them myself. Mr. Snyder would no doubt be glad to see the Woolsey silver.

I stepped through the shop door into a haze of cigar smoke. Inside, one got the impression there were more glass cases in that room than in the entire Museum of Natural History. The walls were filled with floor-to-ceiling cases, and more ran around the perimeter of the room, counter high and a body's length from the wall. All showed the linty evidence of fresh Windexing and stood choked with household artifacts arranged according to category: swords in ornate, tasseled sheaths; coins and paintings and legions of matching stemware. And the sterling silver and silver plate, of course, in separate cases, kept a discreet distance apart.

A trim man, well into his sixties, stood at one of the waist-high cases. He'd spread out pages of *The New York Times* there and was polishing a silver caviar set atop them with his wooden matches, orange sticks, and polishing rags arranged in a ring around an article. I could read the headline upside down: HITLER BEGINS WAR ON RUSSIA, WITH ARMIES ON MARCH FROM ARCTIC TO THE BLACK SEA; DAMASCUS FALLS; U.S. OUSTS ROME CONSULS.

The man introduced himself as Mr. Snyder, unfurled my felt roll, and extracted one oyster fork, as gently as one extracts saffron from a crocus. With his jeweler's loupe to one eye, he examined the Woolsey family crest atop it. Mr. Snyder would no doubt be impressed with that coat of arms, extraordinary in sterling: two filigreed lions in silhouette holding the crest aloft, above it a naked arm, shinbone in hand, rising from a medieval knight's helmet.

Mr. Snyder read the words inscribed on the band of the crest: *"Manus Haec Inimica Tyrannis."*

"It's our family code. It means 'This hand with shinbone shall only be raised in anger against a tyrant or tyranny itself.'" How could Mr. Snyder not be eager to have such history in his shop?

"What is your best price?" I asked.

"This is not a tag sale, Miss Ferriday—Clignancourt flea market is that way," he said, pointing in the direction of Paris with one tarnish-blackened finger.

Mr. Snyder spoke excellent English with just a trace of a German accent. Though his name sounded English, he was of German extraction. I assumed Snyder was once spelled Schneider and was anglicized for business reasons. After World War I, transplanted Germans had been the targets of American prejudice, though that tide had turned recently in the United States, and many Americans were decidedly pro-German. The name Goodrich had probably been added to make the store sound British, for there was no evidence of a Mr. Goodrich.

Mr. Snyder felt the oyster fork all over as a blind man might feel a face, flexed the ends of the tines, then huffed a breath onto it.

"Tines not stretched. That's good. Hallmark is clogged. Have these been dipped?"

"Never," I said. "Only cotton wool and Goddard's."

I fought the urge to curry favor with a smile. With the French at least, smiling was a tactical error, a sign of American weakness.

Mr. Snyder took the four-sided end of a wooden matchstick and twirled it in the hallmark. The pink of his scalp, which shone through his thin white hair, matched the polish on his rag.

"Good," Mr. Snyder said. He waved a finger at me. "But always leave silver tarnished, and polish as you need it. Tarnish protects it."

"The silver belonged to my great-grandmother Eliza Woolsey," I said. I was surprised that I suddenly wanted to cry.

"Everything in here belonged to someone's great-grandmother. I've not taken a lemon, sardine, cherry, or oyster fork in five years, never mind your twelve. No market for them."

For someone who proclaimed the benefits of tarnish, he kept his own sterling well shined.

"Maybe I'll try Sotheby's," I said.

Mr. Snyder began rolling up the brown cloth. "Fine. They don't know a bouillon spoon from a nut scoop."

"The Woolsey silver is featured in the book *Treasures of the Civil War.*"

He waved one hand toward the case behind him. "That Astor punch bowl is from the French Revolution."

Mr. Snyder changed his attitude once I switched to his native tongue. For the first time, I was happy Father had insisted I learn German.

"The book also mentions a loving cup which belonged to my great-grandmother Eliza Woolsey," I said, forcing the German past tense of "belong" from some deep recess.

"How do you know German?" he asked with a smile.

"School. Chapin."

"Is your loving cup sterling?" he asked, continuing in German.

"Yes, and gold. Given to her by the family of a young corporal she nursed at Gettysburg. He would have died from his wounds were it not for Eliza, and they sent her the cup with a lovely letter."

"Gettysburg, a terrible battle. Is the cup engraved?"

"To Eliza Woolsey with deepest gratitude," I said. "It features the god Pan on the front holding baskets of gold flowers."

"Do you still have the letter?"

"Yes, it details the corporal's escape from the swamps of Chickahominy."

"Good provenance," Mr. Snyder said.

I would have taken a bullet rather than part with that cup, but the story softened Mr. Snyder enough for him to make me an offer on the forks.

"Forty-five dollars is my best," he said. "Sterling hasn't recovered since the difficulties."

It had been more than ten years since Black Tuesday. By 1941 our economy was on the mend, but some people could still not bring themselves to say the word "depression."

"Mr. Snyder, you could melt them down and make seventy-five dollars."

"Sixty."

"Fine," I said.

"You are a pleasure to work with," Mr. Snyder said. "The Jews come in here like they are doing me a favor."

I pushed myself back from the counter.

"Mr. Snyder, I am sorry if I gave you the impression I would tolerate any kind of slur. I don't know how they do things in Germany, but I don't do business with anti-Semites."

I rolled up the brown cloth with my forks inside.

"Please, Miss Ferriday. I misspoke. Do forgive me."

"This country was founded on principles of equality and fairness, and you would do well to remember that. I don't think it would help your business to have people think you harbor negative feelings toward any one group."

"I certainly will remember that," he said and gently pulled the forks from my hands. "Please accept my deepest apologies."

"Apology accepted. I don't hold grudges, Mr. Snyder, but I *do* hold the people I do business with to high standards."

"I appreciate that, Miss Ferriday, and I'm sorry I offended you."

I left Snyder and Goodrich that day with renewed optimism and enough cash in my pocket to post both my comfort packages and a case of donated Ovaltine. I comforted myself with the idea that sometimes one must make a deal with the devil in order to help those in need. I'd done business with an anti-Semite, but it was in the service of the beleaguered.

Thanks to Mr. Snyder, fifty parentless French children would know they'd not been forgotten.

CHAPTER 16

Kasia

1941–1942

BINZ SENT ME TO THE BUNKER FOR TWO WEEKS FOR MY IN-
subordination toward Irma Grese. The punishment block lived up
to its reputation: Solitary confinement in a cold, dark cell furnished
only with one wooden stool. Armies of cockroaches. I spent my time
mourning Mrs. Mikelsky and plotting revenge scenarios against the
Germans, the blackness growing in my chest. They would pay for
what they did to Mrs. Mikelsky. I played out scenes in my head
there in the dark cell. Me leading a mass escape. Me murdering
Binz with a stool leg. Me writing coded letters to Papa, naming
names. I would have to be patient, but that day would come.

The following spring, Matka visited us one Sunday, a gift from
heaven since she'd been moved to the elite barracks and we rarely
saw her. She surprised us at our bunk before bedtime, as Luiza, Zuzanna, Janina, and I gathered to play a silly game. We called it What
I'd Bring Down Beauty Road. Beauty Road had taken on another
meaning by then. In the event of an execution, this was the road
one was forced to walk down to the shooting wall. If a girl was
lucky, she had time to have her camp family fix her hair and arrange her clothes so she'd look beautiful taking that final walk.

In this game, each of us competed to come up with the funniest thing we'd bring if marched to our death at the shooting wall. Strange as it may sound now, we took comfort in many such morbid games then, such as Pink Smoke, Blue Smoke, where we would predict the color of a girl's smoke at the furnaces in town. Tired and terribly hungry as we all were, after twelve hours of work, it helped to laugh at it all.

Matka climbed into my bunk and kissed me on the forehead. She wore the electric yellow armband of those privileged prisoners who could roam the camp. I ran my finger across the raised, red script embroidered on the cloth band and felt a queer chill run through me.

I shook off my bad feelings. How good it was to see her! My eye caught the little length of blue string she'd tied around her ring finger. To remind her she was still married to Papa?

"I can only stay a little while," she said, out of breath from running all the way from Block One. The doors were locked at nine each night, no exceptions. Even with her yellow armband, if Matka was caught outside her block for the night she would face the bunker or worse. Plus, there were new rules to eliminate friendships, especially among the Poles: No visiting through block windows. No assisting one another at *Appell*. No speaking to one another without permission.

Matka hugged each of us in turn, and I breathed the sweet scent of her in. From under her skirt, she produced a bundle, wrapped in clean white linen, and opened it to reveal a whole loaf of white bread. The top of it was browned golden and flecked with bits of salt. The yeasty smell of that bread! We each touched it in turn.

"Another loaf?" asked Zuzanna. "Where are you getting it?"

Matka smiled. "Don't eat this all at once, or you'll be sick."

Zuzanna slid the loaf under our pillow. Such a gift!

Luiza huddled closer to Matka. "I think I found my greatest talent."

"Well?" Matka said. "Don't keep me in suspense."

Luiza produced a ball of baby-blue yarn from her pocket.

I took it from her hand. "How did you get that?"

She snatched it back. "I traded a cigarette I found in the *platz* for it. My supervisor says she's never seen a person knit so fast. I finished two pairs of socks just today. I am no longer assigned to grading rabbit fur. I am only to knit from now on, at the *Strickerei*."

The *Strickerei* was the camp knitting shop, a queer place reserved for the fastest, best knitters. A peek inside revealed women sitting in rows knitting insanely fast, like a film going too quickly through the reel.

I touched her arm. "You know those socks go to the front to warm the feet of German soldiers."

Luiza pulled away. "I don't care. When we get out of here, I'm opening a knitting shop with every color yarn and will just knit all day."

"How wonderful," Matka said, drawing Luiza near. "That's bound to be any time now. Surely Papa and others . . ."

Her gaze flicked to me. *Others? Lennart?*

". . . are working on our release."

"We were about to play What I'd Bring," Janina said. It was still strange to see Janina without her flame-red hair. After they'd shaved her bald on our first day at camp, her hair had grown in fine and brown, like the down of a baby sparrow. Many others were allowed to keep their hair, but Binz had made a point of having Janina's head shaved, since she put up such a fuss about it.

"Matka doesn't want to play that," Zuzanna said, her face serious.

"It's a silly game, but will you play with us?" Janina asked.

"Of course," Matka said. "If we hurry." She would do anything to make us happy.

Janina pulled us all closer. "You have to say what you'd bring down Beauty Road."

Matka tipped her head to one side. "You mean—"

"If it's your last walk. For example, I'd bring the prettiest pair of the highest high heels. In black calf—no, suede—to walk tall in. Oh, and hair like Rita Hayworth—"

"That's two things," Luiza said.

"And a pair of falsies."

"Janina—" Zuzanna began.

"What? I want to have a chest for once in my life. If I'm going to die, I want to look good doing it."

Zuzanna leaned in. "I'd bring a box of the best Polish chocolates, every type—vanilla creams, caramels, hazelnut—"

"*Stop* it," Janina said. She hated it when anyone talked about food and covered her ears when girls recited their favorite meals and recipes over and over.

Luiza sat up straighter. "I'd bring my knitting. Once Binz saw how beautiful it was, she'd spare me."

Matka grinned, taking it all in. It was good to see her smile.

It was my turn. I heard a *Stubova* call to someone from the washroom. She was close by, so I kept my voice low.

"I'd bring a mattress with a giant goose-down comforter and sleep on the way. Binz's guards would carry me, with Binz herself fanning me with a giant pink ostrich feather."

Janina stifled a snort-laugh.

"What would you bring?" Zuzanna whispered, still laughing, to Matka.

Matka thought for a long moment looking down at her hands, so long we thought maybe she wouldn't play after all. When she finally did speak, it was with a queer look on her face.

"I would bring a bouquet of flowers—roses and lilacs."

"Oh, I do love lilacs," Luiza said.

"I'd walk with my head high and on the way hand this bouquet to the guards and tell them not to blame themselves for what they did."

Did Matka not understand the lighthearted aim of the game?

"When we got to the wall, I'd refuse the blindfold and shout, 'Long live Poland!' before . . ."

Matka looked down at her hands.

"I would miss you all very much," she said with the barest smile.

This serious answer made Zuzanna lose her happy face in an instant. The rest of us lost any laughter we'd had as well, and all became quiet. The thought of this happening was too horrible to dwell on.

We all must have looked about to brim over with tears, so Matka changed the subject.

"The *Revier* is running much better now—"

"How is the woman doctor?" I said. So many questions and so little time.

"Pleased it's more organized, but I can no longer allow the sick to linger." She leaned in and lowered her voice. "Prisoners unable to work are done away with, so stay away from there. The woman doctor is not to be trusted. It's best you all keep your distance."

"*Germans,*" Zuzanna said. "I'm ashamed for the part of us that's German, Matka."

"Don't say that. You should meet the good pharmacist from town, Paula Schultz. When she comes to deliver SS medicines, she slips me supplies—hair dye so the older women can look younger and escape selections. Heart stimulants so the weak can stand at *Appell.* She told me the Americans are—"

A *Stubova* walked by our bunk, brushing her teeth, and spat into a tin cup.

"Lights out!" she shouted.

I held Matka tight, unable to let go, weeping like a child, until she had to pull away and sneak out, afraid she'd be caught. I felt such shame acting like this, but watching her through the window as she rushed off down Beauty Road and turned to throw us a kiss from the darkness was worse than the hunger or any beating.

Such terrible agony.

———

LATER THAT WEEK ROZA came to the bunk room before morning *Appell* and read a list of ten prisoners to report to the *Revier.* Luiza, Zuzanna, and I were on the list.

After the others were marched off to work, Roza led us down Beauty Road toward the *Revier.* "Come along, girls," she said in a kind way.

Where was the old Roza who'd slap us for dallying? One of my bad feelings was coming on, rising in my chest. The sunrise that morning turned the sky pink and blue as we approached the gray *Revier* block.

I turned to Zuzanna. "What is happening?"

"I don't know," she said, squinting in the morning sun.

"We have Matka," I said.

"Of course," Zuzanna said in a distant way.

The *Revier* was oddly quiet that day. Matka was not at her post at the fat wooden desk in the front room. My gaze fixed on the yellow stool on which she usually sat to check patients in each day, now empty.

"Where is your mother?" Luiza whispered as we passed it.

Zuzanna looked about. "Here somewhere."

Roza handed us over to two sturdy SS nurses in brown uniforms, their caps, like clear, white cakes, bobby-pinned to their upswept hair. They led us down a hallway to a ward, a whitewashed room crammed with three sets of bunk beds and six singles. One window, the size of a doormat, sat up high on the wall, almost touching the low ceiling. Suddenly the walls closed in. Why was there no air in the room?

A girl I knew from Girl Guides named Alfreda Prus sat on one of the beds dressed in a hospital gown, hands folded in her lap.

I wiped the smear of wetness off my upper lip. What was happening to us?

One of the nurses told us to remove our clothes, fold them neatly, and put on hospital gowns with the backs open. I puffed my chest up with air to the point of bursting, then released it slowly. I would be calm for Luiza's sake.

Once the nurses left, Zuzanna paced about the room. She pulled a clipboard from a hook at the end of one bed and studied the blank chart attached.

"What do you think is going on here?" Luiza asked.

"Not sure," Zuzanna said.

"Just stay next to me," I said.

"I've been here for two days already with only a crazy Gypsy woman for company," Alfreda said. "They took her away this morning. What do you think they're up to? There are more girls in the next room. I heard one crying."

Zuzanna walked to the door between the two rooms and wrapped her fingers around the metal doorknob.

"Locked," she said.

Soon the nurses ushered more Polish girls into the room, including a tall, quiet one named Regina who wore round reading glasses and taught a clandestine English class in our block. Janina Grabowski came in too. We put on our gowns, and Janina and Regina laughed since the open backs left our rear ends exposed to the breezes.

"Maybe they're sending us to a subcamp and have to give us special exams?" Alfreda said.

"Maybe they're sending us to the brothel," Regina said.

We all knew about the brothel being set up at another camp. Binz had made more than one recruitment announcement at *Appell*. She promised that in exchange for a few months of service volunteers would receive the finest clothes and shoes and guaranteed release from camp.

"Stop, Regina," I said.

Luiza took my hand, and our palms met, both moist. "I'd rather die," she said.

"I brought my English phrasebook," Regina said, placing it

under one of the pillows. She'd made it from eighty sheets of toilet tissue, inscribed with the tiniest writing.

"A lot of good a book will do us," Janina said. "We are their laboratory rabbits. Need a picture drawn for you?"

"I hope we don't get needles," Alfreda said.

Luiza pressed herself closer to me. "I can't take needles."

To calm ourselves, Luiza and I sat on one bed and watched a house wren build a nest outside the window, flitting off, then coming back with more building materials. Then we quizzed each other from the English book. *Hello. My name is Kasia. Where might I find a taxicab?*

Soon a nurse came into the room with a thermometer, a metal bowl, and a razor.

"Why would they shave us?" Luiza whispered.

"Not sure," I said. Were they operating on us? There must have been some mistake. How could Matka let this happen?

Pretty Nurse Gerda bustled in with two other nurses, one holding a tray of needles and vials. Gerda walked straight to Luiza.

"No, please," Luiza said, wrapping her arms about my neck. I held her fast around the waist.

"Please don't hurt her," I said. "Take me instead."

Zuzanna came to sit next to Luiza on the bed. "Have some mercy. Luiza is only fifteen and afraid of needles."

Gerda's helpers pried Luiza's arms from my neck.

"It won't be so bad," Gerda said to Luiza with a smile. "Soon you will see flowers and hear bells."

They wrestled Luiza onto a wheeled cot and stretched her arm out. I covered my eyes as she cried out at the stab of the needle. At once Luiza grew sleepy and Gerda and the other nurses wheeled her out.

Zuzanna came to my cot at the far end of the room.

"I'm afraid they're ..."

"Operating on us?" I felt a stab of fear just saying the words.

"They'll take me next," she said. "Want to take the difficult ones first." The sound of the wobbly wheels of another gurney echoed in the hallway.

"We must get word to Matka," I said.

Gerda steered the gurney into the room and beckoned to Zuzanna. *"Auf die Bahre,"* she said with a smile. Onto the gurney.

"What is happening here?" Zuzanna sat up straighter. "We have a right to know."

Gerda came to Zuzanna and pulled her by the arm.

"Come now. It's better you don't fuss. You must be brave."

I held Zuzanna's other arm as Gerda pulled her toward the gurney.

"You cannot do this to us," I said.

Zuzanna punched Gerda in the arm, causing her to call for a pair of stocky green-triangled kapos. They rushed in, pushed Zuzanna onto the gurney, and tied her down with strips of white cotton.

"It's best you don't struggle," Gerda said. "Soon this will be over, and you will be released to go home to Poland."

Could that possibly be true?

I stepped up to one kapo. "Where are you taking her?" Janina and Regina watched it all, hugging each other on one of the bottom bunks.

The kapo pushed me back as Gerda managed to get a needle into Zuzanna's arm.

"We are prisoners, not guinea pigs," I said.

Zuzanna grew quiet, and Gerda pushed the gurney out of the room.

"I love you, Kasia," she said as they wheeled her out.

Within minutes, Gerda came for me. I fought as her kapos pushed me to the gurney, but once pinned, I shook all over as if covered in ice. She held my arm out straight, and I felt the sting of the injection in the crook of my arm.

"You girls, you're worse than the men," she said with a little laugh.

Men? What men? Where were they?

Time melted away. Was it morphine? Someone wheeled me into a room with a round light hanging from the ceiling and draped a towel over my face. I felt an intravenous injection and a woman told me to count backward. I counted in Polish, and she counted in German, and I drifted off.

Sometime that night I woke. Was I hallucinating? I was lying back in the ward, in my bed, only a dim glow coming from the window. A slice of light flashed into the room as the door opened and closed. I caught my mother's scent and thought she stood by my bed for a few seconds, and then I felt her tuck me in, lifting the mattress and pulling the sheet extra tight underneath as she always did. Matka! I felt her lips meet my forehead and linger there.

I tried to reach out but could not. *Please stay.*

Soon there was another slice of light, and she was gone.

THE NEXT MORNING I woke as if rising from the depths of the ocean floor.

"Matka?" It was Luiza, calling from her bed next to mine. "I am so thirsty, Matka."

"I'm here, Lou," I said.

I raised myself up on my elbows and saw every bed was full. All the girls except Zuzanna wore a cast or paper bandages on one leg. Some were moaning and calling out for their mothers or husbands or children. We were all so thirsty. They'd put me in the bed closest to the window, Zuzanna down the row from me, closer to the hallway door.

"Zuzanna?" I called to her, but she did not answer. She had thrown up on herself and her bedclothes.

"Matka!" I called as loud as I could. Had she really visited me the night before? Had it been a dream?

My own nausea and pain were terrible. When I first woke, I wasn't sure I still had a leg, but then saw it was wrapped in a heavy plaster from the top of my toes to the top of my thigh. I could feel some fuzzy material inside as if it was lined with cotton. Some of us had symbols written on our plasters and bandages down near the ankle: *AI, CII,* and similar writing. Some had been operated on on their left leg, some on their right, some on both. On my plaster, I found a Roman numeral one was written in black marker. What did it mean?

How we prayed for water! None was given, except when Dr. Oberheuser gave us a glass with vinegar in it. Undrinkable.

I was in and out of consciousness. We were all groggy, but Alfreda and Luiza were in especially bad shape. There was a big letter *T* marked on their plasters. At first Alfreda just cried out in pain, but soon her neck went rigid, and her head arched back. As the morning wore on, her arms and legs grew stiff.

"Please help me," Alfreda said. "Water. Please."

Janina somehow got up that first day and hopped from bed to bed doing the best she could to comfort us all, straightening our blankets and delivering our one bedpan.

"Water is coming," Janina said, suffering from terrible dry heaves herself.

"Matka, it's Kasia!" I called out, hoping she would hear me from her desk in the *Revier*. But we didn't see a soul, except Dr. Oberheuser and Nurse Gerda, who came to our beds.

Sometime in the middle of the night, Luiza woke me. How long had we been there? Two days? Two weeks? Hard to tell, for one hour blended into the next.

"Kasia. Are you awake?" Luiza asked.

Arcs of light from the tower searchlights crisscrossed the room at regular intervals, lighting up Luiza's pale face, tight with pain. She shuddered all over from terrible chills.

"I'm here, Lou," I said.

She reached out her arm across the space between our cots, and I held her cold hand.

"Please tell my mother I was brave."

"You'll tell her yourself."

"No, Kasia. I'm so afraid. I may go mad with it."

"Tell me a story. Keep your mind busy."

"About what?"

"Anything. The one about Pietrik's scar."

"The baby bottle? I've told you one hundred times."

I waited for the arc of light to visit my face and gave her my sternest look. "Tell me again."

"I can't, Kasia."

"Don't give up, Lou. Tell me the story."

She took a deep breath. "When Pietrik was a baby, my grandmother, God rest her soul, gave him a glass baby bottle of water to drink in his crib."

"Was he a good baby, Lou?"

"You know he was. But somehow he broke the bottle on the rails of the crib and cut himself across the bridge of his nose. Our Matka came running when she heard his cries."

"Don't forget the blood."

"So much blood his face was awash with it. My grandmother fainted dead away on the nursery floor. She was a fainter . . ."

Luiza drifted off.

"And then?" I asked.

"The doctors stitched him up. The glass didn't hurt his beautiful blue eyes, but now he has that terrible scar across the bridge of his nose."

"I don't think it's terrible at all," I said.

The light caught Luiza's smile, but it only made her seem sicker somehow. "He could have two heads, and you would still be crazy about him. Am I right?"

"I suppose. But he loves Nadia. And she him. A girl doesn't buy all ten of a boy's dance tickets if she's not in love."

"You can be wrong, you know. Nadia told me she left something for you. In your secret spot."

Luiza knew of our secret spot? Nothing was sacred. "You need to get some sleep now."

"I will, but only if you tell me first: Is it a sin to break a promise?"

"Depends on the promise," I said.

Luiza turned her face toward me. Even that small movement seemed to cause her great pain.

"But I crossed my heart. Will God disapprove?"

"God owes us one for putting us here."

"That's *blasphemy.*"

"You can tell, Lou. Whose promise?"

"Well, Pietrik's."

Everything quickened. *About me?*

"Swear you will never tell him I told. I'll probably never see him again, but I couldn't bear him remembering his sister as a loose tongue."

"You can't think that way, Luiza. You'll see him. You know I can keep a secret."

"He said he knew something when you danced at the casino."

"What?"

"Something important."

"Luiza. I'm not going to drag it out of—"

"Well, he told me he loves you. There it is."

"No."

"Yes. He said he would tell you himself."

"I'm afraid I won't be doing much more dancing after this," I said.

"Don't pretend you don't care. You love him too. I can tell."

"If you must know, yes. But he is crazy for Nadia."

"No, he loves *you.* He would never lie to me. You're lucky to have my brother, Kasia. You will grow old together and have babies." She was quiet for a moment. "I will miss him. And my parents. Do tell them I was brave even if I am not in the end?"

I held Luiza's hand until she fell asleep. I then drifted off myself, thinking of how good it felt to be loved and of Pietrik as a baby and of how I would never forgive myself if I did not bring Luiza home for him.

SOON WE WERE ALL running high fevers, and more girls grew sicker. The pain in my leg was terrible, as if a nest of bees were attacking my calf.

We didn't see Dr. Oberheuser until the following evening, and by then Alfreda and Luiza were both unable to move, their whole bodies stiff, backs arched. I tried to hold Luiza's hand, but her fingers were clenched like claws. She could no longer talk, but I saw it in her eyes—she was terrified.

Zuzanna had spells of wakefulness, but most of the time I was unable to rouse her. The short periods she was awake, she lay curled up and clutched her belly, moaning. What had they done to her?

Dr. Oberheuser came into the room with Nurse Gerda.

"*Es stinkt hier,*" was all Dr. Oberheuser said when she entered.

Could we help it if the room stank? Rotting flesh will do that.

"Please, Madame Doctor, may we have some water?" I asked, but she ignored me and went from bed to bed writing on her charts. "*Gleiche, Gleiche, Gleiche,*" was all she said as she went bed to bed, comparing our operated legs to the healthy ones. "Same, same, same."

"Zuzanna!" I called. How could she not answer? She lay sleeping on her side, knees to her chest.

Dr. Oberheuser stepped over to Luiza, checked her pulse, then gestured to the nurse.

"You can remove that one," said the doctor, pointing to Luiza.

My blood went cold. "Oh no, please, Madame Doctor. Luiza is only fifteen."

Nurse Gerda pulled a gurney from the hallway to Luiza's bed.

"She just needs more medicine," I said. "Please."

Dr. Oberheuser put one finger to her lips, signaling for me to be still.

"Please let me keep her."

Together, two nurses lifted Luiza onto the gurney.

I reached out to the doctor. "We'll be quiet. I promise."

Dr. Oberheuser came to my bed and rested her hand on my arm. "You mustn't wake the other girls."

"Where is my mother?" I said. "Halina Kuzmerick."

Dr. Oberheuser froze there next to me and slowly pulled her hand away, her face suddenly blank of expression.

"I need to speak with her," I said.

The doctor stepped back. "Your friend will be fine. Don't worry. We are just moving her."

I reached for the doctor's jacket lapel, but my plaster weighed me down. Nurse Gerda jabbed a needle into my thigh.

"Tell my mother I need her," I said.

The room grew blurry. Where had they taken Luiza? I tried to stay awake. Was that her crying in the other room?

I THOUGHT I'D GO insane after that. Those of us in casts just lay in the same spot for days listening to classical music played over and over again somewhere in the *Revier.* Where was my mother? Had she helped Luiza? We'd lost all track of time, but after what seemed like a few months, Zuzanna had improved to the point where she could sit up. She pleaded with Dr. Oberheuser to remove or change our plasters, but the doctor ignored us and went about her work, most days in a foul mood, banging her charts around and handling us roughly.

The bedsores were awful, but they were nothing compared to the deep pain of the incisions.

One day Anise Postel-Vinay, Zuzanna's French friend whom she worked with at the booty piles, tossed a gift she'd organized from the SS kitchen through our high window. It all showered down around me on my bed. Two carrots and an apple. A square of cheese and a sugar cube. Such heavenly rain.

"That is for the Rabbits," she said just loud enough for us to hear. She would go to the bunker for sure if she was caught.

I'd wrapped a note for Matka, written on paper Regina supplied me with, around my soup spoon and tossed it out the window.

"Can you get that to my mother?"

"I'll try," came Anise's reply.

The spoon came flying back into the room, relieved of its letter, and safely landed on my bed.

"They've banned many of the prisoner-nurses from the *Revier* since the operations," Anise said.

Such news! So that was why Matka could not come.

"Thank you, Anise," I said. How wonderful to be able to tell Matka we missed her, even by means of a note.

After that, the name Rabbits stuck, and everyone at the camp called us this. *Króliki* in Polish. Medical guinea pigs. *Lapins* in French. Even Dr. Oberheuser called us her *Versuchskaninchen*. Experimental rabbits.

FOR WEEKS AFTER THAT, all of us with plaster casts had a terrible time using the bedpans, and the itching from my wound drove me crazy. When I woke from it at night, I lay there feverish, unable to get back to sleep, worrying about Luiza. What would I tell Pietrik? His parents? They would never recover after losing their Lou.

One day I pulled a long piece of bent wire from the metal frame of my bed and pushed it down inside my cast to scratch the incision.

That helped.

We composed a hymn to bread pudding. Regina read to us from her English book and told us stories about her young son, Freddie, who had just started to walk when she was arrested. I spent hours watching the bird Luiza and I had seen making its nest on the day we came to the *Revier*. It was charming until I realized the little wren was feathering her new home with fluffy bits of human hair, blond, auburn, and chestnut, woven in with her reeds.

One morning the nurses came to get the girls with plasters.

"It is time to remove your casts," Nurse Gerda said, as if it were Christmas morning.

They took me first, and I was overjoyed we would finally be released. A nurse helped me onto a gurney, put a towel over my face, and took me to the operating room. I could hear several people in there, men and women, including Dr. Oberheuser and Nurse Gerda.

I lay on the gurney, gripping the sheet beneath me, glad I had a towel over my face. Did I even want to see my leg? I prayed I would be able to walk and dance again. Would Pietrik think me hideous? Maybe my leg wouldn't be so bad once the cast was removed.

"I will do the honors," a male voice said, as if he were opening a bottle of fancy champagne. Was that Dr. Gebhardt?

I felt cold metal run up the side of my leg as some sort of scissors cut through the cast. Air rushed to my skin as the two pieces of the plaster separated, and someone lifted off the top. The stench reached me under the towel. I sat up, the towel falling away, to see the doctors and nurses recoil. Nurse Gerda gasped.

"God in heaven," Dr. Gebhardt said.

I tried to support myself on my elbows so I could see my leg, but Gerda stretched the towel back over my face to keep me down. I managed to push her away, sat up, and saw the horror my leg had become.

CHAPTER 17

Herta

1942

WE GERMANS WERE OPTIMISTIC COME THE SPRING OF 1942.
True, there were rumors that Hitler's two-front war would be
our downfall, but every morning at Ravensbrück we woke up to find
more good news in *Der Stürmer*. According to the paper, our führer
dominated Europe, or at least the parts of it we needed. The war
would certainly be over by summer.

The end of the previous year had also brought success for our
Japanese ally against the Americans at Pearl Harbor, and we celebrated their continued military advances that spring. A Japanese
delegation had toured Ravensbrück and had been impressed with
the neatness of the Bible girls' quarters and the window boxes filled
with flowers. It was Himmler who'd ordered those window boxes
built, since at a show camp such as Ravensbrück, it was essential to
make a good impression.

I had an entire scrapbook devoted to Germany's successes in
Russia. The capture of Kiev. The advance toward Moscow. True,
we'd suffered our first major retreat there just miles from the Kremlin due to the early, cold winter and the fact that our soldiers were
fighting in light uniforms. But when the Führer asked the German
people to send warm clothes to the boys, we had all sent skiing

boots, ear protectors, and half a million fur coats! The paper predicted that, with warmer weather coming, developments would progress rapidly in our favor.

My career at Ravensbrück was progressing rapidly as well. In the summer, Commandant Suhren replaced Koegel, and it was a welcome change. Where Koegel had been corpulent and long-winded, Suhren was trim and concise. He was a charming man who appreciated the hard work I had put into cleaning up the *Revier*, and we got on well from the start.

The commandant threw a welcome party for himself at his home, a snug beige stucco place with an A-line roof and forest-green shutters, high on the ridge overlooking the camp. I left my quarters at five minutes until seven that night and climbed the steep steps to the commandant's residence.

From that perch, Suhren enjoyed a complete view of the whole camp and surrounding area, including Uckermark, the youth camp, and the Siemens subcamp a few kilometers in the distance. As night fell, I could see lines of *Häftlings* returning from work to the main camp, and the powerful camp lights came on, illuminating the blocks below. The siren sounded and *Häftlings* streamed out onto the courtyard for *Appell.*

We were doing a test run of the new ovens. Two towering chimneys rising from the new *Krema* sent smoke and fire into the sky. The view of the lake was impressive, the gray water stretching to the shore beyond, to the clusters of brick homes and the church steeple of quaint Fürstenberg. A bank of gray clouds gathered on the horizon.

I stepped to the doorway with several fellow members of the camp staff, and Elfriede Suhren, the commandant's slender, blond-haired wife, waved us in. Unlike her predecessor, Anna Koegel, who shouted at the prisoner hairdressers in the camp beauty salon, Elfriede was a gentle woman, whose chief duty appeared to be rounding up their four children much as a farmer wrangles geese.

I walked through the house, past an old man dressed in a Tyrolean jacket and cap who sat at a piano playing German folk songs and into a small library where Suhren stood in the corner, enjoying beer and cigars with Fritz and Dr. Rosenthal. Hunting trophies cluttered the walls: Deer heads. Taxidermied fish. A Russian boar. Suhren's bookshelf held a vast collection of Hummel figurines, though curiously, only the boy Hummels.

The men were too engrossed in their favorite topic to notice me at first. They were discussing the brothel Suhren was sending Ravensbrück *Häftlings* to at Mauthausen and the details of how the lucky winners would be sterilized before leaving. Fritz caught my eye and winced for my benefit.

Suhren and Rosenthal drifted away and I joined Fritz under the gaping mouth of the decapitated Russian boar, a fake pink tongue lolling out of its mouth.

Things had been going well with Fritz and me. We'd seen a movie together at the camp cinema above the garage complex: *Stukas*, a sentimental story about a German pilot who is cured of his depression by listening to Wagner. Fritz squirmed in his seat throughout the film, saying it was all ridiculous, but it was nice to enjoy an evening together. And Fritz had given me a potted hyacinth. It sat on my desk perfuming the air. How smart he was to choose a potted plant over cut flowers, which died so quickly.

"Suhren has a lovely home," I said.

Fritz sipped his beer. "Unless you like your animals with a pulse."

A dog yapped from the kitchen, a small one from the sound of it. The worst kind. At least large breeds had a purpose—to guard against intruders or hunt for food.

We walked to the kitchen, which was clean and modern, with sleek oak cabinets and the latest lighting. Guests helped themselves to cherry-red punch from the cut glass punch bowl on the kitchen table.

"Do you think Gebhardt will send Himmler updates on the sulfonamide trials?" I asked. "Mention our names?"

Fritz held the kitchen door for me as we walked into the dining room. "That's of no concern to me. I'm leaving."

I stopped short, a little light-headed. How could Fritz just *leave*? He was one of my few allies. Leave me with Binz and Winkelmann?

"Why so suddenly? Maybe think about . . ."

Fritz finished his beer and placed the empty stein on a glass box containing a stuffed frightened partridge, frozen in midflight.

"I've had enough of Gebhardt, in case you haven't noticed."

"Stress affects us all differently—"

"You don't know half of what's going on at Hohenlychen. Arm transplant yesterday. Half of Berlin was there at his spa to watch it all, arm courtesy of some poor Gypsy *Häftling.*"

Gebhardt was not only a *Gruppenführer* in the SS and *General-leutnant* in the Waffen-SS, personal physician to *Reichsführer-SS* Himmler, and Chief Surgeon of the Staff of the Reich Physician SS—he was also chief of staff at Hohenlychen, the sprawling spa-hospital fourteen kilometers from the camp.

"Why was I not invited?"

"Count your blessings, Herta. It's a sideshow. Now, with this sulfa project . . ."

"At least you get to operate."

Fritz felt the stubble of his beard. "It's disgusting, doing that to healthy women. It stinks in those recovery rooms."

"They keep asking for more morphine."

"So give them more morphine," Fritz said. "It won't change the results. The whole thing is inhumane."

"Gebhardt says to keep pain meds to a minimum. Why the change of heart about sacrificing prisoners all of a sudden?"

"I'm tired of it, Herta. The suffering—"

"We have no other option."

"There are other options, Herta. If we stop operating on them, they'll stop suffering. Gebhardt just uses us to do his dirty work. Don't you see?"

"It can't be helped, Fritz." How could he let sentimentality interfere with his judgment? The operations were for the greater good of Germany.

"Well, I'll be gone. They need surgeons at the front to stitch up our boys who are dying in a war we can't win."

"How can you say that? Such a defeatist—"

Fritz pulled me closer. "Before I go I want to tell you: Be careful with your new nurse."

"Halina?"

"I've heard things—"

"Men are such gossips. What's being said?"

"I don't . . ."

"Tell me."

"They say there's something going on with you two."

"That's the most—"

"Something not in keeping with the Führer's wishes."

Suhren and Dr. Gebhardt pushed through the crowd and stepped closer to us, all smiles, Suhren tall and trim, redheaded Gebhardt more compact.

Commandant Suhren shook my hand. "Fräulein Oberheuser, I have some good news for you."

Why did he not address me as doctor?

"I'm happy to say one of my first duties will be to bestow a great honor on you."

Gebhardt stepped closer. "Not just any honor. You've been recommended for the War Merit Cross."

The War Merit Cross? Mutti would have a nervous collapse if I brought that home—the silver cross on a ribbon of red and black. The award was created by the Führer *himself.* I would be among Hitler's chosen few who'd received this honor. Adolf Eichmann and Albert Speer to name just two. Was it for my participation in the sulfa experiments?

I turned to share my excitement with Fritz.

It wasn't until then that I realized he'd gone.

I WAS THE FIRST DOCTOR in the OR the next morning, ready for my first day assisting in a new round of sulfonamide operations. I stepped to the sink to scrub up. I removed Halina's ring, the one I'd taken from the files in the *Effektenkammer*, where prisoner property was stored, and secreted it in my pocket. No need for Dr. Gebhardt to see such a fine ring on my finger, since camp guidelines forbade the wearing of any conspicuous jewelry. I would give the ring back to Halina one day. Such a pretty diamond. If I hadn't rescued it, there was no telling where it might have ended up. On the finger of Elfriede Suhren, no doubt.

Nurse Gerda had the patients prepped and sedated. Nurse Marschall had done an adequate job compiling the lists of patients for the experiments. Each lay, covered by a blanket, on a separate gurney. I checked the surgical instruments, opened a box of Evipan vials, and set it on the tray.

We had prepared objects to insert into the wounds to simulate battlefront injuries. Rusty nails, wood and glass splinters, gravel, and a mix of garden soil and a bacterial culture of *Clostridium tetani*. Each patient would have a different infectant introduced into her wound. Dr. Gebhardt arrived from Hohenlychen Sanatorium by private car that morning.

"Glad you are in early, Dr. Oberheuser. Dr. Fischer is not able to join us."

"Is he ill, Doctor?"

Gebhardt removed his jacket. "Transferred."

I tried not to let my disappointment show. Fritz really gone?

"If I may ask, where, Doctor?"

"The Tenth SS Division as chief surgeon of a medical company assigned to the Tenth Panzer Regiment on the western front," Dr. Gebhardt said, his face flushed. "Apparently thinks he can be of more use there . . ."

How could Fritz leave without a goodbye?

"I understand, Dr. Gebhardt. By the way, prisoner-nurse Gerda Quernheim is on today as well."

"Good. I have been very impressed with your attention to detail," Dr. Gebhardt said. "Would you like to take the lead today?"

"Operate, Doctor?"

"Why not? You'd like the practice?"

"Yes, thank you, Doctor," I said.

Was this really happening?

"Make sure the faces stay covered, Doctor," Dr. Gebhardt said. "Just a precaution for anonymity. And be aggressive. Jump right in. No need for gentle tissue handling."

One after the next, Gerda wheeled the patients in, towels across their faces.

We worked well into the evening. I was careful not to rush the closing, crafting my square knot sutures, spiky and black, like tracks of barbed wire guarding each incision.

"I don't compliment often, Dr. Oberheuser, but you have a gift for surgery that cannot be taught. All you need is practice."

Such praise!

We finished the night with a few sterilizations, a new treatment ordered by Himmler himself. I walked back to my room through the quiet camp and slept soundly thanks to my sleep aid of choice, Luminal, waking only once, to the sounds of Binz and her boyfriend Edmund making love in the bathtub.

I TOOK MY TIME getting dressed the next morning, knowing the nurses would record patient vitals and Halina would handle the *Revier* for me, but when I arrived there, things were chaotic. I found a new camp staff nurse sitting in for Halina, and the line of those awaiting medical attention was out the door.

"Madame Doctor, we have run out of paper bandages," the nurse said, as she shook a thermometer.

"Where is Halina?" I asked.

"I don't know, Madame Doctor. Wardress Binz told me to sit here."

I went to the recovery room to check on my patients from the previous day, and the smell there was terrible. I knew that meant the cultures were doing their jobs, but the charts were untouched, no vitals recorded. One of the patients was already out of bed, hopping on one foot, visiting with the other patients.

"Please, we need water," she said. "And more bedpans."

I left the room and found Gerda in the hallway enjoying a cigarette.

"Keep them in bed," I said. "Movement prevents the infection from taking root."

I locked the door and went to locate Binz. After trudging about half the camp, I found her at the Angora rabbit pens, a vast complex of cages heated and kept spotless by the Bible girls. She and one of her subordinates were cooing over a baby rabbit, a white ball of fluff with ears like feather dusters.

"What is going on in the *Revier*?" I asked.

The other *Aufseherin* slid the rabbit back in the cage and beat a hasty retreat.

"You come out here without a word of hello?" Binz said. "Someone had to take charge in there."

"You have no right—"

"It could not be helped," Binz said, folding her arms across her chest.

"Make some sense, Binz."

"You don't know?"

It was all I could do not to shout at her. "Where is Halina?"

"Maybe we should talk about this elsewhere."

"What have you done, Binz?"

"For God's sake, don't cry. You don't want my girls seeing you emotional. I warned you about the Poles, didn't I? You have no one to blame but yourself."

"I don't understand."

"Well, that makes two of us. Suhren couldn't believe what that Pole of yours was up to. Let's just say you'll be needing a new assistant."

CHAPTER 18

Caroline

1942

"ALL THE WAY TO THE BACK, AND FACE THE FRONT," SAID OUR new elevator operator, Estella.

In her orthopedic loafers and nylon knee-high stockings, Estella was a far cry from Junior Rockefeller's ideal elevator attendant. Since the Japanese attack on Pearl Harbor the previous year, America had finally entered the war, causing young men of all walks of life to enlist, including our elevator boy.

"Any word from Cuddy, Estella?"

"The U.S. Army does not send me updates, Miss Ferriday. Seems you've got big problems in France right now. That's what Pia says."

Estella was right. Once Germany invaded France's so-called free zone, in November 1942, all of Vichy France had become a puppet state. The French transit camps began sending transports to a complex network of concentration camps throughout Poland and Germany. I was on my third box of red pins.

"That's what Pia says?"

For someone who handled secure information, Pia was playing a bit fast and loose with it.

Once in the reception area, I took the long way back to my office to avoid Pia's desk, but she sensed movement, like a black mamba.

"Roger wants you, Caroline."

"Fine," I said, doubling back. "By the way, Pia . . . must you share our business with Estella? This is supposed to be secure information—"

"When I want your opinion, I will ask for it," Pia said, bringing to mind a sign on the baboon cage at the Paris zoo: CET ANIMAL EN CAS D'ATTAQUE VA SE DEFENDER. This animal, if attacked, will defend itself.

I hurried to Roger's office and stopped short, for it looked as if a squall had blown every book and paper in it about. Below his window on the Rockefeller Ice Rink, a line of skaters followed a scrawny Santa on skates. He stopped short, and they fell like dominoes.

"We have to double our orphan-aid boxes, Roger. I got the new numbers. Over two hundred thousand French children parentless. Hundreds of them with parents lost to the underground."

"We need a lot of things, Caroline, but Pearl Harbor changed everything."

"I can use *some* personal funds—"

"You know the rules. Can you close the door?" he said in a voice that could only be described as tremulous.

"What is it?" I braced myself against the cool marble of Roger's fireplace. Please, not Paul.

"A few things. Do you have much information on Drancy?"

"Six files full."

Drancy, a former housing complex on the outskirts of Paris, had become a clearinghouse of sorts for prisoners from all five French subcamps on their way out of the country. From the few reports I'd read, it was a hellish place, a waiting room for deportation. It was under the control of the French police, but supervised by the Gestapo Office of Jewish Affairs.

"Why, Roger? What did you find?"

Could Paul be in such a place? True, Rena was Jewish, but did that put him at risk? She was a French citizen after all, but even in the supposedly free Vichy zone, anti-Semitism had become the law of the new state, and foreign Jews were rounded up. The spirit of freethinking France had seemed to disappear overnight.

"Roger, just tell me. Did you find him?"

"Several transports have left with French prisoners, to camps all over Hitler's real estate."

"Paul?"

Roger nodded.

"Oh no, Roger."

"A group of French men was taken to Natzweiler-Struthof, Caroline. There is good evidence to suggest Paul may be among them."

I pulled a chair from the conference table and sat. The dampness from my palms left two silver handprints on the polished wood and then disappeared. Natzweiler.

It was terrible news to be sure, but oddly hopeful, for at least he was alive.

"How can you be sure?"

"There were only a few men in Paul's transport processed at Drancy, and they all went to Natzweiler."

"In the Vosges Mountains?"

Natzweiler-Struthof was the only permanent Nazi concentration camp in France, located fifty kilometers southwest of Strasbourg. My mind ran ahead to forced labor and corporal punishment.

Roger nodded. "Near a little town my grandparents used to visit. Quaint but isolated." He tossed a manila packet on the table. I sifted through the documents, scanning for anything about Paul's captors.

From the Royal Air Force reconnaissance photo, it appeared to be a small camp, only twenty rows of barracks and four other buildings, all wedged into a walled area surrounded by thick, snow-covered forest. So much snow. Was Paul freezing to death while I sat in a warm office? I scanned the photo, looking hard at the groups of prisoners gathered outside, trying to spot Paul among them.

"Thank you, Roger. I'll have Pia run a search on it."

"No more searches, Caroline. Washington has officially broken off diplomatic relations with France." Roger pawed through the mess of papers on his desk.

"How can that be? You have to call—"

"Call *whom*, Caroline? The embassy in Paris is no more. And *this* office is officially closed. Just heard. I've been ordered to destroy anything of consequence."

"What do we do?" I asked.

Roger stood and looked out the window at the skaters.

"I've been told to go through the Swiss Consulate."

"Please. They're in Germany's pocket."

"Our flag has to come down. I'll keep the lights on as long as I can, but it won't be easy. No more funds will be transferred here until further notice."

"Will we at least have contact with France?"

"Hopefully we'll get packets from Free France in London, but they'll have a hell of a time finding boats willing to bring them. The Swiss may come through and the Brits have been reliable."

"I appreciate your help locating Paul, Roger."

"Well, there's one more thing, Caroline. About Paul."

I braced myself. What could be worse?

"I found his wife's name on the deceased list. Auschwitz-Birkenau. Rena Rodierre."

"Rena? Oh no, Roger. It can't be."

"Typhus. Or so it said. I'm sorry, Caroline."

I sat stunned. How was it possible? Poor Rena. Paul surely didn't know. Paul. How would he react to Rena's death? It was all too horrible.

I picked up a magnifying glass and searched the photo. If Paul was alive, I would find him. I would be there for him if I had to swim the Atlantic.

IN THE DAYS THAT FOLLOWED, I made more trips to Snyder and Goodrich. The little money Mr. Snyder provided helped keep my

French Families Fund afloat, and Roger didn't seem to notice. But the specter of shutting down the consulate for lack of funds loomed large. With no official contact in Paris and the rest of France in chaos, the shutdown made sense. But closing down just when people needed us most seemed so unfair. Plus, it was my only link left to Paul.

"You're going to tear a retina with all this research," said Roger one night as he headed home, attaché case in one hand, hat in the other.

"I'm fine," I said, stuffing the frustration down deep. "I guess it's just hard on the nerves, with our own navy planes bombing German submarines in Long Island Sound. And now this news about Paul."

"I know, C. Are you going to the Vanderbilt party? You need to get out of here and have some fun."

Roger was right. I was no use to anyone frazzled and burned out.

I ran home and changed into my best black dress, slipped Father's retailored tux jacket on over it, and put my hair up. Did it make me look taller? I took it down. I looked pretty good for forty years old.

By the time I made it to the Vanderbilts' brownstone home at Fifth Avenue and Fifty-first Street, just around the corner from our apartment, I was looking forward to getting out, even if it meant seeing Betty, who'd probably deny knowing me. I shuddered at the thought of seeing Jinx Whitney, for I'd inherited an intense dislike of the fatuous Whitneys from Father. I would simply avoid Jinx and reconnect with old friends. Didn't I owe it to myself to at least stay on speaking terms with society? I couldn't work *all* the time.

The Vanderbilts' home was a lovely old place, one of the last remnants of the Gilded Age, and it was a shame to tear it down, but the area had become somewhat unfashionable, and the Queen of Fifth Avenue needed to downsize after her husband's death. She had cut her staff from thirty to eighteen and moved to an even lovelier mansion. Mrs. Vanderbilt used the occasion to have one last party at the house, a fundraiser. It was a curious mix of bridge tournament, dancing, and feasting, all for twenty-five dollars admission, the proceeds going to charity.

It was the public's first and last time invited into those hallowed halls, and many stood and stared. A young couple, still in their hats and cloth coats, walked about the first floor, mouths agape. They ogled the gold-inlaid woodwork and caressed the onyx pillars. A group stood before a Pompeian fresco in the entryway. That foyer alone could have housed ten needy families.

"Merle Oberon is here," said a little man, fedora in hand.

The bridge players drifted into the library and took seats at the thirty card tables under the rock crystal chandeliers. The teams were arranged according to group: Junior League. Chapin School. Collegiate. Princeton. The Chapin group was one of the largest.

In front of a fireplace so large I could almost stand upright in it, two waiters in tuxedoes chalked in names on an enormous bridge scoreboard that looked like the pari-mutuel machine at Hialeah. The points of a compass designated the players. North and South. East and West.

As the jeunesse dorée took their seats at the bridge tables, I wandered the dining room, lured by the heavenly scent of rib roast and popovers. Trays of cold meats and seafood on the half shell, a stiff hothouse iris centerpiece, and a silver punch bowl of syllabub big enough to bathe in sat on a landing strip of white damask. The orchestra played Cole Porter and Irving Berlin while a waiter stood guard. Counting the silver?

Since the Japanese had attacked Pearl Harbor, it seemed every young man in New York had enlisted. Some college boys had come home at Christmas break and gone right into the service. Overnight, the armories filled with soldiers gearing up. Mrs. Vanderbilt allowed servicemen free admission to the party, and it was quite a sight to behold all of them in their uniforms. Naval aviators from Floyd Bennett Field in their navy-blue jackets with gold trim discussed war strategy with army reservists.

Most of our set trained at the lovely Park Avenue Armory, drilling in that soaring hall reminiscent of Europe's great train stations. One could always tell those boys from the others, for they often had their uniforms custom made by the best bespoke tailors in New York. As long as they followed uniform protocol, servicemen could have their uniforms made of the best wools and silks, with the finest brass and tortoiseshell buttons.

"Not playing, Caroline?" asked Mrs. Stewart Corbit Custer, Mother's bosom friend.

My lips brushed the smooth powder on Mrs. Custer's cheek. It was especially good to see her that night, done up in aquamarine chiffon. She and Mother loved to tell the story of how angry Father got when they took me to the poultry show at Madison Square Garden a few weeks after I was born. They had brought me home to Southampton in a Moses basket atop stacks of feed bags in the backseat of the car.

"Trying to give the other girls a chance?" said Mrs. Custer. "Good of you, dear. You would surely skunk them all."

From the looks of the scoreboard, the bridge teams were formidable. Mrs. M. Field and Mrs. Cushing. Mrs. Noel and Mrs. Dykman. Mrs. Tansill and Mrs. Auchincloss.

"I'm sorry Mother couldn't make it," I said.

"Me too, dear. Would you mind doing the tally for me? Your mother usually does it, and you are the most honest person in this room, I'm sure of it."

"I'm happy to, Mrs. Custer."

"We're doing a two-hour time limit. Just gather the tallies at the gong and bring me the winner. You've seen it done a million times, of course."

I dropped a pack of tally sheets and a box of little green pencils at each table and found Betty in the library, standing with Prudence Bowles, a sweet, doe-eyed Vanderbilt cousin; Jinx Whitney, a not-so-sweet Rockefeller cousin; and Kipper Lee, a dim girl with a gummy smile, one of Jinx's furies.

The four stood in a huddle—something between rugby scrum and papal synod—as Jinx told a story. Was Betty still cross with me? Surely she'd soften once I made an effort.

". . . and then I told her," Jinx was saying, "the man is the member. We can't make an exception. I don't care if her father was the president of the United States. We're simply full up now."

Seeing her companions' eyes flash to me, Jinx turned.

Jinx, who'd somehow managed to marry money, resembled a Frigidaire in both shape and hue.

"Oh, Caroline," Jinx said. "My goodness, you're in costume?"

"Nice to see you, Jinx."

"Aren't you lovely in black?" Jinx said.

"Yes, you look pretty," Pru said. "It takes a certain skin tone to wear dark colors."

"True," Jinx said. "My grandmother wore that very shade for her viewing. Everyone said she looked so natural."

Pru chimed in. "But Caroline, of course you look lovely. You *were* chosen as Poppy Girl after all."

Jinx turned away. She still hadn't recovered from me beating her in the contest to be Poppy Girl in 1921. It had been quite an honor to be singled out from all of that year's debutantes. At nineteen, I became the face of the new poppy effort, sponsored by the American and French Children's League, my photo in every magazine and newspaper to promote the sale of silk boutonnière poppies. It was all to aid wounded American Great War servicemen and sick French children back in France.

"Of course, *half* of that poppy money went back to France," Jinx said.

"To help tubercular children. It was a reciprocal effort, Jinx. Half of the proceeds from the poppies sold in France were used to mark the graves of American soldiers."

"Who's ready for bridge?" Jinx said in Betty's direction.

"Does anyone need a partner, Betty?" I asked.

"I'm playing with Pru," Betty said, suddenly interested in the baguettes of her engagement ring.

"I hate to say it, but we're full up for bridge," Jinx said with a pout. "The teams have been set for weeks, darling. I'm so terribly sorry."

"Caroline's been busy at *work*," Betty said.

Jinx stepped closer to Betty. "Who are you and Pru playing for, Betty?"

"Haven't a clue," Betty said. "Not that we'll win."

Betty was right. She and Pru were miserable at bridge.

"Kipper and I are playing for the American Soldier Services," Jinx said.

"Delightful," I said.

Jinx turned to me. "You have a problem with that, Caroline?"

"Well, it's just that most of that money goes to parties."

"Someone has to support our troops," Jinx said.

"I guess. If you call civilians drinking gin while the troops are off fighting support, then yes."

"Betty, do let's partner next time," Jinx said. She fiddled with the accordion-pleated scarf at her neck, which brought to mind the undergills of a toadstool. For fun, I considered pulling the scarf tight around her neck. This crowd would be happy to see someone do that, something they'd all imagined themselves.

"So where's your mother, Caroline?" Jinx asked. "Does she even come to town anymore or just stay up in the country in that big house alone?"

"The cook is there," I said.

Jinx sipped her club soda through a tiny straw. "Alone with the Russian chef?"

"I really need to be going," I said.

"And that handsome Negro gardener? Well, times have changed."

"Mr. Gardener has been a tremendous friend to our family through difficult times, Jinx. Certainly a better friend to us than many others in so-called polite society."

"Caroline, I sent a check for your French children," Pru said, one hand on my arm. Trying to defuse the tension? She had a lovely feline way about her and gave one the impression that, given the right circumstances, she would curl up in your lap and purr.

"Thank you, Pru. We can use the donation."

"You know, they don't allow soliciting here tonight," Jinx said. "It's printed in the program. I was thrilled to see that. There's a limit to charity."

"At your house, certainly," I said.

"We can't all nail ourselves to the cross, Caroline, like your mother the wet-wool type. Not happy unless she's wearing it, attending the needy."

Betty stirred, shifting from one foot to the other. Breaking in new alligator pumps or uncomfortable that my mother was being maligned?

"How *is* Big Liz?" I asked. Jinx was named Elizabeth after her mother, who became known as Big Liz to differentiate them, a name that suited her. "Home from the ranch? You know they sell Slenderella courses by mail now."

"She's loving Southampton," Jinx said. "The Murrays had her over to Gin Lane. They've gutted the place, your Mitchell Cottage. They brightened it up considerably. It was so *dreary*, they said, with the roof practically coming down and all."

"I'm happy for them," I said.

"So sad you had to give that place up," Jinx said. "All because of your poor young lungs."

"Don't you need to be getting to the tables, Betty?" I asked.

"Poor little you, not being able to take the Southampton air. I adore that salt air rolling in off the Atlantic. Comes all the way from Africa."

"Jinx, stop," Betty said.

"So your parents ended up in Connecticut because of you, Caroline?" Jinx said.

What would happen if I slapped Jinx right there in front of everyone? It would feel good—my hand grazing her fat cheek.

"Yes," I said.

"Ironic, isn't it?" Jinx said.

"Honestly, Jinx," Betty said. "That's enough."

"Ironic because, after all that, your father's lungs were the ones to go. Tragic, really."

"I'm sorry for your loss," Kipper said.

"It was years ago, Kipper, but thank you," I said.

"I can't imagine the guilt, him lying there in your apartment, nothing to be done," Jinx said with the pained look of concern she did so well. "I just hate the word 'pneumonia,' and I imagine you do too, dear. Such a terrible word."

At least Betty had the good manners to look away.

"If you'll excuse me, I need to go . . ."

I spent most of the match eating more shrimp than was socially acceptable and then pretending to listen to a corporate lawyer discuss his wife's difficulties with her maid dressing better than she did while considering ways to bring Jinx Whitney down.

At last, the gong sounded. I walked to the library and collected the tallies, the tension in the room palpable, for the only people more competitive than those bridge groups were Wall Street traders and Brazilian jiu-jitsu competitors. At least the Brazilians had banned eye gouging.

Guests mingled close to the scoreboard, bordering on jostling but trying to appear casual while awaiting results. Jinx stood with Kipper, Betty, and Pru, and after her strenuous rounds of bridge, looked more rumpled than a Bergdorf catalog at a Smith College reunion.

"How did you do, Betty?" I asked, attempting to mend our fence.

"Well, Pru got lucky on a slam."

"I think we edged you out, Pru," Jinx said.

I flapped my stack of tallies. "We'll see," I said.

"You're tallying?" Jinx said. "Have someone double-check your math. I'd hate for you to make a mistake."

"Don't worry, Jinx," I said. "How could anyone but you and Kipper come out on top?"

I ferried the fat stack back to the powder room, a gilded affair with golden swan-headed lavatory taps Marie Antoinette would have liked, and tallied the scores. Jinx and Kipper were the team to beat, having trounced Betty and Pru.

The gong to gather sounded, and I hurried to the library. Mrs. Custer stood with Mrs. Vanderbilt near the chalk tally board. Mrs. Vanderbilt, ablaze with old mine diamonds, was lovely in steel-gray taffeta and matching turban. Was it the champagne or the exertion of the noblesse oblige that brought high color to her cheek?

"Come, dear, who are our winners?" Mrs. Custer asked. "I'm afraid there's no time to put it on the board."

I handed her the stack, the winning tally on top. Mrs. Custer showed it to Mrs. Vanderbilt, and they shared a smile. As I stepped to the back of the room, Mrs. Custer sounded the gong, and guests gathered from all parts of the house. Men in evening clothes gave way to those in uniform, and all craned their necks for a better view.

"It is with *great* pleasure that I announce the winners of to-night's bridge tournament," Mrs. Vanderbilt said. "My late husband would see this as a fitting send-off for our old place, raising twenty *thousand* dollars for the Red Cross."

The crowd clapped and shouted, and Jinx and Kipper edged their way to the front of the room.

"And another five thousand to a very lucky charity. I know you're all eager to know the names of the talented winners who can call themselves the best of the best. So without further ado, say hello to your winning team . . ."

The orchestra played an anticipatory riff.

Jinx took Kipper's hand and started toward the board.

"Mrs. Elizabeth Stockwell Merchant and Mrs. Prudence Vanderbilt Aldrich Bowles."

Mrs. Custer tossed the remaining tallies in the fire as Betty and Pru pushed their way through the crowd. Mrs. Vanderbilt handed the check to Betty, who seemed nonplussed by the whole thing.

"And what charity are you girls playing for tonight?" Mrs. Vanderbilt asked.

"One close to my heart," Betty said, hand to her chest. "Caroline Ferriday's French Families Fund."

The crowd clapped and the applause, polite at first, swelled as Mrs. Vanderbilt wiped a tear. Betty's smile made me glad our splinter had worked its way out.

The crowd surrounded Betty and Pru, and I made my way to the door, eager to breathe the night air. On the way, I passed Jinx and Kipper.

"Sorry for your loss," I said.

"Math never was your strong suit," Jinx said. "Don't think I won't get the word out about this."

"Thank you, Jinx," I said. "I hope you do."

I made it outside and tried to shake off the nipping of my conscience. So I'd been dishonest. It was in the service of a friend. I tried to focus on all the good Roger and I would do with five thousand dollars.

I walked home with a lighter step, for that night had knocked something loose in me, something long overdue to be knocked. At long last, I saw that group for what they were, with a few exceptions—a queer assortment of layabouts and late risers, most overdrawn at the bank or at least cutting into principal, only interested in who's going in the drawer at the Maidstone Club or their wedge on the fifteenth hole at Pebble Beach or dressing down the staff about a bit of shell in the lobster while shoveling canapés in. Jinx had done me a favor, freed me of any lingering allegiances to New York Society, snipped my fear of being on their bad side.

I was free of spending my life pleasing them, free to go it alone.

CHAPTER 19

Kasia

1942–1943

WHEN GEBHARDT CRACKED OPEN MY CAST AND I SAW MY
leg, it no longer looked like a human limb. It was swollen fat as a
log, covered in dark blue and greenish-black patches. Black sutures
strained to hold the flesh together along the incision from ankle-
bone to knee.

I don't remember screaming, but later the girls back in the ward
said they thought I was being operated on again, this time with no
anesthesia, and others heard my screams in the courtyard at *Appell*.
Dr. Gebhardt rolled a towel and forced it into my mouth as one of
the nurses gave me a shot of something that put me to sleep.

I woke up back in the ward, my leg wrapped tight in gauze, the
incision feeling like a thousand knives cutting it. Zuzanna slipped
out of bed to look at it. She pried a corner of the gauze back.

"Is it bad?" I asked.

"It isn't good, Kasia. I think they've removed bone. And maybe
muscle."

It didn't make sense. Why would muscle just be taken out of a
person? "What is all this for?"

"It might be some sort of experiment," Zuzanna said. "They
give you tablets, but some of the others received nothing."

"I'm so hot," I said.

"Hang on, Kasia. Matka will help us soon."

I WAS OPERATED ON three more times, and each time the suffering began anew. Each time the fevers were higher, and it was harder to recover, as if the doctors were seeing how far they could go before I'd die. By the last operation, I'd given up all hope of dancing again and just hoped for walking. I lay on my back all day all mixed up, sometimes conscious, sometimes not, dreaming of Matka and Pietrik and Nadia, thinking I was back at home.

I grew angrier as I lay there completely in their control. Though it was hard to track time, I knew it was the late winter of 1942 and I tried to stay positive and think of seeing Matka again.

As we lay there, Regina drilled us on English verbs and told us funny stories about Freddie and his habit of climbing out of his crib. Janina taught us all French, for she'd learned many phrases working at the hair salon in Lublin. She taught us phrases such as "'This dryer is too hot," *Ce séchoir est trop chaud,* and "May I have a cold overnight permanent wave, please, with medium curl and extra end papers?" After Janina's tutoring, I had a working knowledge of French, with a heavy emphasis on things like asking for help with dandruff.

"I can't just lie around like this any longer," I said.

"Sure," Janina said. "Let's go out and ride bicycles."

"I'm serious. I have a plan."

"Oh no," Zuzanna said.

"I think we should write secret letters home to our families."

Regina propped herself up on her elbows. "Like in *Satan from the Seventh Grade?* I loved that book." What schoolchild had not read Kornel Makuszynski's adventure story about the boy detective?

"Yes, exactly," I said. "We did it in Girl Guides."

Zuzanna looked up from the bread bead she was rolling for her homemade string of rosary beads. Why was she not *eating* that bread? Prayer had long since proved ineffective. Even my favorite saint Agnes had forsaken me.

"That's a good way to get us all killed, Kasia," she said.

"The boy in that book used lemon juice," Regina said. "He coded his letters so the first letter of every sentence spelled out a message."

I sat up as best I could. "Our own urine would work just as well. It's acidic. We could code in *letters written in urine* . . ."

"It's ingenious," Regina said.

"It's insanity," Zuzanna said. "Put it out of your head."

ZUZANNA WAS RELEASED BEFORE I was, and I missed her terribly. We heard new girls arriving in the room next door.

Then one morning Janina made a comment while old Nurse Marschall was in the room, walking about taking vitals, a towel to her nose to stem the stench. It was a harmless comment about how tired we were of being there. Nurse Marschall walked out of the room in her prickly way, and a moment later Dr. Oberheuser came back with her.

"Well, if you don't want to be here, then get out," Dr. Oberheuser said. "Right now. Stand up and get back to your block."

At first we thought she was joking, since none of us were fully healed. We realized she was serious when Marschall poked and prodded us out of bed.

"But we haven't been issued shoes——" I began.

"Out," Dr. Oberheuser said, one arm outstretched toward the door. "Hop if you cannot walk."

I tried to stand but fell. My plaster was gone by then, but I couldn't put weight on the leg without the worst pain.

"Get up and be off with you, quickly," Dr. Oberheuser said.

I froze there on the floor. Dr. Oberheuser curled her strong fingers around my upper arm and pulled. She dragged me out through the *Revier* front entrance as one pulls carpets out on cleaning day.

Dr. Oberheuser tossed a wooden crutch out after me and left me there in the cold, the sharp slag that covered Beauty Road like glass jabbing my skin. I looked to see if Matka was anywhere around and tried to sit up.

It was strange to be outside again, like being on the moon. It was cold and overcast, everything gray, and no birds flew in the sky. Pieces of ash floated in the air, like black snowflakes in a grimy snow globe, and there was a new stench. A cleaning detail was sweeping the windowpanes of the blocks, for black soot had drifted there the way snow does. In the distance, just behind the bunker, outside the camp walls, twin crimson tongues shot into the sky from new chimneys. You could hear the roar of that fire from almost anyplace in the camp, a giant belching furnace from the mouth of hell.

How good it was to soon see Zuzanna hurrying toward me, a look of deepest concern on her face! I leaned on her as she helped me stand and take a step. Zuzanna, already in our new home for a few weeks, led me toward the block. I was eager to see Matka again.

I hadn't taken more than one step in months, and even with the crutch the walk was too much, especially barefoot across jagged pieces of slag. I stopped.

"I can't make it. Leave me. Please."

"Come now," Zuzanna said as she half-carried me. "Baby steps."

Block 31 was our new home, an international block: some Poles, including all the "Rabbits," as we'd come to be known; French women arrested for working in the underground; and Red Army nurses, all political prisoners. This block was even more crowded than our previous one.

Since I'd been in the *Revier*, there had been a new development. Some prisoners, including the Poles, were now allowed to receive packages from their families. The soup had become even thinner by then, so it was easy to tell who was receiving food packages from home and who was not. Those who got packages walked about relatively healthy. Those who did not were reduced to skeletal wretches who lay in their bunks no longer able to clean the lice off themselves.

I dozed and then woke as the girls were coming in for lunch. Zuzanna knelt by me and held my hand. Her friend Anise, a quick-witted, handsome woman who gave the impression she could solve any problem, stood behind her.

"We missed you," Anise said. "We have a new *Blockova*. Marzenka. A tough one."

"I missed you too," I said. "What is that smell outside?"

Zuzanna squeezed my hand. "They've built a crematorium. Furnaces."

"For what?"

Zuzanna hesitated. "To burn—" Zuzanna said, not able to finish. I figured it out, of course. To burn those of us unfortunate enough to die there.

"I'm sorry to tell you, sister, but everyone has heard about Luiza," Zuzanna said. "I thought it best for you to hear it from me. One of the Norwegian girls told me she saw her in the room they use for a morgue—"

"No, it's a mistake."

Poor sweet Lou, who never hurt anyone. Pietrik would never forgive me.

"No mistake. She said it broke her heart to see such a young thing lying there. Alfreda too."

Luiza and Alfreda both dead? It was hard to understand. Why had they killed such loving girls?

"You mustn't dwell on it," Zuzanna said. "Only think of getting better. At least you don't have to work this week. Nurse Marschall issued you a bed card."

"Such an angel," I said.

"The whole camp is up in arms over what they did to you all," Anise said. "There've been more than fifty Polish girls operated on now, and word is they're planning more. The Girl Guides have organized—over one hundred strong now."

"We call ourselves Mury," Zuzanna said. The Walls. "Someone found a Girl Guide badge in the clothing brought back from the shooting wall, and we swear in new Guides on it."

"They've collected all sorts of good things for you," Anise said. "So much bread. And the French girls wrote a play for you all called *The Rabbits.*"

"Did my mother see it?"

Anise and Zuzanna just looked at each other.

Anise squeezed my hand. "Oh, Kasia."

"What?" Why was everyone looking so scared? "Tell me. Zuzanna, please."

"No one has seen Matka since we were taken for the operations," Zuzanna said. Her eyes were glassy, but how could she be so calm?

I tried to sit up, but a stab in my leg sent me back down. "Maybe they sent her to a satellite camp. Maybe she's in the bunker."

"No, Kasia," Anise said. "She was never there. We think it happened the first day you were operated on."

How could it be? There'd been a terrible mistake.

"She's gone, Kasia," Zuzanna said.

"Impossible. No one saw anything? She was always so good at hide-and-seek. Remember? The time she hid under my bed?"

"Kasia—" Zuzanna said.

"And we spent all morning trying to find her, and she had fallen asleep under there?"

"I don't think so, Kasia."

"She is probably with the Bible girls," I said. "Maybe Suhren has her cutting hair."

"No, Kasia."

"You just don't care enough to look," I said to Zuzanna.

Zuzanna pressed her homemade rosary into my hand. "Of course I care."

I threw it to the floor with a clatter. "You never loved her like I did." A black ink spot grew over my face, seeping into my eyes and nose and taking me down with it. "No wonder you've given up."

Zuzanna retrieved her rosary.

"I will forget you said that, Kasia. It's just the fever talking, and the shock."

"Don't forget it. I mean it. I am going back to the *Revier* right now to find her. I don't care if they kill me."

I tried to get out of bed, but Zuzanna pinned me down. I raged against her until I'd lost all strength. I slept, waking only to fall deeper into despair.

IT TOOK A FEW DAYS for it to sink in that Matka was not coming back.

At first I hoped that our Polish network just failed to find her and she was tucked away somewhere safe or transferred to another camp. When I asked girls from the block to help me find her, they were kind, but after a few days, it was clear they all believed she was dead.

There would be no funeral. No birch cross. No black cloth nailed to our door.

Before I learned to use my crutch, I depended on Anise and Zuzanna to carry me to and from the latrine. Janina needed an escort too. Our helpers were gracious, but I hated being a burden. I imagined my own death. What a wonderful, quick death it would have been to throw myself on the electric fence. Of course, no one would carry me there.

Until that time, all through our arrest, our arrival at the camp, and the operations even, I had always found good things to think about and Polish optimism to fall back on, but once Matka was gone, I could not pull myself out of the darkness. I felt like a fish I read about when I was a child, the African mudskipper. Each year when the drought came, it burrowed deep into the mud and lived there for weeks, neither dead nor alive, waiting for the rains to come and bring it back to life.

LIFE WENT ON AS USUAL after our release from the *Revier*—the brutal waking, the endless hours of *Appell*, and the most terrible gnawing hunger, our bosom companion. The only thing that interrupted this pattern was the terror that accompanied our *Blockova* reading the names of those in our block to be executed.

The procedure seldom varied. It was preceded by warnings from the prisoner-workers in the front office that the courier had arrived from Berlin with an order of execution and that the male guards who served as executioners had been approved for extra schnapps rations. Then Binz would order certain blocks locked down. Once the noon soup was delivered but before it was served, the *Blockova* would read the numbers of "the pieces to be called." The unlucky ones prepared their things, and Binz and friends came to get them shortly. My reaction seldom varied either: The cold fear my name would be called out. The relief it was not. The terrible stabs of sadness watching a blockmate go through her final ritual.

The day the first executions of Rabbits were announced we waited, barely breathing, on the benches of the dining table, packed tight—Zuzanna on my right, Regina to my left. Those of us who'd been operated on had just graduated to eating at table, a big event, for it meant our soup no longer had to be brought to our bunks. There were many rumors that the commandant would schedule the Rabbits for execution, liquidate us to eliminate the evidence of the crime, but could we believe rumors? There was always a new one, like that the Americans were on their way to save us or that there would be steak in the soup.

"Attention," Marzenka said as two Russian girls struggled the soup boiler into the block. "*Häftlings* with numbers called up will finish here, collect their things, and await further instruction."

Marzenka pulled a square of paper from her jacket pocket and unfolded it, the crinkling of it the only sound in the room.

"Number 7649."

To my left, Regina stiffened.

Marzenka read the names of three other Rabbits, all still recovering in the *Revier*.

"No," Zuzanna said. "There must be a mistake."

I wrapped one arm around Regina.

"No hysterics," Marzenka said.

How could this be happening?

I whispered in her ear, "We can fight this, Regina."

She didn't answer, just placed her spoon in her bowl and handed it to Zuzanna. "I'd like you to have this," she said.

Zuzanna took the bowl, water shining in her eyes. Such a gift!

Regina stood. "Janina, would you fix my hair?"

Janina nodded and we followed Regina to the bunk room, bringing her full bowl with us, since left unattended it could be stolen in seconds.

"Do you know the first thing Spartans condemned to death did before their executions?" Regina asked. "Had their hair styled."

Janina pulled Regina's dirty kerchief off. Ordinarily, fixing one's hair was a punishable offense. The rule was hair must be kept back, tied with a regulation kerchief, but Binz relaxed the rules when a prisoner was about to die. Regina's hair had grown longish when she was recovering from her operation, thick and dark. Janina swept it back in the prettiest French twist. Someone from a top bunk handed down a hairpin she'd probably traded a bread ration for.

"Kasia, I want you to have my English phrase book," Regina said. "Homework tonight is prepositions. And if you could get my *Troilus and Cressida* to my Freddie once all this is over . . ."

I nodded.

"I'm going to refuse the drink," Regina said. We all knew a sedative drink was offered to those taken to the wall to make things easier for all. "Do you think I'll be brave enough to shout 'Long live Poland'?"

She handed it back. "You addressed it to the Lublin post office. Take it back—"

I kept my hands clasped behind me. "In care of Adalbert Kuzmerick. My father works there, Madame *Blockova.*"

"Oh," Marzenka said. She slapped it onto her pile and moved on.

I wished that letter safe travels on its way. *Be careful with it, Marzenka. It's our only chance.*

I held her hand. "It doesn't matter—"

"It does, Kasia. You know they hate that."

Prisoners faced death in different ways. Some cried and raged. Others grew quiet or prayed. Regina stood near her bunk and read us her favorite lines from *Troilus and Cressida,* rushing to fit in as much as possible before Binz arrived:

O brave Troilus! Look well upon him, niece: look you how his sword is bloodied, and his helm more hacked than Hector's, and how he looks, and how he goes! O admirable youth! He ne'er saw three and twenty.

As Regina read, we pinched her cheeks to bring color to them. A girl who worked in the kitchen had some beet juice, and Janina smoothed a bit of it on Regina's lips.

It wasn't five minutes before Binz and her guards burst into the block. Regina leaned close to me, book clutched at her chest.

"Tell everyone this happened," she said.

"Hand it over," Binz said. She snatched the book. "What are you so worried about? The commandant himself has said you are to be freed."

Was that possible? Surely it was another lie.

Janina untied the string from her own waist and cinched it around Regina's, making her uniform look more like a real dress.

"*Out, out,*" Binz said, jabbing at Regina with her rubber stick.

Regina limped to the door, her leg not yet fully healed. At the door, she handed her reading glasses to Zuzanna and turned to smile at us. She'd taken on a radiance, a new sort of glow, and there was high color in her cheeks.

Binz tossed the book to an *Aufseherin* and pushed Regina out to the road. Not one prisoner who watched Regina go could keep from crying. How brave she was. The name Regina means "queen," and this was fitting, for she looked regal that day. If not for her uneven way of walking, Regina could have been a movie star or fashion model, standing tall and proud on her way down Beauty Road.

With heavy hearts, Zuzanna and I shared Regina's soup with Janina. How guilty we felt eating that, but she'd not meant for it to go to waste. We split the sweet little carrot, such a delicacy. I would get strong on Regina's soup and live to tell the world about it all.

Soon Zuzanna and I reported to the *Strickerei* to knit, but we listened all afternoon, hoping not to hear the shots. Maybe Binz was right, and the girls were being released? Sent to a subcamp?

Later that day we heard a truck drive toward the lake and four muffled shots, one after the other, and we prayed silently to ourselves, for praying was a punishable offense. Later, Anise told me she'd heard from the girls working in the kitchen, which was adjacent to the shooting wall, that Binz had taken all four of the Rabbits there for execution. One had to be carried, her wounds not healed enough for her leg to support her.

"We wept," they told her, "when all four of them cried, 'Long live Poland!' at the end."

After that, I could no longer just be angry and not act. Would we be the next to go to the wall? Who would be left to tell the world? Even if it got me killed, I would launch my plan.

THAT SUNDAY, WHILE ZUZANNA slept trying to shake a nasty case of dysentery, I loosened the boards above an upper bunk and shimmied up into what we called the Annex, an attic of sorts, where girls went to smoke cigarettes sometimes. With my bad leg, just getting up into the Annex was an ordeal. There was little light up there to see, and my eyes adjusted to the dark as I assembled my tools for the secret mission.

1. A letter I'd written in German on a single page of camp stationery in which the first letter of each line spelled out "letter written in urine."

2. The toothpick I'd paid half a bread ration for.
3. My water cup, into which I sent my warm secret ink.

My first tries left puddles on the page, but I soon grew better at writing between the lines and wrote of the operations and the names of the Rabbits who'd been executed. Regina first, then Romana Sekula, Irena Poborcówna, Henryka Dembowska. It felt good to tell Papa about the firing squads and the operations and ask him to send word to everyone he could. By then seventy of us had been operated on. It would take many more letters to get Papa all the names. I asked him to send back a spool of red thread as a signal he had received and understood our secret letter.

THE NEXT MORNING WE WOKE to a cold drizzle and lined up ten abreast at *Appell*, waiting for letter collection before we went to the *Strickerei* for work. I kept my letter dry under the sleeve of my jacket. As Marzenka came down my row to collect letters, I took it out and ran my finger over it. It was just a bit warped from where urine met paper. Would Marzenka see? The censors?

Marzenka stepped closer and stretched out her arm, her palm up. My hand shook as I placed the letter on her palm. A gasp caught in my throat as the letter slid off and fluttered toward the ground.

"Clumsy," she said.

I lunged to catch it as it fell, but it ended up on its back in the mud.

"I'm not touching that," Marzenka said.

I picked the letter up and wiped the mud off with the hem of my dress and handed it to her. "Please, Madame *Blockova*."

She took it with two fingers and squinted one eye. "Why so worried about one little letter?" She held the letter up to the spotlight overhead.

I could barely breathe.

CHAPTER 20

Herta

CHRISTMAS 1943

COME CHRISTMAS OF 1943, MORALE AMONG RAVENSBRÜCK
staff hit a new low. Earlier that year German troops had fought
hard at Stalingrad, despite being underclothed and underarmed,
but in the end capitulated. We also faced increased Allied bombing
in Berlin, but our troops retaliated in Great Britain, and we seized
control of northern Italy and rescued Mussolini, who'd been arrested by the Italian military. So there were still things to celebrate.

As the war dragged on, though, life at Ravensbrück grew more
difficult. Fresh transports arrived around the clock, loaded with infected prisoners from the Führer's conquered territories.

Without Halina the *Revier* was a madhouse, teeming with disease carriers from every country. There was little time to spend
missing Fritz or Mutti. I stayed in my office most days, but the place
had to be managed. The camp doctors in particular needed a break,
and we received one in the form of an especially fine Yuletide celebration. Across Germany, citizens suffered with reduced rations,
but the camp staff still enjoyed real coffee, salami, Polish vodka,
and good champagne.

Our party began with a pageant. Binz and her guards shuffled
into the canteen dressed as angels, in white satin robes tied at the

waist with golden ropes. She'd even convinced me to wear one such outfit, which was good, because the bell sleeves covered the few cuts on my arms and helped me avoid embarrassing stares and questions. This cutting of mine was a phase, a typical tensional outlet, not surprising given the stress of my duties.

Binz and each angel on her staff wore a foil headpiece with a cross rising from the forehead and carried a tall pole topped with a gold-painted swastika that almost scraped the low ceiling. As they filed in, each lit a candle on the tree in the corner, which was fitted with candles on every branch and strewn with the usual silver tinsel threads. Then SS men entered, dressed as shepherds in costumes of robes and long headpieces made of shimmering blue material. Bringing up the rear of the procession was Commandant Suhren, our Father Christmas on stilts. He wore a long red felt robe trimmed with white fur and carried a rod in one hand. He tipped his pointy cap forward to enter the doorway.

"Who's been naughty or disobedient?" he shouted, a twinkle in his eye.

Soon Father Christmas threw down the rod and opened his sack of sweets. Where was he getting such treats in wartime? Beer, the chosen beverage of the group, flowed freely. Even Father Christmas had a mug.

When the new religion ushered in by national socialism first appeared, it had seemed strange, but one adjusted. According to the Führer, one could be a German or a Christian but not both. He suggested we be Christ *ourselves,* which seemed a practical solution.

Many German people resisted this change, but all members of the SS converted to this new religion. Gradually, religious aspects of Christmas were replaced with symbols of nationalistic pride, and we celebrated the winter solstice instead of Christ's birth. Soon even Father Christmas was replaced by Odin the Solstice Man. Mutti chafed at all this, for she was raised a devout Protestant and my father a Catholic, but eventually even Mutti had both a "People's Tree" topped with a Germanic sun wheel and a traditional Christmas tree. This new religion suited me, for it freed me from trouble-some theological issues.

I sat alone and watched the angels and shepherds enjoy their dancing.

Commandant Suhren approached my table, his Kris Kringle pil-low belly bouncing as he walked. "You're not eating, Fräulein Ober-heuser."

He slid his plate of meat and buttered potatoes onto the table.

I turned my face away from the smell of the bloody beef. "It's 'doctor,' Herr Commandant."

"You must keep your strength up. Meat has protein and iron, you know." Why did it never occur to him not to lecture a doctor on nu-trition?

"We're counting on you. I know it isn't easy with Fritz gone and Dr. Gebhardt off lecturing so much. And with the incident—"

Why did everyone refer to what happened with Halina as "the incident"? "I'm fine, Herr Commandant." It was true. Chronic in-somnia was common among concentration camp staffers.

As Suhren shook at least a jigger of salt onto his potatoes, Binz and her boyfriend Edmund kissed in the corner. It looked like an angel giving a shepherd mouth-to-mouth resuscitation. Binz, re-cently promoted to deputy chief wardress at the camp, was not let-ting her new position disrupt her love life.

"I'd be better if we could manage the situation of the Rabbits, Commandant," I said.

"I have a lot to deal with right now. Seventy subcamps, all with their own problems. Siemens complaining the prisoners are dying at their benches. Besides, my hands are tied on the Rabbits situa-tion, Fräulein. Since Berlin slapped my wrist, I don't even receive reports about what's happening at my own camp. And Gebhardt doesn't communicate."

Suhren had protested the sulfa operations, claiming he needed the Polish girls as workers. Gebhardt appealed to his friends in high places, and Suhren was overruled. He was forced to apologize to

Gebhardt face-to-face, a humiliating blow to his ego by all indications.

"So what is the latest?" Suhren asked, rolling a potato with his fork. He'd seen it all from his office no doubt. Why did he need my version?

"Well, after the Rabbits marched in protest—"

"Marched? Half of them can't walk."

"They were carried to the square and demanded to see Binz."

"I heard some of this part."

"They handed her their manifesto, demanded *in writing* a halt to future operations."

"You're lucky it didn't incite a scuffle. So you operated anyway?"

"In the bunker this time. Couldn't use anesthesia down there but we needed the extra security. The whole camp has become very protective of them."

"How can I help?"

"Berlin heard about the protest, and they are reviewing the situation. Gebhardt says there'll be no more Rabbits at the shooting wall until further notice."

"So?"

Suhren watched Binz and Edmund in their corner. I was losing him.

"If we can't make the results of this experiment go away, we may be the ones left holding the sack. Fritz is gone. Gebhardt's traveling."

That got his attention. "I can't overrule Gebhardt, I'm afraid. He speaks to Himmler himself every day."

"Well, something must be done soon. If this leaks . . ."

Suhren waved that thought away. "Our security is near perfect. Only three escapes, and two of the escapees apprehended. Himmler himself complimented our censors. They do not allow leaks."

This was a blatant falsehood. I'd heard all sorts of things got through our censors. Binz found evidence of this daily. A bottle of hair dye in a box of rolled oats. Antibiotics in a toothpaste tube.

"Besides, the surgeries were performed in secret with the patients blindfolded. None of them can identify you."

"But—"

"Patience, my dear. I'll see to it the problem is addressed. Leave this to me."

Suhren wandered off leaving his napkin wadded up on his plate, beef blood seeping into the linen. As Binz's chorus of misshapen angels gathered to sing a medley of German folk songs, I felt my first shiver of fear about it all. I knew too well that loose ends tend to unravel.

CHAPTER 21

Caroline

CHRISTMAS 1943

ANY SPARE TIME I HAD THAT DECEMBER I SPENT CHASING commuters at Grand Central Terminal, selling war bonds. Seemingly overnight, a 125-foot war-themed photo mural had sprung up on the station's eastern wall. Warships and fighter planes loomed over the sea of commuters, many of whom were in uniform themselves. The caption left no ambiguity as to the mission: BUY DEFENSE BONDS AND STAMPS NOW!

One afternoon, one of the station's organists, Mary Lee Read of Denver, who volunteered to play each holiday season, launched into a rousing version of "The Star-Spangled Banner." This brought the main concourse to a standstill, all commuters holding hands to their hearts as they stood to listen, causing legions of missed trains. The stationmaster asked Mary not to play that song again, and she became the only organist in New York ever barred from playing the United States national anthem.

Security at Grand Central was tight, since two German spies had been caught trying to sabotage the station, but a small corps of volunteers, including Mother and me, were allowed in to sell bonds. All agreed Mother had missed her calling, for she was quite the rainmaker. Woe to the weary traveler who refused to part with at least ten cents for a war stamp, for once in her thrall, they all ended up forcing additional funds on her, which she happily accepted.

There were large numbers of women commuting through the station then. With so many men at war, women joined the work-force in droves. Even Betty had a job typing reports at the armory. Not exactly Rosie the Riveter, but it was a big step for her.

Mother and I spent Christmas morning of 1943 at Saint Thomas Church, not far from Grand Central Terminal at Fifth Avenue and Fifty-third Street. We listened to Rector Brooks at his magnificent carved-oak lectern, resplendent in his Christmas finery, as he did his best to lift our spirits. The war weighed heavily on the congrega-tion, mostly women and older men at that point. There were a few uniformed servicemen in the pews, but most had been deployed to Europe or the Pacific theater by then, including our elevator boy, Cuddy. Every one of us knew someone who'd been impacted by the war. I said a prayer for those aboard the French ship Roger had been forced to turn away the day before, thousands of Europe's displaced seeking asylum, still waiting off the coast.

I couldn't bear to count the months since I'd heard from Paul. Roger's best guess was that he was still at Natzweiler concentration camp. From what information I could gather, many French men had ended up there in the Vosges Mountains doing hard labor in extreme cold. Could anyone survive two years at such a place?

That year another development had surfaced, troubling and om-inous. It was clear not only from the scanty reports we got from the Swiss Red Cross but also from New York and London papers that Hitler was moving ahead with his plan to annihilate Jews, Slavs, Gypsies, and any other people he considered *Untermenschen*, sub-humans, in order to make room for his Lebensraum. Reports of gas vans at Chelmno, Poland, and mass exterminations had surfaced. Hitler even stated his plan openly in his ranting speeches, yet Roo-sevelt was slow to react and kept immigration at a bare minimum.

Saint Thomas was our life raft of hope. Kneeling there in that great church, the air perfumed with frankincense, the magnificent stone altarpiece behind the altar, I felt the world might just untangle itself after all. When I was a child, Father and I began memorizing all sixty saints and famous figures carved in stone there. Saint Polycarp. Saint Ignatius. Saint Cyprian. We'd made it to number forty-six, George Washington, when Father died, so I'd never learned the rest. Being there made me feel close to him, especially when the organist got all 1,551 of the organ's pipes playing "God Rest Ye Merry Gentlemen," Father's favorite Christmas song. Just hearing the flush-cheeked choirboys sing of God's glory renewed one's sense of positivity.

As Rector Brooks told us of his plans to enlist in the military and join "the old Seventh Regiment" of New York as chaplain, I read the names cut into the wall of those who served in World War I. Twenty of those, their names painted in gold, gave their lives for their country. How many more would we lose to this second world war? Our parish had more than four hundred members in uniform, and we had already surpassed World War I in the number of those mortally wounded.

I'd snuck one of Paul's letters into my hymnal, a straggler that had arrived well after France had been invaded. I'd read and reread it so many times it had become thin as facial tissue. I read as Rector Brooks continued:

Thank you, my love, for the packets of Ovaltine. Believe me, this is a welcome change from the hot beverage Rena's father makes from ground acorns. Do not be alarmed if this letter is my last for a short while. Every newspaper is predicting an invasion soon. But in the meantime know that I miss you and you are not outside my thoughts for more than a few minutes and that is when I am asleep. Please keep us in your prayers and sleep soundly on your pink satin sheets, knowing we will be at H&H Automat soon, enjoying the air conditioning and the apple—

I felt someone's gaze and turned to find David Stockwell across the aisle from me one pew back. He stared openly at me. What was that on his face? Curiosity? A bit of sadness? I closed my hymnal as Sally Stockwell, who even in the chill of the great hall appeared to be perspiring in earnest, leaned forward and smiled in my direction. Betty leaned forward as well and rolled her eyes for my benefit, a commentary on Rector Brooks's lengthy sermon.

At the end of the service, Rector Brooks left the altar and followed a sparse procession of choirboys and old men. As they made their way down the center aisle, it was clear their ranks had been decimated, since many had gone off to war, trading their scarlet cassocks and white surplices for military uniforms. Once they made it to the rear of the church and back to the sacristy, the congregation began filtering out.

Mother and I caught up with Betty, David, and Sally in the narthex of the church, the exquisite entryway with its lovely coffered ceiling. All three stood out in the crowd, Betty since she wore a suit of pure white under her Denmark mink coat; Sally since she was about to burst with twins, her crimson coat fighting a losing battle trying to cover her belly; and David because he was practically the only man in Manhattan not in a uniform. He claimed his job at the State Department was an equal sacrifice, but compared to going to war, long lunches at "21" didn't seem a hardship.

Mother and I reached the three as Sally fanned herself with a church program.

"Oh, hello, Caroline," said Sally with a tremulous smile.

"Looks like we'll have two Christmas babies?" Mother said.

"Three," Betty said. "Now it's triplets. Mother's having fits. She has to have three baby nurses lined up." It wasn't enough that the Dionne quintuplets were on every billboard, reminding me of my own childlessness. Sally Stockwell had to be an overachiever as well.

I took David by the elbow. "Can I speak to you? Privately?"

David looked startled. Afraid I wanted to discuss our past? Despite my still-bruised feelings, I couldn't help but notice he seemed to be getting better looking with age.

"I hope he's not in trouble," Betty said.

"I can spare a minute," David said. "But we do need to get home. Cook has a roast on."

I pulled David to a quieter corner, and he smiled. "If this is a last-minute bid for my affections, maybe church isn't—"

"Why won't you return my calls?" I said.

The war had not impeded David's ability to dress well—classic, but almost to the edge of fop, his necktie arched, the pockets of his camel-hair coat with perfectly swelled edges.

"When was the last time you did *me* a favor?"

"I just need you to call someone about—"

"Only Congress can loosen immigration quotas, Caroline. I told you."

"You're in a powerful position, David."

"To do what?"

"Roger had to turn down another boat this morning. Sailing from Le Havre. Half of them children. If you could just ask—"

"The country doesn't *want* more foreigners."

"Foreigners? Half this country just got here a generation ago. How can you just let people die, David?"

David took my hand. "Look, C. I know Paul Rodierre is over there in a bad situation—"

I pulled my hand away. "It's not that. How can we just do *nothing*? It's appalling."

Rector Brooks joined Mother, Betty, and Sally in the narthex. He waved his hand in a sign of the cross over Sally's belly, which only seemed to cause Sally to fan herself more.

"We're at *war*, Caroline. Winning it is the best thing we can do for those people."

"That's a smoke screen and you know it. Seventy thousand Romanian Jews refused asylum here? The *St. Louis* turned away? How many innocents sent back to certain death?"

Rector Brooks turned to look at us, and David pulled me farther into the shadows.

"It's a slow process, Caroline. Every visa form must be perfectly vetted. Nazi spies might come here posing as refugees. It's in the best interests of the United States."

"It's anti-Semitism, David. There was a time when you'd have done the right thing."

"Brother dear," Betty called.

David held up an index finger to her. "Let's admit what this is really all about. If you weren't pining away like a schoolgirl for your lost married boyfriend, you'd be back at the Junior League knitting socks for servicemen."

"I'll forget you said that if you promise to at least try——"

"David, *now*," Betty said.

"Okay, I'll ask."

"I have your word?"

"*Yes*, for God's sake. Are you happy?"

"I am," I said with a smile. For a moment, I thought I caught a flicker of sadness move across David's face. Regretting our breakup? It was hard to tell, for it retreated as quickly as it had come.

We turned to see Mother and Betty ease Sally down into a back pew. Rector Brooks watched like an anxious father as Mother dispatched choirboys in search of a basin. Sally's cries echoed about the church as Mother wadded her coat to cushion the poor thing's head.

"My God," David said, stricken.

Betty ran to David and pulled his arm. "Get over here. She's about to erupt. No time to get to St. Luke's."

It seemed David would not be going home for Cook's roast after all.

CHAPTER 22

Kasia

CHRISTMAS 1943

CHRISTMAS OF 1943 WAS AN ESPECIALLY GRIM ONE FOR Zuzanna and me. With Matka and Luiza gone and my sister wasted almost to nothing, there was little reason to celebrate. There'd been not one letter or package from Papa in so long. Was he even alive?

We had off from *Appell* on Christmas afternoon, so the camp guards could have their celebration. Zuzanna lay next to me, so thin from dysentery one could see the sharp edge of her hip bone jut through the thin blanket as she slept. As a doctor she knew what was happening and tried to instruct me on how to make her well, but even when the girls in the kitchen snuck her salt and clean water, nothing worked. Though many of our fellow prisoners shared their own precious food with all of the Rabbits, without packages of our own from home, we had become living skeletons.

Zuzanna lay on her side, hands clasped under her chin, and I dozed next to her, my chest to her back, her breath my only happiness. The women in our block had voted to allow us to have a bottom bunk to ourselves in light of our situation as Rabbits. This was an extraordinary gesture, since some bunks hosted more than eight prisoners! The Russian women, many of them doctors and nurses captured on the battlefield, were especially kind to us and had organized the vote. As a Christmas gift, Anise had given us a louse-free scrap of a blanket she'd taken from the booty piles, and I'd wound it around Zuzanna's bare feet.

I watched a few Polish girls stuff some grass under a piece of cloth. This was a Christmas tradition we'd followed in Poland since we were young where fresh straw is put under a white tablecloth. After supper some maidens pull out blades of the straw from beneath the cloth to predict their future. A green piece predicts marriage, a withered one signifies waiting, a yellow one predicts the dreaded spinsterhood, and a very short one foreshadows an early grave. That day they all looked very short to me.

With Marzenka away for the moment, some Polish girls sang one of my favorite Christmas songs, "Zdrów bądź Królu Anielski," "As Fit for the King of Angels," in low, hushed tones, since singing or speaking in any language except German was forbidden and could land one in the bunker.

The song took me back to Christmas Eve in Poland, our little tree covered with silver paper icicles and candles. Exchanging gifts with Nadia, always books. Dining on Matka's clear beetroot soup, hot fish, and sweets. And going to church on Christmas Day, our family there in the same pew as the Bakoskis. All of us crowding in with Pietrik and his gentle mother, like a dark-haired swan. She'd been a ballet dancer before she met Pietrik's father and always wore her hair gathered in a knot at the nape of her neck. Mr. Bakoski standing tall in his military uniform and Luiza in her new pink coat snuggling close to me. His family smiling as Pietrik pulled me close to share a prayer book. His scent of cloves and cinnamon from helping his mother bake that morning.

I spent more time in memories then—anything to escape that freezing block—but I could feel the hunger taking the place of any love I had. Most of the day I thought only of bread and ridding Zuzanna and me of our lice. Zuzanna had developed a rigorous delousing routine for us, since she was terrified of typhus. As a doctor, she knew too well the consequences of contracting the disease.

My thoughts were interrupted when the old electrician from Fürstenberg came to work on the wires in our block. He was a frequent visitor and one whose presence was much anticipated. He stepped into the block, stooped and white-haired, toting his canvas bag of tools and a wooden folding stool, the shoulders and sleeves of his tweed coat dark with wet patches. He shook the rain off his mustard-yellow hat and then did something he always did, something extraordinary.

He bowed to us.

Bowed! How long had it been since anyone else had done this for us? He then walked to the center of the room and opened his folding stool. On the way he glanced at Zuzanna, asleep next to me, and smiled. For some reason, he seemed especially fond of Zuzanna. She had that effect on people. Did she remind him of his own child? On a previous visit, he'd snuck her a sugar cube, wrapped in white paper, that we made last for days, waking up at night to take little licks of it. And once, he "accidentally" dropped a headache powder packet near her bunk.

Why, you ask, would starving girls be happy to see this German man? Because Herr Fenstermacher was no ordinary workman. He was a kind, cultured man with a voice like warm molasses. But this was not the best thing.

He sang for us. In French.

But not just any songs. His own songs, made up of the newspaper headlines of the day. Yes, we knew about some war events just by listening to the distant thud of bombs to our south. But Herr Fenstermacher brought us, at great risk to himself, a gift more precious than gold. News of *hope*. The name Fenstermacher means "window maker" in German, and he was our window to the world.

He always started the same way: He stepped upon his stool and fiddled with the bare lightbulb and sang: *"Recueillir près, les filles, et vous entendrez tout ce qui se passe dans le monde."* Gather near, girls, and you will hear all that is happening in the world.

That Christmas Day he sang of American troops landing on European soil; of Stalin, Roosevelt, and Churchill meeting in Tehran; and of the British Royal Air Force successfully bombing Berlin. So that was who'd been flying overhead! I pictured handsome, young English pilots in their planes causing the air-raid siren to sound, sending Binz and her *Aufseherinnen* into panic. Did those pilots even know we were down here waiting to be freed?

Those who knew French whispered translations to the rest. You can't know how happy we were to get this gift. The electrician ended with a pretty "Merry Christmas to you, dear ladies. May God help us all soon."

He gathered his tool bag and settled his hat back on his head. Tears pricked at my eyes. Would he catch a chill in this weather? We'd been forgotten by everyone. Did he know he was our only ally? He walked by our bunk and tipped his hat to me. *Please take care*, I thought. *You are our only friend.*

I was happy Zuzanna slept through it all. One day of rest not having to stand in the sleet for hours as Binz and her guards counted us would help her recover. It wasn't until Herr Fenstermacher was out the door and on his way that I saw what he'd left at the foot of our bunk.

The most beautiful pair of hand-knitted socks!

I reached for them and could not believe the softness. I stroked my cheek with them. They felt like Psina's downy underfeathers. And the color! The palest blue, like an early summer sky. I slid them down under Zuzanna's chin, between her clasped hands and her chest. A Christmas miracle.

No sooner had Herr Fenstermacher left than the door to the block opened and Marzenka trudged in, stomping the mud off her boots. How we envied her boots, since bare feet in oversized wooden clogs in the middle of winter is a torture unto itself.

Marzenka carried an armful of packages. My chest thumped at the sight of them. It was too much to ask for, a package for us on Christmas after waiting so long.

She walked about the block, called out names, and tossed packages and letters into some bunks. How strange, I thought, that we were allowed parcels, being political prisoners and all. But lucky for us, Commandant Suhren was practical. A prisoner's family sending her food and clothing saved the camp money. It meant fewer funds were necessary to keep a worker alive.

By the time Marzenka made it to our bunk, she only held two more parcels.

Please let one be ours.

She slowed as she approached our bunk. "Merry Christmas," she said with a rare crack of a smile. Even she had become sympathetic to the Rabbits.

Marzenka lobbed a parcel onto our straw mattress, and it landed with a thump. I sat up and snatched it. I was a little dizzy and held the box wrapped in brown paper for a few moments, letting it all sink in. A package. Little splotches of rain had spotted the brown paper, giving it an animal-skin look, and the rain smudged the ink of the return address, but it was from the Lublin Postal Center.

Papa.

Had he somehow cracked the code and ironed the letter? Should I wake Zuzanna so we could open it together? The package was already half-open, having been rifled through by the censors, so I went ahead and pulled off the brown paper. I was left with an old candy tin, cold to the touch. I popped off the lid, and the smell of stale chocolate came up to meet me. Oh, *chocolate*. I'd forgotten about chocolate. Even stale chocolate made my mouth water.

In the tin were three cloth-wrapped bundles. I unwrapped the first to reveal what was left of a poppy-seed cake. More than half! Ordinarily the censors would take a whole cake. Were they being generous since it was Christmas? I tasted a crumb and thanked God for creating the poppy flower, then wrapped it back up with haste, for I would save it for Zuzanna. Polish cake would be good medicine for her.

The next bundle I unwrapped was a tube of toothpaste. I almost laughed. Our toothbrushes were long gone, but how wonderful it was to see something so familiar from home. I twisted off the cap and breathed in the cool peppermint. I tucked it under our mattress. With proper bartering, such a treasure would trade for a week's worth of extra bread.

The last bundle was small and wrapped in Matka's little white kitchen towel, the one she'd cross-stitched with two kissing birds. Just seeing that sent me into choking sobs that delayed my progress, but I finally loosened the little bundle, hands shaking so hard I could barely untie the knot. Once the towel fell open and lay in my lap, all I could do was stare at the contents.

It was a spool of red thread.

"Joy" is an overused word, but that was what I felt there that day, knowing Papa had understood my secret letter. It was all I could do to keep from standing in the middle of the room and calling out with happiness. Instead, I kissed the little wooden spool and slipped it into my sleeping sister's clasped hands.

That was the best Christmas in my life, for I knew we were no longer alone.

Herta

"VILMER HARTMAN IS HERE TO SEE YOU," NURSE MARSCHALL
said with a knowing look. Why did she continue to enter my office
without knocking?

I'd woken that morning in a foul mood and with a strange buzzing sound in my head. Maybe it was due to the fact that the camp
was bursting at the seams. Ravensbrück had been built for seven
thousand prisoners but by that summer held close to forty-five
thousand. Maybe it was the constant air-raid sirens or the ominous
war news. In early June word reached camp that the Americans had
landed in France. Or maybe it was the fact that the camp was overrun with infectious prisoners, and every other week I had to cleanse
the *Revier* completely of patients not fit for work and send them on
black transports. Even after a few cuts to relieve the tension, I still
couldn't sleep.

To make it all worse, Suhren had made no headway in the case
of the Rabbits. The blocks were so overcrowded and mismanaged it
would be impossible to find them without a camp-wide lockdown.
Gerda told me their friends exchanged numbers with them and hid
them everywhere, even in the TB block.

I was in no mood to visit with old friends.

Vilmer Hartman, a psychologist I had known at medical school, wanted to tour Uckermark, a nearby former youth camp for girls, where Suhren sent prisoner overflow. I knew psychologists did the rounds of the camps checking the mental health of the camp staff—a waste of time when there were so many more important tasks. I hoped to take him to Uckermark, conduct his tour in five minutes or less, and be on my way without complications. I planned on an early evening and a cool tub, for we were in the middle of a heat wave. It was the hottest July on record.

I found Vilmer out in front of the administration building, waiting in the passenger side of a *Wagen*. I took the wheel, started the engine, and switched on the radio to discourage conversation.

Germany continues to be victorious. Allied supplies continue to dwindle as German troops continue Operation Watch on the Rhine. In other news—

Vilmer switched the radio off. "Victorious? Such lies. How can we delude ourselves? We've already lost the war. It was over back in Stalingrad."

"So what brings you to camp, Vilmer? The last time I saw you was in biology class. You were having a hard time with a fetal pig."

Vilmer smiled. "That class almost did me in."

Vilmer was a good-looking man with a slight wave to his blond hair and a gentle way. He wore civilian clothes, I assumed to gain the trust of the patients he spoke with. His expensive-looking pair of cordovan brogues somehow stayed polished even through the dust of the camp.

"The medical doctor path is not for everyone," I said.

"It certainly pays better," Vilmer said. "But I'm happy being a psychologist."

Once we reached Uckermark, I parked and Vilmer, a typical German gentleman, opened the *Wagen* door for me. We surveyed the three newly built blocks and the enormous canvas army tent set up on the *platz*, under which hundreds of *Häftlings* stood and sat, still in their civilian clothes.

Vilmer had excellent manners, typical of a cultured German man, but was a dull sort. He'd asked me for a date once, but I'd been too busy to go.

"You publish so much, Vilmer. What a career you've made for yourself."

I brushed the sleeve of my white coat, for black ashes had collected there.

"It is too warm for long sleeves today, isn't it?" Vilmer said. "No need to dress formally for me."

"Why are you here, Vilmer?"

"Studying the connection between trauma and psychosis."

"Another study? You will have endless subjects here, starting with the officer's canteen."

"I am more interested in the prisoners."

"Who cares about them? Don't touch them unless you want to catch something."

"I care very much," Vilmer said. "It's only part of my assignment, but through talk therapy with prisoners, I've learned a great deal."

"What's your official assignment?" I asked.

We reached the tent, and Vilmer turned to smile at a *Häftling*.

"To evaluate the population's ability to contribute based on a variety of criteria."

What he meant was *to cull those mentally unable to work*. Before he marked them for special handling, he dabbled in a little research of his own.

"Observing the rats in the maze," I said.

"I like to think it helps them to talk about it. Since when did you become so callous, Herta?"

"Should I be on a couch for this?"

"It would do you good. I'm not surprised, really. You have been systematically desensitized for years after all, starting with medical school. I remember a sword fight with human limbs in the dissecting lab."

"And you are here to observe only prisoners?"

"Oh no. Select camp staff as well."

"Does that include me?"

Vilmer shrugged. "We all have a job to do."

"So everything I say will be recorded and fed to Suhren?"

"I report to Berlin."

"Did they tell you to evaluate me?"

"You are one of many, Herta. The camp doctors are especially at risk. As a group, you show a deep respect for authority. You accept, even crave, the status quo."

"I can't live in a place so dirty as this." I brushed more cinders off my coat. "What does my file say?"

"You tell me."

"I'm sure the whole incident with the Pole is in there."

"Perhaps."

"What is there to tell? I found a prisoner, a former nurse, who helped me transform the *Revier*, and Nurse Marschall became jealous and put an end to it. Marschall. There's one to study."

"Do you know why they have you playing chess with Dr. Winkelmann?"

"We don't exactly chat about it, Vilmer."

Though I had at first railed against the forced visits with my rotund colleague Winkelmann, I had come to find them oddly relaxing. I dabbed mentholated jelly under my nose to fight his body odor and watched him eat an endless queue of fish sandwiches as he lectured me on the benefits of fish as brain food. I'd had worse dates.

"I assume they suspect I became overly close with another woman and would benefit from male company."

"How do you feel about that?"

"It is not my job to feel."

"Internalizing your emotions won't help you, Herta."

Vilmer was so *soft*, with his sad brown cow eyes. Never the sharpest student, medical school had been wasted on him.

"I was simply sad about it all. She was a hard worker and a good person."

"My notes say you took to your bed for several days. Acute anxiety."

"I got over it." Anything can be overcome with hard work and discipline. Why was he making such a production out of it all?

"You seem upset that your jacket is becoming dirtied by the *Krema* cinders. Care to talk about it?"

"I happen to prefer wearing a clean white coat, Vilmer. Is that a violation of some behavioral rule?"

"No need to raise your voice, Herta. Have the episodes become more frequent?"

How much more did I have to take?

"How are you sleeping?"

Suddenly it felt hot like hell standing out there in the sun. "Not well, Vilmer. Might have something to do with the four A.M. siren. Not that anyone cares if I sleep."

"You feel like no one cares?" Vilmer asked.

"Would you stop asking me about feelings? *Mein Gott*, Vilmer. What good does that do? How do I feel? How do I feel?"

My raised voice attracted the attention of an *Aufseherin*. That was all I needed—more reports in my file.

"Look, this is not an easy place to call home," Vilmer said. "Your chart indicates your camp responsibilities. You can't possibly be indifferent to it all. It's not in your nature to end lives, Herta. You're no doubt experiencing psychic numbing."

"I do my job," I said, pulling the sleeves of my dress down over my wrists.

"Any more cutting?"

What if there was? I could handle it.

"No, of course not," I said. "No cutting."

Vilmer put a cigarette to his lips and flicked open his lighter, the glint of sun on the aluminum case blinding me for a moment. "You can't have it both ways, Herta. Kill and still be seen as a healer. It takes a toll."

"On my time off, I think of other things."

"That's doubling, you know. It's unhealthy."

"So is smoking."

Vilmer winced and tossed his cigarette away, causing a scuffle among the *Häftlings*. "Look, a certain amount of compartmental-izing is healthy, but you might be better off with a change of pace."

"You are transferring me?"

"I think you could do with a change, yes. At this point, there isn't a lot you can do to help the Reich."

"So you'll stick me in some small-town hospital ward with a tongue depressor and a bottle of aspirin? You may not have taken your medical education seriously, but I have worked hard to get where I am."

"No need for hostility, Herta."

My dress was like a furnace, causing perspiration to roll down my back.

"So now I am hostile? Please. Have you ever done something so well you think you are destined to do great things? No, don't write 'suffering from grandiosity' on my chart. This is real. I am a *medical doctor*, Vilmer. It is my oxygen. Please don't let them send me away."

"This mess is not ending well for Germany, Herta. You must see that. You will be in line for the gallows."

I started back to the *Wagen*. "Suhren is managing things."

Vilmer followed. "You think Suhren will protect you? He will make a run for Munich. Or Austria. Gebhardt is already lobbying to have himself made president of the Red Cross, as if that will ab-solve him. Why don't you just take a leave of absence?"

It was sickening. Such weakness. Had all Germans turned to jelly overnight?

"I will leave you to your research." I stepped back into the *Wagen* and tossed him the bag of sandwiches we'd brought. "I can handle this, Vilmer. I have come this far. Please don't take it all away."

As I drove out of the Uckermark gates, a truck passed me in the opposite direction, coming to pick up a special-handling transport. I found Vilmer in my rearview mirror, squatting near the tent, talking with some Hungarian Jews. Chatting with them about their feelings, no doubt. As if that would help the Reich.

A FEW MONTHS LATER Suhren called me to his office, his face earthworm gray.

"Our sources tell me news of Gebhardt's Rabbits has leaked. Berlin intercepted a Swit broadcast from the Polish government-in-exile in London that gave details of the Rabbits. Called it vivisection and mentioned me by name. Binz too. Said our crimes will be avenged with a red-hot poker."

"Any doctors mentioned?"

"Just Gebhardt. They said a Catholic mission in Fribourg sent word to the Vatican."

"I told you, Commandant."

He paced. "How did word leak? We were so careful. I suppose we need to make sure those Rabbits are well tended then."

"No, Commandant. Just the opposite. As we discussed—"

"The security office says the Polish government-in-exile has condemned Gebhardt to *death*, you know. This is international opinion we are dealing with. Must be handled carefully. It can make a difference once things are, well, *over*."

"It's better if the Rabbits are never found. Hard for public opinion to comment on something that never existed."

"But Himmler is talking to Sweden about transporting *Häftlings* out of here. To Sweden in Red Cross buses. Thinks it might encourage leniency. Perhaps this will help us. I hope it is well noted that I objected to the operations."

How could Suhren be so naïve? There would be no *leniency*. If Germany lost the war, the victors would not exactly be lining up asking who had objected to what. Suhren would head straight for the gallows.

"Do you think the world will look kindly on that walking evidence of what went on here? Commandant, you will be held responsible no matter what you say. Me too."

Suhren looked out his window over the camp below.

"How do we find them? *Häftlings* are not going by their real numbers anymore." His eyes were bloodshot. Had he been drinking? "At *Appell*, they just slip away. They exchange numbers with the dead."

I stepped closer to him. "Most should be in Block 31—or hiding underneath. With the new facility—"

"Please, Oberheuser . . ."

Suhren didn't like to talk about the new facility, and certainly no one spoke the word *gas*. His new staff members, just arrived from Auschwitz, had helped him cobble together a makeshift facility in an old painter's shed next to the *Krema*. Not fine workmanship but it would make the whole business of silencing the Rabbits much simpler.

"I will have Binz secure that block and then call *Appell*," said Suhren. "You will personally see to it that each Rabbit is caught."

It was about time.

"Are you giving me permission to—"

"Do what you need to, Doctor. Just make sure no trace of them is found."

CHAPTER 24

Caroline

1944–1945

ON AUGUST 25, ROGER PHONED ME UP AT THE HAY AND SAID
the Free French and American troops were at the outskirts of Paris.

We were back in business.

It was a Saturday, so traffic was light as I drove into the city with
the gas pedal to the floor, screeching by cars on the Taconic Parkway, until I saw blue flashing lights in my rearview mirror. Once I
told the baby-faced officer the circumstances, he turned on his flashing lights and escorted me to the consulate.

In Roger's office, we grabbed information from every source we
could. We read telegrams and cables and listened to the radio all at
once. When our troops made it to the Arc de Triomphe, we were
overcome with joy and on the phone with Bordeaux and London.
The U.S. troops, accompanied by General De Gaulle and the Free
French army, marched into Paris from the south, along the Champs-
Elysées in jeeps and on foot. Hordes of Parisians surged into the
streets shouting, *"Vive la France!"* People streamed out of their
homes, frantic with the joy of liberation, even while German snip-
ers and tanks still fired here and there. Soon the Germans waved
white flags of surrender from behind their bunkers, restaurateurs

brought their last few bottles of champagne out of the cellars, and Paris went mad with happiness.

Later that day we watched from Roger's office as Lily Pons, the Metropolitan Opera star, sang "La Marseillaise" to thirty thousand people gathered below us on Rockefeller Plaza to celebrate the victory.

We all agreed it was just a matter of time before Hitler capitulated and Berlin fell. The Allies would liberate all of the concentration camps. I sent telegrams and letters to possible repatriation centers across France inquiring about Paul. How would he get back to Paris?

THOUGH FRANCE HAD BEEN LIBERATED, the war dragged on. I sat at the dining room table up at The Hay the following April, still in my pajamas, writing a press release for orphans in freed France: *These common things are most urgently needed in France TODAY: Rice. Sweetened cocoa. Powdered whole milk. Dried fruits. Tea and coffee for older children are next in importance....*

How long had it been since I'd had that first letter from Paul? None of my inquiries had borne fruit. One last snowstorm had hit Bethlehem, but even winter was tired of winter, and quiet flakes covered the crusty snow in the yard like white flannel. Terrible snowball snow, Father would have called it.

Serge threw the mail he'd picked up from the post office onto the half-moon table near the front door with a thump and went about shoveling the front walk.

I made tea in the kitchen as the afternoon grew dark. On my way back to the dining room, I flipped through the mail stack. I found the usual envelopes. A flyer for Mother's annual spring Bethlehem Horse Show, held on Ferriday Field behind our house to benefit the library. The monthly Elmwood Farm milk bill. An invitation to a handbell concert at the grange.

One envelope stopped me in my tracks. It was ecru just like the others he had sent, addressed in Paul's handwriting—somewhat less crisp and strong, but unmistakably his. The return address read, *Hôtel Lutetia, 45, boulevard Raspail.*

My hands shook as I ripped the side of the envelope and read the letter's contents.

I grabbed my boots from the kitchen, threw Mother's coat on over my pajamas, and ran across the front yard to Merrill Brothers General Store, cracking through the top crusty layer of snow with each step. I bounded up the stairs and found Mother standing near a wall of shelves with Mr. Merrill, a clear bottle of witch hazel in her hand. They separated, startled.

Mr. Merrill smiled when I entered, a porcupine of keys at his waist.

"Caroline. How've you been—"

"Not now, Mr. Merrill," I said, grabbing the doorjamb as I tried to catch my breath. Though generally a concise man, handsome Mr. Merrill would discuss the pros and cons of the paper grocery bag ad infinitum if even slightly encouraged.

Mother turned. "Good Lord, what is it, dear?"

Unable to catch my breath, I waved the envelope.

Mother stepped to the door. "Close this, Caroline. For goodness sakes, what is wrong with you?"

"It's from Paul. He's at . . ."

"At where, dear?"

"The Hôtel Lutetia."

"Why didn't you say so, Caroline?" she said, handing the witch hazel back to Mr. Merrill. "We'll go tomorrow."

After all, our bags had been packed for months.

CHAPTER 25

Kasia

1945

BEAUTY ROAD WAS NO LONGER BEAUTIFUL COME FEBRUARY 1945. The Germans used the window boxes and many of the linden trees for firewood. The road's black slag was covered with frozen slush, and snow was still piled high about the camp, a layer of ash collected atop it—fallout from the furnaces. The cage of exotic animals was long gone.

I dodged groups of women out braving the cold, some in gangs, some wandering alone. On Sundays, Beauty Road teemed with a rowdy jumble of women of all nationalities, some carrying a rinsed pair of bloomers or a uniform shift between them, airing it out to dry. The camp had become impossibly crowded as the Red Army pushed west across Poland and transports of prisoners the Germans evacuated from concentration camps like Auschwitz and Majdanek arrived hourly. We soon had prisoners from twenty-two countries. Poles were still by far the largest group, but we now had among us British prisoners, Chinese, Americans. Everyone knew Himmler kept many of his *Prominente*, special prisoners, in the bunker, including an American pilot who'd been found near Ravensbrück, having parachuted from his failing plane.

Though most of us wore the same blue and gray striped uniforms, we could guess a prisoner's nationality by the way she wore hers. You could always tell a French girl. Each tied her kerchief in a unique, charming way, and they all sewed chic little bags called *bautli* from organized scraps to hold their mess kits. Some even stitched little white collars onto their uniform shifts and made lovely bows from rags. The Russian prisoners, many of them Red Army nurses and doctors captured on the battlefield, were unmistakable as well. They were a disciplined group and all wore their camp uniforms in exactly the same way. Each had kept her Russian-issued leather army boots and wore the camp head scarf tied in a perfect square knot at the nape of her neck.

It was easy to recognize newly arrived prisoners to the camp. Once camp authorities ran out of uniforms, new prisoners wore a crazy assortment of mismatched clothing taken from the booty piles. They looked like exotic birds in their parrot frocks, as we called them, a gaudy mix of ruffled skirts and bright blouses. Some were lucky enough to find warm men's jackets, all chalked by camp staff with a big white Saint Andrew's cross across the back in case the wearer escaped.

Two Russian girls stood at their makeshift store between Blocks 29 and 31, where one could buy a sweater or stockings or a comb, for the price of a bread ration. Their lookout stood close by, alert for signs of Binz.

Rumor was, Gemma La Guardia Gluck, sister of New York City's Mayor Fiorello La Guardia, was our fellow prisoner. A group of female British paratroopers captured by the SS in France too. Charles de Gaulle's niece Geneviève. And everyone knew Himmler's own sister had been a Ravensbrück prisoner, arrested for race defilement—relations with a Polish man. The girls in the front office said even she was not spared the twenty-five lashes that came with her sentence.

Binz turned up the music that was playing throughout the camp even higher and pelted us with war songs and marches. I looked to the sky as three planes flew overhead—German. I could tell by the sound of the engines and the lack of an air-raid siren.

The previous summer we'd heard about the Normandy invasion thanks to Herr Fenstermacher, but no one needed to tell us Germany was rapidly losing the war. The signs were everywhere. Daily air raids. Shorter *Appells*. Fewer work details.

The Nazis were giving up.

They did not give up killing us, though. The windowless black transport buses came to the blocks with new urgency. Fat Dr. Winkelmann in his long leather coat and his partner old Nurse Marschall prowled the camp, looking for sick prisoners to mark down for the buses.

Sick women hid everywhere to escape: under the blocks, above the ceilings, behind the coal bins. Zuzanna invented a method of scraping the arms of women arriving from evacuated Auschwitz to cause their tattooed skin to appear infected to hide their blue numbers. Everyone in the camp continued to hide the Rabbits when roll call came. Some even traded numbers with us at great peril to themselves.

Rumors flew. A prisoner-nurse told Zuzanna that out at the former youth camp, the *Jugendlager*, not ten minutes away from camp by truck, they were sending in older women restricted from work. The food was more filling, and there was no roll call. Could it be true?

Early that evening I was given permission to go to the administration building and collect a package addressed to me. I left the block, happy I could finally walk without my crutch, but before long, Karol, a *Jules* from the Netherlands, caught me by the arm and pulled me into the shadows.

My heart contracted. I was wary of most every *Jules*, for this was a new sort of character that emerged in the last year of the camp. Usually a German prisoner with a green or black triangle, a *Jules* would gather a man's sport coat, trousers, and even men's underpants from the booty piles, cut her hair in a masculine way, and swagger about the camp with a cigarette and a nasty attitude. Some would use a blade to carve an *X*, called a "cow's cross," into the forehead of a girl they liked, marking her as theirs. The *Jules* were not all bad. I knew several nice ones, and it was often an advantage for a girl to go steady with a *Jules*, for it meant protection and food, but the objects of their affections were powerless to refuse since a *Jules* always had connections in high places. They could starve a girl if she did not cooperate.

"They are doing another selection next door," Karol said. "Let's take a walk."

We walked away from the truck, taking the long way to the administration building, but I glanced back and saw Winkelmann and Nurse Marschall loading women onto one of the windowless black vans. A death transport. Neither of us had to say it: Anyone caught close to that hurricane could have been swept up for no good reason.

As terrifying as some *Jules* were, Karol may have saved my life that day. Once the danger was over, I thanked her and continued on my way.

I soon passed a long white canvas tent set up for a group of newly arrived prisoners in an open area just off Beauty Road. The camp had become so horribly crowded, and the transports kept coming from all countries. Suhren set up these tents right in the middle of camp. This one was so jam-packed with women and children that they were barely able to sit down under there. Many stood, trying to soothe their babies.

"Kasia," someone called. I turned, surprised to hear my name.

I didn't recognize her at first in the shadows under the tent, for her face was drawn and gaunt and her short blond hair gray with dust.

Nadia.

She sat on an old suitcase, and a woman lay next to her with her head in Nadia's lap. Nadia stroked the woman's brow and murmured something to her. I watched for a second to make sure it was her and then walked closer to the tent, just out of sight of the *Aufseherin*.

"*Nadia?*" I said. Was this a hallucination?

She looked up as if her head was too heavy for her neck.

"Kasia," she said, her breath a puff of white steam. How beautiful my name sounded when she said it. She put one hand out to stop me from coming closer.

"We just saw a girl dragged away for talking to us. Plus half of us have typhus. Be careful."

I took a step toward her. What a happy day this was! How quickly could I get her to our block?

"How long have you been here?" I asked quietly, so the guards would not hear.

"We just arrived last night from Auschwitz. They said we are going to the youth camp. There is shelter there."

"When?"

"I don't know," she said, looking down at the woman in her lap. "We're all so thirsty, and she needs a place to die in peace."

"Nadia, come quickly. I can hide you."

"I can't leave her."

"Someone else can tend to her." I stepped closer.

"You don't recognize her, do you? It's my mother, Kasia. I would never leave her."

Mrs. Watroba. How had they been caught?

"Come," I said. I knew I could hide them both.

"I know what you are thinking, my friend, but I am staying here with my Matka."

"What can I get for you?"

Binz's guards began waving prisoners into the truck.

"Nothing. Don't worry. We'll all be back in Lublin before you know it. Back with Pietrik. He will be happy to see you." She said this with a real smile. The old Nadia.

"It's you he loves," I said.

"Do you know how many times he asked me if you liked him? Hey—I left the book for you before I went. In the spot. You'll love chapter five."

"I think the spot may be long gone, but we'll both check it together when we get back."

"Yes."

Nadia gasped, one fist to her chest, her gaze fixed on my bad leg. One of the mismatched woolen men's socks I'd traded some of our toothpaste for had slid down to reveal it—by then healed, but withered and shrunken, missing whole tendons and bones, the skin shiny and taut. "My God, Kasia, what happened to your leg?" Water came to her eyes.

To be crying for me while in her situation? This was a good friend.

"I'll tell you later, but now I can get you a drink—I have a bit of rainwater saved."

Nadia smiled again. "Always resourceful, Kasia. Matka would love that."

"I'll be right back," I said and set off back to my block.

My leg slowed my progress, and by the time I returned with the water, the guards were loading the last of the prisoners into the open truck. They closed the back gate and banged twice on it, and the truck started off down Beauty Road.

Nadia. It had been like medicine to see her! Would she be safe at the youth camp? I'd never heard of anyone going there from Ravensbrück before. I said a prayer that what I'd heard about the new camp there was true. Was God even listening to prayers from us?

The truck continued down Beauty Road, and tears came to my eyes as I caught a glimpse of Nadia cradling her mother.

"I'll see you soon, Nadia," I called, running as best I could after the truck.

She craned her neck above the crowd, smiled, and raised her hand.

I watched the truck rumble off, the red taillights a blur. I wiped the tears away. Were they really going to a safe place? It was hard to believe anything the Germans told us, but no matter what, the Danish girls in the front office said the Russians would be arriving soon to liberate the whole camp. At least Nadia and her mother would have shelter. Nadia was the strongest person I knew.

I hurried on to the administration building to pick up my package, darkness descending on the camp. A family of rats, big as cats, walked across the road ahead of me, no longer afraid of people. I claimed my bundle at the postal window and glanced at the return address: *Lublin Postal Center, Lublin, Poland,* written in Papa's hand. I opened it as I walked back down the hallway, my wooden clogs echoing on the polished floor, and pulled out another spool of red thread.

I never tired of seeing that. He'd sent two more since the first. Had Papa gotten word out to the world? If we were to die before the camp was liberated, at least everyone would know what happened, and the Germans would be punished for what they'd done. His packages had helped Zuzanna with her dysentery, but she'd then caught something else going block to block to doctor other prisoners. Headache, chills, fever. From the rash on her arms alone, we both knew what it was: typhus. Nothing but liberation could help with that.

I passed the desk of Brit Christiansen, a Danish girl I knew, one of many Scandinavian prisoners who worked the front office. She was tall with a short blond bob and a pretty constellation of beige moles scattered down her cheek. I'd never even met a Danish person before the camp and now found they were among my favorite people. Gentle. Trustworthy. Kind.

"I have two things to tell you, and we must be quick," Brit said in a soft voice. "One is an SS man, high up, came today inquiring about your mother."

"What? *Who?*"

"Not sure, but he was very tall."

Lennart! Here at Ravensbrück? Was Matka here too somewhere?

Brit pulled me closer. "And also, they are hunting Rabbits today."

Those words gave me gooseflesh all over. "But it's almost dark. A night selection?"

"Binz is on the warpath. Suhren is coming too. They doubled the liquor ration for the guards."

"We'll have to hide," I said.

Could I get Zuzanna under the block? Or Anise could hide us with the Hungarian Jews again. The typhus ward?

"They know you've been hiding under the block, Kasia."

"We'll go up to the Annex."

"They know that too. And there are new buses here."

Buses. A jolt of fear shot through me. There was no time for hysterics.

I hurried back to the block.

An inky blackness settled in around me, for there was no moon that night. The floodlights above clicked on as I ran the best I could despite my bad leg, pushing women aside on the way to my block.

Just don't feel anything. If you are to live, you cannot feel.

I knew as I entered the block that word of the hunt preceded me, for girls were crying and holding one another. I pushed through women from every country Hitler had plundered, the room a jumble of different languages: Russian, French, Hungarian, Polish. I found Zuzanna on our bunk, knees to her chest, shaking with chills. She barely lifted her head.

"Have you heard?" I said. I sat next to her on the bunk and stroked her forehead. "They are coming for the Rabbits. You need to get up, my darling."

Zuzanna opened her eyes and then closed them. "No, Kasia."

Anise pushed through the crowd, calling my name.

"Get out now, Kasia," Anise said in her calm way. "They are coming. Binz and Suhren and the woman doctor. The Red Cross already took the Swedish girls, and French girls are being taken next. From the linen shop. I'll keep the back window open for you."

"In buses?" I said.

"Yes. Use the number 9284. It's safe. I could only get one."

I grabbed her wrist.

"Don't go, Anise. How do you know it's not a death transport?"

How many times had we seen them trick women into buses? Some looked like ambulances, with red crosses painted on the sides. We heard them drive around to the little painter's shack and cut their engines. After that, those prisoners' clothes would come back to the linen shop, smelling of the sweet, unmistakable odor of gas.

"It's the Swedish Red Cross, Kasia, the real thing, and you need to hurry."

"Girls, we have *Appell*," said Marzenka, banging a pot with a wooden spoon.

Anise ran out with one last look back.

I pulled Zuzanna by the hand. "We need to—"

"No, Kasia. You go."

She tried to lie back down on the bunk.

"We need to get under the block," I said as I pulled her up, held her around the waist, and guided her through the crowd toward the door, her weight light against me, like a dried branch.

Marzenka stood on a dining bench, hoarse from yelling above the din.

"Please. Binz has given me her word no harm will come to any of you."

That only increased the panic, and many ran for the door, but Binz and her dog appeared there ahead of her *Aufseherinnen*. Just outside the doorway stood Commandant Suhren and Dr. Oberheuser, she with clipboard in hand. I was close enough to see light snow on the shoulders of Binz's gray cape. Her dog nipped at Zuzanna's leg, and we drew back.

"Everyone out here now for *Appell*," said Binz. "Disobey orders, and you will be shot."

Dr. Oberheuser at a block selection? We were trapped with no choice but to comply. No time to get to our hiding place. I pulled up my socks. Would the doctor recognize me?

I supported Zuzanna as we all filed out onto Beauty Road in front of the block and stood at attention in the cool night air, the lights above shining bright. What if we ran? Even if we had good legs to run with, the dogs would finish us. Though it was cold, I felt hot all over. This was it. Why had I not been faster?

Binz and Dr. Oberheuser walked up and down our ranks and checked our numbers. Binz stopped in front of me, crop in hand.

"Roll down your stockings," she said.

So this was how it was to end.

I rolled down one sock. It revealed my good leg. Binz motioned to Dr. Oberheuser.

The doctor paused.

"Well, Doctor?" Binz said.

I held my breath. The doctor seemed frozen in a dream as she stared at me. Was that hatred or pity? She motioned to my other leg.

"The other one," Binz said. I rolled my other sock down, over the smooth ridges of indentations where my muscles once were. The doctor must have recognized her handiwork, for she nodded a quick yes to Binz, and they moved on to Zuzanna. Zuzanna looked at me. *Be strong,* that look said. Next we would go to the wall. Would I be able to be brave like the others and walk down Beauty Road, head held high?

Dr. Oberheuser seemed puzzled by Zuzanna at first, for her scars were not as obvious as others'. Would she let Zuzanna go? Send me to the wall, I prayed. Let my sister live. Let one of us go home to Papa.

The doctor nodded to Binz.

Yes.

Zuzanna took hold of my hand. We'd go to the shooting wall together as we'd always planned, there for each other until the end.

Then something very strange happened.

The lights went out.

Not just the floodlights but also every light in the camp. It was as if the hand of God had come down and drenched us in the kind of velvety black where you can't see a single thing. Girls called to one another. Suhren, Oberheuser, and Binz barked orders in the darkness. The confused dogs growled. You would not have believed how loud it was in the camp with everyone on Beauty Road, crying and calling out.

"Adelige, *sit*," said Binz, her tin training clicker chirping in the darkness.

I grabbed Zuzanna by the waist and pulled her away from the group. Would the lights come back on any second? I felt my way along and brushed Dr. Oberheuser in the darkness. A wave of the terrible perfume she wore washed over us. I stepped on Binz's foot and felt her arms windmill.

"*Verdammtes Arschloch!*" she said.

I headed for the linen shop, heart beating out of my chest, guessing the direction in the darkness, one arm around Zuzanna, the other outstretched in front of me like the cowcatcher in front of a train, bumping into people in the darkness. The fire from the crematorium in the distance was not bright enough to illuminate the camp, but I navigated by it. I practically dragged Zuzanna, her full weight against me.

I knew we were in the right area when I saw a bus in front of the linen shop, the vehicle lit from within, the only light in the camp. As we drew closer to the shop building, I heard French girls talking. I felt for the back window and helped Zuzanna climb in, then followed her, pulling my bad leg in with great effort. It was warm in the room, and the crowd smelled good as I pushed through, a mix of perspiration and perfume.

Zuzanna leaned against me. "I can't go much farther."

"We are almost there," I said. "You can rest soon."

I saw Anise's friend Claire in the glow of a flashlight.

"Kasia," she said.

I grabbed her arm. "Binz has us on her list. As soon as the lights come on, Zuzanna and I will be taken."

"The lights won't come on tonight," Claire said. "The Russian girls turned them off. Szura flipped the switch at the transformer station once they heard Suhren was coming for the Rabbits. The whole electrical grid is down, and they'll not turn it back on until morning."

"How do you know these buses are really Red Cross?"

"Suhren has been stalling them, but they threatened to ram the gate. The girls in the office said Himmler himself authorized Count Bernadotte of Sweden to take us."

Elaborate hoaxes had been made up before to get girls to go peacefully, but it was our only chance.

"Anise gave me a number," I said.

"Make sure you move along," said Claire. "This is the last bus. Two have already loaded and are waiting at the gate to go."

I held Zuzanna and pushed through the crowd in the darkness. From the French I'd learned, I could tell the girls were all excited to be going home. As the last of them loaded, there were few left in the shop.

Once I made it to the front of the line, I saw two men stood at the back of the bus checking numbers. One I did not know. The other was fat Winkelmann, dressed in his long leather coat. The rear door of the bus was swung open wide to reveal French girls packed into the bus, standing, waiting. A blond nurse dressed in a white uniform stood inside, helping people up the few steps. If this was a Nazi hoax, it was an elaborate one, but German guards often wore the uniforms of doctors and nurses in order to fool us.

I breathed easier once I told Winkelmann the number Anise had given me and I helped Zuzanna into the bus. When my turn came to step up into the bus, the nurse bent toward me.

I set one foot on the wooden step stool.

Was this really happening? Going home? To Lublin? To Papa . . . The nurse smiled and reached her hand to me and I took it.

Winkelmann placed his white stick across my chest.

"Stop. Number?"

The nurse clenched my hand tighter. "Their numbers have all

been checked. We don't have time to argue." She spoke German but with a Swedish accent. We were going home.

Winkelmann pushed me back with his stick, and the nurse released my hand.

"My orders are French *Häftlings* only. If this girl is French, I am Charles de Gaulle."

"I am indeed French," I said in German. Did he see my legs shaking?

"Yes?" Winkelmann said. "Say something in your native tongue, French girl."

Without hesitating, I said in the most forceful French I could, "This dryer is too hot. Can you cut a little more off the sides? May I have a permanent wave, please, with medium curl and extra end papers? And use the boar-bristle brush, for it seems to help with my dandruff."

Winkelmann looked at the other man. "She's a Pole for sure," he said.

"Just get on the bus," the other man said and waved me on.

"We need to move," said the nurse, pulling me up to join Zuzanna. "Come in quickly."

As the nurse began to shut the doors, a prisoner ran to the bus with a bundle of clothes. "Wait, your baggage!" she called out, and handed the package up.

"That's mine," said sweet Pienotte Poirot, a friend of Anise's, from the front of the bus. The girls passed the bundle down to her, and her friends drew near.

The bus jerked forward, and we started on our way toward the open gates. Just a short way to freedom.

Please let this be a real hospital bus.

The white pole at the guard station lifted, the bus driver gunned the gas, and we left the gates behind. Why did I not feel the joy of liberation? We made our way down the road along the lake, and Pienotte opened her bundle.

"My God, it is Guy," said Claire to me. Pienotte opened the blanket to show a tiny newborn, pink and healthy, with a head of dark hair. "He was born two days ago. Thank God he didn't cry. Smart boy."

We rumbled down the road, the bus lights showing the way, illuminating the backs of our escorts, three German soldiers on motorcycles.

How strange to be on a bus once again. How I had missed the pleasing pull of it: gears shifting then hesitating, gliding and pushing on, *going* somewhere. The road went from cobblestones to smooth paving made flat by the road crew's concrete roller. What a fine job you did, ladies, I thought. If only you could feel the smoothness of it.

A teakettle cried somewhere close, already at a boil.

A bomb.

The earth shook, rocking the bus, and the lake lit up like a camera flash.

"It's the Allies, bombing," the nurse said. "They must think we are a German caravan."

The driver cut the lights, the engine too, as the Germans left us and buzzed back to camp, their taillights growing smaller and smaller in the darkness. The teakettle whined again, and we cried out as the ridge above us split and our faces lit up, as if around a campfire. At least the impact felt like something, like we were alive, and sent us to the rubber floor. I held my sister to me, bone on bone, and we fell against the others. Did she breathe? Did I? I pressed her to my chest, warm against me.

Soon the bus engine came alive, and we lurched on toward Sweden, our two hearts one.

CHAPTER 26

Herta

1945

By APRIL OF 1945, GERMANY HAD LOST THE WAR, THOUGH
the news media would not admit this. They clung to their fairy-tale
world until the end. I knew the war was lost from listening to foreign broadcasts in my quarters. According to the BBC, the western
Allies had pushed past the Rhine, and German casualties soared.
Suhren said it was only a matter of time before Germany reclaimed
Paris, but I knew we were defeated. On April 18 we heard that
American tanks rolled into my hometown of Düsseldorf and easily
captured the city. The British and Americans were headed full speed
toward Berlin.

One afternoon I left camp and stole along the lakeshore, my
steps muffled by humps of moss, suitcase handle slippery in my
hand. The lake was angry, and whitecaps whipped across it. Was it
stirred by the breeze or by those whose ashes were buried there,
settled into silt? How could I be blamed? I had only taken the job of
camp doctor out of necessity. It was too late for the lost to raise their
bony fingers and give testament against me now.

As I neared Fürstenberg, I met a sea of German men, women,
and children walking, some with luggage, some with only the
clothes on their backs. Half of Fürstenberg's civilians had headed

south months before, and it seemed the other half was evacuating that day to escape the Red Army. From their posture alone, one read the humiliation of defeat. I joined that great autobahn of the displaced and was swept up in the crowd, half-numb. It was hard to believe it was all over, that I was running away. The shame of it was near debilitating.

"Where are you going?" I asked a German man in a tweed overcoat and mustard yellow hat. He carried a birdcage strapped to his back. The bird swayed, perched on its little wooden trapeze, as the man walked.

"We are taking side roads to avoid Berlin, then south to Munich. There are American troops advancing from the west, Russians from the east."

I joined a group headed for Düsseldorf, and our passage on foot was long and unremarkable. We avoided main routes and followed wooded trails and field tracks, slept in abandoned cars, eating anything we could find to stay alive.

I imagined how happy Mutti would be to see me. She had been living with a man named Gunther in a nice apartment upstairs from our old place, and I'd stayed with them one holiday break. He was a nice enough magazine salesman. Rich too by the looks of the apartment. I imagined the fried onions and mashed potatoes with applesauce she would make in that kitchen when I got home.

It was drizzling when I reached Düsseldorf, and I had to be careful to keep a low profile, since there were American soldiers everywhere. Not that I was high on the authorities' list of suspects. Did they even care about me? They had bigger fish to fry.

The streets of Düsseldorf were littered with abandoned suitcases and horse and human corpses. I walked by the Düsseldorf train terminus, bombed to rubble. As I neared Mutti's building, I passed a looted wagon tipped on its side as two elderly women tried to strip off its wheels. Along the street, people came and went, some with all their worldly possessions. I tried to blend in with them, to look like just another displaced person.

Once I made it to Mutti's doorstep, I was happy to see the apartment building not only still standing but in perfect order. All I could think of was her bathtub and a hot meal. The smell of fried onions hung in the lobby. Some lucky person had squirreled away some food.

I made it to the third floor and rang Gunther's apartment bell.

"Who is there?" came a voice from behind the closed door. Gunther.

"It is Herta."

He hesitated. What was that buzzing sound in my head? Was it due to dehydration?

"Is my mother here?" I called through the door.

The lock clicked, and the door swung open.

"Quickly," Gunther said. "Come in." He grabbed me by the arm, pulled me inside, and relocked the door.

The apartment was still well furnished, with thick carpets and chairs upholstered in velvet. Someone had removed a portrait of the Führer from the wall, exposing a rectangle of brighter wallpaper behind. That was fast.

"Two looters tried to break the door down this morning. It's anarchy out there."

"Really, Gunther—"

"Everyone steals from everyone now. Goods belong to those who can hold on to them."

"I'm starving," I said.

"*Everyone* is starving, Herta."

"They were still cooking food at the camp—"

"That's not all you and your friends were doing there. The truth is getting out, you know."

I walked to the radio. "There must be rations. They will broadcast—"

"No *rations*, Herta. No broadcasts. Women are prostituting themselves for a spoonful of sugar."

Gunther did not appear to have missed many meals. He'd lost a bit of weight, but his skin was still taut. Just a slight creeping at the neck. How had he managed to stay out of military service? Things were not adding up, and the buzzing sound in my head grew louder.

"I'm in need of a bath," I said.

Gunther lit a cigarette. How was he getting cigarettes? "You can't stay here. They know what you've done, Herta."

"Where is Mutti?"

"She had to go down to the station. They came looking for you."

"Me? What for?" I didn't have to ask *who*.

"Crimes against humanity, they said."

How could they be on my trail so quickly?

"You are putting your mother at risk, Herta, just being here. Take your bath, but you need to find other—"

"My mother may feel differently," I said.

"Take a bath, and then we'll talk."

I set my suitcase on the sofa. "I may need Mutti's help with some matters."

He tapped cigarette ash into the ashtray. "Money matters?"

"Among other things. Legal fees maybe."

"Oh, really? If anything should happen to you, the state pays the fees."

"Happen?"

Gunther strolled to the hall closet and came back with a towel. "Take your bath while we still have hot water. We'll talk later."

I dropped my things in the guest room and ran the bath, one ear to the lavatory door, half-expecting Gunther to call the authorities. There was sure to be some sort of Allied military hierarchy set up. Gunther would never turn me in, I assured myself. Mutti would be livid. But Gunther had never been a real patriot, and the new power shift made almost everyone suspect.

I locked the bathroom door and took my time running the water extra hot. I slipped into the tub, sliding down the enameled cast iron into that glorious burning sea.

I felt every muscle slacken there in the hot water. Where was

Fritz? I would ask for my old job back at the skin clinic. If it was still standing, not under a pile of stones. I rehearsed my talk with Mutti as I soaped my legs, feet black with dirt from the walk. She would support me, no matter what Gunther said.

"So what?" she would say when I told her about the camp. "You were doing your job, Herta." Where was she? Probably out doing her best to find some bread.

I closed my eyes and recalled Mutti's breakfasts: hot rolls and fresh butter, her coffee—

Were those footsteps in the living room?

"Mutti?" I called. "Gunther?"

A rap at the bathroom door.

"Herta Oberheuser?" came the voice through the door. The speaker had a British accent.

Shit. Goddamned Gunther. I had known he was not to be trusted. How much had they paid him to turn me in?

"I am coming!" I said.

I lost control of my limbs there in the tub. Could I make it out the window? Something hard hit the door, and it cracked open. I may have screamed as I reached for the towel. A British officer entered the bathroom, and I sat back in the tub, the diminishing soap bubbles my only protection.

"Herta Oberheuser?" he asked.

I tried to cover myself. "No."

"I hereby place you under arrest for war crimes against humanity."

"I am not she," I said, in shock, like an imbecile. How could Gunther do this to me? Mutti would be furious. "I have done nothing."

"Step out of the tub, Fräulein," said the man.

Another British agent came to the bathroom with a canvas raincoat in hand. I motioned for the two to turn their backs.

"I will leave for a moment," said the first agent, red-faced. He handed me a towel, averting his eyes. "Wrap yourself in this."

I took the towel, and he left, pulling the door closed. I hoisted myself out of the tub. Goddamned Gunther, I thought as I stepped to the medicine cabinet. I found his razor blades and slid back into the tub, the water cooling.

"Fräulein?" called the first man from outside the door.

"Just a moment," I said as I pulled a blade from the pack.

I felt for the radial artery and found it easily, since my heart was pumping hard. I drew the blade down my wrist, deep into the artery, and watched it open like a peach. The water grew pink, and I lay back in it as it cooled, light-headed. Would Mutti cry when she saw what I'd done? At least I'd done it in the tub. Cleanup would be easy.

Before I could get to the other wrist, the agent came back in.

"*Christ,*" he said when he saw me, the water squid-inked with red by then. "Teddy!" he called to someone somewhere. "*Christ,*" he said again.

After a great deal of shouting in English, they pulled me from the tub.

So much for modesty.

I was losing consciousness, not about to tell them how to treat me, but noted with satisfaction they were doing just fine without me, for some reason elevating my legs. A sure way to make me bleed out. My feet were still filthy black, in each toenail a crescent of dirt.

I lost consciousness, but regained it as they carried me out on a stretcher, my wrist nicely bandaged. Someone knew what he was doing. There was a doctor among them? Was he surprised a German doctor had done such a poor job?

Why did you turn me in? I tried to say to Gunther as the British agents carried me down the stairs to the street.

They started to load me into an ambulance.

I saw Gunther watching from a window above, his face impassive. More faces came to windows. Old men. Women. They brushed aside curtains and peered down.

Just curious Germans. A girl with yellow braids came to the window, and her mother pushed her away and drew the shade.

"She is only curious," I said.

"What?" said an Englishman.

"She's in shock," said another.

Unter schock? Incomplete diagnosis, English doctor. *Hypovolemic* shock. Rapid breathing. General weakness. Cool, clammy skin.

More faces came to the windows. A full house.

Something wet drifted down to my face. Was that rain?

I hoped no one would mistake it for tears.

Part Two

Part Two

CHAPTER 27

Caroline

APRIL 1945

Mother, waylaid with the grippe, sent me off to Paris alone. She was terribly worried, of course, since the Allies may have helped liberate France, but the war was far from over. How many rogue U-boats were still out there in the Atlantic? I would not be deterred, however, on the eve of seeing Paul again after five long years. I'd taken a bit more silver to Mr. Snyder in order to make the trip. The petit four tongs. Butter knives. A few dinner forks.

I docked at La Rochelle, north of Bordeaux, on April 12, 1945. When we disembarked, the first mate announced that President Roosevelt had died at his home in Warm Springs, Georgia, and a collective groan went up from all of us gathered there. The president died before he got to see the Germans surrender in France. He never know Hitler took his own life.

Roger had arranged for a car and driver to get me up to Paris, and I took in devastated France from the backseat. It's one thing to read of war in newspapers and chart the action with pins, but it was quite another to see France ripped asunder. It had been more than seven months since the Allied forces helped liberate Paris, but the destruction was still fresh. Entire blocks were decimated, buildings imploded, and the walls of many apartment buildings had been sheared off, showing a cross section of still-furnished rooms. Our drive was repeatedly detoured since black craters and tank-sized sections of macadam blown off the roads were still not repaired. South of Paris, not a bridge over the Seine was left standing. Yet even with all the devastation, it was spring, and the city was still lovely rising from the ruins, the Arc de Triomphe untouched, five flags draped under the arch.

Once in Paris, I borrowed our caretakers' old Peugeot, which was powered by an improvised wood-burning stove fixed to the back. A wartime lack of gasoline had led to widespread use of these home-made gasogenes, wood gasification units mounted on the backs of buses, taxicabs, and private cars. It was quite a sight to see these vehicles on the streets, each with its own combustion tank fixed to the rear. Drivers stopped at filling stations to stoke the stove with firewood, not to get gasoline. Driving such a car in Paris was challenging, for the streets were choked with bicycles, and they owned the roads. As a result, the Métro was more popular than ever. Even the wealthiest counts were seen in its depths.

I arrived at the crossroads of the boulevard Raspail and rue de Sèvres that night and choked back a sob at the sight of the Hôtel Lutetia, still there. Freed from her Nazi occupiers, the towering Belle Epoque hotel stood fearless, her name in lights above, the tricolor flying again.

I pushed through the hotel entrance, past a tangle of the mothers, husbands, wives, and girlfriends of deportees, and who waved pictures of the missing and called out their names, hoping for news. The lobby, its black and white tiled floor strewn with trampled notices and lilac sprigs, was packed with journalists, Red Cross workers, and government officials, all jockeying for position at the front desk.

A frail woman in black, her back hunched, seized my arm as I squeezed through the crowd.

"Have you seen this man?" she said, as she thrust a photograph of a white-haired man in my face.

"No, I'm so sorry," I said.

In the dining room, groups of dazed survivors, still in their striped camp uniforms, sat at tables under the crystal chandeliers as waitresses brought them the best of everything. Veal, champagne, cheese, and fresh bread, from the provisions the Nazis left behind. Many deportees sat and stared at the food, unable to eat. Some who ate more than a few bites headed for the lavatory.

Searchers elbowed their way into the Great Gallery, to walls plastered with notices and photos of missing loved ones, many inked with black *X*'s, meaning those deportees would never return. That is where I found it.

Paul Rodierre. Suite 515.

I sprinted to the elevator but found it so choked with people the door would not close and ran on to the stairs. On the way, I passed men, skin stretched taut over their skulls, wandering the back halls, their camp uniforms hanging from them. What would Paul look like? I prepared myself to find him in that state or worse. I didn't care as long as I could be with him every day. I'd pay whatever it took to get him well.

I passed guest rooms turned hospital wards, fitted with extra cots, the doors propped open. 511 ... 513 ... In the hallway, two gendarmes chatted with a pretty nurse. Love was back, now that the war was over.

I found the spacious fifth floor suite, tall windows open to the city below, the Eiffel Tower in the distance, a lovely French Louis Seize Beauvier cane bed against one wall. The royal treatment for the famous M. Rodierre.

From the doorway I watched Paul as he sat in an overstuffed chair playing cards with three other men, the curtains on the windows stirring in the gentle breeze.

Paul was dressed in a plain button-front shirt, and a nurse sat behind him, one arm across the back of his chair, the other hand on his pulse. It was so strange to see him in that lovely suite with the damask drapes and fine wool carpets. I stepped closer and looked over Paul's shoulder at his cards.

"I wouldn't bet the farm on that hand," I said.

Paul turned his head and smiled. To my relief, he looked fine. Gaunt, and his head was newly shaved, but he was *alive*, awash in that white cotton shirt. I couldn't wait to get him home to his own bed. I would spend every penny I had on doctors if I had to.

"Have you brought no money for me to bet with?" Paul asked. "No Russian cigarettes? Come here and kiss me."

I stepped around the chair and saw, with a jolt, Paul's legs extended out from the bottom of his shirt, long and thin, knobbed at the joints, like the legs of a cricket.

"I won't break, you know. And don't believe a word the doctor says. If my winnings are any indication, I'm fine."

"I don't know where to start," I said as I knelt by the side of his chair, afraid to touch him. Was it painful to be so thin?

A young doctor approached us, his orange hair piled atop his head like frizzled saffron.

"You are a relative?" the doctor asked.

"She's a friend," Paul said. "Miss Ferriday from New York."

The doctor looked me over, his eyes red rimmed. Had it been days since he'd slept?

"Can you walk with me, please?" the doctor said.

I sensed a tenuous criticism, as if he disapproved of me somehow.

"I am Dr. Philippe Bedreaux," he said once we stood in the hallway. "I have been treating Paul for a few weeks now. He made an excellent recovery from typhus, due in part to chloramphenicol, a new drug. Then he took an inexplicable turn for the worse. Pneumonia."

"Pneumonia?" My breath caught in my throat. Like father. *Pneumonie*. So much prettier in French, but just as deadly. Something Mother still referred to as "lung fever."

"He recovered but is by no means out of the woods. Are you staying in the city?"

"At my mother's apartment close by. Does Paul know about his wife's death?"

"Yes. It was a great shock, and he refuses to speak of it. Right now he needs to sleep. At some point, he'll need aggressive physical therapy due to muscular atrophy."

"Will he recover completely?" I asked.

"Too early to tell, Mademoiselle. We are dealing with a ruined body here. He has lost almost half his overall body weight."

"Mentally, he seems fine," I said. "Playing *poker*—"

"He is an actor. Of course he puts up a good front, but we must be very careful. His heart and lungs have been through a great trauma."

"So are you guessing two weeks? Three?"

"He may not wake up tomorrow as it *is*. You must let him *recover*."

"I am sorry, Doctor—"

"A young man was set to go home last week—vital signs good—and he died of cardiac failure the morning he was to leave. Who knows when we can consider these patients cured?"

"I'm just eager to—"

"He must not exert himself in any way—no cooking, extended walks, and certainly no, well—"

"What, Doctor?"

"Certainly no extracurricular activities . . ."

"I beg your pardon."

"Complete bed rest."

With Paul *alone* in the bed, he wanted to say.

After the doctor left, I sat at Paul's bedside, watching his chest rise and fall under the blanket.

"Don't leave," Paul said.

I smoothed the back of my hand across his cheek.

"Never," I said.

I SAW PAUL EVERY DAY and decamped to Mother's apartment each night. I was relieved the old place had survived the war relatively unscathed thanks to our caretaker's wife, Mme Solange. The apartment was surprisingly untouched, not a crack in the floor-to-ceiling casement windows or the hornbeam parquet floors, though fine white powder covered every surface, the silver-topped jars on my mahogany vanity table now two inches deep in silty dust. The carriage clock in Father's study had stopped at 9:25, and there'd been a leak in Mother's bedroom. A section of damask wallpaper curled down off the wall there like a stained sow's ear.

Paul slept for much of those first two weeks, but soon asked to go home to the house he and Rena had shared in Rouen. Dr. Bedreaux reluctantly agreed, with additional vague references to a ban on lovemaking that made Paul smile. Dr. Bedreaux insisted a doctor had to visit Paul every day, for Rena's house was several miles outside of Paris, with limited access to hospital care. I agreed, happy to pay whatever it took to make Paul happy, and with the help of three strong nurses, we managed to get him into the front seat of the Peugeot.

On the road to Rouen, fresh evidence of combat was everywhere, and many buildings were nothing more than façades. The imposing Rouen Cathedral, made famous by Monet's paintings, was one of the few buildings left intact. Paul directed me to a bunker-like house on a side street in Rouen, not at all what I'd expected.

I helped Paul up the front walk and considered the house, which resembled a military pillbox, cold and standoffish. It was designed in the Bauhaus style, another abhorrent thing Germany had foisted on France.

Would the neighbors come out to greet him? Would they think me an interloper? After all, Rena had grown up in the house and she and Paul had lived there together. Did they have friends, couples on the street who missed her?

Paul and I walked into the front hallway and inched our way across the living room. It was a dark house, but the rooms were done in the bright prints of Provence. I considered asking Paul if we could live at Mother's apartment with its lovely morning light and pastel boiseried walls, filled with the pieces Mother and I had found at the Marché aux Puces and other *antiquaires.* My Louis Seize commode. The fin de siècle metal garden table in the kitchen. Mother had gone a bit toile crazy, but it was nicely done. All it needed was a good dusting.

I helped Paul up the stairs and past a snug little room with yellow, fabric-upholstered walls and on to the master bedroom, where Paul and Rena once slept. The bed was small for a man as tall as Paul and wore a white matelassé bedcover and blue-and-white ticking pillows.

I pulled a chair next to Paul's bed and watched him sleep well into the night. Eventually I moved to the padded window seat and slept for a bit. Before dawn, Paul spoke.

"Rena?"

"No, Paul, it's Caroline."

"Caroline? I am so cold."

I brought my blanket to the bed and smoothed it over him.

"I thought I was in the hospital," he said.

"No, you're home, dear."

He was back asleep before I finished the sentence.

It was strange to cook in Rena's kitchen, the copper pots still burnished bright, her drawers filled with pressed cotton napkins folded in neat stacks. There was little food to cook, for all over France, meat and vegetables were hard to come by. At first, I improvised. With a ration card, a lucky sort could hunt down some potatoes and bread, perhaps some anemic carrots, but most of the country existed on thin soups and toast. Then I raided Mother's pantry at her apartment and struck gold: molasses, oatmeal, and tea bags. Eventually I found one could buy anything for a price on the black market.

Each day I served Paul an old family remedy my great-grandmother Woolsey gave her soldier patients at Gettysburg: one egg and soda water beaten into a glass of wine. Several other Woolsey remedies were on the menu as well, including beef tea, milk punch, and rice with molasses. I told Paul they were old New England favorites from my distaff side. Thanks to them, he grew stronger every day.

"Would it help to talk about the camp?" I asked one night.

"I can't talk about it, Caroline. You have good intentions—"

"You have to at least try, Paul. Maybe start with the night you left here. Baby steps."

He was quiet for a long moment.

"They came for me with no warning thinking I might be good for their cause. Rena was sick in bed with the flu. Took me to headquarters and told me very nicely they wanted me to film some things: propaganda, of course, but I wouldn't do it. They kept me in Paris for a while and then sent me to Drancy. I guess they came back later to get Rena and her father. That was the beginning of the roundups, taking the Jews."

"How did they know Rena was here?"

"They knew everything. Maybe from the visa application. I don't know. Drancy was horrible, Caroline. They took the children from their mothers."

Paul bent his head, chin to chest, and pressed his palm to his mouth.

"I'm sorry, Paul. Maybe this is too much for you."

"No, you are right. I have to talk about it. You would not have believed the camp—Natzweiler."

"In Alsace? Roger thought you might be there."

"Yes, in the Vosges Mountains. Many died from the cold and the high altitude alone. I was such a coward. I prayed I would die. We built part of the camp. New barracks and . . ." He tried to take a sip of tea but put the cup back in the saucer. "Maybe we can finish later."

"Of course," I said. "Doesn't it help to talk about it?"

"Perhaps."

I tucked Paul into bed that night, happy to be making progress.

———

THE AFTERNOON OF MAY 8, I was ankle deep in the stream behind Paul's house picking watercress from the banks, marveling at the chestnut blossoms and emerging wisteria. Purple foxglove, a flower I'd had to pamper back in Connecticut, sprang up everywhere like weeds. I could hear Paul whistling in the house, and it made me smile. Men only whistle when they are happy. At least that was true for Father.

All at once the whistling stopped, and Paul called out.

"Caroline . . ."

I ran through the grass toward the sound of his voice. Had he fallen? Heart pounding, I raced into the kitchen, tracking wet footprints.

"De Gaulle is on," Paul said.

I found Paul, right as rain, standing near the radio. I caught my breath, relieved, just in time to hear General De Gaulle announce the end of the war in Europe.

> Forever honor our armed forces and their leaders. Honor our people that terrible trials could not reduce or decline. Honor the United Nations, which have mingled their blood with our blood, their sorrows our sorrows, their hopes our hope, and now triumph with us. *Ah, vive la France!*

Paul and I hurried to the front garden and heard the cathedral bells.

"It's hard to believe it," I said.

Though the first act of the German capitulation had been signed in Reims the day before, it wasn't until we heard General De Gaulle and our neighbors in their cars, honking horns and flying a *tricolore* out the window, that it all sank in.

The war in Europe was over.

I threw on one of Mother's scarves and drove us to her apartment in Paris. We flung the windows open wide expecting to hear a great celebration, but Paris was strangely quiet that afternoon considering the momentous news of the war's end. All that changed, however, as the afternoon wore on, and young people streamed out into the parks and squares.

"Let's go to the Place de la Concorde," Paul said.

"Why don't we just listen to the radio here?" I said. "The crowds may be too much for you."

"I'm not a cripple, Caroline. Let me enjoy this."

It was a lovely warm day, and we walked to the Hôtel de Crillon at the Place de la Concorde. The lovely old building rose up from the square, the *tricolore* flying between the columns. It was all so surreal, to celebrate a free France, in the same square where King Louis XVI was guillotined.

As the shadows in the square grew long, the crowds thickened, and American military police wearing white helmets appeared here and there in the crowd, making sure people made it in and out of the American Embassy. We pushed through the crowds, the din of horns and singing all around us, waving white handkerchiefs above our heads, jostled and knocked as American army jeeps rode by. Young French men and women on the running boards popped champagne and threw flowers to the crowd.

As the sunlight waned, the lights came on at the Place de la Concorde for the first time since the war started. A cry from the crowd went up as the Fontaines de la Concorde were turned on once again and the fountains' sculpted fish, held by bronze sea nymphs, sent great plumes of water into the night sky. People danced in the fountain fully clothed and soaked to the skin, mad with happiness that Paris was back.

Paul dropped his handkerchief, and a teenaged girl stooped to retrieve it for him.

"Here you go," the girl said. "For a minute, I thought you were Paul Rodierre."

"He is," I said.

The girl danced off. "Very funny," she called over her shoulder.

"She doesn't know what she's saying," I said, but Paul knew the truth. He was barely a shell of his old self.

The wind seemed to go out of Paul's sails after that, and we left after sunset to head home. As we drove toward Rouen, fireworks exploded over the Seine.

Once home, we changed into comfortable clothes, me in Paul's soft trousers and an oversized shirt and Paul in his favorite ivory flannel pajamas. He seemed withdrawn and more tired than usual. He sat slumped at the kitchen table as I prepared dinner.

"Are you sad Rena's not here?" I asked.

"It doesn't help to bring it up. As it is, you can't stop trying to be her."

"I'm not," I said.

"Cooking her recipes, dressing like her. Please don't do that."

"Because I wore a *scarf* today?" I asked.

"Just relax and let it be like it was in New York."

"I've never been happier," I said.

It was true. We had our differences, but since I stopped typing up medication and exercise schedules for Paul, our relationship strengthened every day. Plus, thanks to the Woolsey remedies, Paul was finally filling out.

"Then why don't you move in? For good, I mean."

"Oh, I don't know, Paul. It would help to hear how you feel."

"I'm crazy about you."

"How so?"

Paul thought for a second. "You are a very hard worker. I respect this."

"That's it?"

"And I like the way you speak French with your American accent. *Very* sexy."

"Certainly that isn't—"

"And I never tire of being with you."

He stood and came to me at the sink.

"I like your imperfections. Your lopsided smile."

I touched my lips. Lopsided?

"And you don't have a giant handbag you're always pawing through."

He took my hand. "I like that you wear my clothes." He unbuttoned one button at my chest. "And your white skin. So smooth all over—I thought of that a lot while I was away."

He wrapped his arms around my waist. "But my favorite thing about you is . . ."

"Well?"

". . . the way you kiss. Sometimes I think I may not recover when I kiss you. It's like going to another place."

Paul pulled my shirt collar aside and kissed my neck.

I smiled. "Funny, there's one word you never use."

Paul stepped back. "Why do Americans have to have every detail spelled out? You say 'I love you' to the garbageman."

"I believe the phrase was invented here."

"If that's all it takes, I *love* you. I can't imagine a life without you. Now move your things in, your clothes, your books. Make the house ours."

"You mean not go back to New York?" It was too wonderful to imagine, being with Paul for good.

"Yes. Make this your home. We can always visit New York. And your mother can move here. You already have the apartment."

"I'll miss the consulate, but Roger has Pia."

"He certainly does."

"Of course I'll stay," I said.

"Good then," Paul said with a smile. It was like medicine to see that smile again.

Was it too late to have a baby together? I was over forty years old. We could always adopt. There was a file in my suitcase full of darling French babies who needed homes. We'd have a real family. Mother would be thrilled to have a wedding at last. Roger had wrangled her a visa, and she was on her way to Paris for a visit after all. I could tell her in person.

"Why not start tonight?" he said.

"I'll go get my things." Was this really happening? Did I have any silk stockings at Mother's apartment?

"Don't bring any makeup," Paul said. "You are perfect as is."

"Not even a lipstick?"

"Hurry. I'll finish making dinner."

"Please don't, Paul," I said. "Dr. Bedreaux says . . ."

Paul stood and walked to the counter. He scooped a few dusky new potatoes, the color of violets, from the bowl. Would it be too much for him to make a meal?.

"Don't say another word, or I will change my mind," he said.

I grabbed my purse. "Nietzsche said a diet predominantly of potatoes leads to the use of liquor."

"Good. Bring a bottle of your mother's wine. We're celebrating."

In the almost two-hour drive back to Paris, I made a mental list of what to pack. Capri pants. Silk stockings. My new lingerie. I would eventually need a proper French driver's license.

At the apartment, I drew the shades, threw a suitcase together, and headed out. As I locked the door, the phone rang in the kitchen, and for once in my life, I ignored it. If it was Mother, I needed more time to tell her the whole story.

On the trip back I stopped at our favorite market and found one sorry-looking baguette, small, but a good omen. I stopped again to stoke the engine with wood and headed for Rouen, the car radio turned up, windows open, as Léo Marjane sang "Alone Tonight."

I am alone tonight, with my dreams. . . .

The papers all chastised the cabaret singer for having entertained the Nazis a little too enthusiastically during the occupation, but no song captured the war like that one. I sang along.

I am alone tonight, without your love. . . .

It was wonderful not to be the one alone for once. Sad songs are not so sad when you have someone who loves you. I turned onto Paul's street singing with abandon. Who cared what the neighbors thought?

I rounded the bend and saw a white ambulance parked at the curb outside Paul's house, engine running.

Time stopped. Was it parked at the wrong house? I drove closer and saw a nurse standing outside the front door, a navy-blue cape over her white uniform.

My God. Paul.

The car barely stopped moving before I jumped from it.

I ran up the walk.

"Is Paul hurt?" I said, my breath coming in great gulps.

"Come quickly," the nurse said as I followed her into the house.

CHAPTER 28

Kasia

1945

"AM I DREAMING?" ZUZANNA SAID AS THE FERRY DOCKED AT Gdansk, the salt air filled with the wild cries of gulls and terns. I lifted my hand to shield my eyes, for the sparkling water, alive with diamonds, blinded me.

We had spent two months in Malmö, Sweden, the place for which God saved all the most beautiful things in nature. The greenest grass. Sky the color of cornflowers. Children who seemed born of that landscape, their hair spun from white clouds, eyes of cobalt sea.

We were sorry to leave, for we were treated like royalty there, feasting on princess cake and *pitepalt* dumplings with butter and lingonberry jam. Once we regained our strength (both Zuzanna and I were up to forty kilos), many of us wanted to get home to wherever that might be. Poland. France. Czechoslovakia. A few women with little left to go home to stayed in Sweden to start new lives. Some waited to see what would happen with the proposed new elections in Poland before they ventured back. We'd heard the repressive Soviet law enforcement agency NKVD was in charge in Poland, but Zuzanna and I never hesitated. We ached to see Papa.

While I was grateful beyond words for my rescue, the stronger I became, the angrier I got. Where was the joy at being rescued? I watched women around me recover, eager to resume their old lives, but for me, the rage just grew, black in my belly.

Once we'd made it to the northern coast of Poland by ferry, a driver met us at the landing. He was a young man from Warsaw, one of more than one hundred former Polish Air Force pilots who'd joined Britain's Royal Air Force and risked their lives fighting the Luftwaffe. He was only a few years my senior, but at twenty-two, I had the limp and posture of an old crone.

He reached for Zuzanna's cloth sack and helped us into the car. I felt the leather of the backseat, cool and smooth. How long had it been since I'd been in an automobile? It may as well have been a spaceship.

"So what is happening in the world today?" Zuzanna said once we were under way, opening and closing the little metal ashtray in her door handle. I opened my own and found two crooked cigarettes stubbed out there. What they would have given for those in the camp!

"Heard what's going on with the government?" the driver asked.

"There are to be free elections?" Zuzanna said. We drove through the port of Gdansk, bombed heavily during the war.

"The government-in-exile wants to come back," the driver said. "So the Polish Workers' Party says there will be a vote."

"You believe Stalin?" I said.

"The Polish Workers' Party is—"

"*Stalin.* Just what we need."

"They say we'll be our own free and independent country. People are hopeful."

"Why do we keep believing liars?" I asked. "The NKVD will never let go."

"Don't let anyone hear you say that," the driver said.

"That sounds free and independent," I said.

Zuzanna and I slept much of the way to Lublin and woke once the driver stopped at our front door.

"Time to wake up, ladies," the driver said as he pulled on the hand brake. We sat in the backseat and stared at the bare lightbulb next to our front door, bright in the darkness, inviting a frenzied party of fat moths and other bugs. At Ravensbrück prisoners would have happily eaten those.

"Can you believe we are here?" Zuzanna asked.

We stepped out of the car as if we were arriving on the moon. I circled Zuzanna's waist with my arm. She leaned against me, and her hip bone knocked mine. The pain in my bad leg spiked as I climbed those beautiful front steps.

We had sent Papa a telegram. Would he be waiting with poppy-seed cake and tea for us? I turned the old porcelain knob of our apartment door. It was locked. Zuzanna fished the extra key out of the old hiding place behind the brick. Still there!

One step into the kitchen, and the realization knocked the wind out of me: My mother was gone. The room was dark, save for a small lamp on the kitchen table and the halo of a candle flame on the fireplace mantel. Too-happy yellow curtains hung at the windows, and a new family of red canisters stood on Matka's wooden counter. Yellow and red. Matka loved blue. Someone had hung a painting of a field of wildflowers over the wall where Matka once pasted her bird pictures. A few sparrows peeked out from behind the painting, the mucilage holding them to the wall yellowed with age. I walked to Matka's drawing table. Someone had laid it flat and covered it with a cheap lace tablecloth, atop it a Virgin Mary picture from a shrine in Gietrzwald and a china frame containing a picture of an old woman waving from a train.

I stepped to the mantel, to Matka's picture there, the one where she looked quite serious and was holding her little dog Borys. Someone had set a black bow beneath the photo, the curled ends hanging down off the mantel. I felt dizzy standing there looking at my mother's solemn face as it danced in the candlelight. A dog barked in the bedroom, and Zuzanna caught her breath.

Felka?

"Who is there?" Papa said, creeping down the hall from the back bedroom.

He came toward us in his striped underwear. His hair, thinned and gray as a squirrel's coat, poked out in all directions, a black revolver I'd never seen before in his hand. Felka emerged behind him, her tail beating quite a rhythm. She was all grown up and fatter than the last time I'd seen her, right in that kitchen with Matka.

"It is just us, Papa," Zuzanna said.

Papa stood as if struck dumb, his mouth open. How had he aged so? Even the hair on his chest was gray. Felka came to us and ran back and forth from Zuzanna to me, digging her wet nose into us.

"We're home," I said. My eyes pricked with tears. Papa opened his arms wide, and we went to him. He set his gun on the counter and hugged us both as if he would never let us go. How happy we were to be there in his embrace! Zuzanna and I both cried on his bare shoulders.

"Did you not receive our telegram?" I asked.

"Who receives telegrams these days?"

"You got a letter about Matka?"

"Yes, the handwriting on the envelope looked like hers, so I thought it was a letter from her. But it was a form letter. They said it was typhus."

I took his hand. "It wasn't typhus, Papa."

"What then?" He was like a small child. Where was my strong papa?

"I don't know," I said.

He stepped back, hands on his hips. "But were you not together?"

Zuzanna led Papa to a kitchen chair. "They moved her to a separate block, Papa. She worked as a nurse——"

"And drew portraits for the Nazis. That's what got her killed. Getting too close to them." Why did I say such a thing? I knew too well that her bringing me a sandwich that night at the movie theater had gotten her killed.

Zuzanna knelt next to Papa. "You received Kasia's letters. How did you know how to read them?"

"It took the whole postal center to figure it out. We knew there was some sort of code, but none of us knew how to read it. I dabbed water on the first letter. But then we figured it out. I told certain people, and they got the message to our underground in London, who spread the word. But it was Marthe who said we should iron the letter. That it was a trick from a book she knew."

Marthe?

I knelt at Papa's other side. "Thank you for the red thread."

"I got the word out as best I could. Did you know the BBC broadcast it? What they did to you both . . ." Papa dissolved into another pool of tears. How hard it was to see our strong papa crying!

I took his hand. "Have you seen Pietrik? Nadia?"

"No. Neither of them. I post the lists every day. Red Cross Center does too. I wish we'd known you were coming." Papa took up a linen dishcloth and dried his tears. "We've been frantic with worry."

We?

Zuzanna noticed her first, in the shadows of the bedroom doorway, a thickset woman in a dressing gown. Zuzanna went to her and put out her hand.

"I am Zuzanna," she said.

A woman in Papa's bedroom?

"I am Marthe," the woman said. "I've heard so many nice things about you both."

I stood, took a deep breath, and considered the woman. Marthe was a few inches taller than Papa, her dressing gown belted with twine. Brown hair worn in a braid hung down over her lapel. A country woman. Papa had certainly lowered his standards.

Marthe came to stand near to Papa, but he made no move toward her. "Marthe's from a village outside of Zamosc. A great help to me these years you've been away." Papa looked embarrassed Marthe was there. Who wouldn't, introducing his girlfriend to his dead wife's children?

"Why don't we sit?" Marthe said.

"I would like to go to bed," I said. It was like a swap out at the market. My eyes went to Matka's picture on the mantel. Did Papa not miss her? How could he do it?

Papa waved me to him. "Sit with us, Kasia."

Marthe sat on Matka's favorite chair, the one she had painted white, with the calico pillow seat. I watched Zuzanna bond with Marthe. Papa looked on, happy to see them connect.

"I wish we could offer you something to eat, but we just finished the last of the bread," Marthe said.

Papa felt the stubble of his beard. "It is worse than ever now. Since the Russians came, there is barely any food at all. At least the Nazis kept the bakers in flour."

"So we've traded Nazis for Stalin?" I asked. "Even trade if you ask me."

"I get on well with them," Papa said. "They have let me keep my job at the center."

"Let you?" I asked.

"You can get all the Russian cigarettes you want now," Marthe said, a little too brightly. "But few eggs."

"It is just a matter of time before we are all calling one another 'comrade,'" I said.

"We'll get on just fine," Zuzanna said.

"They are looking for former underground members," Papa said with a pointed look at me. "They took Mazur last week."

A volt of current went through me, and all of a sudden I could barely breathe. Mazur? He was Pietrik's childhood friend, a most skilled agent at the highest ranks of the underground. He'd read me my AK oath. A true patriot.

Big breath in, big breath out.

"I'm done with all that," I said.

"They took us from the camp on a Swedish bus," Zuzanna said. "You should have seen it as we crossed the border to Denmark, all the people gathered there with welcome signs. They were very nice to us in Sweden too. We flew the Lublin Girl Guides banner some-one had found in the Ravensbrück booty piles as we drove in, and you should have heard the cheers. We spent the first night on the floor of a museum."

"With dinosaurs with big teeth crouched over us," I said. "No different from the camp."

Zuzanna fetched her cloth sack. "Then we stayed with a princess at her mansion. Look what they gave us before we left Sweden." She opened the sack, set a white box on the table, and opened it. "They gave each of us one. Tinned sardines. White bread and but-ter. Berry jam and a piece of chocolate."

We had each taken only nibbles of the food, saving it.

"And evaporated milk?" Papa said. "It's been so long."

"How kind of them," Marthe said. "I have a flour ticket I've been saving. I can make—"

"Don't trouble yourself," I said.

Papa bowed his head and ran his fingers through what was left of his hair.

"I am sorry about your mother," Marthe said, standing.

"It looks like it," I said.

"Kasia," Papa said.

I picked up the white chair, the cushion still warm from Mar-the's rump.

"Good night, Papa," I said. "Good night, Zuzanna."

I carried Matka's chair toward my room, passing the mantel, careful to avert my eyes from Matka's picture there. It was too hard to look at her face, a new knock to the belly every time. I entered my room and closed the door. No mistress of my father's would park in my mother's seat, no matter how much help she was to him.

CHAPTER 29

Caroline

1945

I FOLLOWED THE NURSE INTO THE HOUSE AND SAW AN AMBU-lance attendant in the kitchen at the end of the hall. Even from the front door, I could see the potatoes scattered on the floor, the shine of olive oil on tile. How could I have left Paul alone after Dr. Bedreaux's warnings?

As we neared the kitchen, I saw Paul seated at the table, a nurse taking his pulse. A gush of warmth rushed through my arms.

"You're okay, Paul. Thank God."

Paul looked at me. Had he been crying? "We tried to phone you. Can you believe it, Caroline? It's almost like a dream."

I shook my head. "I don't understand."

"They rang the doorbell," he said. "It's all so . . . surreal."

"*Who* rang the doorbell, Paul?"

"Rena."

"Rena rang the doorbell? You're not making sense."

"They just took her upstairs."

"She's back?"

My voice sounded distant, foreign.

Paul rubbed a spot on the tablecloth. "She has been at the American Hospital."

Did he seem happy? Not really. It was all so confusing.

"She hasn't been able to talk much. Seems a German family took her in."

I slumped against the doorjamb.

"How wonderful," was the only thing I could think to say. "I'd better go now."

I turned to leave.

"Caroline, wait," Paul said. "Where are you going?"

"This is all so overwhelming."

"I know. I am sorry, Caroline. Rena has been in the hospital for weeks, too ill to speak."

I am sorry. I hated those three words. How many times had people said that when Father died? *Je suis désolé* sounds beautiful in French, but it only made things worse.

"Well, I have to go home," I said.

I needed time to think and didn't want to break down in front of him. After all, a woman was alive and had not died a tragic death in a concentration camp. She was no doubt tucked into Paul's bed upstairs as we spoke.

Paul stared at the potatoes on the floor. "Yes. We'll talk tomorrow."

"I mean home to Connecticut," I said.

"You can't go home now. This is a shock for all of us."

"I can't think straight. I have to go."

Why didn't he throw his arms around me and beg me to stay?

"We'll talk tomorrow and figure all of this out," Paul said, still rooted in his chair.

Somehow I made it out to the car and back to Mother's apartment, where I committed myself to voluntary confinement, mostly in bed, dressed in pajama bottoms and Paul's shirt I'd worn home from his house. The kitchen phone rang a few times until I took the receiver off the hook and left it dangling. *"Si vous souhaitez faire un appel, s'il vous plaît raccrochez et réessayez,"* said the recording over and over again until there was a series of short beeps and then nothing.

The door buzzer rang several times a day, but I didn't answer it.

I self-flagellated by day—allowed my hot tea to cool and then drank it tepid and overmilked—and steeped myself in could-have-beens. Could have been lasting love. Could have been a wedding. A baby. Had I really hocked half of Mother's silver to nurse another woman's husband back to health? Betty was right. I had wasted my time.

One morning Mother let herself into the apartment and planted herself in my bedroom doorway, her umbrella dripping on the carpet.

Mother. I'd forgotten she was due to arrive.

"It's pouring out there," she said.

Good, I thought. At least others were inside and as miserable as I.

"Heavenly day, Caroline, what is wrong? Are you ill? Why don't you answer the phone?"

I may not have been French, but was I not allowed to take to my bed and marinate in my own despair?

"Paul's wife came back," I said.

"What? From the dead? How is this possible? Where was she all this time?"

"I don't know. Some hospital."

"That is incredible," Mother said. "Well, you have to pull yourself together."

"I can't," I said and pulled the duvet up over my shoulders.

"You are taking a bath, and I'm making you tea. A bath makes everything better."

There was no fighting Mother. And she was right about the bath. I emerged in fresh pajamas and sat at the metal garden table in the kitchen.

"I knew this would never work," I said. "I'm not meant to be happy."

Mother brought me a Mariage Frères Earl Grey tea bag in a cup and a pot of hot water.

"Sorrow is knowledge—"

"Please, Mother. No Byron just now. This whole thing has been a ridiculous fantasy. How did I let myself get so carried away? I should have known. I had to try so hard to make it work."

"Just because he has a wife doesn't mean you can't be with him," Mother said. A few hours in France had thrown her moral compass for a loop.

"I suppose. But why is it always so hard, Mother? There's always some catch."

The doorbell buzzed.

I reached for Mother's wrist. "Don't answer it."

Mother went to the door anyway, an action that made me regret inviting her to France.

"Whoever it is, I'm not here," I called after her.

Mother answered the door. I heard a woman introduce herself as Rena.

Oh God, Rena. Anyone but her.

Mother came back to the kitchen with Rena in tow and then left us alone. Rena stood in the doorway in a cotton dress that clung to her like wet laundry, showing the ridge of her collarbone and a hollow the size of a soup bowl below.

"Sorry to interrupt your tea, Caroline," she said, a tired schoolgirl, all eyes and sunken cheeks. "I tried to call." Her gaze drifted to the dangling receiver.

"Oh," I said.

Rena shifted in her shoes. "Paul is sorry as well. Tried to call you too . . ."

"Please sit," I said.

Rena ran one finger behind her ear, as if to tuck a piece of hair there—an old habit, it seemed, for there was no hair there to tuck.

"I will not take up too much of your time. Just wanted to say how sorry I am."

"Sorry?" I poured hot water over the muslin bag. The scent of bergamot orange triggered a violent craving for one of Serge's violet scones.

"For how this all turned out," she said.

"No need to apologize, Rena."

"Maybe I will sit. I won't be long."

"Of course," I said. "Tea?"

"No thank you. I still can't keep much down. I told Paul he should come over soon and visit. Explain it all . . ."

I tried to sip my tea but could not see the cup because my head throbbed so, my vision blurred.

"I am afraid Paul is not happy to see me," she said.

Somewhere out on the street children laughed, their voices echoing off the buildings as they splashed in the rain.

"You probably wish I were dead after all," Rena said. "Believe me, I wished that myself so often. I would have sent word if I could have. It was just luck that kept me alive."

"I understand."

"No, I don't think you do. How could you? It was just luck they broke with the usual procedure. They had taken our shoes, so we knew."

"Rena, you don't have to—"

"We were on the train from Majdanek, to a subcamp, we thought. The train slowed somewhere in Poland, and they made us get out."

Rena paused and looked out the window.

"I was sick. Typhus, I think. So I barely made it when they marched us through the woods. Paper money lay scattered on the ground along the path. People before us had thrown it away. Lest the Germans got it, I suppose. Someone whispered we were going to work, but I knew. We came to a shed, and they told us to strip."

"Please, Rena. You don't have to tell me—"

"I am sorry. Is all of this too hard for you to listen to?"

I shook my head no.

"It happened so quickly. They lined us up along the edge of a great pit . . ."

Rena lost her thread and drifted away somewhere. After a moment, she began again.

"When the girl beside me saw what was below, she cried out. Her mother took her in her arms, and they shot them first. The blasts threw them against me, and all three of us slid down the dirt sides . . ."

Rena paused, and I barely blinked, afraid to interrupt.

"I lay still as more bodies fell atop me. Soon the shots stopped, and I could tell it was close to night, since the light through the spaces around the bodies above me grew dim. I crawled out of the pit in the dark and rooted around in the shed for some clothes."

She looked at the ceiling. "You should have seen the stars that night, thrown across the sky in great bunches. It was as if they were watching, looking down on all that, sad they could do nothing. I walked through the woods to a house, and a farmer and his wife took me in. A German couple. Their son had been killed at the Russian front. At first, the wife was afraid I would steal her wristwatch, a nice one, a gift from her son, for the wristwatch is valuable currency. But the couple ended up being very kind. They put me in their boy's old bed and nursed me through my sickness as if I were their own. Fed me warm bread with strawberry jam. I returned their hospitality by passing on my disease."

I handed Rena a napkin, and she held it to one eye for a moment, then the other.

"The old man died first. When the Russians came, I told them we all had typhus, but they laid a rug over my face and raped me anyway. Then they raped the farmer's wife and took her wristwatch. She died sometime that night. I don't remember much else, just bits and pieces, until the hospital here. So, you see, I would have come home earlier, but it was—"

"I'm sorry that happened to you, Rena. Why are you telling me all this?"

"I know what Paul means to you—"

"He told you?"

"When he first returned from New York. I didn't care at the time, but things are different now."

Of course things were different. In ways none of us could undo.

"I wish I could make you happy, Caroline. But I can't give Paul up. Maybe once, but not now."

Rena held the edge of the table. She needed to rest.

"I think you should go home to him, Rena."

"Yes, but I need to tell you something."

There was *more*? "I don't think——"

"I haven't told Paul yet." She drew herself up with a deep breath.

"Rena, it's not really——"

"They took Paul before any of us. I was very sick, could eat nothing. Thought it was the flu, but then I found . . . I was, well . . . waiting for a child."

The world stopped for a moment, suspended in air. Waiting for a child? That lovely French phrase.

"Pregnant?"

Rena held my gaze and barely nodded.

"Was it——" I began before I could stop myself.

"His?" Rena looked at her hands for a long time. "War does funny things to people, I am afraid. In our case, it drew us closer. The child must have known what was happening. She arrived the day the Gestapo came for me. Easter morning."

She? Paul had a daughter. I pressed cold fingers to my lips.

"We were tipped off that a raid was coming. My father took the child, said he would go to a convent he knew. He took her in a shoe box, she was so small."

"Where?"

"I don't know. They came for me that night. My father had not returned."

"I'm terribly sorry for your loss, but I——"

"The convent was abandoned during the war, so I am writing to orphanages, but Paul told me——"

"I'm really not in a position to help if that's what you're asking."

I stood and carried my teacup to the sink.

"I understand your reluctance, Caroline. I wouldn't want to be involved if I myself were in your place. But if you reconsider——"

"I'm leaving for New York soon," I said, one hand on the cool porcelain of the sink.

Rena stood. "Of course. Thank you for your time, Caroline."

I saw Rena to the door and watched from our front window as she walked to the end of the block, holding her purse over her head to deflect the rain.

The thought of contacting orphan asylums in search of Paul and Rena's child sent me back to bed. Despite the fact that he had once claimed otherwise, it seemed there was room in Paul's life for a child after all. Why should I put myself out to find her? Paul hadn't exactly considered my feelings through all of this. I may have been taken in once, but I'd learned my lesson. There were plenty of private detectives making a living searching for lost loved ones. Many who'd do a better job than I.

By the time evening fell in the apartment, I'd decided. Paul and Rena were on their own.

CHAPTER 30

Caroline

1945

THE NEXT MORNING I WOKE UP HUNGRY, MY BELLY ONLY FULL of regret. It was shocking how easily my life had become derailed. The French word *dépaysement* ran through my head—the sense of disorientation one feels upon having an immense change forced upon oneself. Mother had done a yeoman's job of dusting, but all at once, the apartment looked especially unkempt, the windows in need of washing, the telephone cord impossibly tangled. Mother's solution to my situation was to force-feed me eggs as if I were a foie gras goose. Midway through her *oeufs pochés,* I shared my situation.

"Did you hear my little chat with Rena?"

"Only bits. She seems like a dear thing."

"I suppose. But she's not giving Paul up."

"That's a pickle."

"Not really. Isn't it obvious? He still loves her."

Mother cracked another egg into the boiling water. "How would you know? You don't answer the phone. Paul leaned on the doorbell for an hour last night, poor thing."

"Five minutes, Mother. Don't exaggerate."

"It's too bad, really. Under different circumstances, you and Rena could have been good pals."

"I have enough friends, Mother, thank you."

"Well, you can't just turn your back on the whole thing, dear."

"I'll never have a child of my own."

"But that doesn't mean it's right to abandon theirs. Before you know it, you'll be wondering—"

"Summarize, Mother. You think I should find that child."

She slipped another egg into my bowl. "Well, it's the Christian thing to do."

"I'm not feeling very Christian this morning, I'm afraid."

"Well, splash some cold water on your face. That will help."

Why was Mother's solution to every problem a splash of cold water? Already a day with her in the apartment felt like an eternity. How would I last the week? Soon her Paris friends would be stopping by. Would I have to suffer their pitying looks?

EVENTUALLY I CAME TO MY SENSES and set about finding the child if for no other reason than to put it all behind me. And to escape the apartment, for Mother was staging a tribute to T. S. Eliot—*The Paris Years*—and the guests had been instructed to come in costume. Among the visitants would be some of Mother's men friends, no doubt. Though I'd not been able to keep even one male admirer, within weeks of coming to Paris, Mother had attracted a bevy of male devotees, mostly bereted older Frenchmen and American expats. They sat in our living room sipping tea, watching Mother be Mother, and were happy to be in her orbit.

Finding an unnamed child in postwar France was not an easy process, and I arrived, at the end of my rope, after many stops, at Orphelinat Saint-Philippe in Meudon. It was one of the orphanages I'd sent comfort packages to from the consulate and now one of many clearinghouses for the war's displaced children, collected from safe houses, boarding schools, and crumbling châteaux all over France, mostly in the south. It stood southwest of Paris in an imposing old stone mansion, complete with its own Romanesque church.

The location rivaled Mount Olympus, set high on a hill, head in the clouds that day.

I darted through the warm rain, having forgone an umbrella, and navigated the mossy steps. I tried not to think about what would happen if I found the child. It would be the official end of our relationship, despite everything Paul and I once had. Apparently he was in love with Rena after all. At least enough to father her child.

The orphanage's front office was packed with people on missions similar to mine. Those wise enough to bring umbrellas held them at their sides like wet bats, for there was no stand at the door. A phone rang unanswered, and cardboard boxes were piled up in the corners. Stacks of white diapers sat on the desk, like layered millefeuille pastries, diaper pins scattered about.

The crowd parted and a man pushed his way in carrying a wailing infant wrapped in linen. He made it to the desk and held out the infant as if it were a live bomb.

"An old granny just handed me this."

The proprietress behind the desk took the child. She was a hawk-like woman dressed in black, her only embellishment an exquisite collar that looked like Queen Anne's lace. She placed the bundle on the desk and unwrapped layers of linen. She looked up, a mauve crescent beneath each eye.

"This is a boy. We take only girls."

The man was already on his way out the door.

"Guillaume!" she called as she reswaddled the baby, quicker than a deli man wraps a sandwich, and a man came at a trot, took the child, and spirited it away.

A young woman approached the desk. "Madame——"

Madame raised one finger without even looking up from her paperwork. "Wait your turn. The children are at lunch. No one sees them until three."

Drips of water from the leaky ceiling fell on the desk blotter, leaving darker green amoebas growing there.

"Pardon me, Madame," I said. "I am looking for a child."

She scanned the list on her clipboard. "Fill out the form," she said.

I edged closer. "I have a special case."

"You are the fifth special case today."

"My name is Caroline Ferriday. I worked with Mme Bertillion. Sent comfort boxes for the children. From the French Consulate in New York."

The woman looked up, tipped her head to one side. "*You* sent the boxes? The children cherish the clothing. Exquisitely done."

"In fact, I sent that Ovaltine over there as well." I indicated an empty cardboard box.

"Thank you, Mademoiselle, but we sold that for next to nothing. The children complained it tasted like bird's nest and wouldn't drink it, I'm afraid. We need *money*, Miss Ferriday, not Ovaltine."

I took from the desk a tin can containing withered tulips, tossed the flowers into the wastebasket, and placed the can on the blotter to contain the drip.

"I know you are terribly busy, Madame, but I am looking for a child."

Madame eyed me. "Your child?"

"No, the parents were deported and are just now getting on their feet."

"I am sorry, but I can only deliver a child to the parent or blood relative. Two forms of identification required."

"I am just trying to locate the child. Her parents will collect her."

"Come with me," Madame said.

She grabbed her clipboard and a towering pile of nested tin bowls, and I followed her up wide stone steps. As we walked, Madame placed a tin bowl here and there as she found more drips.

"Any chance I can meet Mme Bertillion?" I asked.

"I am Mme Bertillion."

How was that possible?

"You wrote such lovely letters," I said.

"Some people are better on paper," Madame said with a tired shrug. Had she slept at all the night before? "What is the child's name?"

"I'm not sure, Madame. It was all done in a hurry. The mother was deported on the birthday."

"Which was?"

"April 1, 1941. Easter Sunday."

"Nazis deported people on Easter? Shocking those good men were not in church."

"Could you check your records?"

"You are looking at my records, Mademoiselle." She held up the clipboard, a sheaf of paper thick as a telephone book clamped there, ragged and marked with cross-outs and burgundy Olympic rings of wine stains. "We are a collection point for children from all over Europe. This will be a difficult search."

We walked into a high-ceilinged room filled with cots, each with a pillow and folded blanket at the foot.

"How do you identify the children?" I asked.

"Each is assigned a number. This number is printed on a small disk pinned to the chest. Some children came with names. Many did not." Madame placed her bowls on a chair. "During the war, some mothers wrote their child's name on a paper note and pinned it to the child before they dropped them here, but most notes fell off or were blurred in the rain. Some sewed trinkets to their children's clothes so they could identify them later, but many children changed clothes and swapped names with others. We still get several anonymous drop-offs daily."

"Surely *some* children remember their own names."

"The older ones, perhaps, but many arrive here mute from their terrible experiences, and a baby doesn't remember its name, does it? So we assigned them. We named them after their birth month if they knew it . . . You will find many Mais and Juins here. We named some after the patron saint of their birth month or after our friends and relatives . . . even pets."

"Can you at least check which children came in on that day?" I asked.

"It is not consistently noted. These children are coming from all over. Safe houses. Boarding schools. From farmers who've found them sleeping in haystacks. Some brought here by the only parents they've ever known find out for the first time they are not who they think they are."

"You must be overrun with parents searching."

"Some, but most of the children here will not be placed. Their parents are long gone. Or don't want them."

"No one would not want their own child."

"Really, Mademoiselle? You are an expert on this? Over one quarter of the children here are mixed. German father, French mother. Kraut kids, they call them. No one will be picking *those* children up. Others were born in Lebensborn production homes, Hitler's baby factories where racially good mothers anonymously gave birth to illegitimate children of SS men."

"But those homes were only in Germany—"

"No, Mademoiselle. There was quite an active one here in France. We've heard of them in Denmark, Belgium, and Holland as well. Several in Norway. Those babies are now pariahs. And who knows how many of these little blond ones were kidnapped from their mothers' arms—hundreds of thousands from Poland alone, meant to be raised as German. There is no record of their parents."

"I will check the list myself, Madame, if it would spare you the trouble."

Mme Bertillion stopped short and turned to me.

"You are used to getting your way, I can see." She picked up the tin bowls and thrust them into my hands, the pile tall and cold against my chest, reaching almost to my chin.

"If you distribute these, only *one* to a child—and they will try to get two out of you—I will look through my list, Mademoiselle. I will fetch you if I find a match. I am not doing this to help you because you came from the consulate, but because I have been on my feet since five this morning."

"Thank you, Madame. Where do I distribute the bowls?"

"Out there, of course," she said, holding an open palm toward a pair of doors.

"What do I do with the extra bowls?" Surely there were too many.

"There will be no extras," Madame said and bent her head to the list.

I pushed through the doors to a vast hall wainscoted in oak, probably once used for dancing and parties. The ceiling rose up one hundred feet, trompe l'oeil painted to give the impression of radiant summer sky, a nice substitute for the actual heavens that day. There must have been fifty refectory tables there, at which girls sat grouped by age from toddlers to teens. They sat still on their benches, hands in their laps, each quiet as a picture. Behind them, six white-frocked women stood beside steaming vats of soup, ready to serve once my bowls were distributed.

As I approached, all eyes were on my bowls and me. I stood for a moment, overwhelmed, and then recovered. These children were hungry.

I placed a bowl before the first child at the table.

"Merci, Madame," a child said.

I placed a bowl before the next child.

"Merci, Madame."

I checked the faces for any trace of Rena or Paul, but my task was soon overwhelming. Who knew if the child favored her parents? Was she even still alive?

I became skilled at handing out bowls and worked my way to the teens. At the beginning of the row, a girl of no more than thirteen sat with a toddler on her lap. The child was dressed in a periwinkle blue velvet shirt, its mother-of-pearl buttons still holding fast. Mother's handiwork. She would be happy.

"You are taking good care of her," I said to the girl.

"No need for two bowls, Mademoiselle. We share."

The toddler on her lap watched me go by as a stargazer watches a shooting star, and I continued down the row with my bowls.

Before long, Madame hurried down one row toward me.

"You are in luck, Mademoiselle." She paused to catch her breath, one hand to her lace collar. "We have a few children with that drop-off date, one girl that age."

I followed Madame down one row and up the next to a table of four-year-olds eating their soup, the only sound the scrape of their spoons against tin. The noise in the room magnified as I followed Madame. Colors sharpened. Would this be Paul's child? Finding her would mean extreme happiness for her parents but the opposite for me.

"A child born on April 1, 1941, would be in our four-year-old group, here," Madame said, as she checked a child's tag and presented her with a flourish. "Now, we have Bernadette."

She was a towheaded sparrow of a child, her skin almost translucent. She glanced up at me with a wary look.

"I don't know," I said. "It's hard to say, but I don't think so."

"That is the best I can do," Madame said. "I will keep an eye out for that birth date. Have the parents come in when they are well."

I lingered in the great hall that day and helped serve the rest of lunch. Madame and I ladled fragrant onion soup, thick with carrots and turnips, into the children's bowls and handed each child a small piece of bread. Their only words, *"Merci, Madame,"* were tremendous thanks. A plane flew overhead, and some hid under the tables, thinking they were still at risk. Many were shod with wooden blocks tied on with rope. I made a note to send shoes. And money.

I did my best to peer into the face of every child of about the right age, looking for any familiar sign. As Madame and I finished collecting the empty bowls on a tray, a teenager handed me hers. The child at her hip stopped me short.

"Madame, could you come?" I asked.

I set the tray down on the table. "Would you please look up the number of this child?"

Madame noted the child's number and went for her clipboard.

I couldn't tear my gaze away from the child. She was dark-haired and had almond-shaped eyes like Paul's and also his coral lips, but everything else about her was Rena. The copper skin, the curve of her nose—down to the ears peeking out from her hair.

"This child has no drop-off date," Madame said. "I am very sorry."

"This is the child, Madame. I'm certain of it."

"Her name is Pascaline," the teen said.

Mme Bertillion forced in a quick lungful of air.

"What is it?" I asked.

"I hate to admit it, but your intuition may be right, Miss Ferriday," Madame said, almost smiling.

"How so?" I asked. The room closed in on us.

"The child's name is *Pascaline*," Madame said, as if I had missed something obvious.

"So what, for heaven's sake?"

"Every good French Catholic knows the name Pascaline means born on Easter."

CHAPTER 31

Kasia

1945

THE SUMMER THE YEAR THAT ZUZANNA AND I CAME HOME TO Lublin I tried to stay optimistic, but it was hard. Once I learned what had happened during our almost four years at Ravensbrück, I couldn't understand why the world had never come to our aid. First with Hitler's invasion in 1939 from the west, then with the Soviet invasion the same month from the east. Though these invasions had caused Britain and France to declare war on Germany, not one Allied soldier had been sent to help us fight. Our first reports of Auschwitz, sent to the Western world by our Polish underground at great risk, had received no response either. Our reports of thousands of our Polish officers murdered in the forests near Katyn, Pietrik's father possibly among them, were ignored by the world as well.

So when this world rejoiced at Japan's surrender and the war was officially over, I did not rejoice. The war continued for us, just under a new dictator, Stalin. Though it was not fully apparent right away, Stalin's hand was already over us. Many of the leaders of the Polish resistance, several of them Pietrik's friends, were taken and eventually murdered by the Red Army and the NKVD, Stalin's brutal law enforcement agency. The NKVD were the nice people in charge of ferreting out "enemies of the people." They executed tens of thousands of Polish political prisoners and sent thousands more to the gulags. Instead of a fresh start, Poland got new forms of injustice.

As a result, we were careful about where we went and spent much time looking over our shoulders. One of the first things I did once I came home was check the secret hiding place Nadia and I had used to exchange books before the war. This was simply a place where teenaged girls had played detective once upon a time. I walked over to Nadia's old street, and the stone wall was still there, crumbling near the edges but still strong! Would the book Nadia left for me still be there?

I slid the stone from the spot in the wall, pulled out the book, and brushed the dust from the yellow cover. It was Kornel Makuszynski's *Satan from the Seventh Grade,* our favorite book we'd exchanged so many times. How had Nadia been able to leave it after she'd gone into hiding? I looked carefully about, to make sure no one was spying on me, sat with my back to the wall, and held the book. The musty scent of the cover brought back earlier days when life had been simpler, when the worst thing we had to worry about was a bad exam grade or an aching tooth.

The book opened naturally to chapter five, and Nadia's gift to me sat there, all ten of Pietrik's dance tickets she'd bought for me. I was too angry to cry at the wall that day, for the childhood we'd lost came rushing back. We had only wanted to chat with boys and dance and read mysteries. Now Nadia was gone, maybe forever. All I had left of her was a book and the photo buried in the back garden.

It was late afternoon by the time I made it home, and I brought up the idea of retrieving the photo of Nadia and the other treasures we'd buried at the start of the war.

"Maybe we should do this another time," Zuzanna said. This was not like my sister at all, to be standing there in the backyard wringing her hands. "Maybe once we are more acclimated it would be better. This can take an emotional—"

"Don't be so nervous," I said. "Why leave the only valuables we have in the *ground*?"

Papa and I shooed away her protests as he paced off the steps.

Ten, eleven, twelve.

Had the tin cans kept our most precious things safe?

Papa stood there for what seemed like a full minute, arms at his sides, the shovel loose in his hand. Was he crying? He then came alive, struck his shovel into the hard-packed earth, and dug like a man whose life depended on what was buried below.

He didn't have to dig long before we heard the shovel blade hit tin. All three of us scooped dirt out of the hole with our hands and helped Papa pull out the cans we'd buried so long ago. We sat, out of breath for a while, staring at the cans. Zuzanna cried just looking into that hole. Missing Matka? Part of me was happy to see her cry, since she seldom showed her grief.

Next Papa lifted out the tin box with the hinged lid. He opened the top, and it let out a little sigh as air was released. He closed it right away, but not before I saw his old silver revolver there. How many guns did we own now?

The millet was next, still surprisingly dry and maybe even edible, and then we started opening the tin cans. Papa handed one to me, and I scraped away the wax. I pulled the scarf from the can, and it unwound, the scent of Pietrik still there! I opened the next can to find the picture of Nadia and me on the cow. Even my Girl Guide uniform was in perfect shape and the corduroy dress that Matka had sewn for my sixteen-year-old body was still bright red. I pulled it on over my skirt and blouse, and it was even loose on me, since I'd still not gained back much weight. None of this caused me many tears, for I was happy to have my precious things back.

The last can I opened was a biscuit tin. I broke the wax seal and lifted off the lid. I pulled out Matka's sable brushes, like new inside their flannel wrap, and a surge of sadness rose up and crashed over me there in the yard. Matka was gone, and she would not be coming back to use her brushes. It was my fault too. I deserved to die for killing my mother. Papa and Zuzanna surrounded me with their arms as we crouched there by the hole, all crying by then.

THROUGH IT ALL, I kept up hope that Nadia and Pietrik would come back and checked the list of returning deportees each morning on the corkboard of the Red Cross Repatriation Center at Lublin Hospital. One especially fine late-summer morning I stopped there first thing to check. The staffers were polite, but I could tell they were tired of seeing me limp in every day. The pain in my leg slowed me up and gave them plenty of time to avoid me. When they saw me approach, they made themselves scarce or busied themselves with shuffling papers. If I did get a response from someone, it was curt.

"No. No Pietrik Bakoski. No Nadia Watroba either," the girl at the desk called out that morning before I said a word.

Next I walked to the postal center, to check the list Papa tacked up in the cool front lobby. By summer's end, the thick lists posted on the corkboard there had dwindled to one sad page. I ran my finger down the list, first by the W's and then the B's. Badowski, Baginski, Bajorek, Bakalar, Bal, Balcer. It felt good to read the names of those lucky few that returned, and I was often at the bottom of the list before I realized the name Pietrik Bakoski was not included there.

Papa came from his office, saw me at the list, and waved me to him.

"Kasia, my love, could you come see me in my office for a moment?"

Why was he being so formal all of a sudden?

I walked to his office, the same one he'd had for as long as I could remember, with its high tin ceiling and his wide oak desk covered with packages of every sort, all soon to be expertly delivered by Papa or one of his staff. Something seemed to be missing, and it took me a few seconds to realize what it was.

"Where is the flag, Papa?"

The Polish flag was one of the first things Papa had put back up in his office, once the Nazis left Lublin, much to the happiness of the postal center patrons. Had the new authorities pressured him to remove the flag? He was cooperating with them; it was clear.

Papa stepped to the window and pulled down the shade. "We don't have much time, but I had to tell you I've heard something. Don't be alarmed. This is something we can fix."

I don't know about you, but when someone says, "Don't be alarmed," I have trouble listening to the rest of what they say, since fear starts running up and down my body.

"What are you talking about, Papa?" I hadn't seen him so frightened since the night we buried our treasures in the backyard with Matka.

Matka. Every thought of her was still a fresh stab.

"I heard that there are rumors going around about you girls who came back from Ravensbrück."

"From who?"

"This is serious, Kasia. They are saying that you are not to be trusted."

"Don't believe all—"

"Zuzanna too."

This sent a real quake of fear through me. "Who is saying this?"

"The authorities—"

"Who? NKVD? Let me talk to them."

"This isn't something to take lightly, Kasia."

" 'Not to be trusted'? What does that even mean?"

"They think, because you were at Ravensbrück, a German camp, that you were working for the Germans. Contaminated by fascism."

"That's ridiculous."

"And you've been seen partaking in suspicious activity. Do you have a secret hiding place?"

"The wall by Nadia's house? That's child's play, Papa—"

"Well, stop it. You are being watched."

"Who can live in such a—"

"Do you want to go away again? This time for good? Get Zuzanna, and destroy any evidence you were there—"

"You're serious."

"Your Girl Guide uniform. Your letters I saved."

"But if they read the letters, they'd see—"

"They are not easily *reasoned* with, Kasia. Go. Now."

Zuzanna and I made a fire in the backyard that afternoon, as one often did to dispose of household trash, and burned the few things we had from the camp. We threw the bags we'd made from our old uniforms on the pyre. Regina's English book. My Girl Guide uniform.

I hesitated when it came to the urine letters I'd sent. Papa had kept them in the kitchen drawer, a neat stack that told the world of our troubles.

"I can't burn these," I said, my grip on the envelopes tightening.

"You listed every girl's name in those," Zuzanna said. "You have to protect them. Who cares about some old letters?"

I still hesitated.

Zuzanna snatched the top letter and handed it to me. "Here," she said and tossed the rest on the fire. At least I would save one.

As the fire burned, black bits of ash floated about, much as they had from the Ravensbrück chimneys. When we were done, almost all evidence of our camp life was gone.

Who needed such things anyway, we told ourselves. Souvenirs of a terrible time. But it made the black spot in my chest grow larger. I was a *patriot*. I took an oath to serve my country. I gave up my youth, my mother, my first love, and my best friend for Poland. For this I was accused of being an enemy spy?

I TRIED TO FOCUS on good things. Even with the terrible shortage of food and the confusion of people returning to Lublin, there was a ray of optimism surrounding the reopening of demolished factories. The universities were not up and running again, but the Red Cross taught basic nursing classes at the hospital.

I headed there one late-summer morning, hoping to get some nursing practice. I stepped into the back wing of the hospital, happy to see it had survived the bombings somewhat intact. The massive ward on the second floor was filled with rows of canvas cots divided almost equally, half occupied by Russian soldiers, the other half by Polish civilians from the camps and other places. Russian nurses and medics brought the wounded, presenting with every type of injury imaginable, in on canvas stretchers.

"We're off to Warsaw soon," said Karolina Uznetsky, one of my favorite nurses, as she unfolded a cot. "The army is taking over the hospital." She filled a basin with warm water.

"I'll miss you all," I said, instead of what I really wanted to say: Please stay. You leave, and who will be here when Pietrik comes back? Leaving means you've given up on survivors.

"How about a free class on the bed bath?" Karolina said.

"Yes, please," I said.

Such an opportunity! The bed bath was known to be more complicated than it sounded.

"Let us start over here," Karolina said.

She carried a basin of water and a stack of towels straight toward a particularly damaged row of soldiers. The facial injuries were the hardest to deal with. They'd taken the mirrors in the lavatories down for a reason. I forced myself to look. How could I be a nurse if I couldn't deal with such things? Suddenly I could not recall even basic Red Cross training. Karolina stood at the cot of one of the worst, a dark-haired man who slept curled on his side. The blood that had seeped through the gauze wrapped around his head had dried black.

"First, introduce yourself to the patient," Karolina said, indicating the man on the cot. "We can skip this step, for the patient is unresponsive."

It would not be exaggeration to say I idolized Karolina. She was everything a good nurse should be. Smart. Levelheaded in the face of gruesome injury. Pleasant. I would have to work on *all* these things.

"Ordinarily we would pull the curtain for patient privacy," Karolina said, "but we will go right to the washcloths and rubber gloves."

I pushed my hands into the gloves, smooth and powdery inside, the smell of the rubber somehow hopeful. Karolina folded a washcloth over my gloved hand like a mitt.

"Begin the bath with the face, no soap used there. Eyes first."

I sat on a chair next to the patient and started with the eyes, reaching the cloth into the deep sockets and moving outward. Could he even feel it?

The soldier next to him lay on his back, arms splayed, snoring louder than any person I'd heard snore before, and there had been many candidates at Ravensbrück.

"Try to use a different part of the washcloth for every stroke," Karolina said. "You are a natural, Kasia." Her words made me puff up with pride. My mother had been a nurse after all. Maybe it was in the blood?

There was something satisfying about washing the survivors, revealing clean swaths of pink skin under all that grime, the dirt drifting to the bottom of the bowl. When I finished, the water in the bowl was dark brown so I replaced it with clean water at the tap.

When I returned, medics came with two more Russian soldiers and placed them near us, one with a skull fracture, the other unresponsive. I started a fresh bed bath on one. These men had not washed in months. I knew how that felt.

"You're good at this, Kasia," Karolina said. "You really should think about coming with us to Warsaw. We could use the help."

I wiped the washcloth down the soldier's forehead and across one cheek.

Why not go to Warsaw? Papa might miss me, but his ladylove Marthe wouldn't care.

"The training is first-rate," Karolina said.

"Maybe," I said. I was ready for a new adventure. Warsaw would be a fresh start. And I was good at this.

I moved on to the next patient and began with the face. I was making good time. Soon, I would be done with the whole row.

I ran the washcloth across the bridge of the nose to uncover fresh pink skin, and . . .

I froze, midwipe.

"What is it, Kasia?" Karolina asked.

My mind registered it all, but my body was stuck. I breathed deeply through my nose and grabbed the stretcher handle for support. It would not look good to have a nurse in training faint right there in the ward.

CHAPTER 32

Kasia

1945

IT COULDN'T POSSIBLY BE HIM. PIETRIK. HOW MANY TIMES HAD my mind played such tricks? *The tooth.* I pulled his upper lip up with my thumb.

"What are you doing, Kasia?" Karolina set her basin on the floor and walked over to me.

My God, *yes.* The chipped tooth, just a little off the side. That gorgeous tooth. I sat for a few moments waiting for my body to catch up with my brain. Yes, it was he. I kissed him all over his face, dirt and everything. He stayed unconscious through it all.

"Kasia," Karolina said, eyes wide.

I called to the other nurses, waving—I must have looked like a castaway on a desert island—unable to get the words out. The nurses ran over, and Karolina told them I was having a mental breakdown of some sort, kissing and crying over a Russian soldier.

"It's him, it's him," was all I could say.

"*Who*, Kasia?" Karolina asked. "Who is it? Calm down, now."

"It's Pietrik," I said.

"Your Pietrik? Are you sure?"

I could only nod yes, and the girls hugged and kissed me.

They helped me change Pietrik out of his dirty uniform and finish his bed bath. He remained unconscious, and I sat with him holding his hand, reveling in my good fortune. I asked the nurses to go and get Zuzanna while I stayed with Pietrik, afraid he would disappear.

Through a translator, we learned the Russian man in the next cot had fought alongside Pietrik. Once the Russians liberated Majdanek concentration camp, the Red Army had pressed Pietrik into service. He said Pietrik had been at Majdanek since he'd been arrested and had worked with the rest of the slave laborers there to finish building the camp.

Zuzanna and Papa helped me move Pietrik home to my bedroom that evening. He had lost much of his body fat, but Zuzanna examined him and said it was possible he would recover. She had seen a lot of head trauma. Many times, once the swelling subsided, the patient regained normal brain function.

IT WAS WEEKS BEFORE Pietrik opened his eyes and even longer before he spoke, but I was grateful for every small step. I carried a matchbox in which to place a piece of sausage or a bit of ham for him whenever I had a chance, and in time he grew stronger. Zuzanna and I celebrated his first words, "Turn up the radio, please," with our own private party while Pietrik watched from his bed with the trace of a smile on his lips. He was like a bird I'd seen once knocked unconscious after flying headfirst into our kitchen window. He came to be himself slowly. And then suddenly one day he was up and walking again.

We didn't press for details of his years at Majdanek, and he didn't volunteer them. We each carried our own bag of troubles.

Once he could walk, Pietrik made up for lost time and was hired to be the caretaker for the glassworks factory, which the owner reopened. As his body filled out, he also took a job driving ambulances for the Lublin Ambulance Corps. But for all his physical improvements, it was as if Pietrik had a piece missing. The kissing piece mostly. He sank all effort into his work, avoiding any chance of romance with me. I devised excuses for this: He was too tired. Too sad. Too happy.

ONE MORNING I WOKE to the rumble of thunder, thinking I was back at Ravensbrück, the bombs thudding in the distance. I relaxed once I saw the drops on my bedroom window, though—once I remembered I was to ride alongside Pietrik in the ambulance that day. As a nurse in training, I got to sit up front with the driver. Since he avoided being alone with me then, barely even *touched* me, it was nice to be so close to him all morning with nothing but the stick shift between us. The rain would keep him in the ambulance cab, windows up, all to myself.

I arranged myself there in the front seat of the ambulance, feeling smart in my white nurse-in-training uniform and cap. Maybe he would kiss me. Could I kiss him first? That was terribly forward of course, but what did I know about such things? I'd been locked away for some of my teen years, the time you learn the rituals of romance.

Did Pietrik even still find me attractive? The white stockings we all wore did little to camouflage my bad leg. Every so often people would stop and stare, openmouthed, a "what happened to *you*" look on their faces. Did he find me grotesque? What if I told him what Luiza had said? That he loved me? But I could never betray her dying wish.

"Such traffic," he said, downshifting. "Where is everyone getting gas in this town? We'll take the long way to the hospital."

Since he'd come home, Pietrik got impatient and angry at the smallest thing. Snarled traffic. A mispronounced word. A sprinkle of rain.

"There's no rush," I said. "Just delivering stretchers."

The rain was coming down harder now, the windshield wipers

fighting a losing battle. A gully washer, Matka would have called it. Matka.

We turned down Nadia's street.

"We are going to drive by her house," I said.

"I know, Kasia. I can see."

"You never told me what 'Zegota' meant. On the envelope I picked up."

"The Council to Aid Jews. Nadia's mother knew one of the founders."

"Where did you hide them?"

"I'd rather not—"

"You can't avoid talking about it forever."

He downshifted and busied himself with driving, his gaze directed at the road.

"They lived in different safe apartments," he said eventually. "Until they weren't safe anymore. Z's basement for a time. Once we were arrested . . ."

Traffic slowed as we drove closer to Nadia's old apartment, the orange door shiny with rain.

I saw it first: the black heap of wet fur on the doorstep.

"Stop, Pietrik. It's Felka."

"Again?" Pietrik said.

He pulled the emergency brake, turned on the flashing lights atop the vehicle, and jumped out. I scrambled out too, as best I could from the high ambulance cab, and got to the top of the stairs. There was Felka curled on the doormat, drenched with rain, but looking only a bit sheepish.

The new residents were the Riskas, a nice teacher and his wife, who had been bombed out in Warsaw. Mrs. Riska was a cousin of Mrs. Bakoski's, and they'd moved to Lublin, lured by the new government's offer of free housing. The government had to make this offer since many Polish people were wary of the new government and stayed away, worried that Poland might not end up as free and independent as Stalin claimed. Even with free houses offered, so many still stayed in London or other places, waiting to see.

The Riskas were understanding about Felka showing up on their stoop so often and called us whenever they found her there. Papa tried everything to keep her home. Locked her in the house. Tied her up. But she still managed to escape. We all knew who she was waiting for.

Cars started lining up, blocked behind the ambulance, as we tried to lure her back to the dry cab.

"Come, girl," said Pietrik, sweet as could be, but Felka wouldn't budge. "You take her front. I'll take the rear," he said.

We carried Felka back to the street. Once the drivers in the cars saw the ambulance was stopped for a canine and not a human needing care, the horns started honking.

We managed to get her into the cab of the ambulance and lay her between us, and I wrapped a terry cloth towel around her. As Pietrik pulled away from the house, Felka shivered and shook, sending water flying about the cab and onto our faces. I brushed a smear of dirt off the front of my uniform. So much for the kiss.

"Nadia could still be out there somewhere," I said.

"Dry behind Felka's ears. She likes that."

I brushed the towel over the dog's head and under her grizzled muzzle.

"DPs are still coming home."

"Don't call her a displaced person, Kasia. Tell the truth. She was murdered by the Nazis and is gone. Just like the rest."

"At least your mother gets a memorial service tomorrow."

"It's not just hers, Kasia. It's for two hundred people, and it's going to be a circus. Please don't go."

"Papa said there will be NKVD agents there."

"What will they do to me? Kill me? As long as it's quick, I'll welcome it."

"They are looking for AK members. Any high-ranking member of the underground—"

"I was a Red Army *soldier*, Kasia——"

"Against your will . . ."

"So that gets me a pass for now."

"Papa said——"

"Enough '*Papa said*,' Kasia. Don't you think for yourself any-more?"

I rubbed Felka's belly with the towel, and she turned over onto her back, legs in the air.

"Maybe I shouldn't have done your couriering for you," I said.

"Don't you think I live with that every day? Not only my sister, who was barely out of braces, but your mother, who was dear to me too, Kasia, dead. And what they did to *you*? And here I am, healthy and fine. What kind of a man am I? Sometimes I think, if I didn't have you . . ."

He turned and looked at me.

". . . I wouldn't want to be here."

I searched his face. Had he really said that? He fixed his gaze back on the road, but I'd heard it. *If I didn't have you.*

I reached for his hand, resting on the seat.

"Don't say that, Pietrik. It's a mortal sin, and——"

He pulled his hand away.

"Never mind," he said, two hands back on the wheel. He drove on, lost in thought. "Forget I said it."

It was good to see a bit of Pietrik's old self. But like the sun coming out on a cloudy day, it disappeared just as fast as it had emerged.

I DIDN'T HONOR PIETRIK'S request not to go to the memorial service at Lublin Castle. It was held to honor the lives of the forced laborers murdered there by the Nazis before they withdrew, including Pie-trik's mother. I had loved Mrs. Bakoski and needed to mourn with the others. All of Lublin would be there. And besides, I knew many of the families with mothers, sisters, and husbands who'd died that day. Everyone knew someone impacted by that mass murder.

I started the day in the castle chapel, once Matka's favorite place, kneeling high above the gathering crowds below. The chapel had become my special place to steal away to as well. To pray and talk with my mother and stay warm. The beautiful Byzantine frescoes had not yet been completely uncovered then, but I could see bits of them along the high ceilings between the Gothic arches. I prayed for my usual list: Papa. Zuzanna. Pietrik. For the souls of the dead and missing. Nadia. Matka.

From the chapel window I considered the gathering crowd below, scattered down the grassy slope outside the great wall of the castle. People had come from all over Poland to pay respects. The church choir sang as people, old and young, clustered there in groups, jockeying for the choicest front spots with the best views of the service. Collections of black-frocked priests. A gaggle of Dominican nuns, their white headpieces like giant swans. Lublin families. Papa and Marthe in there somewhere. Zuzanna would be listening to it all from an open window at the hospital.

I descended the spiral staircase slowly, for my bad leg and slippery stone stairs were a scary combination, and emerged out in the stone courtyard where we'd all once been rounded up to be transported to Ravensbrück. Had I been standing there with Matka, Luiza, and Zuzanna just five years before?

I made my way down the grassy slope and pushed through the crowd. Though it had been a warm fall, it was cold that day. People in the crowd carried bouquets. Mostly globeflowers, scarlet corn poppies, and other wildflowers. I held some fall daisies I'd found growing in an empty lot. I'd wrapped them in a wet dishrag, and the cold water burned my hand even through the glove I wore.

I blew on my free hand as I scanned the crowd for Pietrik. What I wouldn't give for two gloves! I had split a pair with Zuzanna after a dying woman had gifted it to her at the hospital. I had the right one; Zuzanna the left.

It was hard to imagine more than three hundred people buried there under that slope in the shadow of the great fortress. Family members stood along the base of the castle grounds where townspeople had hastily buried the murdered in that mass grave. Someone had pounded a great wooden cross into the heart of the hill, and six priests stood below it.

The priests blessed the grave site, and I made my way through the crowd looking for Pietrik. Would he be angry I came? Should I just give up on him? A girl could only take so much rejection.

I approached a group of nuns clustered at one end, prayer candles and cards in their hands, a few of them with wreaths draped over their arms. I spotted Pietrik off to the side of them. He stood alone, back straight, hands deep in his glassworks canvas coat pockets, eyes on the service. He was near the edge of a great pile of flowers that mourners had assembled there, a growing mound of reds and pinks and yellows. I inched down the slope to him, pain stabbing my leg with each step.

I shimmied through the group of nuns, lingering briefly in their warmth, swishing through the sea of black habits, rosary beads long at their waists. I emerged and walked toward Pietrik. If he saw me approach, he gave no sign of it. As I drew closer, I saw his face was splotched red about the eyes. I made my way to him and stood nearby. I fisted my naked hand and blew hot breath on it.

Pietrik turned to look at me, his eyelashes spiky with tears. I stepped to the mound of flowers and set my daisies atop it, then turned and walked back to him.

Should I stay? I'd left my flowers, had done what I'd come to do, paid my respects. He'd asked me not to come, after all.

Receiving no gesture from Pietrik, I turned to go and just then felt his hand on my arm. I almost could not believe it as I watched his fingers make their way around my wrist. He pulled me to him to stand by his side.

"Proud" is a word that is too commonly used, but that is how I felt there that day, listening to the choir sing to heaven. Such pride that Pietrik wanted me to share it all with him. The good and the bad.

He reached for my bare hand and held it, his warm fingers around mine, brought it to his lips to kiss, and tucked it in his pocket, the flannel warm inside.

CHAPTER 33

Kasia

1946

THE ARMY ARRIVED FROM ALL DIRECTIONS. NOT SINCE HITLER'S blitzkrieg had there been such an organized onslaught. In flowered dresses and sensible shoes, they came, hauling pots and dishes, some still steaming, fresh from the oven. General Marthe coordinated the effort at the postal center, resulting in enough pierogies and beet soup and hunter's stew to feed six wedding parties.

You think a postal center an odd place for a wedding party? Maybe, but it served well for our purposes. It is a big, open space with a high ceiling, and you can kill two pheasants with one stone there: pick up your mail and dance with the bride. Not that the bride could dance, but guests pinned money to my dress anyway. I wore a pale pink dress, not my choice, for Marthe had surprised me with a product of her own sewing machine. I'd wanted white, but it was impossible to turn down this dress, for I was trying to be civil, for Papa. I just wanted it all to be over so I could be alone with Pietrik.

It had been a difficult morning for two reasons. One was that the Riskas had phoned to say Felka had died the day before. They'd found her on their front stoop one last time. We buried Felka in our back garden. Zuzanna and Papa came by and watched as Pietrik dug his spade into the earth, and I wrapped Felka in Nadia's blanket I'd brought her home in so many years ago. We all cried saying goodbye to our old girl, Papa harder than any of us.

I couldn't help think that Felka had been a loyal friend to Nadia, waiting for her till the end, unlike me, who'd moved on with my life, planning my wedding with barely a thought that Nadia would not be there. Some friend I was.

The other difficult thing on my wedding morning was the blessing by the mother of the bride. So important is this blessing at a Polish wedding that if the bride's mother is deceased the wedding party walks to the cemetery to visit her grave before going to the church. Of course we could not visit the lake at Ravensbrück, where Matka's ashes had probably gone. Marthe had prepared a long blessing, but I chose Zuzanna to give the blessing instead, causing the heat to rise in Marthe's face. Resigned as I was to making amends with Marthe, it was not always easy. Zuzanna came first in my life and always would.

The ceremony at the church was brief. Though free elections had still not taken place and the Stalinist authorities were not in official control, Moscow's Polish Workers' Party was becoming more entrenched by the day. They discouraged anything that distracted workers from the collective needs of the people, including church weddings. They considered them gaudy spectacles, so people were wary of being seen at them. As a result, only three of my nurse friends braved the ceremony, though it could have cost them their jobs. The few friends Pietrik had left from the underground were still hiding out in the forest. We all were careful, since just putting flowers on a former AK member's grave was cause for arrest.

Guests were not shy about celebrating at the postal center, though, for it was somewhat private there. As soon as I arrived, guests surrounded me and pinned paper money to my dress, my favorite tradition of all. Where had Marthe and her friends gotten such food? Cold cuts, sausages, salads. Tree cake and delicate pastry angel wings! Maybe the food came from *na lewo*. The black market.

"Come. It's time for *oczepiny*," Marthe said.

Oczepiny is the ritual of taking off the bride's veil and replacing it with a cap to show she is officially married. First the single women surround the bride and take her veil; then the married ones circle the bride and pin the cap.

Marthe clapped her hands above her head, and the single girls came around. "Zuzanna, remove the veil."

"She knows what to do, Marthe," I said.

The band played, and the young girls circled me, hands together, as my sister took the hairpins from Pietrik's mother's veil. My bad leg ached from standing so long, but how could I go sit with the old ladies on their folding chairs lined up against the wall? I'd dreamed of this wedding ritual since childhood.

Zuzanna handed the veil to me and joined the circle. I covered my eyes with one hand and tossed the veil with my other, timing it perfectly for it to land in Zuzanna's hands. God willing, she would be next.

"Now married ladies assemble," Marthe called to the crowd.

She held the white cap in her hand. Where was Pietrik? He was missing it all.

"Who will pin the cap?" I asked.

"I will," Marthe said.

"But a married woman must do that." The married women gathered about me in a circle, hands together.

Marthe stepped closer. "Kasia, that's just an old folk tradition."

The married women began circling around Marthe and me to the music. The smell of violet perfume and beet soup was overpowering. I grabbed a hand at random and pulled the tanner's wife into the middle of the circle. "Mrs. Wiznowsky will pin my cap."

Marthe took my hand. "Kasia. Please let me do this."

One look at her brown eyes tearing up was all I needed. She had been good to me after all. Had fed Pietrik, Zuzanna, and me back to health. I let Marthe pin my cap and she burst out in a smile. You've never seen a happier person in your life.

I broke out of the circle, the paper bills flapping as I walked. Where was Pietrik? He'd been so quiet all day. I stopped on my way to find him to let a friend of Papa's pin another zloty note to my dress.

I found Pietrik in Papa's office, alone, slumped in the old leather desk chair, hands in his lap. The lamps were off, and a glint of light from a streetlamp hit the glass on a picture on the desk. It was Papa's favorite, though my eyes were half-closed in it. The one with his arms around Zuzanna and me, taken by my mother.

"Come and join the party." I brushed the millet from Pietrik's hair, still there from when guests had thrown it as we left the church. The millet Papa had buried that night so long ago. Dangerous as it was to call attention to the ceremony, I was happy some had not been able to let the tradition of throwing millet go.

I knelt beside Pietrik.

"You haven't eaten a thing. The hunter's stew's almost gone, and they just brought more of those sausages you like. Plus they're going to dance the kujawiak."

"Soon, Kasia."

Pietrik was a quiet person, but he had never been given to such brooding.

"They are wondering where the groom is," I said.

He was quiet for a long minute, his face in shadows. "What a coward I am, Kasia. My old underground reports hiding in the woods eating grass while I'm here feasting."

The music in the other room reached a fever pitch.

"It's not your fault Papa wants to protect his son-in-law. We have our troubles too, you know——"

"I am just thinking. About what my father would do if he were here. He was no coward."

Though Pietrik seldom spoke of it, more rumors had surfaced about Katyn Forest, and though the Russians blamed the Nazis, we all knew it was the Russian NKVD who'd murdered thousands of

Polish intelligentsia there. Captain Bakoski had most likely been among those executed.

"What are you talking about?"

I put my head in his lap and felt something cold and hard in his hand. As he pulled it away I saw a glint of light on silver.

"Papa's gun?" I said. "Are you——"

"It makes me feel better to hold it," Pietrik said.

I eased the gun from his hand.

"You'd better get back," Pietrik said. "The bride can't just disappear."

Simply touching that gun, smooth and heavy, made my whole body cold. "They want to see you as well," I said.

He made no effort to grab the gun back.

I opened Papa's desk drawer and placed it inside.

"Oh, Pietrik," I said, kneeling next to him.

We stayed there in the dark together for some time and listened to the guests sing as the band played "Sto Lat." One hundred years of happiness for the bride and groom.

CHAPTER 34

Herta

1947

THE SO-CALLED DOCTORS TRIAL AT NUREMBERG WAS A FARCE from beginning to end, and the trauma of it caused me a series of debilitating bronchial infections. The waiting. The reams of paper that could have been burned to keep good Germans from freezing. The 139 trial days, eighty-five witnesses, and endless defendant cross-examinations.

Dr. Gebhardt's testimony alone was three days long and especially difficult to watch. As he explained the operations in great detail, he only dragged Fritz and me down with him. Gebhardt even offered to have the same operation performed on himself to prove how harmless the procedures were, but his offer was ignored.

And why did I ask my lawyer, Dr. Alfred Seidl, to tell me the fates of Binz and Marschall from the trial of Ravensbrück camp staff, the so-called Ravensbrück trial at Hamburg, on the day I was to testify? It only roused more fear about going on the stand that morning.

"They took Elizabeth Marschall first," Alfred said, "then Dorothea Binz. And Vilmer Hartman last. Ladies first, I suppose."

My abdominal muscles contracted as he indicated the picture in the newspaper. It showed Vilmer, hands fastened behind his back, neck broken at the fifth vertebra, his feet hanging there in their beautiful shoes. He had dropped well. The noose knot, placed under his left jaw, had broken the axis bone, which in turn severed the spinal cord. I scanned the pictures of the others, all hung like ducks on a hunter's rack, and was convulsed with a terrible fear, which sent tremors to my hands. Many of them had turned to religion before they walked up the thirteen steps to the gallows. All were buried in nameless graves.

That day's events in court did nothing to calm me either. First up, a Rabbit from Ravensbrück on the witness stand.

"Can you identify Dr. Herta Oberheuser?" Alexander Hardy, associate counsel for the prosecution, asked. He was a reasonably attractive man with a receding hairline.

The Rabbit pointed to me. How could that be? They remembered me? I had no memory of them. They knew my name? We'd been so careful. Alfred had told me the Poles asked to have me extradited to Poland to stand trial. Only *me*. Had others not done much worse? Alfred had challenged this request and won.

Soon it was my turn.

"We call Herta Oberheuser to the stand," Hardy said.

Fritz gave me a look designed to instill courage. I took a deep breath, the blood pounding in my head. I made my way to the stand, the crowd a blur, and scanned the balcony for Mutti.

"How could you participate in the sulfonamide experiments in good conscience, Herta Oberheuser?" Hardy asked.

"Those prisoners were Polish women who were sentenced to death," I said. "They were scheduled to die anyway. That research helped German soldiers. *My blood.*"

I found Mutti in the balcony, fingers raised to her lips. No Gunther?

Hardy waved a sheaf of papers in my direction. "Were any persons shot or executed after they had been subjected to these experiments?"

"Yes, but they were political prisoners with—" The red lightbulb attached to the witness stand in front of me lit up. The interpreters were having trouble keeping up. I would have to slow down. "Political . . . prisoners with . . . death sentences."

"And in your affidavit in connection with lethal injections, you admit that you gave five or six lethal injections. Is that correct?"

Why had I admitted that in my affidavit? Could I pretend not to understand the translator?

"No," I said.

"Well, you gave injections, and after such injections the persons died, did they not?"

"Yes, but as I've said in previous examinations, it was a matter of medical aid to patients in their dying agony."

"And this medical aid resulted in death, did it not?" Hardy asked.

I kept my gaze fixed on my hands in my lap. "No."

"I said, 'And this medical aid resulted in death, did it not?' " Hardy said.

My heart pounded as I studied my hands. "As I said, these patients were in their dying agony."

"Miss Oberheuser, were you ever given any awards or medals?"

"I received the War Merit Cross, if I remember correctly."

"And for what reason did you receive that medal?"

"I don't know."

Hardy leaned on his podium. "Was it for your participation in the sulfonamide experiments?"

"Certainly not."

"I have no further questions, Your Honor."

Though evidence of American experiments similar to those we were charged with was presented and visibly shook the American judges, in the end, the verdicts hinged on the issue of whether the subjects of the experiments had been volunteers. All I could do was wander the orchard in the prison exercise yard and wait.

Fritz seemed devastated by the trial. While some of the doctors took it in stride and tried to research their way out of convictions, Fritz became withdrawn. We were not allowed to talk while in the courtroom, but he once spoke to me as he entered the elevator down to our cells.

"They may as well hang me now," he said. "I'm finished."

Fritz was the only Doctors Trial defendant who was openly repentant, a fact that did not go unnoticed among the other doctors, the rest of whom stayed resolute to the end.

The day of our sentencing, August 20, 1947, I wore a black, long-sleeved wool coatdress with a white bow collar provided by the court. My heart hammered at my sternum as I listened to my colleagues' sentences announced one at a time in the great room. I waited my turn in the hallway behind the wooden courtroom door, a silent American guard at my side. I knew enough English by then to understand Dr. Gebhardt's fate.

"Dr. Karl Gebhardt, Military Tribunal One has found and adjudged you guilty of war crimes, crimes against humanity, and membership in an organization declared criminal by the judgment of the International Military Tribunal, as charged under the indictment heretofore filed against you. For your said crimes on which you have been and now stand convicted, Military Tribunal One sentences you, Karl Gebhardt, to death by hanging."

It was becoming increasingly difficult to breathe. When my turn came, the door slid open, I stepped into the courtroom, and put on my translation headphones. The room took on a vivid color, saturated and intense, as I searched the crowd for Mutti.

"Herta Oberheuser, Military Tribunal One has found and adjudged you guilty of war crimes and crimes against humanity, as charged under the indictment heretofore filed against you."

Once I heard the word *"schuldig"* in my translation headphones, I grabbed the railing.

Guilty.

Then came the sentence. I listened, numbed. "For your said crimes on which you have been and now stand convicted, Military Tribunal One sentences you, Herta Oberheuser, to imprisonment for a term of twenty years, to be served at such prison or prisons, or other appropriate place of confinement, as shall be determined by competent authority."

I was careful to show no trace of reaction to the sentence. Fritz was sentenced to life in prison, and many of the others were doomed to join Gebhardt at the gallows. I would be an old woman when released. In the one minute and forty seconds it took to sentence me, they stripped me of a lifetime of work.

ON JUNE 2, 1948, Dr. Gebhardt was hanged on one of the three portable gallows in the prison gymnasium. I read in the paper that the nooses they used that day were not adjusted properly and several of the defendants lingered, alive, for almost ten minutes. The Americans couldn't even execute a death sentence properly. I was glad the Führer had taken his own life and had not been able to see that travesty. They soon bused me to War Criminal Prison Number 1 in Landsberg, Bavaria, to begin my sentence. The thought of not practicing medicine for all those years was debilitating, and I started my letter writing campaign.

To the mayor of Stocksee went my first.

CHAPTER 35

Kasia

1947

I SCREAMED MOST OF WEDNESDAY, MARCH 25, 1947. AT PEOPLE'S Hospital in Lublin, we nurses were happy to hear such screams, for it meant a healthy mother. A quiet birth was often a sad one. I was pleased that my baby's lung function was productive as well, for as a maternity nurse myself, I'd seen things go wrong in seconds. Breech births. Blue babies. Our doctors were excellent (including my sister), but it was the maternity division nurses who made it hum. I was lucky it was a routine labor, since pain medication and other drugs were in short supply.

Pietrik stood next to my bed, swaddled baby in his arms, and every nurse on the floor gathered around him. He wore a white hospital smock over his factory coveralls and held her in a most natural way, not stiff and awkward like so many new fathers. As kind as my visitors were, I just wanted to be alone with the baby and get to know our girl.

"Give her back, Pietrik," I said, my vocal cords raw.

Pietrik laid the baby back in my arms. I was soon sleepy, since it was warm for such a large ward—over fifty beds. My ward supervisor had reserved the best one for me, on the far wall away from the drafty windows, next to the radiator. I breathed the baby's sweet-sour scent and watched the fontanel atop her head beat out a soft rhythm. She was as blond as Mrs. Mikelsky's baby. Jagoda would have been how old by now? Eight? Should we name our baby Jagoda? That might be too sad. Maybe a name like Irenka.

Hope.

Pietrik lobbied for the name Halina, arguing my mother would have wanted that. But didn't he see it would be too painful to say my dead mother's name ten times a day?

The series of bells signaling visitor time rang, and the nurses scattered. Marthe was first to arrive. She carried a plate of *paczkis* in one hand, napkins in the other.

"We come bearing gifts," she said. "*Paczki* for the mother?" Papa brought up the rear bearing Marthe's purse.

"No, thank you," I said. I felt as round and fat as a *paczki* myself. When would Zuzanna be back to fend off Marthe? She'd assisted at the delivery but had been called away to set a fracture.

Marthe placed a sugar-frosted *paczki* on a napkin and set it next to me. "This is no time for a slenderizing course."

I resisted sweets since I not only had baby fat to lose, but a cavity in my left canine tooth as well, a souvenir from Ravensbrück, and which stung when it met with sugar.

My father kissed my hand, then my forehead and the baby's too. "How are you, Kasia?"

Pietrik lifted the baby from my arms, leaving me cold. He handed Papa the baby, Marthe's purse still on Papa's arm.

"We are thinking of naming her Halina," Pietrik said.

"Well, I like the name Irenka," I said. "It means hope——"

"Halina, of course," Papa said. "How nice."

Were those tears in his eyes?

"She favors you, Pietrik," Marthe said. "Will you christen her at home? Don't even think about a church."

She was right. The Polish Workers' Party no longer simply suggested a ban on religious ceremonies, including baptisms and weddings. It openly discouraged them and made life terribly difficult for those who disobeyed. Marthe and Papa were still not married, though many priests wed couples in secret.

Marthe scooped the baby from Papa's arms. "This may be hard for you, Kasia, with your bad leg once you come home. I will take care of the baby."

As Marthe cooed over the baby, a dark wave crashed over me. Why wasn't my mother here? Matka would walk the ward with the baby and show her off. She would tell me stories of myself as a child and make me laugh about it all.

All at once, my face was wet with tears. I'd helped hundreds of mothers fight baby blues, but it was harder than it appeared, like being sucked down into a dark hole.

"I need the baby back, please," I said.

Suddenly I wanted them all gone, Pietrik too. If I couldn't have my mother, I wanted no one.

Pietrik took the baby from Marthe, who looked pained to release her, and placed her back in my arms.

"Kasia needs to rest," he said.

Marthe gathered her plate of *paczkis*. "We'll be back tomorrow with pierogies."

"No thank you," I said. "They feed us well here."

Once they left and Pietrik went back to the factory, the baby and I drifted in and out of sleep. When the radiator started hissing steam, I woke with a start thinking I was back on the train to Ravensbrück, the train's whistle screaming as we came to the platform. My heart raced, but I calmed once I looked at the baby. She shifted in my arms.

Halina? So she would have my mother's name after all? As it was, I could barely look at my mother's picture without falling to pieces. More terrifying, could the child's name somehow cause her to follow Matka's terrible path? To live a wonderful life, cut short? A shiver ran through me. Stranger things have happened.

Once Pietrik and Papa started calling the baby Halina, I gave in and soon called her that myself. I needed to grow up after all. I was a mother now, with responsibilities, no longer a child. Plus, everyone said it was a beautiful name, and it suited the baby. It honored my mother, and she would have been pleased.

But somehow I couldn't shake the notion I should have named her Hope.

CHAPTER 36

Caroline

1946–1947

ONCE I FOUND THE CHILD AND ARRANGED FOR HER PARENTS to fetch her, I stayed in Paris doing my best to avoid Paul. He was a father now, and I wanted no part in disrupting his family. It was easy to avoid him since they remained at Rena's house in Rouen.

You might think there is no better place to salve a wounded psyche than the City of Love, but that year, after the war ended, every park bench teemed with lovers kissing in public, some before breakfast, vivid reminders of my lost love. Even the news from home was grim, for Roger wrote that our elevator boy, Cuddy, had been killed in action in the Pacific.

I became like a drug addict, the withdrawal from Paul hellish. No sleep, no appetite. Why could I not move on to a higher purpose? So I would remain unmarried, alone for the rest of my life. Worse things had happened to people.

It didn't help that letters from Paul choked our letter box. Mother lobbed each one into a basket in the living room with a labored stage sigh. More than once I flipped through them admiring Paul's handwriting and held a few to the light. But why read them? It would only prolong the agony.

I felt like Paris had cheated on me. We'd both been dealt a blow, but only she was recovering, starting to rebuild and clear the rubble. If the fashion industry was any indication, Paris was back, already holding elaborate fashion shows in the grand haute couture houses and magazine shoots against backdrops of ruined buildings, while I was still reduced to tears by a crippled pigeon or an old fruit man with three wormy apples arranged on a towel to sell.

MONTHS PASSED. I WOKE one November morning and vowed to immerse myself in work and not think of Paul even once more that day. There were no new letters in the basket, and fortunately there was still much to be done in Paris since rebuilding was in full swing. Turning oneself to the misfortunes of others is the best way to dispense with personal troubles. Hadn't Lord Byron himself said, "The busy have no time for tears"?

Gasoline remained in short supply, so Parisians still rode their bicycles everywhere. Things like plates, matches, and shoe leather were still in short supply, not to mention decent food. Workers continued to cultivate beans and potatoes on the Esplanade des Invalides with horse and plow, but there were few eggs to be found, and ridiculously long lines formed at the bread and butcher shops at the hint of a rumor that a few scraps were available.

Mother secured a supply of old K rations from a friend at the military post exchange store to supplement our diets. Each cardboard rectangle held a miniature American breakfast: a tin of diced ham and eggs, Nescafé coffee, cellophaned crackers, a pack of Wrigley's gum, and a pack of Chesterfield cigarettes. It was a miracle our boys had stayed alive to fight in spite of those breakfasts, but any food was precious then.

Mother volunteered for the ADIR, the National Association of Deportees and Internees of the Resistance, a new organization that helped women deportees returning from Nazi concentration camps get back on their feet. These "lucky" women often had lost everything. Their husbands and children. Their homes. To make matters worse, the French government focused on the men who returned, military men especially, but any males who'd survived the war. Somehow the returning women were an afterthought.

I volunteered here and there as well. Since so many children in Paris lacked coats, Mother and I appealed to Le Bon Marché department store to allow us to set up a donation station just outside the store's doors and they agreed. They carted out coatracks and folding tables to the cordoned-off area, and Mother and I hung donated children's coats by size. The price of admission into our little shop was one child's coat. A parent could choose from any of our coats and jackets in a larger size, and the donated garment was cleaned and redistributed. Le Bon Marché even advertised our event, running a grim little photograph of Mother and me at the bottom of their newspaper ad.

We chose a perfect sunny November day to set up, when all of Paris was out to see what fashions the stores held for the coming season. Dior had debuted his revolutionary New Look, with its nipped waists and full skirts, that spring, and Paris was abuzz about what he'd unveil next. It was hard not to feel optimistic that day, with the scent of roasting chestnuts in the air and the one-man band in the adjacent park playing a lively version of "Le Chaland qui passe."

Soon people queued up and crowded in. Mother had left me in charge, for she'd already achieved field marshal status in the post–World War II French charitable world and had gone to oversee a soup kitchen on the other side of town. I was thrilled, for I desperately needed a new mission of my own. Besides, I'd become good at picking the perfect coat for a child. The key was in the coloring. This was Paris after all. A yellow coat on a sallow child was almost worse than no coat at all.

The coat exchange was packed by midmorning when I realized I'd never opened my ration box. Before I could reach for it, an elderly woman approached me.

"Excuse me, Mademoiselle, would you assist me, please?"

She was gaunt but had the bearing of a countess, well dressed in her wool skirt and cardigan and clean white gloves. She wore a faded pink Hermès Saumur scarf fastened with a jeweled partridge brooch, the belly of which was a South Sea pearl. Even in dire circumstances, or perhaps because of them, the women of Paris continued to pull themselves together with unexpected touches, still subscribing to the fashion truism that too much simplicity is timid. In one hand the woman held a white paper package, a malacca walking stick hooked over her wrist. In the other she held the leash of an ebony-colored standard poodle. It was a magnificent animal and, like its owner, thin but beautifully groomed.

"I have brought a coat," she said.

I took the package, broke the cellophane tape, and lifted out the coat, releasing a musky scent of rose and lavender. I'd seen many lovely garments that day, some with hand-embroidered flower plackets and enameled buttons or glorious rabbit fur linings, but this coat was in a category all its own. Cashmere? It was the color of a robin's egg and surprisingly heavy, but soft and lined with quilted white satin.

"Thank you for your donation, Madame. Please choose another. We have many good coats, perhaps maybe none as fine as this one—"

"It is lined with goose down. It was made for my granddaughter. Never worn."

"Help yourself to the rack. What size is your granddaughter now?"

The woman smoothed her hand down the dog's neck. Upon closer inspection, I saw she'd misbuttoned her cardigan, giving her sweater a cockeyed skew. Her jeweled brooch was missing a diamond. Sold or lost?

"Oh, she is gone. Taken with her mother and brother years ago now. My daughter and one of our maids had been printing leaflets in our pantry."

The underground.

"I'm so sorry . . ." My sight blurred. How could I comfort others if I couldn't control my own emotions?

"I kept it thinking she might come home, but then they took me. Can you imagine? What would they want with an old woman? My housekeeper kept my dog in Saint-Etienne while I was, well, away. He's my family now." She shook her head, unable to continue, then straightened. "Perhaps someone can use the coat?"

I returned the coat to the wrapping. "Thank you, Madame. I will make sure it finds a good home. There is hot coffee inside."

She laid her gloved hand on mine for a long moment, the cotton warm and smooth. "Thank you, dear."

I pulled a card from my pocket. "This is the ADIR, a charity my mother supports. They help women coming back from, well, from the camps. Run by women who were deportees themselves, out of one of their apartments. Near Le Jardin du Luxembourg."

"Thank you, Mademoiselle." She took the card and turned.

"Wait, Madame." I pulled my K-ration box from beneath the table. "I have an extra. Would you like it?"

She eyed the box. "Oh no, dear, give it to someone more—"

"Please take it."

"Well, I do have a neighbor—"

I smiled. "A neighbor. Good then. I'm glad it will be well used."

The woman tucked the box under her arm and made her way out of our little coat exchange, jostled and pushed by the crowd.

There were many such stories that afternoon, and by day's end I was ready to rest, but the crowds only grew larger. To make things worse, the temperature dropped, making me all too aware of my own coatlessness. Mother had mistakenly added our own coats to her donation piles and carted them off, and as a result I had no outerwear of my own. The wind picked up, blowing coats off their slippery wooden hangers.

I stooped to retrieve a jacket and stopped short as I stood. I couldn't miss Paul in the crowd, taller than most, working his way toward me. My first instinct was to dive into the crowd myself and avoid seeing him, but who would man the booth? He'd in all probability moved on by now, I thought. Adjusted to his new life. Forgotten me.

As he came closer, it was hard not to notice he looked good in his aubergine velvet jacket. He had been eating, it seemed—still thin but finally filling out.

Paul made his way to me, both of us jostled about by the crowd. He held out a small tweed coat the color of ripe wheat with a wilted tricolor ribbon pinned to the breast. I took it, careful not to touch him. One touch and I'd be back into it all, and the pain would return. It might even be worse.

"Remember me?" he asked.

It had been almost two years since we'd last seen each other at his kitchen table.

"Thank you for your donation, Monsieur. Please choose another."

It was Pascaline's coat, of course. Thin and light. A wool-cotton blend? The sleeves had been let down twice, leaving lines, dark as graphite, around each cuff, and two lovely little patches had been sewn into the warp of the tweed with tiny, regular stitches. Rena.

"I'm sorry you have to talk to me, Caroline. You obviously don't want that."

"We have many good coats—"

"Would you please look at me?" He passed the fingers of his free hand across his lips. Paul nervous? That was a first. The velvet at the elbow of his jacket was worn. Had Rena not cared enough to mend his too?

Paul reached for my arm. "It's been terrible without you, C."

I stepped away. Was he acting? He was good at that, after all.

"You are free to choose any coat . . ."

Why could I not stop babbling about coats?

Paul stepped closer. "I'm in a bad way, Caroline."

If he was acting, he was doing a remarkable job. He clearly

hadn't slept anytime recently. Overcome, I turned and held a coat-rack to keep it from toppling over in the breeze.

Paul grabbed my wrist and turned me toward him. "Did you even read my letters?"

I shook off his hand. "I've been busy. You should see the apartment. Mother's been boiling cottons on the stove—"

"If you would just read them, you'd know—"

"You should see her on a stool stirring the pot with a canoe paddle."

I turned away and straightened the coats. He followed.

"So this is it? We'll never be together again?" He stood taller for a moment.

Misery looked good on Paul. Unshaven, messy, lovely misery. I buttoned a tiny pink coat.

Paul stepped back. "I had to see you when I read you'd be here. Hitchhiked all the way from Rouen."

"You'd better start back soon. It looks like rain."

"Is it someone else? I've heard you were with a man—"

"What?"

"Holding hands. At Café George. You're well known, Caroline. Word gets around. You at least owe me an explanation."

I'd lunched with one of Mother's admirers, a bearded count from Amiens twenty years my senior. Disconsolate that Mother had little time for him, he'd spent half the lunch with my hand in his, pleading for me to intervene, keeping me from my vichyssoise.

"How can you be so unfeeling, Caroline?"

"*Unfeeling?*"

"I still can't even work, and you go about your do-gooding here as if I'm no one to you."

Do-gooding? I felt my Irish temper rise up my back in warm prickles despite the cold. I turned to face him.

"How unfeeling were you when you decided to have a child?" I said.

"You knew I was married—"

"Incompatible, Paul. You said children complicate things, remember? 'No place for that in an actor's life'?"

"Things happen. Adults deal with them. Unless they're rich and spoiled—"

"Spoiled? Really? Is it spoiled to give up my own happiness for that of a child I don't even know? Do you have any idea what it's like waking up every morning knowing you and your family are together and I'm alone? Don't talk to me about unfeeling."

It wasn't until he opened his jacket and wrapped me in velvet that I realized I was shaking.

"Be sensible, Caroline. When will either of us find what we have again?"

"True," I said into the cotton of his shirt. "You may be the only man left in Paris."

He laughed and pulled me closer.

"I miss you, C." His heavenly scent surrounded us, cocooned in that jacket, his fingers interlocked at the small of my back. I'd missed that musky essence of pine and leather. He brushed his lips against my cheek.

"Come and get something to eat," he said. "Even over that terrible band, I can hear your stomach growling. A friend of mine has a place in the Latin Quarter you'll love. He's made an apple tart. With real crème fraîche."

How wonderful it would be to slide into a bistro booth with Paul, the leather seat allowing us to sit hip to hip as so many lovers before us had done. The offerings would be meager, but there would at least be warm bread and wine. We'd talk about everything. Which crème fraîche is best? From southeast or southwest France? Which new play should he do? How much he loved me. But then what? He'd go home to his family and leave me worse than before.

"I'll come to New York," Paul said, his lips soft against my ear. "It will be like before."

I felt his chest against me, only the silk of my dress and the cotton of his T-shirt between us.

"You can't just leave here, Paul."

Even if he didn't have a family, it could never be like before. The world was so different now.

Paul stood back, held me at arm's length, and smiled his most dangerous smile. "I need to get back to New York. Broadway's rebounding, you know."

I pulled away and shivered as the wind ballooned the skirt of my dress. Was he using me to escape his new responsibilities? Did he want me or just relief from family life?

"C'mon, C. We could do something together. I'd consider Shakespeare. Let's talk about it at dinner."

I felt a drop of cold rain on my hand. I would have to move the coats under the overhang of the store.

"You need to get back to your family, Paul."

Paul stepped back. "You're infuriating."

"You're a father."

"But I love you——"

"Love your daughter. If you don't, I'll have given you up for nothing. So *act* if you have to, and soon you'll find you mean it." I touched his sleeve. "It's not that hard. Just be there. When she wakes in the night afraid. If she stumbles at school."

"Rena doesn't want me there——"

"Your daughter does. She wants you to teach her to sail a boat, show her off in the park. You don't know how powerful your love is, Paul. Without it she'll fall for the first boy who says he loves her, and he'll shatter her for good."

"Why throw away everything we have? It's ridiculous, your pilgrim ethics."

"Puritan," I said.

"I don't think I can do it."

"You can. Funny thing about grief: It gets easier with practice."

I held out a white package.

"This coat's perfect," I said. "A bit large, but she'll grow into it."

"I love you, C. And I'm stubborn too, you know."

"Love her, Paul. If not for you, then do it for me."

"You're going to wake up one morning and know you've made a terrible mistake."

I suppressed a smile. Like every morning?

Paul stared at me for a long moment, then slipped off his jacket and draped it across my shoulders. He wore only an old white T-shirt underneath, threadbare in parts. It was a prewar shirt, no doubt, for it hung somewhat loosely, but the sight of Paul in it, even thin as he was, caused more than one woman in the booth to stare.

"This always looked better on you," he said.

The satin lining of his jacket felt good against my skin, still warm from him.

Paul kissed me on both cheeks and took the white package. I smoothed the flap of one velvet pocket in my fingers, soft as a cat's ear.

I looked up just in time to watch Paul's beautiful back as he retreated through the crowd, and then I turned and pushed the racks out of the rain.

IN THE MONTHS THAT FOLLOWED, Paul sent a few more letters, and I tried to distract myself with volunteering. At least I had Mother, though she would not be with me forever. Our life became reduced to a routine well known to those in homes for the aged—tea with Mother's friends, the conversation revolving around inflamed sacroiliacs; the odd errand at the embassy for Roger; and church choral concerts.

They were pale days, one indistinguishable from the next, so a visit from a friend of Mother's one morning threw me for a loop. Mother had told me a friend of hers named Anise Postel-Vinay, who'd been arrested while working for the French underground during the war and held at Ravensbrück concentration camp, was stopping by our apartment. Anise and friends had founded the ADIR. Though Mother was uncharacteristically evasive when I asked for details, I agreed to this favor, expecting Anise to appear at our apartment asking for gently used clothing or canned goods.

That day, Mother, midway through her unfortunate poncho phase, was sporting a red-checked, caftanesque affair she'd resurrected from somewhere when Anise arrived. Parisians stared when Mother wore that poncho, as if picturing it where it belonged, flung over a café table under a plate of good cheese.

The doorbell buzzed, and Mother showed Anise in. Two men followed behind carrying a canvas stretcher on which a woman lay wrapped in a white cotton blanket.

"Dear God," I said.

Anise, a handsome, no-nonsense woman, planted herself on our living room Aubusson and ran the fingers of one hand through her cropped hair.

"Good morning, Mme Ferriday. Where should the men take her?"

I took a step back. "She's staying? Here? We knew nothing of this."

Mother went to the stretcher. "Anise asked if we could help this Polish friend of hers," she said to me. "She's unconscious, Anise?"

Anise laid her hand on the woman's blanketed leg. "Heavily sedated. Just flew her from Warsaw."

"She needs a hospital, Mme Vinay," I said.

"Her name is Janina Grabowski. I knew her at Ravensbrück concentration camp. Operated on by Nazi doctors." Anise felt the woman's forehead. "We need to handle this privately. She was brought out of Poland, well . . . without the knowledge of the authorities."

We were to take in a sick Polish fugitive?

"Could she get no help in Warsaw?"

"Most of Warsaw has been reduced to rubble, Miss Ferriday. Their healthcare system is a mess. Antibiotics in short supply."

Anise threw back the blanket to show us the woman's leg. Under the gauze, an angry infection raged.

"Take her to my room right away," Mother said. "I'll cut some fresh bandages." At last, Mother could relive the nursing days of the Woolseys on the Civil War battlefield. "We'll call our personal doctor for her."

I held one hand to the stretcher. "Wait. I listened to the trial on the BBC. The Germans are supposed to be providing reparations——"

"None, Miss Ferriday. Germany decided they do not recognize Communist Poland as a country. They consider it part of Russia."

"That's ridiculous."

"Janina is a charming person who once gave me the medicine she could have used to save herself, allowing me to stand here now. She has suffered more this morning than you will in your lifetime and could quite possibly be dying as we speak."

I waved the men along. "We are happy to have her," I said.

"Good. Thank you, Mademoiselle."

I walked to the window. "Put her in my bed. First door on the left."

The men carried the stretcher down the hall to my bedroom and Mother followed. As they passed, I saw that blood from Janina's leg had seeped through the blanket. What had we gotten ourselves into?

"We are at your service, Mme Vinay," I said.

Anise walked to the door. "Your mother told me you'd help." She turned and almost smiled. "That's good. Because there are sixty-two more where she came from."

Part Three

CHAPTER 37

Kasia

1957

I PICKED HALINA UP FROM DAYCARE ONE NIGHT AFTER MY LAST nursing shift. The facility was housed in one of many government-controlled childcare centers. In Lublin at the time, any child with two working parents was assigned to a childcare facility where school-aged children spent their days learning basic math, reading, and Communist Party rhetoric. I walked toward ours, which was situated in a drab former housing complex requisitioned by the Party, a beige, humorless place that smelled of cooked potatoes and cabbage, a smell I still could not tolerate twelve years after Ravensbrück. At least the government paid for it.

As I waited for the class to be released, I leaned against the wall to take the pressure off my bad leg and considered my new bracelet, the result of a plan Father Skala and I had worked out. Father, Papa's dear friend, was our former parish priest, now retired. At Zuzanna's urging, I approached him for advice about my being overwhelmed as a mother. With trying to juggle work, caring for a young daughter, and being a wife, I was often worn to a frazzle and lost my temper more and more. Father Skala suggested that, in addition to prayer, I might also wear a rubber band on my wrist and snap it every time I felt my temper getting the better of me. I wore the dull red band on my wrist and did a good deal of band-snapping each day. By week's end, my wrist was raw from snaps.

"No running," Comrade Jinda, Halina's unit leader, called out as the children made their way to their parents.

It was easy to spot my daughter in the crowd. She had Matka's golden hair and was a hand taller than most of the other children. At ten years old, Halina was a year behind the children her age, for she had been held back for not knowing her multiplication tables. How lovely it was to see her—my reward, the prize God had given me for all I'd been through. The children walked up to meet their parents and exchanged the accepted greeting. Halina shook my hand and gave me a perfunctory kiss on the cheek. She had a lovely scent all her own, of soap and fresh air, even after being in that dreary place.

"Good evening, Matka," Halina said.

Comrade Jinda noted with a smile that all children were accounted for and turned to assemble the next group.

"A real kiss for your mummy, Halina?" I said.

She reached her small hand to mine. "You know it's not allowed."

We headed for the door. What a serious little thing she'd become!

"So how is the most wonderful daughter today?"

"Not more wonderful than any other," Halina said.

"Was rest time better today?" At daycare, the children were taught to eat and rest and even use the toilet on cue.

"I just pretended to rest," Halina said

By the 1950s, the Polish United Worker's Party, or PZPR, Moscow's thinly disguised Polish proxy, was in complete control. Though Stalin was dead by then, his policies lived on. He had promised the Allies at Yalta that he would provide free elections in Eastern European countries and allow them to operate as democracies, but instead installed a Communist Party government in each country, Poland being no exception. We ended up with rigged elections, no independent political parties, and no criticism of the Party allowed.

All policy was based on the collective needs of the people. I was reassigned to be a trauma nurse at the new state hospital and Pietrik to factory work just outside Lublin, where he was bused daily.

"I'll talk to your teacher," I said. "She must make sure you are getting a good sleep." With morning drop-off at 5:00 A.M. and pickup at 7:00 P.M., a child needed a rest during the day.

"No, Matka. I'm not a baby. Besides, Comrade Jinda would just put me at the end of the lunch line again if you complain. Plus, it's fine. It let me think about what I would paint this weekend."

My leg burned as I hurried her past a breadline.

"We have no paints, Halina."

"We have your mother's brushes."

"How was math class?"

"Comrade Jinda made flash cards. I may be in baby math until I am as old as you. I hate times tables."

"I use math every day as a nurse."

"Marthe said she would buy me paints for my name day."

"When is the placement examination?" I asked.

"I don't know," Halina said. She picked up a stick from the road and dragged it, drawing lines in the dirt along the side of the road.

"Did Comrade Jinda let you be on the blue team?"

"Yes," Halina said.

"Without any trouble?"

"Yes. Once I told her there was no proof Jesus rose from the dead, she let me do anything I wanted."

I stopped short, sending a ripple of pain up my calf.

"Who told you that?" I asked.

"I don't know," she said with a shrug.

I tucked that shocking bit away to discuss with Comrade Jinda. Religion was supposed to be off-limits at school. It was bad enough we had to sneak around to go to mass. Every trip to church meant a black mark on one's record, and there were people paid by the authorities to note such things.

The childcare facility was a twenty-minute walk from our apartment. My leg ached from standing most of the day caring for patients, but I was luckier than most, since I lived within walking distance of childcare. Many of the other nurses were assigned to housing outside the city and only visited their children on weekends.

We were also lucky that Papa, somehow still working in his postal center job, managed to keep us all in our apartment. Pietrik, Halina, and I lived in my old bedroom; Zuzanna slept in her old closet room which only fit her bed; and though I tried not to think about it, Papa and Marthe slept in the room he and Matka once shared.

The smell of buttery pastry met us at the door. Marthe had been baking Halina's favorite *kolaczki* again.

Halina ran to Marthe. *"Babcia!"*

"My little *ciastko*," Marthe said as she turned from the stove and gathered Halina in her arms.

"Did you buy me paints?" Halina asked.

"Halina," I said. "That's not polite."

"It's fine," Marthe said, sitting Halina at the table with a plate of apricot *kolaczki*. "She is just a girl."

"She knows better," I said.

I walked down the short hallway to my room, feeling as if a hot poker were stabbing my calf with every step. My old bed was pushed to one side, and a small bed for Halina stood along the other wall, the bed I shared with her most nights. When had Pietrik and I started sleeping separately? Pietrik sat reading a book, still in his gray coveralls from the factory. He'd been assigned to the Lubgal Ladies Garment Factory in the new suburb of Helenów on the edge of the city. It had its own training school and on-site residences for which we'd put our name on the waiting list.

It may sound strange, but I loved those coveralls. They fit him well in all the right places—his broad shoulders and long legs.

"What are you reading?" I asked. My leg ached, and I wanted more than anything to stretch out on the bed.

Pietrik did not answer. His book wore a brown paper cover, but it was *Doctor Zhivago*, one of many books on the banned list. His friend Aleksander had been sent away for reading Thoreau's essay "Civil Disobedience," so Pietrik was smart about where he read.

I tossed my bag onto the bed. "How was work?"

"They took Symbanski today. Right from his bench. Didn't make quota. He gave them a bottle of vodka, but they still took him."

"We need to make the best of it——"

"We need a third world war."

I stepped out of my uniform so that I was only wearing my slip, the one he'd once said made me look like Myrna Loy. "Halina needs to study for the math exam. Can you help?"

Pietrik kept his gaze on his book. "Does it matter how she places? She will end up on the assembly line next to me."

"If she can get on the medical track——"

"Let her be." Pietrik dog-eared a page. "And stop badgering her teacher."

The room closed in on me. I snapped my rubber band. It smarted the inside of my wrist, but it did little to stop my mounting temper.

"I don't badger anyone," I said.

"They'll have you on some list before you know it. Your father won't be able to get you off it no matter how cozy he is with the Kremlin."

I reached for Pietrik's arm. "You understand—I need some say in my child's life. Let's find time to talk about it, alone——"

"Keep your voice down, Kasia." Pietrik tossed his book on the bed and walked to the door. "Marthe knows enough of our business."

He left and shut the door behind him. He enjoyed his little rebellions. The rubber band wasn't helping me, so I filled my lungs with air to combat the anger.

Once I heard Zuzanna return from work, I hurried to change. I came out from my bedroom to see her kiss the top of Halina's head and steal some *kolaczki* from her plate.

"Did you eat today?" I asked Zuzanna.

"Some greet their sisters with hello," she said with a crooked smile. She had a dark smudge beneath each eye.

"How was the hospital?" Marthe asked.

"Good," said Zuzanna. "We may be getting ten new beds."

"That's a good thing?" I asked.

"More work for the same pay," Pietrik said.

I noticed the tin box of paints near Halina's plate. A fancy British brand.

"Where did the paints come from?" I asked, trying to keep my voice steady. Certainly not from a store. There were no more private shopkeepers at that point, and government shops did not sell foreign brands. These were black market paints.

"A friend got them for me," Marthe said. "An early name day gift—"

"I told her no paints," I said.

"Let it go," Pietrik said under his breath.

I closed my eyes and took a lungful of air. "Give me the paints, Halina."

"Kasia," said Zuzanna, her hand on my shoulder. I shrugged it off. That was when I noticed the brush, the sable-hair tip of it under Halina's plate. Matka's Kolinsky watercolor brush, the gleam of its nickel throat in the shadow of the plate.

"Where did you get that?" I said, short of breath.

"Marthe gave it to me," Halina said.

Marthe stepped toward me. "She has such a talent—"

"Give me the brush, Halina," I said, my arm outstretched, palm up.

Halina curled her hand around the paints and brush and put them in her lap.

"Give them to me," I said, stepping closer.

"Let it go," said Pietrik.

The blood rushed in my ears, heart thumping against my chest. Halina stood and ran to Marthe, paints and paintbrush in hand.

"Give them to me," I said, following.

"It is my fault," Marthe said, one arm around my daughter.

I grabbed for the paintbrush.

"No," Halina said, pulling back.

"I am your *mother*. You must listen to me. Not to Comrade Jinda. Not to Marthe. To *me*."

Halina stood her ground, clutching the paints and brush to her chest.

"No," Halina said.

"She is——" Marthe began.

"Stay out of this. Would you once allow me to speak to my own child?" I stretched out my arm. "Give me the paints, Halina."

"Never," Halina said in a matter-of-fact way, looking me straight in the eye.

It couldn't have been my hand that placed the slap there, for it happened before I could even think about it, yet I slapped her hard across the face. As soon as my hand left her face, I wished I could take it back, but nothing could fix that.

"Kasia," Pietrik said, his tone not so much accusatory as— *worse*—disappointed.

Halina did not even cry, just dropped the paintbrush and paints on the floor next to her. I picked up the black-lacquered brush and, one hand on either end, cracked it over the back of a kitchen chair, which resulted in a satisfying snap, leaving the two shattered ends like cat's whiskers.

I retreated to my bedroom, vibrating with shame, and stood in the tiny room looking at the bed Halina and I shared. Her stuffed bear sat upright against the pillow. I lay on the bed and held the bear to my own chest. It smelled of Halina. Of sweetness and honesty. What kind of a mother had I become?

Before long the bedroom door opened, and Marthe stepped in. I sat up with a groan.

Marthe shut the door. "I may be the last person you want to see, but no one else would come in."

"Please, Marthe . . . this isn't——"

"I've watched you for twelve years now, Kasia. I understand a lot more than you may think."

"I'm not feeling well. My leg—"

"I understand that your mother favored you. That you lost her, and that is a terrible thing, but it's time to move on. Time for some honesty."

"Honestly, you get in my way. I'm the only one who disciplines my daughter. You just cook and give her things."

"Your daughter needs love."

"Don't lecture me. Of course I love her."

"You have to rise above all this and show her." Marthe sat beside me on the bed. "And you can't force Halina to be something she's not."

"Nothing good comes of art."

"What happened to your mother was tragic, but let's move on."

"I'd like to rest now."

"And your husband? He needs help, Kasia. It's your life, but your mother would want Halina to be cherished. Your papa and I are going to stay with friends tonight. Pietrik and Halina will take our room so you have some time to think. You have a choice. To wallow in the unfairness of it all or rise above it. Fix it. Let other people in."

"Easy for you to say. You don't feel the heavy load of it all. You're not even a mother."

Marthe stepped to the door. "And neither are you right now, dear girl."

She left, and for the first night in so long, I had a room to myself. A quiet space to think and work things out. I looked at my rubber band limp on my wrist. From now on, I would use my own resourcefulness and intuition.

By the time I fell asleep, I had a plan. I would make things better. I would look for help, let other people in. Make sure I spent more time with Halina. Pietrik and I would find time to be alone together. I'd survived Ravensbrück. How could ordinary life be harder than that?

CHAPTER 38

Caroline

1957–1958

MOTHER AND I TRAVELED HALF THE GLOBE ONCE WE FINALLY
left Paris after the war. India and Italy. A cruise up the British coast
to Scotland.

The first thing I did when Mother and I landed back in New
York for good was help organize that year's April in Paris Ball. It
was an elaborate fundraiser that supported any number of charities,
French and American, including my new Ravensbrück Rabbits
Committee. It had been over a decade since Anise Postel-Vinay had
introduced me to the cause, and Mother and I had grown terribly
attached, corresponding regularly with the Polish women. Wallis
Simpson, formally known as the Duchess of Windsor, the American
divorcée who'd married England's former King Edward VIII, would
be attending the ball, and I planned to ask for her support.

The Waldorf ballroom had never looked better. The cavalcade of
Hollywood glitterati and Washington VIPs went through endless
rounds of how-do-you-dos, highballs in hand. But one woman was
stealing the show. Man or woman, it made no difference—all eyes
were on Marilyn Monroe.

Betty and I were worker bees on a committee that turned the
ballroom into a Manhattan matron's idea of a French wonderland.

A massive dance floor anchored the center of the room, flanked by long dining tables. We festooned tricolor bunting above the stage and helped drag an enormous golden statue of General Lafayette on horseback center stage, where he reared up out of a sea of white lilies. The decorating committee was well funded, for this was a group with assets to spare. Men wore tuxedoes and ladies wore red, white, or blue. Marilyn Monroe wore a midnight-blue sequin gown that did a marvelous job of showing off her own assets.

I felt like a screen siren myself that night, dressed in a hydrangea-blue Schiaparelli with a flirty little train that dusted the floor as I walked along the tables, performing the last of my decorative duties. I thought I looked pretty good for being on the other side of fifty.

I set a red rose, dethorned, in a plastic water vial at every female guest's plate, reading place cards as I went, a *Who's Who* of A-list Hollywood stars and political bigwigs: Senator John Kennedy. Jacqueline Kennedy. Mr. Winston Guest. C. Z. Guest. Raymond Bolger. Gwendolyn Bolger.

Mr. Paul Rodierre.

A cold splash washed over me. Paul? How could I have not known? It had been ten years since I'd seen him. Next to him, Leena Rodierre. He was remarried? Delightful. What had happened to Rena? I set a rose next to Leena's place and finished quickly, wanting to distance myself from Paul. I'd seen his name in the news here and there in connection with new acting projects, but I'd never seen his films. What could I possibly say to him?

Actor Jean Marais and actress Françoise Arnoul, dressed in French military uniform, started off the evening by entering the ballroom in an open carriage drawn by two black horses. As I watched, Betty, radiant in blue organza, found me and handed me a glass of champagne.

"You should see the gift bags this year, Caroline. All Dior. And *good* caviar finally . . ."

The gift bags at the ball were actually suitcases packed so tight with luxury goods, guests needed porters to carry them to waiting cars.

"Can you believe all the movie people? You would've been big in pictures if you'd stuck with acting."

"Right there with Gloria Swanson—"

"Well, you're ready for your close-up tonight. You look fabulous, honestly. Wish I could say the same for poor Wallis Simpson. She's positively fossilized. Saw her in the powder room, and she complimented my dress. 'Is that Wallis blue?' she said. Really. It's always about her."

"It's good she came."

"It was no hardship, Caroline. She lives upstairs in the Towers. The staff has to call her 'Your Royal Highness,' even though she's not officially allowed to use that title. And the Duke is here. Looking a bit dazed. I think Wallis has him medicated."

"At least it's good press for the cause."

"Really? Try and get the reporters away from Marilyn and Arthur."

"I'm going to ask Wallis to support the Polish ladies."

"Good luck, Caroline. She's tight as a tick."

"She and the Duke do nothing but charity work."

"As long as there are cameras around. Speaking of cameras, I was going to let you find out on your own, but Paul Rodierre is here."

I drank half the flute of champagne in one gulp, the bubbles like fizzy fireworks going down.

"How do you know?"

"I saw him. With his new wife. Some child actress. He looks good, tan as a Palm Beach matron. They must both be wearing girdles." Betty waited for my reaction with a sidelong look. "Don't go running off now."

"It's fine," I said, my stomach doing somersaults. "I actually saw their place cards. I have nothing to say to him."

"Well, if you two do speak, stay away from the knives."

"Don't be ridiculous," I said, draining the glass. It had been years since I'd seen the man, and I was hardly carrying a torch.

Betty went to find her husband, whom she'd spotted winding his way through the crowd with two champagne flutes, and I went in search of Wallis Simpson. Though reviews on her were mixed, she seemed like a compassionate woman. I hoped she'd be sympathetic to the plight of the Polish ladies and lend her support.

I squeezed through the crush of guests, the train of my gown trod upon by more than one patent leather dress shoe. I found Wallis off to the side of the ballroom with Rosemary Warburton Gaynor, wife of a prominent plastic surgeon, Dr. William C. T. Gaynor, and chair of the ball. Up close it was plain to see why Wallis had been fifteen times on the International Best Dressed List. She stood in a pillar of white Mainbocher lace, her dark hair clenched in a tight chignon. Her husband waited nearby, half-listening to the British ambassador, eyes trained on Wallis, like an aged sporting dog ready for his master's whistle.

Wallis and Rosemary stood together—gazelles at a watering hole—a stone's throw away from where Marilyn Monroe sat with her husband, Arthur Miller. I lingered nearby, waited for Rosemary to notice me, and accepted another glass of champagne to help bolster my courage. It isn't every day one asks the Duchess of Windsor for money.

Before long, lovely Rosemary noticed me and reached out, seeming happy for the diversion. "Oh, Caroline, come meet the Duchess."

Dressed in a floor-length off-the-shoulder white gown with a ruffled hem, Rosemary drew me closer. "Your Grace, may I introduce my friend Caroline Ferriday? Caroline Ferriday, may I present Her Grace, the Duchess of Windsor."

Wallis hesitated and then extended one satin-gloved hand. I shook her hand, wondering what one calls a divorcée married to an abdicated king. I went with Rosemary's lead and chose "Your Grace." So much had been written about Wallis Simpson at that time, I felt I already knew her. The press obsessed over every aspect of her life—her French couture, her large hands, the mole on her chin, her dismissive attitude, and above all, her jewelry.

Rosemary waved in the direction of the dance floor. "Caroline has been *awfully* busy helping us put all this together."

"So nice to meet you," Wallis said.

My heart beat faster. How to bring up the Rabbits? Why was I so nervous? I'd once played to an audience of fezzed Shriners in Boston who'd passed a gin bottle down the front row of the theater. That was much scarier than this.

"Can you believe Marilyn Monroe?" said Wallis to no one in particular. She looked toward the horde of people clustered about Marilyn and her husband. A French television news crew, lights bright, was interviewing Marilyn and Arthur at their table. "Every photographer here is smitten with her."

"It's the dress," Rosemary said.

"Not one's even glanced my way," Wallis said.

Mrs. Gaynor turned to me. "Caroline works *tirelessly* for the downtrodden, Your Grace. She has quite a reputation."

"How is that?" Wallis asked, perking up as she accepted a glass of champagne from a tuxedoed waiter, perhaps hoping for scandal. How nice it is, when one's own reputation is damaged, to hear of others' misfortunes.

"A *good* reputation, of course," Rosemary said. "She heads up an American arm of a French organization to assist women in need. She's been awarded *both* the Cross of Liberation and the French Legion of Honor for her work."

"Don't go near those canapés, dear . . . too salty," Wallis called to the Duke, who stood nearby apparently mesmerized by a waiter's tray of liver mousse canapés.

"Yes, I head up American Friends of the ADIR, Your Grace," I said. "We support women who have returned from concentration camps. Help them regain normal lives."

"Still?" said Wallis, drifting back into the conversation. "It's been how many years since the war? Doesn't their government help?"

"Some, but they still need assistance. We're working to get reparations for a group of women from Ravensbrück, a German concentration camp near Fürstenberg."

"The Duke and I try our best to avoid any place with 'berg' in the name."

Since the couple's prewar trip to Berlin, where they were received by Hitler, the press often revisited the faux pas, even twenty years after the fact.

"The women are called the Ravensbrück Rabbits, Your Grace," I said. "Polish women, girls really at the time, experimented upon by doctors there."

"Just terrible," Rosemary said.

"Poles?" said Wallis, a furrow between her brows. "I thought you worked for the French. It's all terribly confusing."

Wallis's attention shifted to a fashion show model who settled near us, one hand on her hip, the other held high, a diamond cuff on the wrist. The Duke raised his eyebrows at Wallis as if asking her opinion of the bracelet. Wallis sent him a noncommittal shrug.

"We help women of any nationality who've returned from the camps," I said. "Conditions are especially difficult in Poland. Many of them are sick—some dying—and still have no reparations, since West Germany doesn't recognize Communist Poland as a country."

Wallis glanced about the room, perhaps looking for the exit. "I'm not in a position to donate to anything these days. We have to bow and scrape for everything we're given. We're not even on the Civil List, if you can imagine. Plus, the world has grown weary of all that death and destruction. Those stories even bore the people who went through it all. Who *hasn't* written a memoir?"

Wallis turned to the Duke, smoothed the royal Peter Pan's hair in place, and fussed with the gold medals and ribbons at his chest. She removed a canapé from his hand, placed it back on the silver tray he'd taken it from, and took the Duke by the hand.

"Let's pop up and check on the dogs." She motioned for the waiter with the silver tray to follow. "Pugs need to eat at least every two hours," she said with a smile and swept off toward the exit.

"If you'll excuse me, Rosemary," I said. Apparently Wallis was not sympathetic to my cause after all.

"Good luck with your fundraising, dear," Rosemary said as I turned to leave. "I'll certainly be donating. And maybe pop in on Norman Cousins at the *Saturday Review*. He and his darling wife helped the Hiroshima Maidens after all."

"I will, Rosemary. Thank you."

I trekked the periphery of the ballroom in search of more champagne, smarting from Wallis's rebuff. I was careful to play the "If I were Paul Rodierre, where would I be?" game in order to avoid him. He would plant himself as far from the whole fashion show spectacle as possible. Probably near the food.

Definitely near the bar.

I circumvented the bar and walked by the Dior models as they twirled and sashayed through the guests. A waiter passed through the crowd, offering microscopic potatoes topped with sour cream and caviar. Was all the food that night to be tiny? I stepped toward the tray but stopped short, my train pinned.

"Would you mind?" I said, turning.

Paul.

And by his side stood a ravishing creature—Leena, no doubt.

"Nietzsche said a diet predominantly of potatoes leads to the use of liquor," Paul said, shoe still on my train.

His voice robbed me of my powers of speech. It didn't help that his ladylove was almost too beautiful to look at, her eyes thick-lashed, with the kind of perfect face a cigarette lends just the right amount of cruelty to. She was tall, impossibly young, and leggy.

"I see you're stalking me," Paul said.

The girl wandered off to the fashion show sipping champagne, apparently not threatened if she'd registered me at all.

"You can remove your foot," I said.

"You have a habit of disappearing," Paul said.

"Only when provoked."

He left his foot there.

I had expected Paul to have recovered since the time I saw him last, but was not prepared for how good he looked, fit and oddly well tanned for April.

"Do I need to take off my dress?"

Paul smiled. "This party is finally getting good."

"Really, Paul. It's Schiaparelli."

He released my train. "I have the exits covered."

"Don't concern yourself."

"Champagne?" asked a passing waiter, flutes bubbling on his silver tray.

"No thank you," I said with massive restraint. "I need to be going."

"I thought about calling you last night," Paul said. "Figured your mother would talk to me at least."

"After all these years? It doesn't matter."

"But I got into some cognac. You know how that is."

"Not really."

"I hoped you'd be here. Among your people."

I shrugged. "It's a good cause."

Another waiter came by. "Champagne?"

Paul took two flutes. "I hoped we could talk about it all."

"That isn't necessary. It's been almost a decade, Paul."

"Have you ever read *one* of my letters?"

"I really need to be going—"

"Aren't you the least bit curious about my side of it?"

I took a glass from him with a shaky hand. "Not really."

"Don't you owe it to me? Leaving me flat?"

"If that's how you remember it . . ." I said.

I watched Paul's new wife consider a model's scarlet shift. Had she ever tasted foie gras? How did she stay so fit in a country that frowned upon vigorous exercise?

A photographer came by. "Can I get a picture, Mr. Rodierre?"

"Why not?" Paul said.

He pulled me to him with more force than necessary, one arm around my waist. He still wore Sumare. Did his new wife like it? Impossible not to.

"Smile, Caroline. Pretend you like me."

The flashbulb blinded us both for a second.

"Thanks, Mr. Rodierre," the photographer said and wandered off.

"Last time we were in this room, I was in command of that stage," Paul said.

I just nodded and pretended to be recovering my eyesight from the flash, afraid speaking would unleash a few tears.

"You've been tanning," I said after a moment.

"Cannes. It was horrible. I hate all that."

"I'm sure. So where is Rena?"

"Who knows? Last seen on the Greek island of Hydra with a young man half her age."

"How wonderful for her." I meant it. Rena deserved her time in the sun.

"You may have kicked me to the curb, but life did go on, Caroline. I guess I don't make the best decisions when it comes to women."

"Maybe give them up for Lent."

Paul smiled. "It's good to see you again, C. You hungry? I'm taking Leena to meet some film people. I know a little place by the Hudson—"

"Look, Paul, I obviously never really knew you. Let's just leave it at that. Maybe remember the good things." I turned. "I have to go."

Paul caught my wrist. "Nothing has ever been as good as our time in New York. You ruined me for love, you know."

"Looks like it," I said, watching his Leena pluck a lobster canapé from a tray.

"What's wrong with you? I've been through hell. You're not the only person affected here—"

"*Mon cher*," Leena called to Paul, "I'm famished."

I really was invisible to her as she waved Paul to follow.

"Come here, darling," Paul called to her.

Leena worked her way toward us. It had been a long night. Did I have to meet his wife?

"Oh, please, Paul. I'd rather not—"

Paul pulled his Leena to him, one arm around her waist. "Leena, I'd like you to meet—"

"Caroline *Ferriday*," Leena said. "How did I not recognize you?" The girl took my hand and pulled me to her. "Of course I know you from photographs. With Helen Hayes. What was it like to be on the same stage with her?"

"Thank you, but I really must be going."

"She runs away, Leena," Paul said. "You need to hold on to her."

Leena held my arm with her other hand. "Oh, please. I'll do anything to have lunch. In Paris. The next time you're there."

"I'd rather not—"

"But, Father, you must convince her."

A chill ran down my arms.

Father?

"Miss Caroline Ferriday, Leena Rodierre," Paul said, his smile still more dangerous than ever at close range.

"*Pascaline* is my stage name, but do call me Leena."

How had I not seen?

"I too played Balthazar, Miss Ferriday. My first role, just like you. Father's told me everything about you."

"Do call me Caroline, dear," I said as I stared at her. Leena was a perfect mix of her parents, tall, with her father's stage presence, no doubt. "You must have been a perfect Balthazar, Leena."

The girl circled me in her arms and held me tight to her. The lovely child I'd found at Orphelinat Saint-Philippe. *Pascaline*. Born on Easter . . .

Pascaline released me. "*Do* say you'll come to Paris, Caroline. I'm to have my first lead role. It would mean the world to have you there."

I nodded. It was all I could do to contain the tears. She was a darling girl with her father's charm. "Of course, dear," I said.

"Well, we must be going," Paul said.

"Father's introducing me to *movie* people," Leena said.

"Au revoir, Caroline." Paul kissed me on each cheek, the familiar scratch of his beard, my hair shirt. "How about you write me back this time? At some point, even I give up."

"You haven't changed," I said.

He smiled. "I guess somewhere in a corner of our hearts, we are always twenty."

Paul disappeared into the crowd, and I felt the old rip of him leaving, but this time it was a little easier somehow. Had that just happened? Paul's daughter had invited me to Paris?

I escaped into a cab after a bellboy heaved my gift bag into the trunk, its contents already earmarked for charity. As the cab drove off, I caught a glimpse of Paul in the crowd and felt a rush of *retrouvailles,* another one of those words that do not translate into English, which means "the happiness of meeting someone you love again after a long time." I hugged myself there in the back of the cab, fine with going home alone.

Would he write? Maybe. I might even write back if I had time.

THE FOLLOWING DAY I took Rosemary Gaynor's advice and called Norman Cousins, famed editor of the *Saturday Review,* hoping to chat with him for a moment in his office. Perhaps have him mention the Polish women in his magazine. He suggested I come by that afternoon.

I sat in the reception area paging through the newspaper. I turned to the society page by habit and saw a full page of photos of the April in Paris Ball. Just under a picture of Marilyn Monroe and the British ambassador, his gaze fixed upon her décolletage, was a photo of Paul and me. I just about fell off my lobby chair. Though his tuxedo was cut in the European style, a bit too nipped at the waist, and my train was soiled, we did make a reasonably handsome couple. The caption read: *Miss Ferriday and Paul Rodierre, back on Broadway?*

I was still reeling from seeing the photo when the receptionist ushered me down a hallway past oversized prints of *Saturday Review* covers in aluminum frames to a conference room. Norman had gathered his staff at the long conference table, a yellow legal pad at each place.

"Nice to meet you, Caroline," Norman said, as he stood to greet me. It was impossible not to be charmed by his old-fashioned good looks and generous smile. Though even the simplest bow tie can be most unbecoming on the wrong man, Norman wore his madras butterfly with aplomb. "You have our undivided attention for a whole five minutes."

Norman went to the far end of the room and leaned against the wall. I was thrown for a moment to be in the presence of such a distinguished editor, known around the world. All at once the butterflies in my stomach would not settle, and my mouth went dry. I summoned Helen Hayes's advice, which had always helped me onstage: "Don't be boring. Use your whole body." I drew myself up and started strong.

"Mr. Cousins, since you and your wife have raised a considerable amount of money for the Hiroshima Maidens—" I paused and looked about the room. Norman's staff was anything but attentive. They fidgeted with their watches and pens and wrote on their pads. How could a person communicate with such a distracted audience? "I thought you might be equally interested in this group of women in similar circumstances."

"These are Polish women?" Norman asked, playing with his handheld tape recorder.

"I'm afraid I can't continue without your full attention, Mr. Cousins. I need to use the little time we have effectively, you see."

Norman and his staff leaned forward, all eyes on me. I had my audience.

"Yes, Polish women, Catholics, political prisoners arrested for their work with the Polish underground. Held as prisoners at Ravensbrück concentration camp, Hitler's only major concentration camp for women, and used for medical experimentation. There was a special Doctors Trial at Nuremberg, but the world has forgotten the victims, and there's been no help or support for the ones who survived."

Norman averted his gaze and looked out the window to the taupe stone rectangles and water towers of Gotham that filled the view ten stories up. "I don't know if our readers will be up for another campaign so soon, Miss Ferriday."

"The Hiroshima project isn't even off the books yet," said a man built like a pipe cleaner, his Dave Garroway glasses at least two sizes too big for his face. I knew him by sight as Walter Strong-Whitman, a man who attended our church, though we'd never been introduced.

"These women were operated upon in a complex series of experiments," I said.

I passed a series of eight-by-ten glossies around the table and watched the staffers' faces as they passed each photo on to the next person, revulsion turning to horror.

Norman stepped to the table. "My God, Caroline, these barely look like legs. This one is missing whole bones and muscles. How can they walk?"

"Not well, as you can imagine. They hopped about the camp. That, in part, is why they were called the Rabbits. That and the fact that they served as the Nazis' laboratory animals."

"How did they even make it home to Poland?" Norman asked.

"However they could. The Swedish Red Cross rescued some. Some were sent home by train when Russians liberated the camp."

"What are their immediate needs?" Norman asked.

I stepped closer to Norman. "They are having terrible trouble in

Poland, behind the Iron Curtain with little access to modern medical care and no help from the German government."

"The Iron Curtain," Mr. Strong-Whitman said with a laugh. "We have no place messing with all that—"

"West Germany has compensated other deportees, but not the Rabbits, since they don't recognize Communist Poland as a country. Some have died from the simplest conditions we can cure here."

"I don't know, Caroline," Norman said. "The Russians aren't cooperating with anyone these days."

"Why should these girls have to suffer because their oppressors won't allow them to leave the country?"

"Murphy got into East Germany for the United Airlines story," one young staffer said.

"This might work as a travel piece," said a woman in a handsome houndstooth jacket.

"The Pan Am client might help," said another.

"This is a terrible idea, Norman," Strong-Whitman said. "We can't go to our readers for every little thing, on the dole for this and that. Our readers couldn't care *less* about Poland."

"Why don't we find out?" I said.

"This is a literary magazine, Miss Ferriday," Strong-Whitman said. "We can't be expected to cover the pet charity story of every clubwoman in New York."

Clubwoman? I took a deep breath.

"You can maintain high standards and still aid the disadvantaged. Norman has proven that with the Maidens."

"We can run a piece in Lifestyle and offer an address for donations," Norman said. "Nothing too fancy, mind you. Maybe a page."

"This country's charitable muscle has atrophied," Strong-Whitman said. "It has been how many years since the war ended? Twelve? No one will give."

"What address should we print?" asked a young woman with a steno pad.

"The Hay, Main Street, Bethlehem, Connecticut," I said.

Were they really doing this? Every muscle relaxed.

"Sure you want mail sent to your home address, Miss Ferriday?" the woman asked.

"How's the post office in Bethlehem?" Norman asked. "Can they handle some extra mail?"

I thought of our postmaster, Earl Johnson, white as Wonder Bread in his summer pith helmet and khaki shorts, often thrown by a misspelled surname.

"Why, it's first-rate," I said. "They are inundated with mail every year, since everyone wants the Bethlehem stamp cancellation on their Christmas cards. Our post office can handle this."

"Bethlehem it is," Norman said. "Congratulations, Caroline. Let's see if we can bring your Rabbits to America."

NORMAN ENDED UP WRITING a lovely article about the Rabbits, four pages long.

It began, *As I start to write, I know my greatest difficulty will be to convince people that what is told here is not a glimpse into the bowels of an imaginary hell but part of our world,* and only got better from there, explaining in careful detail the plight of the girls and their grim situation.

After the *Saturday Review* went to print, a few letters trickled in, one asking if the Rabbits needed a theatrical agent, another inquiring whether the ladies could perform at a 4-H club meeting. I faced the reality that America might indeed have charity fatigue.

The following week, on a glorious, warm fall morning so hazy it was like looking at the world through cheesecloth, I finished feeding the horses in the barn and walked to our Bethlehem Post Office to pick up the mail. Our sow, whom Mother had named Lady Chatterley, followed close behind, apparently unable to let me out of her sight.

I passed Mother's Litchfield Garden Club friends assembled in the garden, washing down Serge's coconut washboard cookies with whirligig punch, their crystal cups flashing rainbows as they sipped. Sally Bloss, Mother's lieutenant, still in garden clogs, her bandana tied like a baby's bib, stood at the front of the group lecturing on their topic of the day: wasps, the garden's friend. Slight, dark-haired Nellie Bird Wilson stood adjacent, skinny as a wasp herself, holding a presumably vacant papery nest aloft. Mother's social calendar was much fuller than mine, filled with garden club, charity fetes at her Nutmeg Square and Round Dance Club, and coaching her baseball team.

Once I made it to the post office, just a few steps across the street from The Hay, the American flag above the door waved me in, and I left Lady Chatterley with nose to the screen door. Our little Bethlehem Post Office was a warren of small rooms tucked under the wing of Johnson Brothers Grocery. Johnson Brothers was a town meeting place with our only gas pump and ice cream counter.

I found Earl Johnson in his mailroom, a tight space no bigger than a closet. He sat atop his high stool, a white wall of mail cubbies peppered with envelopes behind him. For his clothes, Earl favored the neutral part of the color wheel, giving the impression that if he stood still long enough he would become indistinguishable from his mail. Beads of perspiration shone on his forehead, no doubt due to that morning's ten minutes of rigorous mail sorting.

Earl leaned toward me through the window and slid a flyer for the upcoming Bethlehem Fair my way.

"Been hot," Earl said, unable to look me in the eye.

Was I that ferocious?

"It has indeed, Earl."

"Hope you're not here to see the barber downstairs. He's not workin' today."

I took the flyer. "Is this the only mail for me?"

Earl stood and sidled out of his mail closet. "Can you help me with something, Miss Ferriday?"

Country life has its charms, but I had a sudden yearning and appreciation for the Manhattan post office at Thirty-fourth Street, that massive, columned complex of efficiency.

"Must we, Earl?"

Earl waved me down the back hallway, and I followed. He lingered next to a closed door.

"Well?" I said. "Open it."

"Can't," he said with a shrug.

I fanned myself with the flyer. "Well, get the key, for heaven's sake."

"It's not locked."

I took the knob in hand and turned it, then pushed the door with one hip, but it only opened a crack into the darkened room.

"Something's blocking the door, Earl. What do you do here all day? It can't take much to keep things tidy."

"Clyde!" Earl called at the top of his voice. Mr. Gardener's nephew came running.

"Yes, Earl?" said dear Clyde, who was no thicker than two sheets of paper.

"Get in there for Miss Ferriday," Earl said.

"Yes, sir," said Clyde, happy to have a mission that celebrated his size. Clyde slid through the door opening like a stinkbug slipping under a window sash.

I put my lips to the door crack. "Open the door, Clyde."

"Can't, Miss Ferriday. There's stuff in front of it."

"Stuff?" Where was Clyde getting his slang? "You really need to clean this place up, Earl."

Earl toed a knot of wood in the floor.

"Just clear the door, Clyde," I said. "Open the window shades. Then we can help."

I heard shuffling, a groan from Clyde, and the snap of an ascendant window shade.

"Almost there, Miss Ferriday," Clyde said.

Clyde opened the door, and a lovely Steinway smile seized his face, his teeth white and straight as keys.

The room was heaped with canvas bags, each big enough to fit Clyde himself, U.S. MAIL stamped in blue letters on all of them. The bags covered the floor and the counter that ran around the room. Some had burst at their rope handles, belching out piles of letters and packages.

I waded in through an avalanche of envelopes.

"It's all addressed to some rabbits, Miss Ferriday," Clyde said. "Look, one from Hawaii."

"My God, Earl," I said, a bit dizzy. "All for us?"

"Got ten more in the truck. Been dumpin' them in here through the windows."

"Whatever happened to 'Neither snow nor rain nor heat nor gloom of night stays these couriers from the swift completion of their appointed rounds,' Earl?"

"Beg pardon, Miss?"

"Why didn't you *tell* me?"

I scooped up a handful of letters with return addresses from Boston, Las Vegas—Mexico?

"At Christmas I have fifteen extra employees," Earl said. "It's just me here summers. There's more in the basement. So much the barber can't get in there."

Mr. Gardener led Mother's garden club over with a convoy of wheelbarrows, and we ferried the mail back to The Hay, with Clyde astride one bag, riding it like a pony, Lady Chatterley struggling to keep up. We opened every letter, separated them into piles on the dining room table, and called out their contents.

"*Seventeen* magazine is designing a clothing line for the girls!" Sally Bloss said. "Dr. Jacob Fine at Beth Israel Hospital donating medical care—"

Nellie Bird Wilson waved a piece of Roy Rogers stationery. "Kevin Clausen from Baton Rouge sent his allowance."

"How lovely," I said, scribbling it all down.

Mother couldn't rip open envelopes fast enough. "National Jewish Hospital in Denver, Caroline."

"Wayne State University," Mr. Gardener said. "Dr. Jerome Krause, dentist."

Sally held up a letter on blue-castled letterhead. "Disneyland in Anaheim is donating passes . . . The girls are to be Mr. Disney's honored guests."

"The Danforth Foundation is forwarding a check, Caroline," Mother said. "A whopper."

Nellie fanned herself with an envelope as she read. "The Converse Rubber Company wants to design a collection of footwear for the ladies."

"Clothes and handbags from Lane Bryant," Serge said.

We made a pile for the radiologists and osteopaths donating medical care and one for the dentists offering free cleanings. A pile for hospitals offering beds. Families from Bar Harbor to San Diego opening their homes to the girls. By nightfall we added up money and checks totaling over six thousand dollars, more than enough money to support a trip for the girls.

In the next *Saturday Review*, Norman called America "electrifying in its generosity," and I was numb with happiness.

Our Rabbits were coming to America.

CHAPTER 39

Caroline

1958

D R. HITZIG AND I ARRIVED IN POLAND THAT SPRING. IT WAS a pleasure to travel with the doctor, for he was blessed with a razor-sharp mind and a gentle way one generally finds only in the Amish. He was our American medical expert in orthopedic surgery, charged with determining which of the Polish ladies were healthy enough to withstand a trip to the United States later that year. I was along to organize the travel documents and smooth the way.

An official delegation met us and whisked us to the Warsaw Orthopedic Clinic by private car. Once we entered the clinic, Polish doctors surrounded Dr. Hitzig. They pumped his hand, patted him on the back, and escorted him to a conference table in front of a makeshift stage. I took a seat next to Dr. Hitzig as twenty-nine other doctors, Polish and Russian, followed. There were also two members of ZBoWiD there, the Society of Fighters for Freedom and Democracy, an official Polish veterans association, the authority Norman and I worked with to ensure the Rabbits' rights.

The clinic was much like the Bethlehem Grange Hall, wide open and so drafty we felt the breeze from the windows even in the center of the room.

The first three ladies entered the clinic huddled together, clutching their coat collars to their chins. Each wore a cloth purse over one forearm and the strain of the trip on her face, for simple steps appeared to still be painful for all three. Our translator, a severe young man with a Stalin-like head of hair, took a seat next to Dr. Hitzig, and the women walked to the changing screen behind the stage.

The first Rabbit, a pretty woman in her midthirties with short dark hair and dark eyes, emerged wrapped like a Greek goddess in a dull white sheet. She shuffled to the folding chair on the stage, wincing with each step. Once seated, she looked over the audience, her chin high.

The lead doctor, Professor Gruca, an energetic, avuncular man shaped like a fire hydrant, took the stage and read from the document. At seemingly endless intervals, the translator shared the English translation:

"The death of Adolf Hitler's close friend, SS-*Obergruppenführer* Reinhard Heydrich, precipitated the ersatz medical experiments referred to as 'the sulfonamide operations' at the Ravensbrück concentration camp. Dr. Karl Gebhardt, close friend of and personal physician to Heinrich Himmler, was called to treat Heydrich, who'd been critically wounded in an attempted assassination, a car bombing arranged by the Czech underground."

I kept my eye on the woman onstage. She held her head high as she listened.

"In treating Heydrich, Dr. Gebhardt refused to use sulfa drugs, and chose other treatments instead. Once Heydrich died, Hitler accused Gebhardt of letting his friend die from gas gangrene. As a result, Himmler and Gebhardt planned a way to prove to Hitler the decision not to use sulfa had been correct: a series of experiments, first performed on males at Sachsenhausen and then on female Ravensbrück inmates."

The woman onstage brushed her hair back from her forehead, her hand shaking.

"Gebhardt and staff performed surgeries on perfectly healthy women, specially chosen for their sound, sturdy legs, to replicate traumatic injuries. They added bacterial cultures to the wounds to produce gas gangrene, then administered sulfa drugs to some. Each sulfa patient that died proved Gebhardt's case. The inmates operated on"—Dr. Gruca indicated the woman in the chair—"included Kasia Bakoski, née Kuzmerick, currently employed as a nurse for the state."

The doctor pulled back the sheet to reveal the woman's leg. Next to me, Dr. Hitzig took a sharp intake of breath. Her lower leg was shrunken and horribly disfigured, like a gutted fish.

"Mrs. Bakoski was operated on in 1942. She underwent three subsequent surgeries. All Group One: Bacteria, wood, glass, and additional materials were introduced. An incision was made in the left lower extremity and blood vessels on both sides of the wound tied off."

As the doctor continued, Kasia kept her chin high, but her mouth softened. Her eyes grew glassy.

"Ground silica and wood fragments were introduced, and the wound was stitched up and given plaster dressing," said the doctor.

Could the doctor not see she was distressed? I stood and walked toward the stage.

"This cast remained in place long enough for gas gangrene and other conditions to develop," the doctor continued. "Then sulfonamides were introduced."

The doctors scribbled down notes.

"In addition to severe deformity, which affects the entire skeletal system, patient suffers posttraumatic reactions of the brain, depression—"

"I am sorry, but . . ." Kasia said. She stood, one hand over her eyes, the other holding the sheet to her chest.

I stepped up onto the stage. "This cannot continue, Doctor."

"But these women have agreed to this," Dr. Gruca said. "The doctors have disrupted busy schedules to be here."

"So have the Rabbits, Doctor. You may continue the examinations in private. You, Dr. Hitzig, and I will be present."

"This is highly——"

I took Kasia by the hand. "These women were victims once but will not be abused again if I'm here."

"Let us continue in the smaller examination room," Dr. Hitzig said.

I helped Kasia off the stage and to the dressing area and did my best to help her dress.

"Thank you," she said. "I appreciate your help."

"You speak English so well, dear."

"Not so much."

"Certainly better than my Polish."

"My sister Zuzanna isn't here yet, but she is on the list. She's a doctor. And has beautiful English."

"I will look for her," I said.

The exams progressed nicely once they moved to the smaller room, attended only by Dr. Hitzig, Dr. Gruca, and myself. Kasia's sister Zuzanna was the last patient examined. She asked that Kasia be allowed to sit in, and the doctors agreed.

"Zuzanna Kuzmerick," Dr. Hitzig read. "Forty-three years old. A member of the control group of sulfonamide operations. Injected with staphylococcus and tetanus bacteria. One of the few controls who, given no antibiotics, spontaneously recovered. Currently experiences cross-lateral headaches, occasional dizziness, and gastric upset. Possible gastric ulcer, treated with antacids." Dr. Hitzig stopped reading.

"Go on, Doctor," said Zuzanna. "It's fine."

Dr. Hitzig removed his glasses.

"I don't think it's——"

"I've seen it," said Zuzanna. "I wrote it, actually. It says I was sterilized at the camp, doesn't it?"

Kasia stood. "Oh no, Zuzanna."

"It's fine. I wrote the report. Please, Doctor . . . continue."

Dr. Hitzig slid his glasses back on. Zuzanna sat straight in her chair as Dr. Hitzig began his examination, feeling the glands on both sides of her neck.

"Is it hard for you as a doctor to suddenly become a patient?" I asked.

"No," Zuzanna said. "It's important to see both sides. Makes me a better doctor. That is one of the reasons I'd like to come to America. And to take more advanced medical classes and learn as much as I can."

Zuzanna spoke such good English, with her lovely, lilting Polish accent, it was a pleasure listening to her.

Dr. Hitzig rubbed two fingers on the left side of her neck.

"What is it, Doctor?" Zuzanna asked.

"Oh, nothing," Dr. Hitzig said. "I think we are done here for now."

As we cleaned up and the Polish women prepared for the trip home, Dr. Hitzig conferred with his fellow doctors, and I shared the gifts I'd brought from the States.

"Gather round, girls," I said. I held out one of the lovely handbags I'd brought, this one of navy-blue leather. The golden clasp caught the light. "These have been donated by a wonderful American shop called Lane Bryant."

The Rabbits stood still as if rooted in place. Such a serious group.

"Girls, please don't be shy," I said, holding the bag out farther still. "They are free. They have been donated. Blue is the big color this year."

Still not a move. I picked up a Whitman's Sampler box, the name on the package painted in cross-stitch.

"Anyone for chocolates?" Not one moved toward me. "Fig Newtons? They're cookies."

"Maybe we should take a photograph?" Kasia said, motioning toward my Leica. They gathered for the camera, and the photograph arranged itself, like a bouquet of flowers in a vase.

"What will this trip be like?" asked Kasia.

"So far, the plan is the Rabbits will start in New York City and then fan out to stay in private homes across the country. Then the group will meet up in San Francisco and travel to Los Angeles and then return across the country by bus, visiting Las Vegas, Texas, and ending in Washington, D.C."

Kasia translated to the others, who gathered close to hear. I expected at least smiles, but the women remained solemn.

"They would like to know where the ship leaves from," said Kasia.

"Oh, no *ship*," I said. "Pan American Airways has donated the airfare."

There was much excited discussion in Polish and plenty of smiles after that.

"Most of us have never been on a plane before," Kasia said.

Dr. Hitzig stuck his head in the door, and all eyes turned to him.

"We have our final list," he said. "May I speak to you privately, Miss Ferriday?"

I rushed to join the doctor back in our exam room.

"They are all cleared to go on the trip," Dr. Hitzig said.

"How wonderful." I breathed a tremendous sigh.

"Except one. The doctor."

"Zuzanna? Why, for heaven's sake?"

"Sorry to say, I found a hardened Virchow's node," he said.

"What?"

"It indicates a cancerous tumor."

"Can it be treated?"

"Probably not. It is a strong indication of stomach cancer. Her days are numbered, I'm afraid."

I hurried to the women waiting at the door with their coats on, ready to head home. I asked Zuzanna and her sister, Kasia, to meet with Dr. Hitzig and me privately and ushered them to the exam room. They sat on folding chairs.

"Zuzanna, I'm afraid, well ..." Dr. Hitzig said. "The lump I found in your neck is a hardened Virchow's node."

"The seat of the devil?" said Zuzanna.

"I prefer the name 'signal node,'" Dr. Hitzig said.

"It is a symptom of gastric cancer, isn't it?" Zuzanna said.

"I am afraid so, yes."

"Too bad to have one named after a *German* doctor," said Zuzanna with a wan smile, eyes bright.

"How can you be sure?" Kasia asked.

"We should do more tests," Dr. Hitzig said. "But it is the conclusion of the medical group that you are not a candidate for travel to the United States."

Kasia stood. "What? The whole reason for the trip is to get medical attention not available here. How can you bring us all this way and refuse the person who needs you most? She can have my place."

"It is not a matter of space, Kasia," I said.

"You talk about helping us, Miss Ferriday, but you don't really care. You bring us fancy handbags and expect us to snatch them up."

"I thought you would like—"

"We are *ladies*, Miss Ferriday. Ladies who don't all like being called Rabbits—easily frightened, caged animals. Ladies who live in a country where we cannot accept gifts. Is this not obvious to you? A new handbag from an American? People disappear for a lot less. A Polish journalist accepted chocolates from an American, and no one has heard from her since."

I felt my cheek grow hot. How could I have been so cavalier?

"Kasia, please," Zuzanna said.

"You really want to help, Miss Ferriday? Help my sister."

Kasia walked to Dr. Hitzig. "I will pay you anything to put her on that list."

"We will know more after the test—" Dr. Hitzig began.

"My sister is a woman who can save lives. She has done nothing but help others. You treat her, and you treat thousands."

"I wish it were otherwise, but the doctors here agree," Dr. Hitzig said.

"We cannot overrule the ZBoWiD," I said.

"I'm leaving," Kasia said. "This is ridiculous."

She rushed out.

"I'm so sorry," I said to Zuzanna.

Zuzanna laid one hand on my sleeve. "I understand, Miss Ferri-day—"

"Caroline, dear."

"The important thing is the rest of the girls get to America."

I gathered Zuzanna in my arms and held her close. Such a lovely woman. But so thin. How tragic she was so ill. If only we could get some of the Woolsey remedies into her.

When we finally separated, Zuzanna took my hand.

"Don't mind my sister, Caroline. Kasia is just a little tense some-times. We've been through a lot together. But your gifts are very much appreciated."

She smiled.

"And if you want to leave your gifts at the hat check, I'll make sure the girls get them once no one is looking."

CHAPTER 40

Kasia

1958

THE DAY BEFORE I WAS SCHEDULED TO LEAVE FOR AMERICA, our tiny bedroom was scattered with clothes, some mine, most borrowed. Pietrik rubbed his back, sore from taking my suitcase down from the closet shelf and putting it back up, since I'd packed and unpacked six times. Pietrik had won a radio at the factory, a prize for the most productive worker, and we'd turned it up, for good-looking Eddie Fisher, my favorite singer, was on.

> *Dungaree doll, dungaree doll,*
> *Paint your initials on my jeans . . .*

Pietrik held me, and we swayed to the music. It would be nice to be able to dance again. But how could I go to America and have the operation without Zuzanna?

I released Pietrik and continued to unpack.

"How can you be so foolish?" he said.

"I'm not going without Zuzanna."

Pietrik sat on the bed next to my open suitcase, Matka's old green one. "Zuzanna told you to go. How can you pass this up?"

I wanted to get on that plane. More than I'd wanted anything in a long time. I would have the chance to have my leg put back to normal or close to it. Just the idea that I might be relieved of the pain made me giddy. And all the girls were scheduled for dental work. Could the dentists there fix my tooth? It had gotten so bad I hardly smiled. Plus, what would it be like to fly in a jet to New York and see the sights? *California* too. The Lublin papers had already made us celebrities.

I pulled my good dress from the suitcase and hung it back in the closet. "How can I leave Zuzanna here?"

"We'd miss you if you went," he said. "But think of all you'll miss out on, Kasia. Zuzanna's the one who most wants you to go. What about Halina? How does this look, her mother afraid?"

The thought of flying on a plane for the first time made my stomach hurt—never mind the prospect of having to use my terrible English in America and of another operation.

"I'd be gone for months. Who's to say Zuzanna would be alive when I returned?"

Pietrik took my hand. "We'll take good care of her."

His hand felt good around mine. I pulled away and closed the locks on my empty suitcase.

"There's no changing my mind," I said.

Pietrik heaved my suitcase up, returning it to the top shelf of the closet. "You have to learn there are some things you can't change."

"So it would be better to leave my sister here to die? I'm not—"

I turned to see Zuzanna there in our bedroom doorway.

"Oh, I was—" Had she heard?

Zuzanna stepped into the room, hands behind her back. "Don't worry about it, Kasia."

I braced myself, arms folded across my chest. "I won't go without you."

"I'm glad," she said.

"So you're not upset with me?"

She smiled. "Not at all."

I wrapped my arms around her and felt her hard ribs through the back of her dress. "Good, because I would never leave you."

"Well, that makes me happy," Zuzanna said. "Because if I'm going to die, I'll want you near me." She pulled from her pocket a telegram envelope. "Especially since we'll be in New York together."

She pulled a sheet from the envelope, cleared her throat, and read: "Miss Zuzanna Kuzmerick cleared for travel to U.S. STOP Travel documents to follow STOP Report to Warsaw Airport with New York–bound group STOP Bon Voyage STOP Caroline Ferriday STOP."

Pietrik walked to the closet and pulled the suitcase down from the shelf as Zuzanna and I swayed in each other's arms to Eddie Fisher's smooth voice.

Together, together, together.

CHAPTER 41

Kasia

DECEMBER 1958

WE LANDED AT IDLEWILD AIRPORT IN NEW YORK AT 8:30 A.M., thirty-five very excited Polish women. The din of Polish on that plane was so loud, but the other passengers were kind and seemed to enjoy watching it all.

Caroline met us as we came down the steps from the plane— some of us very slowly—and directed a parade of wheelchairs. The name Caroline means joy, so it's no wonder we were all so happy to see her. She looked beautiful in a navy suit, French scarf, and a charming little felt hat with a feather on top.

"Why isn't she married?" all the Polish ladies asked.

Tall, slim, and delicately pretty, with the regal bearing of a queen, in Poland Caroline would have had many marriage proposals each day.

Once we made it through customs, a crush of reporters and Red Cross people and friends of Caroline surrounded us . . . so many camera bulbs flashing!

"How do you like it in America so far?" said one reporter, pointing a microphone at my face.

"If the food on the plane is any sign, it will be a good trip," I said. They all laughed.

"Welcome to the Polish ladies," said Caroline, her arm around Zuzanna's waist. "An olive branch across the miles."

You've never in your life seen so many smiling faces in one place.

That week we all split up and went to different cities. Zuzanna and I stayed in New York with Caroline for treatment at Mount Sinai Hospital. Others went to Boston for reconstructive surgery; to Detroit, Baltimore, and Cleveland for heart operations. Two went to the National Jewish Hospital in Denver for the best tuberculosis treatment in the world, for their lungs were still bad.

My sister and I were lucky to stay in New York, since there was so much to see. Caroline drove us all over, Zuzanna in the front seat, of course. Caroline couldn't get enough of Zuzanna, it seemed, as if they were best friends all of a sudden.

"Here is Central Park, ladies, one of the most beautiful parks in the world."

"We have beautiful parks in Poland," I said.

She talked about her city as if it were the only one in the world.

We drove down Fifth Avenue. Hundreds of cars choked the streets, many with only one person inside. Such wastefulness! How was it allowed?

Our first day at Mount Sinai Hospital was a busy one, packed with blood tests and every other test you can imagine. Mount Sinai was a massive complex ten times the size of any Polish hospital. It took a long time to get anywhere, since the pain in my leg forced me to rest often and since Caroline stopped everyone she saw and introduced us.

"These ladies are here for medical treatment all the way from Poland," she would say.

People were polite but looked at us with pity. It was kind of Caroline to introduce us, but it made it impossible to blend in.

The glass front doors of the hospital parted as if by magic, and Caroline forged ahead with Zuzanna as we hurried to meet the doctor. Zuzanna looked about her, remarking upon every little thing.

"Can you believe this place? So huge."

Caroline turned as she walked. "Six floors. All state of the art."

"How do they get to know the patients in such a big place?" I asked.

Zuzanna dropped back to walk with me. "This is the future of medicine. Can't wait to see their rehabilitation ward."

"We have that at home," I said.

"What? A jump rope and two dumbbells? They have a whole hydrotherapy unit here. Some people would be grateful to receive such care."

We changed into hospital gowns and the nurse affixed a paper bracelet to my wrist. As we went to be x-rayed, I kept my purse and clothes with me, though a locker was offered.

"Can you believe this equipment?" Zuzanna asked.

I slipped a soft robe over my gown. "Ours does the same thing. Just not as new."

We walked to the doctor's office in slippers we were allowed to keep.

"Please, let me take your things," said the doctor's nurse, a tall woman wearing a ruffled nurse's cap.

She tried to take my clothes and purse from my arms, but I held on tight. "I'll keep them, thank you."

The nurse helped me up a little step stool to sit on the examining table. The paper crinkled under me as I sat. Dr. Howard Rusk was a good-looking man with a shock of white hair and a kind face. He held up a small metal box that fit in his palm.

"Do I have your permission to record my notes with this device? It saves me time."

A doctor asking a patient for permission? That was different.

I nodded, and Dr. Rusk spoke into the box.

"The operations at Ravensbrück concentration camp in Fürstenberg, Germany, throughout 1942 left Mrs. Bakoski, a thirty-five-year-old Caucasian woman of Polish-German descent, with reduced muscle function in her left calf, complicated by the introduction of foreign elements."

He slid my x-ray under the metal rim of the light box and flicked on the light.

Zuzanna turned to me, her mouth open. There was a light box in every exam room. We had only one at the hospital back home.

My x-ray showed a scattering of objects in my calf. How strange to see it in such detail! I'd had plenty of x-rays but had never seen such clarity. It brought the operating room at Ravensbrück back in full color. Dr. Gebhardt. Dr. Oberheuser. I started to sweat as the doctor slid another x-ray onto the light box.

"Tibia has been reduced by six centimeters, resulting in antalgic gait. Network of neuromas developed around site, partial source of localized nerve pain Mrs. Bakoski suffers from. Treatment scheduled as follows: procedure to remove foreign elements and neuromas to increase blood flow and reduce pain, and reconstructive plastic surgery. Recommend orthopedic prosthesis, pain medication as needed, and routine post-op psychiatric eval."

By the time Dr. Rusk clicked off his recording machine, I was short of breath. Could he tell?

"Any questions, Mrs. Bakoski?"

"After the operation, will I still have pain?"

"Hard to say one hundred percent. Chances are there will still be some pain, yes, but substantially reduced. Your gait will improve significantly."

"No more questions, Doctor. Thank you." I stepped down from the examining table, eager to escape that room and the x-rays hanging there.

"We'll also schedule the post-op psychiatric evaluation later."

"I'm not crazy, Doctor."

"It's standard. The Hiroshima Maidens found it helpful." The doctor helped Zuzanna up to the table. "Good then. You'll spend the night here, and we'll get started in the morning. You can wait here or in the reception area to check in."

"The operation will happen tomorrow?" I asked.

"The sooner we proceed, the sooner you recover."

Recover? My mind flashed to the *Revier* recovery room. How could I do that again?

Dr. Rusk moved on to Zuzanna, and I left the room, panic jagging through me. Would the surgery be painful? Would I lie in a cast for days?

I changed back into my clothes and made my way down the maze of corridors and out the magic doors. There would be no operation. I was happy to keep my antalgic gait, thank you.

CHAPTER 42

Kasia

1958

ONCE OUT ON THE STREET, I PULLED OFF MY HOSPITAL BAND and tossed it in a trash can. It was good to be anonymous walking the crowded streets of New York.

The crossing sign lit up: DON'T WALK. I stopped there on the sidewalk, but the rest of the crowd continued across the street.

I walked until my leg ached, looking at hats in shop windows, then made it back to the waiting room at Mount Sinai. I sat and paged through magazines—my favorite part of a doctor's visit, especially looking at American magazines. I flipped through the *Saturday Review*. I stopped at an advertisement for *The Diary of Anne Frank*, a new picture at the cinema. A pretty actress sat cross-legged, dressed in a peasant skirt, and smiled from the page, America's idea of what the real Anne Frank was like.

Then I stopped short at an article: THE LAPINS ARE COMING was the title, and it was written by Norman Cousins. *Lapin*. How much prettier the word "rabbit" is in French! The way he told the story it sounded beautiful.

"So far nearly 300 *Saturday Review* readers have contributed almost $6,000 to the general Lapins' fund. . . . The biggest costs are

yet to come, of course. . . ." How generous people in America were
to us.

Suddenly Caroline and Zuzanna were upon me.

"Kasia, where have you been?" Caroline asked. "We paged you."

"I needed some air. Can we go now?"

"Go?" Caroline looked about to fall over. "They're waiting for
you at check-in. Where's your ID band?"

"I'd rather not—"

"Do you know what has gone into all this for you? Dr. Rusk is
one of the best surgeons in America." The little feather on her hat
shook as she spoke.

"No one asked if I wanted this," I said.

Caroline's cheeks flushed pink. "You're risking everything we've
worked for. Now Zuzanna is late too."

Zuzanna took me by the arm, and none too gently. "May I speak
with Kasia in private?"

She steered me around the corner.

"Are you out of your mind?"

"I can't do this again," I said.

"I know this is hard for you, but you won't have this chance—"

"Let me think about it."

"No, Kasia. It's now or never."

"The thought of another plaster . . . and how do I know I can
trust them once I'm asleep?"

"There'll *be* no plaster. I asked. And I'll walk you there. Keep an
eye on things."

"Stay with me?"

"I'll scrub in if they let me. Watch the whole thing. No one will
hurt you, except me if you don't get back in there."

WHEN I WOKE AFTER the surgery, I thought I was back in the *Revier* at Ravensbrück. My pulse raced, but once I felt my leg wrapped in a clean bandage and remembered where I was, relief flooded through me to the tips of my fingers. The best part was I barely felt any pain. The morphine was administered intravenously—there wouldn't be any sticking with a needle! Before long, I ate soft foods, even drank coffee. My bed had six buttons to adjust its position, and I had my own nurse, Dot, from a long island, close to Manhattan. She wore a white cap with black stripes along the top, meaning she had trained at Mount Sinai. Not that different from my cap I wore at home.

The next afternoon I walked for the first time, leaning heavily on two nurses, but it was the best feeling in the world to take steps without the usual stabs to my calf.

Once Dot brought my lunch, I could not stop babbling.

"I'll walk everywhere from now on. Dance with my husband again."

Dot cleared my lunch tray, something a nurse's assistant would have done back in Lublin. "Looks like you're in the clean-plate club."

Of course, I ate everything.

"Today you see Dr. Krazny. She's good to talk to."

I tucked the paper salt packets from my tray in my pocket.

"A psychiatrist? No thank you."

Just what I needed, a report sent back to Lublin that said I was crazy. People had disappeared for less.

"You won't have to walk. I'll get a wheelchair." Was Dot chewing gum? This was allowed? "Dr. Krazny's a doll. Wish I could sit for an hour and talk about *my* problems."

The floor supervisor came to the door. "Dot, your chair is here. Better get it before someone else does."

"Hold on—just a minute," she said. Talking back to a supervisor? Dot wouldn't last long on the trauma floor back home. "So you're going to refuse treatment? Keep it bottled up, and it'll just come out some other way."

"Thank you for your concern," I said. It took getting used to—Americans giving out advice without being asked.

Once Dot told me that all records were confidential and would not be sent back to Poland, I agreed to see Dr. Krazny. I doubted the confidential part but thought it worse to refuse.

The doctor's office was tidy but cramped, which did nothing to ease my nerves. Through the one small window I saw snowflakes dance in the wind. I was surprised to find that the doctor was a young woman. She wore pretty black glasses that curved up on the ends. Her diploma on the wall looked new. Probably just out of school. Inexperienced enough to write me up as mentally ill when that was not the case at all? I would have to stay composed.

She barely glanced at me when the orderly wheeled me in. "You're late. Half your time is up."

"Maybe it was a mistake to come," I said.

"Feel free to leave."

Could they not find a nicer doctor at Mount Sinai? "You're so young—"

The doctor capped her pen and tossed it onto the desk. "We're not here to talk about me."

I pulled on the rubber tires of the chair, but the orderly had braked it.

"I can't stay," I said.

The doctor settled back in her chair. "In this country, you have a choice."

I pressed one index finger with the other. "First of all, I'm not mentally unstable."

"I'm a psychiatrist. Just here to talk."

Could I tell her about the cheese sandwich?

"We have psychiatrists in Poland," I said.

"One for every five thousand Polish people is what I hear. Can't be easy getting an appointment."

"Would have been easier if the Germans hadn't killed them all."

The doctor reached for my chart. "Says here you have trouble sleeping—"

"My sister is a doctor. She told them that."

"And trouble breathing in small spaces. That is known as a claustrophobic adult-onset panic episode."

"I'm a nurse. I know what it's called."

"Then you know how to stop the attacks? How is that working?" She stared at me. "You were in a camp."

"It's on my chart—"

"Ravensbrück. Only women?"

"Yes."

"Tortured?"

"Every day was torture."

That got a crack of a smile from Dr. Krazny.

"I don't need sympathy."

Dr. Krazny sat up straighter in her chair. "I see."

She eyed the chart.

"Your mother . . ." she said.

I took a deep breath. "She brought me a cheese sandwich and was arrested along with me."

"I hope you don't think it was your fault."

I examined my fingernails. Of course it was my fault.

"She didn't return with you? From the camp?"

"She disappeared. I don't know what happened."

"Any ideas?"

"I don't think of it."

"Not an inkling?"

I watched a little tornado of snow swirl around on the window ledge.

"Things happened there," I said.

"Care to elaborate? That's how this works."

I brushed the hair back from my forehead. "She just disappeared. She was helping a doctor."

"Did the doctor do it?"

"I don't know."

"Not an inkling?"

"It's not that *easy*. You don't understand." Snow clung to the windowpanes, closing us in. I breathed hard. Not now. It was no time for an episode. "Many of the doctor's colleagues were executed, but she's in prison."

"How do you feel about that?"

"Good. As long as she stays there."

"And when she's done her time?"

"Not until 1967. I'll deal with it then."

"Do you wish she'd been executed too?"

"No."

Dr. Krazny looked at me, eyebrows up. "Why?"

"She knows what happened to my mother."

"What was your relationship like with your mother? Did you love her?"

"Of course. I was her favorite. What does this have to do with anything?" I pinched my hand to prevent the tears from falling.

The doctor shook her head. "Not sure."

"Not an *inkling*, Doctor?"

Dr. Krazny pulled off her glasses and wiped the lenses.

"I do know unresolved questions can play havoc with a psyche. Produce hostility. Ruin relationships." She replaced her glasses and looked at me for a long second. "I don't often offer advice to my patients, Mrs. Bakoski—"

"No need to start."

"But you're lucky you're alive."

"*Lucky?*" My palms were wet with sweat. "Please."

"You suffered, but you're here."

"Sometimes I wish I wasn't. You don't know what it was like."

"I do know you're holding on to the pain of losing your mother. After all, that's all you have left of her, isn't it? Give that up, and you give up the last thing you have of her."

I turned my face to the window.

"I also know you have considerable work to do, and you need to put your shoulder to it. That's the secret to getting better." The doctor gathered her papers and tapped them on her desk.

"Orderly," she called. "Mrs. Bakoski needs an escort to her room."

"I can make it on my own," I said.

The doctor leaned closer to me.

"Look, Mrs. Bakoski, you'll make no progress until you get to the bottom of that anger. And I would embrace the sympathy people give you. You need all the help you can get."

CAROLINE BROUGHT US UP to her country home she called "The Hay," north of New York City, in Bethlehem, Connecticut, for Christmas. Tears welled in her eyes when she told us her late father had named it "The Hay" after an estate his family once owned in England.

She said the air was cleaner up north, good for recuperation, and maybe that was true for I was taking short walks before long. Zuzanna and I both felt so much better being up there at Caroline's home. Perhaps it had something to do with Caroline's mother, Mrs. Ferriday, treating Zuzanna and me like queens. From the time she met us at the door dressed in Polish folk costume to the minute we left for California, she fussed over us as if we were her own. She'd learned many Polish phrases to make us feel at home.

How wonderful it was to be able to take steps like a normal person again! Mrs. Ferriday lent me her fur coat, and we walked, arm in arm, about their property. To a warm barn that smelled of sweet hay and horses, sun slanting in through the high windows. Out to the playhouse Caroline had used as a youngster, a child-sized version of the main house, complete with a working stove.

But even with the special treatment, I couldn't shake the homesickness for Poland and for Pietrik and Halina. It didn't help that Caroline favored Zuzanna and rose early each morning to take tea with her, the two of them sitting at the kitchen table, heads together to share a little story, laugh at a private joke. It was understandable, for everyone loved Zuzanna. Thankful as I was to the Ferridays, I wanted my sister back.

I tried to count my blessings. Bethlehem was a very nice place to spend Christmas. Caroline took us everywhere. To the small store across from the town green, Merrill Brothers, that sold everything one could want, even melons and green beans in the winter. To mass at the Abbey of Regina Laudis, home to cloistered nuns who sang haunting, beautiful chants. One Sunday, her chauffeur's day off, Caroline drove us to mass in her long, green car, so big it fit all of us, including their Russian cook, Serge, with room to spare. Caroline stared straight ahead and gripped the steering wheel so tightly I thought she'd break it. Mrs. Ferriday told me later that people in town got word out to stay off the roads whenever Caroline took to that car.

But I was happiest just being at the house, for The Hay was the most beautiful one I'd ever seen, tall and white with black shutters and enough room for a family of ten. The furnishings were all quite old, but very nice, including parlor curtains Mrs. Ferriday had sewn herself, with the most intricate crewelwork. The barns out back were home to three horses, a handsome German shepherd named Lucky (whom Zuzanna and I were terrified of at first, until he proved to be a most gentle, loyal companion), many sheep and chickens, and a pig that followed Caroline everywhere. She spoke French to it.

"Come, *chérie*," she said as it waddled after her. "*Dépêchez-vous. Vous pouvez être beau, mais cela ne signifie pas que je vais attendre.*" You may be beautiful, but that doesn't mean I'll wait.

That pig even followed Caroline into the house on occasion, climbing up the front stairs with great effort, and to her bedroom.

Caroline was a different person up in Connecticut. She mucked out the animals' stalls dressed in blue jeans and a hunter's cap, even climbed up onto the roof with her father's old shotgun and shot at some rabbits she said had eaten her lettuce that year. Here was the solution to the mystery of why this woman was not married.

CHRISTMAS DAY WAS A DIFFICULT ONE with Pietrik and Halina half a world away. We wrote letters back and forth, of course, and Pietrik sent a package of my favorite sweets for Christmas and a pencil drawing of Papa and Marthe that Halina had sketched, but I still couldn't shake the tears.

It helped to keep Zuzanna close by. Zuzanna hadn't required a corrective surgery like mine, but suffered through a round of chemotherapy to fight her cancer. She was still weak, so Caroline arranged us side by side in their living room on Christmas Day, warm near the fireplace, me in a wheelchair and Zuzanna in Caroline's father's wing chair. This was my favorite room in that house, for it looked out across the garden, its great hedges and manicured boxwood paths beautiful even in winter.

We sat near the fire facing the Christmas tree in the corner, the angel atop it grazing the ceiling. There was a surprise under the tree from Caroline for each of us: a bottle of perfume Zuzanna had admired at a store called Bergdorf Goodman and a selection of books for me, including *The Power of Positive Thinking* by Norman Vincent Peale. I had not thought to find a gift for Caroline, but Zuzanna made a cut-paper picture for Caroline and Mrs. Ferriday featuring the house and all their animals. The horses and pig, chickens and cats. Even Lucky the dog and their African gray parrot. Zuzanna said it was from the both of us, but it was clear who'd created the work of art.

Mrs. Ferriday had Serge make the traditional twelve Polish dishes for dinner, which we all ate, stopping only for exclamations of true joy. After dinner, Mrs. Ferriday wheeled me into the big old kitchen at the back of the house. This was my second favorite room, with its black and white tile floor and white porcelain sink big enough to bathe a small adult in.

I sat at the kitchen table with Caroline and Mrs. Ferriday and watched Zuzanna and Serge wash the dishes together. My sister was still frail but insisted on washing up. Her hair was gone from the radiation, leaving her completely bald, just as so many of us at the camp once were. She'd tied one of Caroline's French scarves around her head like a milk woman. Serge stuck close to her all night, even after dinner. I knew they had become more than friends. I'd seen her sneak back to our bedroom just before dawn from the servants' wing. The thought of it sent tears to my eyes. How could my sister be so secretive?

Caroline poured us all coffee. How Matka would have loved being there. The coffee alone! Mrs. Ferriday opened a fresh package of my favorite cookies, Fig Newtons, and poured us each a thimble glass of orange liqueur.

"How was Zuzanna's blood work?" she asked.

"It's looking better," Caroline said. "They're optimistic."

"It *is* exciting, but you may still need more treatment, Zuzanna," Mrs. Ferriday said.

Zuzanna smiled. "Maybe then I could stay indefinitely."

Serge smiled back at her. Only a simpleton could miss the fact that they were sweet for each other. A Russian? He was good-looking enough in that simple Russian way, but what would Papa say?

"Let's get to California first," I said. "I can't wait to see the movie stars' homes. They say Rodeo Drive is packed with stars."

"You must get out there and smile for all those Californians," Mrs. Ferriday said. "It is a *lovely* tooth, dear."

I smiled and ran my tongue over my new canine, which had taken the place of my old decayed one. What would Pietrik think of my new smile?

I bit a Fig Newton in half and chased it down with the brandy in one shot as we did back home with vodka.

Caroline sniffed the cream and poured a bit in her coffee. "There are more interesting things to see in Los Angeles than celebrities. The La Brea Tar Pits, for one."

"Dying beasts trapped in tar?" Mrs. Ferriday said. "Gawd-awful. Let these women have some fun, dear."

Too bad Mrs. Ferriday wasn't coming to California with us. She took up the brandy and started to refill my thimble glass.

Caroline took the bottle from her. "No more brandy for the girls, Mother."

"Good gracious, Caroline. It's Christmas."

"Kasia's already had too much. She is *recovering*, Mother."

"A little brandy never hurt a patient. The Woolseys rubbed brandy on babies' gums."

Caroline stood, plucked the bottle from the table, and rested it on the counter. Mrs. Ferriday smiled at me and rolled her eyes. How lucky Caroline was to have her mother!

Zuzanna and Serge hadn't noticed any of it, since you've never seen two people so happy to do dishes, laughing and poking each other with sudsy fingers.

Caroline raised her cup of coffee to toast. "Merry Christmas, all."

"Wesołych Świąt," Mrs. Ferriday and I said, toasting with our empty glasses.

Merry Christmas.

CHAPTER 43

Kasia

1959

THE FOLLOWING SPRING WE ALL TRAVELED FROM OUR RESPEC-
tive cities and met up at San Francisco International Airport. We'd
been away for several months at that point, and all missed home,
but San Francisco had never seen so many happy Polish women.
Janina joined us all the way from France. She'd recovered there
with Anise's help and gone to hair school in Paris, which improved
our hairstyles a lot. How we all loved California! The air fresh and
clean, the sun so welcome to those of us who'd spent winter in cold
New England.

Nice as San Francisco was, Los Angeles was the highlight of the
West Coast. You should have heard the chatter on that bus. Where
to go first? Grauman's Chinese Theatre? Rodeo Drive? Best of all, I
could *walk*. Like a normal person. With some of the old pain left,
but without a noticeable limp. Plus, the plastic surgery had smoothed
out my calf and made my leg look more normal. Dr. Rusk had pre-
scribed some pain pills, but I could have walked Rodeo Drive all day.

We went to Disneyland, a place we'd heard so much about. The
thirty-six of us arrived by air-conditioned bus, Caroline filming it
all with her 8mm camera like a Hollywood director. She brought
her guitar along and played that at the noon meal, but we still had

a good morning. Frontierland was especially fun. We took a ride on a log raft at Tom Sawyer Island. Zuzanna fell in love with the Three Little Pigs. Somehow these three poor souls trapped in overstuffed human clothes, black eyebrows like parentheses painted on their papier-mâché heads in perpetual surprise, touched her heart. When Zuzanna simply mentioned this, it sent Caroline snapping a million pictures of my sister with these oversized, bald pigs.

Things got tense at the Casey Jr. Circus ride. That was the child-sized train that circled the edges of the park. It was not a particularly scary-looking train, but the haunting call of its whistle had followed us around the park all day. When it came time to board, Janina just couldn't. It was hard to forget that other train we'd been on.

After California, we toured our way back across America, stopping at the Grand Canyon and Las Vegas. Zuzanna thought she'd broken the slot machine when the lights started flashing and money poured from it. By the time we made it to Washington, D.C., and were introduced at a special session of Congress, we felt like movie stars ourselves.

Once we arrived back in New York, we all fanned out to stay with different families for our last week, and Zuzanna and I continued to be Caroline's guests, this time at her apartment in New York City. Caroline fussed over my sister like a mother hen, surprising her with a new nightdress and slippers. Once the doctors gave Zuzanna the good news that her cancer was officially in remission, Caroline celebrated and bought us both new dresses at Bergdorf Goodman. You've never seen a woman so happy—you'd have thought Caroline was Zuzanna's mother.

If eating was any indication, my sister was recovering with record speed. It may have had something to do with being in Manhattan, the place of Zuzanna's dreams. Or maybe it was Caroline's Russian cook stuffing Zuzanna with Polish food.

Or maybe it was the Automat.

"When I die, I want to come here," Zuzanna said, holding her white china cup under the silver-dolphin spigot. Coffee swirled into the cup, dark and fragrant.

If New York City was our Land of Oz, the Automat was our Emerald City. As the free matchbook said, it was the HORN & HARDART AUTOMAT AT FIFTY-SEVENTH AND SIXTH. It was warm enough inside to take your coat off, and food appeared there as if by magic. Happy women dressed in black, called nickel throwers, sat in the glass booths and made change for paper bills with rubber tips on their fingers. Put a nickel in a slot next to a food you liked, and the little door would open. Just like that you could choose cooked pullet, apple pie, brown-sugary baked Boston beans. Over four hundred different foods! We wanted to eat there every day.

Zuzanna and I blended in well. In our new Bergdorf Goodman dresses, we lived up to our new name, the Ravensbrück Ladies. It was hard to believe our trip was nearly over, that we'd fly out soon and leave it all behind, but I couldn't wait to get home. To see Pietrik. Halina. Hard as it was to admit, I'd even miss Caroline, who'd done so much for us all, but it would be nice to finally have Zuzanna to myself the whole plane trip home, to laugh and talk about everything.

Zuzanna set her tray across from mine.

"I'm getting fat, Kasia. Don't you love mashed potatoes?"

On her plate emerald peas rolled about a hill of mashed-up potatoes, a puddle of brown sauce on top.

A woman came to our table with a pot of fresh coffee and moved to pour some into my cup.

"No," I said, one hand over it, for I had not ordered extra coffee.

"It's called a free refill," said Zuzanna.

New York was full of surprises like that.

Zuzanna dipped her fork in potatoes, trapped a few peas, and ate. She looked wonderful, like a fashion model.

"What we wouldn't have given for peas back then," she said.

She couldn't bring herself to say Ravensbrück.

"At least now Herta Oberheuser is in a cold cell eating beans from a can," I said.

"You might think about letting it go, Kasia."

"I'll never forgive them, if that's what you're saying."

"It only hurts you to hold on to the hate."

My sister seldom bothered me, but her positivity could be irritating. How could I *forgive?* Some days the hate was the only thing that got me through.

I changed the subject.

"I'm glad you're getting fat," I said. "Papa won't know you. You're like a different person. Although one who has not even packed yet."

Zuzanna kept her eyes on her potatoes.

"I have a favor to ask you, Kasia."

I smiled. What would I not do for my sister? I ran the tip of my tongue over my new tooth, afraid it might not still be there. It was my favorite souvenir, smooth and perfect, the exact color of my other teeth. I practiced my smile just for fun. A group of young men and women came into the Automat and scrambled into a booth. A boy kissed a girl long and hard, right there in public. How free and happy they seemed. I could see it all with my smart new eyeglasses.

"Anything," I said.

Zuzanna pulled a folder from her bag and slid it next to my tray.

"I need your help. To choose . . ."

I opened the folder and flipped through the photographs inside. There were six, maybe seven pictures in there taken from the shoulders up, black-and-white, like passport photos, all of children. Some infants. Some older.

I closed the folder. "What is this?"

Zuzanna pressed little garden gates into her potatoes with the tines of her fork. "Caroline gave it to me."

"For?" I took her free hand. "Zuzanna. What's happening?"

She drew her hand away. "I've been wanting to tell you . . . I was at the hospital last week, and they asked my opinion about a case."

"That happens all the time. What does that have to do with anything?"

"Afterward they asked me if I would teach a class."

"*Here?*" I said.

"Yes, here. Where else, Kasia? I asked Caroline to extend my visa."

"You're not coming home?" Why had I fought to bring her there only to lose her?

"Of course I'm coming home. Don't be ridiculous. It's just that I was granted a special extension for doctors."

"It's the cook, isn't it?" Why had I let that go on for so long?

Zuzanna gave me her serious doctor look. "He has a name, Kasia."

"Papa will have a stroke. *I'm* not telling him."

"The photos of the children are from Caroline. They need homes. One named Julien just lost both parents to an automobile accident in Ingonish, on the coast of Cape Breton Island in Canada."

"That's what orphanages are for."

"He's a *toddler*, Kasia. Caroline says that if Serge and I make things, well, more permanent—"

"*Marry* him? I hope you're joking."

"Then she could help us adopt. Once I'm completely better. We want to open a restaurant together. Mostly crepes and quiche at first—"

"So I am to go home alone while you stay here and marry a Russian cook and open a French restaurant and raise someone else's child?"

"I am forty-four years old with no prospects, Kasia. You already have your family. This is my only chance."

"At home, you can—"

"Do *what?* Work myself to death at the hospital? Delivering other people's babies? Do you know what that's like? I'm going to do what I can to make my life a good one in the time I have left. I suggest you do the same. Matka would want that."

"What do you know about Matka? You think she'd want you sleeping with a Russian cook, turning your back on Lublin?"

Zuzanna snatched the folder and slid it back into her bag.

"I'm going to forget you said that, dear sister."

She walked out the door without a look back, leaving me with her tray, the mashed potatoes hardly touched.

CAROLINE BROUGHT US UP to The Hay for the final few days of the trip. My last morning in Connecticut, I woke with a start from a dream of flying over wheat fields, hand in hand with my mother. It was one of those happy, so-real-you'd-swear-it-was-true dreams, until I realized it was not Matka's but Herta Oberheuser's cold hand I was holding.

I sat up, heart hammering. Where was I? Safe in Caroline's guest bedroom. I felt the bed beside me. Cold. Zuzanna was up already? Visiting her Russian friend no doubt. Maybe it was good she was staying. She'd be safe and well cared for. But how could I go back to Lublin without her?

I padded down the hall in bare feet and through Caroline's high-ceilinged bedroom, past her perfectly made canopy bed, to the tall windows overlooking the garden below. A winged stone cherub stood in the center of the clipped circles of boxwood hedges, guarding the tulips and bluebells. Caroline knelt at a rose bed, steam rising from the white mug next to her on the grass as a sea of lilac bushes swayed behind her in the breeze.

I breathed in the safety of it all and exhaled, my breath on the glass turning the scene into a blur of electric green and lavender. I ached to see Pietrik and Halina again, but there in that old house, nothing could hurt me, a whole ocean between me and my troubles.

I dressed and wandered downstairs in search of my sister and hot coffee. Finding neither in the kitchen, I hesitated at the kitchen window and watched Caroline in the garden. She wore canvas garden gloves, her hair caught back with a scarf as she tugged weeds from soil around the thorny stalks. Caroline's pig lay sleeping open-mouthed a stone's throw away under a lilac bush, pawing at the ground as if running in her sleep. Should I join them? I was in no mood for a lecture.

Caroline spotted me at the window and waved to me with her trowel.

I had no choice but to step out the kitchen door.

"Have you seen Zuzanna?" I asked.

"She and Serge took Mother to Woodbury. Come and weed, dear. It's good for the soul."

So is coffee, I thought.

I walked along the gravel path and knelt beside Caroline. The house rose above us like a great white ship from a sea of purple lilacs waving at its base. You've never seen lilacs in such colors, from deep aubergine—almost black—to the palest lavender.

"Sorry I took the last of the coffee," she said. "The early risers got to it first."

A dig at me? I ignored it.

"I think you designed the perfect garden," I said.

"Oh, it was Mother. We'd just moved in, and Father called the landscapers to come plant a garden, and they surprised Mother when they asked for a garden plan. She took a pencil and sketched the design of the Aubusson rug in the library and handed it to the men. Works perfectly well, I think."

From where I knelt, the scent of rose and lilac was almost solid. "Such a beautiful fragrance."

Caroline pulled out a dandelion, hairy root and all, and tossed it in her bucket. "The scent is strongest in the morning. Once the sun is overhead, things dry out and flowers keep the fragrance to themselves."

Why had I not spoken to Caroline about her garden before? We had a common love of flowers, after all. I slid a trowel from her bucket and pulled a green sapling from the earth with a satisfying pop. We worked without speaking, spearing the dark earth with our trowels, the only sounds the birds chattering in nearby trees and Caroline's pig's gentle snore.

"I must say, you're the rock of your family, Kasia dear."

How nice it was to hear that praise! "I suppose."

"I knew the first time I saw you onstage in Warsaw that you have a special strength."

"Not really. Since my mother . . ."

Caroline rested one canvas-gloved hand on my arm. "Seems like your mother was a remarkable woman, very much like you. Strong. Resilient. I'm sure you loved her very much."

I nodded.

"I thought I might die when my father passed away. It was so long ago, but there isn't a day that goes by that I don't wish he were here." Caroline waved toward the lilac bushes that swayed above us. "He loved these. It's a lovely reminder of him, but terribly sad too, to see his favorite Abraham Lincoln lilacs blossom without him."

Caroline wiped her cheek with the back of her gardening glove, leaving a dark smudge below one eye, then pulled off her gloves.

"But it's fitting in a way—Father loved the fact that a lilac only blossoms after a harsh winter."

Caroline reached over and smoothed the hair back from my brow with a light touch. How many times had my mother done that? "It's a miracle all this beauty emerges after such hardship, don't you think?"

Suddenly, water came to my eyes, and the grass swam in front of me. I could only nod.

Caroline smiled. "I'll have Mr. Gardener pack you up some lilac saplings to plant back in Lublin."

"No need to pack any for Zuzanna," I said.

Caroline sat back on her heels. "I wanted to tell you sooner—"

"It's fine. It's good, really. At first I was sad, but you've helped her in ways I never could. To get well. To raise a child of her own someday. My mother would have liked that. I don't know how to thank you."

Caroline pressed her hand over mine. "That's not necessary, Kasia dear."

"Zuzanna and I have taken so much from you. I wish I had something to give."

"You've been good for all of us, especially Mother."

We continued weeding in silence. I would miss Bethlehem.

Caroline turned to me. "Well, there is one thing, Kasia . . ."

"What is it?"

"Something I've been meaning to discuss with you."

"Of course."

"It concerns, well, someone . . . someone you used to know."

"Anything."

"Well, Herta Oberheuser, actually."

Just the name made me feel sick to my stomach.

I steadied myself, one hand to the grass. "What *about* her?"

"I am terribly sorry to even bring it up, but my sources tell me she may have been released early—"

I stood, dizzy, trowel in hand. "Impossible. The Germans can't let her out . . ." Why could I not breathe?

"As far as we know, Americans did this. Back in 1952. Quietly."

I paced toward the house and then back. "She's been out all this time? Why would they do that? There was a trial—"

"I don't know, Kasia. With Russia trying to woo German doctors away from the U.S., we may've been trying to curry favor. Somehow the Germans lose every war but win every peace."

"Your sources are *wrong*."

Caroline stood and touched my sleeve. "They think the West German government has helped Herta settle up in Stocksee. Northern Germany. She may be practicing as a doctor again . . . A family doctor."

I brushed off her touch. "I don't believe it—she killed people, did this to me." I pulled back my skirt.

Caroline stepped closer. "I know, Kasia. We can fight it."

I laughed. "Fight *them*? How exactly would this happen?"

"First, we need someone to make a positive ID."

"And that someone would be . . ."

"Only if you're comfortable."

The sun came up over the trees, warm on my shoulders. "*Comfortable?* No, I'm not *comfortable* with that." I threw the trowel in the bucket, where it landed with a clatter. "How can you even suggest I visit Herta Oberheuser?" All at once, the sun seemed too hot.

"We need a photograph or an official receipt from her office. Otherwise, it's simply hearsay."

"Snap a picture of Herta Oberheuser? You're *kidding*."

"I'll provide transit papers and money."

Was she really asking me to go see Herta? I conjured up her face. The smug look. The bored expression. My stomach contracted. Was I going to be sick there on the perfect grass?

"I'm sorry. You've been very kind to us, but no thank you." I started along the gravel path toward the house.

Caroline followed. "Sometimes we must sacrifice for the greater good."

I stopped and turned.

"*We?*" So Zuzanna would stay here safe while I alone went to find Herta?

"Please just consider it, dear."

"But—"

"Take your time. We'll go make a fresh pot of coffee."

The pig woke with a start, struggled to her feet, and followed as we walked to the house, our steps crunching in the gravel.

It felt good to be needed by Caroline, but she was asking the impossible. To go see *Dr. Oberheuser?* Would I have to talk to her? Would she recognize me? Remember Matka?

By the time we made it to the house, I realized Caroline was right about the roses. Once the sun was overhead, the fragrance was gone.

CHAPTER 44

Kasia

1959

BACK IN LUBLIN, THINGS HAD CHANGED SO MUCH. I'D BEEN gone less than nine months, but it felt like ten years. Pietrik had moved us to our own apartment at the Lubgal Ladies Garment Factory where he worked, just outside of the city. The whole place was no bigger than Caroline's kitchen in Connecticut, but it was *ours*, just the three of us. No Papa. No Marthe. Zuzanna was with Serge in Connecticut. Two bedrooms all for us.

The kitchen was compact, barely big enough to turn around in. On my day off from the hospital, I sewed blue curtains Matka would have loved, gingham, with birds along the hems, and I arranged the two little bottles of vodka the stewardess from my flight home had given me along the kitchen windowsill.

Pietrik seemed happy to have me home. Had he missed me? He would not say, and I was not about to ask, but he was all smiles when he met me at the airport, a single pink rose in hand. I was all smiles as well with my new tooth. Perhaps things would be better between us? Why did I feel so shy with him, my *husband*? I could walk so much better, too. The pain pills the Mount Sinai doctor gave me to ease the little discomfort I still had were running out, so I was irritable at times. But I was eager to make things right again, to get back to how it was before the war.

ONE LATE AFTERNOON that fall I went to the postal center to see Papa. He handed me a package through the bars of the pickup window.

"I got to this before the censors did," he whispered.

The package was no bigger than a shoe box and wrapped in brown paper.

"Be careful about what your friends mail you."

The return address was *C. Ferriday, 31 East 50th St., New York, NY, U.S.A.* Caroline had been smart not to send it from the consulate. It would have been opened for certain. But any communication from the West was suspect and noted on one's record.

"And a letter from Zuzanna," Papa said.

He looked curious, but I just tucked both under my coat.

I hurried home to our apartment and climbed the three flights of stairs, finally able to walk like a normal person. Halina had pinned a new poster on our door: DISTRICT 10 ART EXHIBITION: PO-LAND IN POSTERS. It was graphic and stark, a new look for her. How had I forgotten the art show was that night? Since I'd left, Halina had attacked art with new vigor. I tried not to think about this.

I set the brown paper package on the kitchen table and stared at it. I knew what was inside.

I heard a pebble hit the kitchen window and went to see who'd thrown it. Neighborhood boys, no doubt. I pulled up the window sash, ready to scold, and saw Pietrik standing below.

"It is a beautiful day!" he said. "Come out and play."

"You will break the window with those stones," I said, resting my weight on my forearms along the windowsill. He was still so handsome, like a boy. A little thicker around the middle, but every-where we went women still glanced at him when they thought I wasn't looking.

"Are you going to make me come up there and get you?" he said with a smile, hands on his hips.

I closed the window, and he was up the stairs in seconds. He arrived in the apartment winded, his cheeks flushed. He came to me and tried to kiss me, but I turned away.

"Remember me, your husband?" he said.

"I think I have the flu. My muscles ache. I can't stop sweating."

"Still?" said Pietrik. "Maybe because you're not taking those pills."

"I don't know," I said.

Pietrik placed his hand on the package. "What is this?"

"From Caroline," I said.

"Well?" Pietrik tossed the box to me. "Open it."

I caught it. "Not yet."

"What are you waiting for, Kasia?"

"I know what's in it. She wants me to go up to a town in Germany called Stocksee. To identify . . ."

"Who?"

I placed the box back on the table. "Herta Oberheuser."

"She's *out*?" Pietrik said.

"They think she might have a medical practice up there. And they need an eyewitness identification from someone who knows what she looks like."

"Still a *doctor*? Are you going?"

I said nothing.

"You'd need special papers, Kasia. And even that doesn't guarantee they let you through."

"That's what is in the package," I said.

"And it isn't cheap. The gas alone—"

"That's in there too," I said. "Knowing Caroline, both zlotys and marks."

Pietrik took a step closer. "We have to go, Kasia. Finally we can *do* something to get back at them. I'll come with you. Just getting across the border is dicey as hell. Do you know how many people have died crossing it?"

"Illegally. People do it legally every day."

"It's harder now. Plus the area's full of booby traps and mine-fields. Fifty thousand GDR guards patrol it, all top marksmen. When in doubt, they shoot first."

Pietrik took up my hands in his.

"I'll come with you. Halina can stay with your parents."

"I'm done with all that, Pietrik. The underground. Ravensbrück. I need to move on."

"That's the problem—you can't move on. Have you even said two words to your daughter since you've been home?"

"She's been busy with art class—"

"She missed you when you were gone. Made a calendar and X'd off the days till you came home."

"I'm working two shifts now," I said.

Pietrik took hold of my shoulders. "Can you make room for her?"

"She's always over at Marthe's . . ."

He walked to the chair where he'd thrown his jacket and reached for it.

"It's always someone else, Kasia." Pietrik headed for the door. "You never learn, do you?"

"Where are you going?" I asked.

"To our daughter's art show."

I stepped toward him. How could he just leave? "What about dinner?"

"I'll eat elsewhere." He stopped at the doorway. "And give serious thought to going up to Stocksee with me. It isn't every day you get a chance to do something like this, Kasia."

I turned away and heard the door close, my stomach ready to erupt. I watched him through the window as he walked off, hands in his pockets. Halina met him in the street, hauling a black portfolio pregnant with artwork. They embraced and went their separate ways, Halina headed up to the apartment. When she reached our place, I was still nursing a grudge.

"You look awful," Halina said.

"Thanks."

"Are you coming to my art show tonight? I was kind of hoping you would."

Halina looked more like an artist every day, that day dressed in one of Pietrik's old shirts, splattered with paint. She wore her blond hair piled on top of her head as my mother used to. It was hard to look at her, almost the exact image of Matka.

I tucked Caroline's package under the table. "I have work to do."

"You've never been to one of my shows, Matka. A teacher wants to buy my poster."

I looked out the window. "Better run and catch Father. He'll buy you dinner."

"They are serving cheese at the show," Halina said.

"And vodka, I suppose."

"Yes."

If the modern art wasn't modern enough, it would become so after a paper cup of two-hundred-proof alcohol.

"Run along and find Father," I said.

Halina left without a goodbye. I went to the window and watched her once she made it to the street below. She looked so small. Would she turn and wave? No. At least Halina connected with one parent.

I opened Zuzanna's letter, a short one and to the point, the way she always handled things when the news was bad. She would not be returning. She had extended her visa again and hinted a wedding was in the works. There was one bright note, though. The doctors at Mount Sinai agreed that her cancer was still in remission.

I drank to that, draining one of my airplane vodkas.

There was only hot cereal in the cupboard, so I made a bowl and poured a glass of Pietrik's vodka. For vodka made in someone's basement, it traveled down the throat easily. As Papa used to say, you could taste the potatoes. It was more flavorful than the airplane vodka, and it stayed down as long as I didn't imagine the contents of my stomach, gray hot cereal and vodka, sloshing around.

No wonder Pietrik drank it on occasion. It made my whole body tingle and warmed arms and fingers, head and ears. Even my brain was numb by the time I slipped into my American dress. I smiled at the mirror. With my tooth repaired, I could look at myself again. Why shouldn't I go and enjoy my daughter's big night? The nylon stockings covered the few scars I had left. Even my husband might be happy to see me.

It was a short walk to Halina's school. I stepped into the gymnasium and found it filled with bright spotlights trained on posters hung on the cinder-block walls. People milled about admiring the students' artwork. Marthe and Papa stood at the opposite end of the room talking to an arty-looking couple. A card table across the room held bottles of vodka and a paper plate of cheese cubes.

"You came, Matka," Halina said with a smile. "First time ever. Come, let me show you everything."

Pietrik stood at the other end of the room, leaning with his hand on the wall, in deep conversation with a woman in a red hat.

"Perhaps some cheese first," I said, my breath suddenly short.

We went to the refreshment table, and I took some cheese cubes and a paper cup of vodka.

"Since when do you drink vodka?" Halina asked.

"It's important to try new things," I said.

I tasted it, then tipped my head back and drank it in one shot. It was smoother and had a more refined taste than ours at home. I was becoming a vodka aficionado.

"Let me show you my self-portrait," Halina said. She took my hand in hers, and my eyes stung with tears. When was the last time she had taken my hand?

Halina's work was grouped along one wall, full of bright color. Graphic and strong. A portrait of a woman, Marthe no doubt, cooking, painted as if through a kaleidoscope. Next, a fish with an automobile body full of gears and machine parts.

"Do you like the one in the kitchen?" Halina asked.

"The one of Marthe? What pretty colors."

"That isn't Marthe. It's you," she said. "I did it in blue. Your favorite."

More tears came to my eyes, and the colors swirled like paint in a water jar.

"Me?" I said. "How nice."

"I have been waiting to show you the best one. Teacher wants to buy it, but I may keep it."

I tried to dry my eyes with my napkin as Halina brought me farther down the wall to her self-portrait. Once I stood there in front of that canvas, it was as if it reached out and bit me, it was so alive.

"Well?" Halina said.

It was the largest painting in the room, a woman's full face, with golden hair, and a wreath of thorns wrapped around her head.

It was my mother.

I became warm all over, and my head spun. "I need to sit down."

"You don't like it," Halina said. She folded her arms across her chest.

"Yes. Yes, I do. I just need to sit."

I sat on a folding chair and watched Pietrik laugh with his lady friend while Halina went to fetch me another vodka. There was a reason I didn't go out much.

Halina grabbed Pietrik's hand and brought him over.

"Here, Matka," Halina said, handing me a cup of vodka.

"What got you to come here?" asked Pietrik with a smile. "Wild horses?"

"Certainly not you," I said.

Pietrik's smile faded. "Not here, Kasia."

"You're enjoying the show," I said with a jerk of my chin in the red hat's direction. My vision was blurry, my tongue loosened by the spirits.

"You've been drinking?" Pietrik said.

"Only you are allowed to drink," I said, taking a sip from the paper cup. I felt a new clarity of thought.

Pietrik reached for the cup. "I'm taking you home."

I snatched the cup back and stood just as Marthe and Papa came by, Halina's art teacher in tow.

"You are Halina's mother?" said the teacher, a pretty, dark-haired woman, who wore round, black glasses and a violet caftan. The teacher put one arm, the sleeve like a batwing, over Halina's shoulder.

"Halina and I have long talks," said the teacher. "She speaks highly of you."

"Oh, really?" I said. "She admits she has a mother?"

The group laughed a little too hard. It was not that funny.

"Oh, yes, *teens*," said the teacher. "Have you seen Halina's self-portrait? My colleague at the university says it's his favorite piece here."

"It's my mother," I said.

"Pardon?" said the teacher.

Marthe and Papa exchanged looks. The room spun like a fun house.

"Halina painted it of *herself*, Kasia," Marthe said.

Pietrik took my arm.

"If you *knew* my mother, you wouldn't be sleeping in her bed today," I said.

"We're going home," said Pietrik.

I pulled away from his tight fingers. "Halina may not have told you in one of those long talks, but I got my mother killed by working in the underground. After all she did for me."

I brought the paper cup to my lips, and it collapsed in my hand, splashing vodka down my dress front.

"Pietrik, we'll take Halina home to our house," Marthe said.

"Yes, my mother was an artist just like Halina here, but she drew portraits for bad people, Nazis in fact, if you must know." I felt my face wet with tears. "What happened to her? Only God knows, Mrs. Art Teacher, because she never said goodbye, but take it from me, the woman in that poster is my mother."

All I remember after that is Pietrik holding me up on the way home, us stopping for me to be sick in an alleyway and to wipe formerly hot cereal off my American dress.

I WOKE BEFORE DAWN the next morning.

"Water," I called out, for a second thinking I was in the *Revier* at Ravensbrück.

I sat up in Halina's bed and saw that my dress had been exchanged for my nightshirt. Pietrik had changed me? The previous night bobbed to the surface, and my cheeks burned there in the dark. What a fool I'd made of myself. Even before rising, I knew I'd go to Stocksee.

I walked past Pietrik's room. He slept with one arm across his face, chest bare. Beautiful. What if I just crawled in with him? Why didn't I have the courage to sleep with my own husband?

As dawn broke outside our window, I gathered my overnight things and pulled open Caroline's package, careful not to make a sound. In the small box I found my transit papers. German money. Polish money. A letter addressed to Germany's largest newspaper detailing Herta Oberheuser's war crimes at Ravensbrück and her early release, complete with German postage. Three maps, a list of approved gas stations at which to purchase fuel, and detailed travel instructions. A note apologizing for only being able to obtain one set of travel papers, and a whole package of Fig Newton cookies. I tossed the box in my suitcase and clicked the locks. Pietrik stirred in the next room.

I froze for a second. Should I leave a note? I scribbled a quick goodbye on the paper from Caroline's package and made my way down the stairs to the old turquoise car Papa loaned me now and then, the one Pietrik had kept alive for years. As Papa said, that car had more rust on it than paint, but it got us wherever we needed to go.

At first, I fretted as I drove. What if it really was Herta? Would she hurt me? Would I hurt *her*? My head cleared a bit once I was under way, one of the few drivers on the road that early. I spread a map and the driving instructions out on the seat next to me, turned the radio volume up, cranked the window down, and breakfasted on a whole cellophane sleeve of Fig Newtons. The box said, NEW TWIN-PAK STAYS FRESHER! and they did taste better than ever, soft and moist cookie outside, sweet figgy middle. Eating these helped my mood very much. Perhaps this trip was a good idea after all.

On my way northwest, I passed through one neglected village after another, the only color in the drab towns the red on white propaganda posters proclaiming the virtues of socialism and the UN-BREAKABLE FRIENDSHIP WITH THE PEOPLES OF THE SOVIET UNION.

The travel arrangements were complicated, since Germany had been stripped of all the land it had taken during the war. In the East it had been returned to Poland under Russian occupation, and in the West it was divvied up between the Western Allies. Two new states had been created out of occupied Germany, free West Germany, no longer fully occupied by the Allies, and the smaller German Democratic Republic, or GDR, in the East.

It took me a whole day to make it through Poland and East Germany. The roads were potholed and often strewn with litter, and it was rare to see other passenger cars. A Soviet military convoy lumbered by, license plates painted out. The soldiers riding in the back of the trucks eyed me as if I were a circus oddity. The first night I slept in my car, one eye open, alert for robbers.

The next day, through dense fog and drizzle, I made it to the inner German border, the 1,393-kilometer boundary between West German and Soviet territories. Caroline had directed me to one of the few routes open to non-Germans, the northernmost designated transit route, to the Lübeck/Schlutup checkpoint. As I approached the guardhouse and the red-striped pole, which blocked the road, I slowed and pulled up behind the last car in line.

Light rain fell on the car roof as I waited and I studied the white concrete watchtower standing along the wall in the distance. Were they watching me from up there? Could they see my dying car spewing lavender smoke as I waited? Somewhere a guard dog barked and I considered the stark surrounding countryside and the long, metal fence that ran the length of the road. Was that where the booby traps were, beyond that fence? I would be fine as long as I didn't have to get out of the car.

My car inched forward in line, my naked windshield wipers useless, the rubber stolen long before by petty bandits. I turned off my radio so I could concentrate. Where was Zuzanna when I needed her? Oh yes. Enjoying her new life in New York City. I rechecked my papers for the tenth time. Three pages thick and signed in ink with a flourish. *Kasia Kuzmerick, Cultural Ambassador,* it said. I ran my finger over the raised seal. I certainly didn't look like any cultural ambassador but those papers made me feel important. Safe.

By the time I made it to the gate, my dress was soaked with sweat under my heavy coat. I rolled down my window to speak with the East German guard.

"Polski?" said the guard.

I nodded and handed him my papers. He took one look and turned toward the guardhouse, my papers in hand. "Don't turn off the car," he said, in German.

I waited and studied my gas gauge. Was the needle actually moving downward as I watched? Two more East German soldiers swept aside the guardhouse curtains and glanced out at me. At last, a middle-aged officer came out to my car.

"Get out of the car," he said in German-accented Polish.

"Why?" I said. "Where are my papers?"

"They have been impounded," said the officer.

Why had I not listened to Pietrik? Maybe he was right. Some people never learn.

CHAPTER 45

Kasia

1959

IT TOOK ME SOME TIME TO GET OUT OF MY CAR AT THE CHECK-point, for the door would not open, no matter how I tried. I climbed across and out the passenger side, much to the amusement of the border guards, standing there flaunting their rifles.

The rain was down to a fine mist, and I watched it collect and bead on the shiny cap brim of the officer who had ordered me out. I braced myself with one hand on the hood of the car, for my legs felt about to fail, then snatched it away, for the metal was hot from the engine. Was the car about to overheat?

"You have fancy papers," the officer said. "They have, however, been replaced with a one-day pass."

"But they are——"

"If you don't like it, turn around," the officer said. "Either way, get this car out of here—it's on its last leg."

I took the pass. Did he see my fingers trembling? The pass, soggy by then and no bigger than a pack of cigarettes, was a miserable exchange for my beautiful papers.

"Make sure you are back here by six tomorrow morning, or you will be living here in this house with us." He waved the next car forward, signaling the end of the conversation.

Back in the driver's seat, I broke out in a cold sweat of relief. The second checkpoint was easier, and once the West German border guards checked me through, I crossed into the West, and drove north toward Stocksee.

West Germany was like a different world, a wonderland of green fields and neat farms. The road was smooth, and modern trucks passed me on that popular trucking route, for my car refused to go over fifty miles per hour. I stopped only once, at the first telegraph office I saw, and sent a wire to Caroline saying I was on my way.

Somewhere on the outskirts of Stocksee, I heard a terrific clank and turned to see my muffler fall on the asphalt and clatter to the side of the road. I backed up and retrieved the lanky hunk of metal and hurled it into my backseat. After that, my car sounded like the loudest motorbike when I pressed the gas pedal, but what choice did I have? I had to keep going.

I chugged into Stocksee in the early afternoon and shivered as I passed the flowered sign: WILLKOMMEN IN STOCKSEE! Herta's home base? It was a rural town close to a lake with the same name, a big lake, tranquil and dark. She always did like lakes.

I drove past rolling farmland and into the heart of Stocksee, a tidy little place. If the dress of the inhabitants was any indication, Stocksee was a conservative place too, for most wore traditional *Tracht*, the men in lederhosen, *Trachten* coats, and alpine hats, the women in dirndl dresses. I slowed my car by a sidewalk and asked a man for help in my best rusty German.

"Excuse me, sir, could you tell me where Dorfstrasse can be found?" The man ignored me and kept walking. A stab of fear went through me when I saw a woman resembling Gerda Quernheim, Nurse Gerda from the camp, pass by on the sidewalk. Could it possibly be her? Out of prison already?

I found the doctor's office, a single-story building of white-painted brick. I parked far down the street, relieved to turn my car off, and sat there attracting hostile looks from passersby. One peered into the backseat in a pointed way, looking at the muffler lying there. I tried to steady my breathing and gain courage. Should I just return home? Call the police and ask for help? That might not end well.

A silver Mercedes-Benz slid by me and docked at the curb in front of the doctor's office. It was an older model but the kind of car Pietrik would have admired.

A woman got out of the car. Could that possibly be Herta driving such an expensive car? Why had I forgotten my glasses? My heart beat like a crazy, flip-flopping fish. The woman was too skinny to be her, wasn't she? My hands were slippery on the steering wheel as I watched the woman walk into the doctor's office.

I slid to the passenger door and exited, the hinges complaining, and shook my hands about like two wet mops, trying to calm myself. I entered the doctor's office, and stopped to read the brass sign next to the door: FAMILY MEDICAL CLINIC. The words WE LOVE CHILDREN were painted below. Children? It couldn't be Herta. Who would let someone like her touch their little ones?

It wasn't a big waiting room, but it was unnervingly neat and tidy. The walls were painted with schools of manic fish and turtles, and an aquarium bubbled in the corner. I sat and thumbed through magazines, glancing now and then at the patients, waiting to see if she'd walk by. It was hard to look at those well-fed infants with their velvety skin and know Herta might be the one touching them. As their names were called, the mothers went in to see the doctor just as we once had. Did she give them their inoculations or leave that to a nurse?

I watched an angelfish in the tank suck in and spit rocks from the pink-gravel bottom. A German mother sat across the room, the picture of Aryan purity. The Nazis would have put her on the cover of every magazine during the war. I considered telling her how they killed babies at Ravensbrück, but then thought better of it. Never volunteer information. The Germans were always suspicious of that.

Though it was cool in the room, sweat ran down my back. To calm myself, I paged through *German Mother* magazine. The war was long since over, but the *Hausfrauen* had not come far. Still working hard, but no longer for their beloved Führer. If the magazine was any indication, the Germans worshipped a new idol—consumer goods. Volkswagens, hi-fis, dishwashers, and televisions. At least that was an improvement. The receptionist scraped her glass window open.

"Do you have an appointment?" she asked, blue eye shadow on her lids. Makeup? The Führer would not have approved.

I stood.

"No, but if the doctor is free, I'd like one."

She handed me a clipboard, a long form trapped under the silver clamp.

"Fill this out, and I'll check," she said.

The Germans still loved their paperwork.

I filled in the form with my real married name and a false address in the nearby town of Plön. It was barely readable, my fingers shook so. Why worry? The war was long over. Hitler was dead. What could Herta do to me?

I listened to the music as I waited. Tchaikovsky? It wasn't calming me.

The last patient went in to see the doctor, and I sat alone. Would she remember me? I was certain she'd recognize her own handiwork.

The receptionist appeared at her window.

"The doctor will see you after the last patient. I will be leaving soon, so may I have your paperwork?"

"Of course," I said and handed her the clipboard.

I'd be there alone with the doctor? Should I just leave?

I went to the wooden coat-tree in the corner, empty except for a white lab jacket, to hang up my coat. The nameplate pinned to the breast pocket said DR. OBERHEUSER. A chill ran through me. How

458 · Martha Hall Kelly

strange to see that name in print. At Ravensbrück the staff had been careful not to reveal their names. Not that we hadn't known them.

The receptionist stood and tidied her desk, ready to go home.

Why stay? If I left then, no one would know I'd been here. Caroline could send someone else.

The last mother walked through the waiting room, baby at her shoulder, and smiled at me as she left the office. I thought of Mrs. Mikelsky's baby with a pang of sadness. I could follow that nice girl out of the waiting room and go home to Lublin. I hurried my coat on and started toward the door, openmouthed, sucking in air. I made it and felt the knob smooth in my hand.

Just go.

Before I could turn it, the receptionist opened the door that led to the back rooms.

"Kasia Bakoski?" she said with a smile. "The doctor will see you now."

CHAPTER 46

Caroline

1959

OCTOBER 25, 1959, TURNED OUT TO BE A PERFECTLY LOVELY day for a wedding. Mother was in rare form, despite the fact the United States had just launched monkeys Able and Baker into space on a Jupiter missile and she was knee-deep in a letter-writing campaign to end such animal cruelty.

It was a year of firsts. The first diplomatic visit to the United States by a Soviet premier, Nikita Khrushchev. The first time the musical *Gypsy* played on Broadway. The first wedding at The Hay.

Serge and Zuzanna were guaranteed good weather for their nuptials, since we'd erected a tent at great expense in the lower yard below the garden. It was Indian summer up in Bethlehem, hazy, hot, and just a bit blustery.

This was not a society wedding, if that is what you are accustomed to—far from it, as our procession back from the church proved. Our raucous little group meandered from Bethlehem's Catholic church, past the town green, to The Hay, attended by a great gonging of bells from the town's churches. All of Bethlehem had come out for Serge and Zuzanna's big day, except for Earl Johnson, who felt duty-bound to remain on his post office stool.

Mother, understated in gray taffeta, led the procession, Mr. Merrill from the general store by her side. She walked backward, conducting her Russian orchestra friends, their instruments festooned with gay flowers and ribbons. They performed a rousing version of Bach's "Jesu, Joy of Man's Desiring," lovely actually, on balalaika.

Next came the bride and groom. Serge was striking in one of Father's gabardine suits we'd cut down for him and wore the kind of wide grin usually found on a man standing next to a trophy marlin on a Key West pier. What man wouldn't be proud to marry lovely Zuzanna? She was part Audrey Hepburn and part Grace Kelly, with the temperament of a spring lamb. She and her strong-willed sister, Kasia, were as different as chalk and cheese. Kasia refreshingly forthright, Zuzanna subtler.

Mother had sewn Zuzanna a dress of ecru lace. It was becoming, even with dollar bills pinned all about it in the Polish tradition, the breeze sending them fluttering like a flapper's fringe. The bride carried a spray of Mr. Gardener's Souvenir de la Malmaison roses, fragrant and blush pink. The groom carried a blossom as well— a ten-month-old named Julien, peach cheeked with a headful of hair that was, as Mother would say, "black and straight as a Chinaman's." The dear boy had officially been theirs for two weeks, and his feet had yet to touch terra firma, so many adults loved holding him so.

After various and sundry cousins and acquaintances came Betty and me. She was resplendent in a Chanel suit, the mink heads on her stole bouncing with each step. I wore a lavender raw silk sheath Mother had whipped up, which Zuzanna said suited the mother of the bride, which sent me into tears even before the service. Bringing up the rear was Lady Chatterley the sow, daisy chain around her neck, and like many of our guests most concerned with the prospect of good cake.

Our procession wended its way to our gravel driveway. Back beyond the house, behind the barns, the hayfield stretched all the way to the next street over, Munger Lane. The hay had been harvested, leaving the naked meadow spiky with tufts of straw, and the maples and elms at meadow's edge, already starting their crimson turn, swayed in the breeze. Back there, one's eye naturally goes to the end of the meadow, beyond the orchard to my old playhouse.

I considered the little house, a white clapboard echo of its parent, with its sturdy chimney and pedimented entryway fitted with child-sized benches. The black door shone in the sun and the silk curtains Zuzanna had sewn, the color of pussy willows, lapped out the windows with the breeze. I was not surprised it had become Zuzanna's cocoon of sorts, where she went when the world was just too much. It was once my place of solace, where I'd spent days reading after Father died.

Once the procession wound around to the back garden, Betty and I went to the kitchen to fetch the petit fours Serge's sous chef had prepared.

Serge had opened a restaurant in nearby Woodbury, weekend home of well-heeled Manhattanites. He called it Serge! and it was an immaculate hole-in-the-wall that had a line out the door on Saturday nights. This was not surprising, since everyone knows New Yorkers, when deprived of good French food for more than twenty-four hours, become impossible and seek it out like truffle pigs. Or maybe it was Zuzanna's Polish desserts that kept patrons lining up.

"I do love the Polish traditions, don't you, Caroline? Pinning money to the bride? Genius." Betty plucked a petit four from the box and popped it into her mouth whole.

I tied on one of Serge's new aprons with his logo, a black *S*, down the front. "Stop pinning hundred-dollar bills on the bride, Betty. It's vulgar."

"It's such a practical tradition."

"At least it's distracting Zuzanna. From dwelling on the fact that none of her family could be here."

"Those two need a honeymoon, Caroline. Must be exhausting tending to a teething child."

"She misses her sister."

"Kasia? Fly her in, for heaven's sake."

"It isn't that easy, Betty. Poland's a Communist country. I had a hard enough time getting her a transit visa to go to Germany—"

"To confront that doctor? *Really*, Caroline . . ."

"I sent everything she needs, but I haven't heard a word from her."

I'd mailed the package to Poland weeks before, express, with more than enough money for her trip to Stocksee, and still hadn't heard a peep. And I wasn't the only one waiting to hear if it truly was Herta Oberheuser. A slew of British doctors was ready to help me pressure the German government to revoke Herta's medical license. Anise and friends were ready to go to battle as well. Herta was just one of many on our list of Nazi war criminals who needed to be held accountable.

"Your persuasive powers are first-rate, dear. You won't catch me traipsing up to some godforsaken German town to identify a deranged Nazi doctor."

How did Betty manage to boil every situation down to the absurd? Had I taken advantage of Kasia by asking her to identify Herta? She would be fine—such a strong, capable person, not unlike myself at her age.

"Well, anyway, don't worry about all that, Caroline. I have a gift for you."

"That isn't necessary."

Betty heaved a Schiaparelli tote onto the kitchen table.

"It's lovely, Betty."

"Oh, the bag is Mother's, and she wants it back—she's become positively miserly in her old age. But the gift is inside."

I reached into the bag and felt the flannel, that unmistakable feeling of metal muffled by cloth, and knew instantly what it was.

"Oh, Betty." I held on to the table to steady myself.

I pulled out one flannel roll and unfurled it to find a row of oyster forks.

"It's all there," Betty said. "I've been buying it from Mr. Snyder for years. You know he calls me first when he has anything good. When he had Woolsey silver . . ."

I pulled all twenty rolls from the bag and piled them into a brown-flannel pyramid on the table. Even the silver petit four tongs were there.

Betty wrapped her arms around me, and I rested my cheek against cool, smooth mink. "Now, don't get all teary on me, Caroline. This is a joyous day."

How lucky I was to have such a generous friend. Mother might pretend not to care, but she would be delighted the Woolsey silver was back.

Betty and I set up the wedding cake on a card table in the garden and used my long-lost silver tongs to serve the petit fours. The happy couple stood, surrounded by wedding guests and the last of the fall smooth-leaf hydrangeas with their white-blossom globes, like bystanders craning their necks to see the festivities. Mother, holding Julien, managed to cut the cake, while the couple took her loving cup between them, sipping vodka from it while Betty and members of the orchestra shouted, "*Gorku! Gorku!*"—Bitter! Bitter!—to urge them to drink.

On my way back to the house for more lemonade, I heard the tinkle of a bicycle bell and turned to find Earl Johnson riding around the corner of the house, his tires leaving a dark snake of an impression across the grass. He rode his red Schwinn Hornet bike, complete with chrome headlamp, the white straw basket peppered with yellow plastic daisies.

Earl removed his cap and had the good sense to look sheepish. "Sorry to ride on the grass, Miss Ferriday."

"Don't worry about it, Earl," I said. So what if I'd asked him ad nauseam not to ride on the lawn? "It's only grass. Just maybe walk around next time?"

Zuzanna spotted Earl and walked toward us, baby on her hip. On her way, she plucked a sprig of late fall lilac. She brushed it under Julien's chin, causing him to draw his legs up and down like a frog in delight. How sure Zuzanna's step was now that she was finally well.

Earl stood straddling his bike. "Got a letter for you. From——" He squinted at the return address.

I plucked the letter from his fingers.

"Thank you, Earl." I glanced at it just long enough to see Paul's handwriting and tucked it in my apron pocket. I ran my fingers across the letter there and felt it was thick. A good sign. Was it simply a coincidence that Pan Am had recently started direct flights from New York to Paris?

Earl produced a second envelope from his bike basket. "And a telegram. All the way from West Germany." He handed it to me and waited, hands on his handlebar grips.

"Thank you, Earl. I can take it from here."

Earl turned with a "Good day" and walked his bicycle back toward the front of the house but was intercepted by Mother, who led him to the cake.

Zuzanna reached me, an expectant look in her eyes.

I tore off one side of the envelope and pulled out the telegram. "It's from Kasia. From West Germany."

I caught the scent of zinc oxide and baby powder as Zuzanna covered my hand with hers—cold, but caring and soft. A mother's hand.

"Shall I read it aloud?" I asked.

Zuzanna nodded.

"It reads: 'Under way to Stocksee. Just me.' "

"That's it?" Zuzanna asked. "There must be more."

"I'm sorry, but that's all, dear. She signs off, 'Kasia.' "

Zuzanna released my hand and steadied herself. "So she's going. To see if it's Herta. By her*self*?"

"I'm afraid so, dear. You know how important this is. She's a brave girl. She'll be fine."

Zuzanna held Julien close. "You don't know what they're like."

She turned and walked in the direction of the playhouse, the baby at her shoulder watching my shrinking form with one shiny fist to his mouth. The band struck up "Young Love" by Sonny James as I watched Zuzanna walk across the meadow.

Once at the playhouse, she stepped inside and gently closed the door, leaving me with a sinking feeling I'd finally gone too far.

CHAPTER 47

Kasia

1959

THE RECEPTIONIST LED ME INTO THE DOCTOR'S OFFICE.

"Wait here," she said.

It was nicely furnished, with an Oriental carpet, pale green walls, and French doors that overlooked a quiet garden. It smelled of leather and old wood, and the furniture looked expensive. An upholstered sofa. A shiny brown side table with feet like lion's paws. A tall leather chair at the doctor's wide desk. Across from the desk sat a black-painted chair with a caned seat, clearly earmarked for the visitor. Could this really be where Herta spent her days? If so, it was quite a step up from her last office. She was certainly not eating beans out of a can.

"You are the last appointment," said the receptionist. "The doctor's had a long day. Two surgeries this morning."

"Some things never change," I said.

"Pardon me?"

I walked to the chair. "Oh, nothing."

My hands shook as I grasped the wooden arms of the chair and lowered myself down. Built-in bookcases lined one wall, and a pink china clock sat on a shelf.

"I'll be leaving now," the receptionist said. "Here is your receipt. The doctor will be in shortly."

"Thank you," I said.

I glanced at the receipt: *Dr. Herta Oberheuser* was printed in pretty script across the top. My evidence!

I almost took the receptionist's hand and begged her to stay in the room with me but instead watched her leave. What could possibly happen? She closed the door gently behind her. If this was indeed Herta's office, how good it would feel to tell her off, then slam that door behind me when I left.

I stood and walked to the bookcase, the carpet muffling my steps. I ran one finger down a smooth, leather-bound book set and pulled out a heavy volume, *Atlas of General Surgery*. Herta's specialty. I slipped the book back into place and stepped to the gilt-framed oil paintings on the wall of cows in a field. The desk held a blotter, a telephone, a facial tissue box, and a silver water pitcher on a china plate. The pitcher perspired. That made two of us.

I looked at the diplomas framed on the wall. DÜSSELDORF ACADEMY FOR PRACTICAL MEDICINE. DERMATOLOGY. There was another for infectious diseases. No surgical diploma? I poured myself a glass of water.

The door opened, and I turned to see the woman who'd stepped out of the silver Mercedes slip into the room. I froze, my mouth suddenly full of sand, and then placed my glass on the desk. It was Herta.

She strode to the desk, clipboard in hand, wearing her white doctor's coat, a black stethoscope draped around her neck. Thank goodness she didn't offer to shake my hand, because my palms were wet.

I sat, my whole body jellying, as she eyed my paperwork on the clipboard, her attitude somewhere between bored and irritated.

"What can I do for you today, Mrs. Bakoski? New patient?"

"New patient, yes," I said, clasping my hands in my lap to stop them from shaking. "Looking for a family doctor."

She sat in the leather chair and pulled herself to the desk.

"Polish?" she asked as she uncapped her fountain pen. Was that a hint of disdain?

"Yes," I said and forced a smile. "My husband is a grocer."

Why was I shaking so? What was the worst that could happen? Commandant Suhren was in a pine box in a German cemetery. Or was he? The way Nazis were turning up in that town, I might see Suhren doing the backstroke in the lake.

"You live in Plön?" She frowned, lifted my glass from the desk, and placed a linen coaster under it.

"Yes," I said.

"On School Street?"

"That's right."

"Funny, there is no School Street in Plön."

"Did I write School Street? We are new to town." Outside the window a magpie fluttered its wings.

"What can I help you with today, Mrs. Bakoski?"

How could she not recognize me when her face was so etched in my mind?

"Can you tell me your background?" I asked.

"I was trained as a dermatologist and have recently made the switch to family medicine after practicing for many years both at Hohenlychen Sanatorium and a large teaching hospital in Berlin."

Once my heart stopped thumping so loudly, I became more comfortable with my role. She really didn't recognize me.

"Oh, that must have been interesting," I said. "And before that?"

"I was a camp doctor at a women's reeducation camp in Fürstenberg."

She leaned back in her chair, fingers steepled. There was no doubt it was her, but Herta had changed. She had become more refined, with her longer hair and expensive clothes. Prison had not broken her but had made her more sophisticated somehow. My whole body tensed at the thought. How was it that the criminal was enjoying such a luxurious lifestyle while the victim was driving around in a tin can?

"Oh, Fürstenberg is lovely," I said. "The lake and all. Pretty."

"So you've been there?"

That was the moment. I had a choice. To walk out having identified her or stay for what I really wanted.

"Yes. I was a prisoner there."

The clock chimed the half hour.

"That was a long time ago," Herta said. She sat up straight in her chair and organized phantom objects on her desk. "If you have no further questions, I have patients to see, and I am behind schedule."

There was the old Herta. She could only be pleasant for so long.

"I am your last appointment," I said.

Herta smiled. A first. "Why stir up old dust? You're here for some sort of vigilante justice?"

All my rehearsed speeches went away. "You really don't recognize me, do you?"

Her smile faded.

"You operated on me. Killed young girls. Babies. How could you do it?"

"I did my job. I spent years in prison just for doing academic research."

"*Five* years. You were sentenced to twenty. So this is your excuse? Academic research?"

"Research to save German soldiers. And for your information, the German government for years has exercised the right to use executed criminals for such research purposes."

"Only we weren't *dead*, Herta."

Herta took a closer look at me. "I served my time, and now, if you'll excuse me—"

"My mother was at Ravensbrück too."

Herta closed her desk drawer a little too hard. "I can't be expected to keep track of every *Häftling*."

"Halina Kuzmerick."

"Doesn't sound familiar," Herta said without a second's hesitation.

"You had her moved to Block One."

"There were over a hundred thousand *Häftlings* at Ravensbrück," Herta said.

"Don't say *Häftling* again."

"I have no recollection of that person," Herta said with a quick glance in my direction.

Was she afraid of me?

"Halina Kuzmerick," I repeated. "She was a nurse. Worked with you in the *Revier*."

"There were three shifts of prisoner nurses. You expect me to remember one?"

"She was blond and spoke German fluently. An artist."

Herta smiled. "I would like to help you, but my memory is not the best. I'm sorry I can't remember every nurse who sketched portraits."

The clouds outside shifted, and sunlight poured through the window onto Herta's desk. Everything slowed.

"I didn't say she sketched portraits."

"I have to ask you to leave. I really am busy. My—"

I stood. "What happened to my mother?"

"If you're smart, you'll go back to Poland."

I stepped closer to her desk. "They may have let you out, but there are people who think you deserve more punishment. Lots of them. Powerful people."

"I paid the price."

Herta capped her pen and tossed it onto the blotter. Her ring caught the sunlight and threw a kaleidoscope of light about the desk.

"That's a beautiful ring," I said.

"My grandmother's," Herta said.

"You're a sick person. Pathological."

Herta looked out the window. "I don't know what you're talking about."

"Relating to or manifesting behavior that is maladaptive——"

"This ring has been in my family——"

"Save it, Herta."

Herta took a fancy leather pocketbook from the drawer. "Is it money you want? Seems like every Pole has their hand out."

"If you don't tell me exactly what happened to my mother, I will go to the people who sent me and tell them you're here, with your Mercedes-Benz and your clinic where you treat *babies*. Then I'll go to the papers and tell them everything. How you killed people. Children. Mothers. Old people. And here you are, like nothing happened."

"I don't——"

"Of course the fancy paintings will have to go. And the leather books."

"All right!"

"The fine clock too——"

"Just *stop* it. Let me think." Herta looked down at her hands. "She was a very good worker, if I recall. Yes, she had the *Revier* running well."

"And?" At this rate, I would miss the border checkpoint time by hours.

Herta tipped her head to one side. "How do I know you won't tell the papers anyway?"

"Keep going," I said.

"Well . . . she stole. All *sorts* of things. Bandages. Sulfa drugs. I couldn't believe it. Turns out a pharmacist from town named Paula Schultz came with deliveries for the SS apothecary and funneled supplies to her. Heart stimulants. Shoe polishes for their hair, so the older women——"

"I know what it was for. Keep going."

"All that was bad enough, but I didn't know about the list." Herta snuck a look at me.

I leaned in. "What list?"

"The surgical list for the sulfa tests. Nurse Marschall discovered your mother took it upon herself to, well, edit it."

"Edit it how?" I asked, but I knew.

"She tried to take you and your sister off. And another prisoner."

"So they killed her?" I said, tears flooding my eyes.

"Sent her to the bunker first. Then Nurse Marschall told Suhren about the coal. How she took it to make remedies for the *Häftlings* with dysentery. I never even told him she broke into the apothecary closet, but the coal was enough for Suhren."

"Enough to kill her?" I said, feeling myself sucked down a drain.

"It was stealing from *the Reich*," Herta said.

"You didn't stop them."

"I didn't know it was happening."

"The wall?" I groped for my purse looking for my handkerchief, unable to continue.

Herta took her cue.

"I really must be going now," she said and started to stand.

"*Sit,*" I said. "Who shot her?"

"I don't think—"

"Who shot her, Herta?" I said, louder.

"Otto Poll," Herta said, speaking faster. "Binz woke him up from a dead sleep."

She *was* afraid of me. Just the thought made me stand straighter.

"How did it happen?"

"You don't want—"

"How did it *happen*? I won't ask again."

Herta sighed, her mouth tight.

"You want to know? Fine. On the way to the wall, Halina kept telling Otto she knew an SS man. Someone high up. Lennart someone. 'Just contact him. He'll vouch for me.' I had sent that Lennart a letter for her, I'll have you know. At great risk to myself."

So that was why Brit had seen Lennart at the camp. Lennart the Brave had come to Matka's rescue after all. Just too late.

"Keep going," I said.

"'Are you sure?' Otto kept saying to Binz. He loved the ladies. Then Halina asked a favor—"

"What favor?"

"'Just let me see my children one more time,' she said, which Suhren allowed . . . big of him, considering her betrayal. I had no idea we'd operated on you and your sister. Binz took her to where you both were sleeping. After that, she went quietly. Once Suhren met them at the wall, they got on with it. 'Just do it,' Binz said to Otto, but his gun jammed. He was crying. She was crying. A *mess*."

"And?" I asked.

"This is all so sordid," Herta said.

Did I really want to know?

"Tell me," I said.

"He finally did it." Herta paused. It was so quiet there in her office, only the sound of children far off in a garden, playing.

"How?" I asked. *Just get through this, and you'll be back in the car on the way home soon.*

Herta shifted in her chair, and the leather sighed. "When she wasn't expecting it."

At long last, the story I'd waited to hear. I sat down, hollowed like a blown-out egg but strangely alive. Hard as it was, suddenly I wanted every crumb of it, for each detail seemed to penetrate and bring me back to life.

"Did she cry out? She was terrified of guns."

"Her back was turned. She wasn't expecting it." Herta wiped away a tear.

"How did you feel?"

"Me?" Herta asked. "I don't know."

"You must have felt *something* once you found out."

"I was very sad." She plucked a tissue from the box. "Are you happy now? She was a good worker. Practically pure German. Suhren punished me for getting too close to her."

"Were you?"

Herta shrugged. "We were somewhat friendly."

I knew the doctor had liked Matka, but would my mother really have socialized with this criminal? Matka had surely only pretended to be friendly in order to organize supplies.

"If you'd known we were Halina's daughters, would you have taken us off the list?"

Herta laced her fingers and stared at her thumbs. We listened to the faraway hum of a lawnmower.

After several seconds, I stood.

"I see. Thank you for telling me the story."

Why was I *thanking* her? It was all so surreal. Why couldn't I rail at her, tell her to go to hell?

I started toward the door and then turned back.

"Give me the ring," I said.

She clasped her hands to her chest.

"Take it off now," I said. "And put it on the desk."

The thought of touching her made me queasy.

Herta sat still for a long second and then pulled at the ring.

"My fingers are swollen," she said.

"Let me see," I said as I took a deep breath and grasped her hand. I spat on the ring and worked the band back and forth. It released and revealed a narrow strip of white at the base of her finger.

"There," Herta said, avoiding my eyes. "Are you happy? Go, now."

She stood, walked to the window, and looked out over the garden. "And I expect you to keep your end of the bargain. You won't tell the newspapers? Do I have your word?"

I rubbed the ring on my skirt, wiped off every bit of Herta, and slipped it on my left ring finger. It felt cold and heavy there. A perfect fit.

Matka.

I walked toward the door.

"You won't hear from me again," I said.

Herta turned from the window. "Mrs. Bakoski."

I stopped.

Herta stood there, one hand balled in a fist at her chest. "I . . ."

"What is it?"

"I just wanted to say that, well . . ."

The clock ticked.

"I would bring her back if I could."

I looked at her for a long moment.

"Me too," I said.

I stepped out of the office with a new lightness, leaving the door ajar, no longer craving the vibration of the slam.

I WAS ABLE TO FIND the Stocksee telegraph office and hurried in to send two short telegrams.

The first was to Pietrik and Halina: *I am fine. Be home soon.*

The other was to Caroline in Connecticut: *Positively Herta Oberheuser. No doubt.*

I ripped up the letter to the newspaper. Caroline would take care of Herta in due time. It was no longer important to me.

I drove to the Lübeck/Schlutup checkpoint and made it through with little difficulty. Though I hadn't slept, I felt awake and alive on the road home to Lublin. My mufflerless engine seemed powerful and revved with each press of the gas as I drove over the gentle hills toward home. The moonlight showed the way past vast, dark heaths, past blue and white cottages, past slivers of silver birch shining in the dark forest.

I relived my conversation with Herta, reveling in the idea my mother had said goodbye. I touched my forehead and smiled. The dream kiss had been real.

I cranked my window down and let the scent of autumn run around the inside of the dark car, the smell of fresh-mown hay taking me back to Deer Meadow, to thoughts of Pietrik warm beside me, to him holding baby Halina at the breakfast table, reading the newspaper with the bundle of her in his arms. Not letting her go. How easy it is to get tangled up in your own fishing net.

By the time I arrived at Lublin's outskirts, it was still dark, that time between when the streetlights turn off and dawn's first light when anything seems possible.

I coasted down the streets so as not to wake the city, past the silent milk women coming with their cows, bells clanging in the dark.

I passed the square under Lublin Castle where the ghetto once stood, now gone, demolished by forced laborers during the war, leaving only a brass plaque. Past our old pink sliver of a house where, at Felka's grave in the backyard, Caroline's lilacs had already taken root, on their way to growing into the prettiest, strongest plant. I rode down the street where Matka once walked me to school. I smiled at the memory of her, no longer a hot knife to the chest. I passed the new hospital and thought of Zuzanna with Caroline and hoped she was well. Maybe Halina and I would go to New York one day. She would like the art museums.

Once in the apartment, I slipped out of my shoes and padded down the hallway to Halina's room. I stood in the darkness and watched her chest rise and fall. Matka's ring sent gleams of light across the bed as my daughter rested there, her hair fanned out like liquid gold. She didn't stir as I slipped the red-flannel bundle of brushes under her pillow, tucked her in tight, and kissed the top of her head.

I went to Pietrik's bed, where he lay in the almost darkness, one arm across his eyes. I unbuttoned my dress, let it fall to the floor, and climbed under the sheets to meet the smoothness of him, breathing in his sweet scent of sweat and Russian cigarettes and home.

He pulled me close, and for the first time in so long, I felt the compact go *click*.

Author's Note

*L*ILAC GIRLS IS BASED ON A TRUE STORY. CAROLINE FERRIDAY and Herta Oberheuser were real people, as were all the Ravensbrück staff mentioned, as well as Herta's parents and Caroline's mother and father, Eliza and Henry Ferriday. In bringing them to life as characters, I have done my best to represent them in the fairest, most realistic way possible. Through reading Caroline's letters, the Nuremberg Doctors Trial testimony, and testimony of the survivors themselves, I found clues to what their motivations might have been. The dialogue throughout is of my own making, but I used actual testimony when possible in the Doctors Trial chapter and some of Caroline's own words from letters and stories she wrote and the stories of those who knew her.

At Ravensbrück, Hitler's only major concentration camp for women, a prisoner's life depended on her relationships with other women. More than seventy years later, survivors still speak of their "sisters" in the camp, so I thought it fitting to use two sisters as the focus of my story. Kasia Kuzmerick and her sister Zuzanna are based on Nina Iwanska and her physician sister Krystyna, both operated on at the camp. I shaped these characters from the qualities and experiences of the seventy-four Polish "Rabbits" I grew to love through the course of my research, and I hope they serve as exemplars of the spirit and courage every one of the women showed.

Having two beloved sisters of my own, five sisters-in-law, and two daughters whose sisterly bond I've watched blossom over twenty-six years, it was impossible to remain unmoved by Nina and Krystyna's story.

I first learned of Caroline Ferriday through an article in *Victoria* magazine published in 1999, "Caroline's Incredible Lilacs." The article showed photos of Caroline's white clapboard home in Bethlehem, Connecticut, which the family called The Hay, now known as the Bellamy-Ferriday House. There were also photographs of her garden, filled with antique roses and specimen lilacs. A longtime fan of all things lilac, I carried the article with me until it was worn smooth. With three young children, I had little spare time, but I visited the estate a few years later, unaware that that trip would lead to the novel you hold in your hands.

I drove up to Bethlehem one May Sunday and pulled into the gravel driveway. I was the only visitor that day, so I was able to breathe in the essence of the house, which remained as Caroline left it when she died in 1990: The faded wallpaper. Her canopy bed. Her mother Eliza's hand-sewn crewel draperies.

At the tour's conclusion, the guide paused on the landing outside the second-floor master bedroom to point out the desk, her typewriter, medals, and a photo of Charles de Gaulle all arranged there. The guide picked up a black-and-white photograph of smiling, middle-aged women posed in three rows.

"These were the Polish women Caroline brought to America," she said. "At Ravensbrück they were known as the Rabbits for two reasons. They hopped about the camp after they were operated on, and because they were the Nazis' experimental rabbits."

As I drove home on the Taconic Parkway, with the lilac plant I bought, which had been propagated from Caroline's lilacs, filling the car with sweet perfume, the story pestered me. Caroline was a true hero with a fascinating life, a former debutante and Broadway actress who galvanized a jaded postwar America and dedicated her life to helping women others forgot. Strongly influenced by her staunchly abolitionist Woolsey ancestors, she'd also helped bring the first black bank to Harlem. Why did it seem no one knew about her?

I devoted my spare time to research on Caroline, Ravensbrück, and World War II. Any afternoon I could get away I spent in the cool root cellar under the ancient barn attached to The Hay, which today serves as the welcome center, paging through old rose books and letters, absorbed in Caroline's past. Once Connecticut Landmarks and their site administrator Kristin Havill cataloged it all and placed it safely in archival boxes, Kristin would lug them up and down the stairs for me to comb through. Caroline also left additional archives at the United States Holocaust Memorial Museum in Washington and at Nanterre, outside of Paris, a trail of clues I felt was calling me to follow.

As I discovered more about Caroline's life, it intersected with others' integral to the story, especially those of the Polish women subjected to operations at Ravensbrück. I began to discover their journeys through memoir and other accounts and learned how Caroline grew to love them as her own daughters. I taped photographs of all seventy-four Polish ladies around my office and planned to go to Poland to see Lublin, where many of the girls lived when they were arrested, for myself.

A third person kept coming up in my research on Ravensbrück, the only woman doctor in the all-female camp and the only woman doctor tried at Nuremberg, Dr. Herta Oberheuser. How could she have done what she did and especially to other women? I taped her photo up too, along with photos of the other Ravensbrück camp staff, but on a separate wall, and added Herta's to the stories I'd tell.

I moved from Connecticut to Atlanta in 2009 and began writing, at first sitting in the concrete and chain link dog kennel behind our home, hoping it would evoke what it was like to be imprisoned, to feel what the Ravensbrück Ladies felt. But as I read more firsthand accounts of the women's stories, I realized I didn't need to sit in a cage in order to feel their story. They brought me there all too well. The terrifying uncertainty. The rip of losing their friends and mothers and sisters. The starvation. I found myself eating constantly, trying to eat for them.

The following summer I traveled to Poland and Germany. With my seventeen-year-old son as my videographer, we landed in Warsaw on July 25, 2010, and set out for Lublin with Anna Sachanowicz, our lovely interpreter, a schoolteacher from a Warsaw suburb.

As we walked through Lublin seeing the places the survivors referenced in their memoirs, the story came alive. We walked through massive Lublin Castle, where the Ravensbrück Ladies were first imprisoned, and spent an afternoon at the incredible Museum "Under the Clock," which still houses the cells where many Polish underground operatives were tortured and where you can see one of the secret letters the girls used to tell the world of the operations. I walked through Crakow Gate, which withstood Nazi bombs, and through the vast plaza at the foot of Lublin Castle where the Jewish ghetto once stood. It gave me new resolve to make sure the world remembered. Everywhere we went, Lubliners told us of their own experiences in the war years and about the Katyn Forest Massacre, the Stalinist years, and what life had been like behind the Iron Curtain.

In Warsaw I was lucky enough to interview a Ravensbrück survivor, Alicja Kubacka. Her story of her imprisonment at Ravensbrück provided incredible historical details, but her attitude of forgiveness toward her captors turned everything on its head. How could she not resent, even hate, the German people? How could she not only forgive them but also visit Germany every year at their request to aid in the healing?

My son and I decided to take a train route similar to that which the Rabbits took on the terrible day they were transported, in September 1941. Riding from Warsaw to Berlin, we watched the simple train stations of Poland give way to more modern *Bahnhofs* of Germany. By the time we reached the sleek Berlin Hauptbahnhof, a sophisticated marvel of engineering, it was clear Poland had been kept back by its years behind the Iron Curtain.

Once we stepped off the train at Fürstenberg onto the same platform the Ravensbrück Ladies had stepped onto, I could only imagine their despair. As my son and I walked the same walk the prisoners were forced to take, the camp came into view, the metal gate at the camp entrance and rows of barracks gone but the massive wall still standing. The crematorium is still there today and the place where the gas chamber, a repurposed painter's shed, now demolished, once stood is still there as well. So is the shooting wall and the lake into which the prisoners' ashes were thrown. The commandant's house still overlooks the camp and the tailor's workshop, the massive complex of buildings where the Nazis sorted their plunder, remains as well.

Once back in the States, I wrote for more than three years, breaking to travel to Paris to sift through Caroline's archives at Nanterre. There, I sat with a French translator who read me every one of Caroline's letters, many between her and Anise Postel-Vinay, one of her partners in what she saw as a life dedicated to justice. Each night after riding back on the Métro from Nanterre, I returned to the grand Hôtel Lutetia and slept in one of the rooms that once served as a hospital room for those returning from the camps.

That same year I also spent time at the United States Holocaust Memorial Museum in Washington, D.C., where Caroline left her third archive, her papers devoted not only to her work with the Rabbits but also to her later work with her French friends in the ADIR, a French organization dedicated to the care of returning concentration camp deportees, helping them pursue Klaus Barbie.

My goal with all this research was to write a fictionalized account of the events that took place at Ravensbrück, to take readers to the places that the people involved in the story of the Rabbits passed through, and perhaps give some insight into what they might have been feeling in order to breathe new life into a story that had fallen from public view.

When I tell people the story of the Rabbits, many wonder what ultimately happened to Herta Oberheuser. She and Fritz Fischer escaped the hangman at Nuremberg. She was sentenced to twenty years in prison, but after five years was quietly released in 1952, her sentence commuted by the American government, perhaps to curry favor with the Germans as a result of pressure from the Cold War. She established a flourishing medical practice in Stocksee in northern Germany as a family doctor. Once a Ravensbrück survivor recognized Herta, Caroline and Anise Postel-Vinay urged a group of British doctors to pressure the German government to revoke Herta's medical license. Herta fought back with powerful friends of her own, but Caroline took to her typewriter and lobbied the press in America, Great Britain, and Germany. In 1960 Herta's license was revoked and she was forced to permanently close her doctor's surgery.

Another success came for Caroline in 1964. After a successful lobbying campaign by Caroline, Norman Cousins, Dr. Hitzig, and lawyer Benjamin Ferencz, on behalf of the Ravensbrück Ladies, the West German government finally granted the women reparations in 1964. It was one of Caroline's greatest triumphs, for it was a particularly harrowing process, since Poland was under Russian control and Bonn refused to recognize it as a country.

Through the years that followed, Caroline stayed in close touch with many of the Rabbits. She hosted them often at her home, and they came to see her as their godmother, often using that term as a salutation in their letters to her. She wrote that they felt like daughters to her.

Readers often ask if Caroline's relationship with Paul Rodierre is based on fact and indeed it is, inspired by a relationship a dear friend of Caroline's shared with me. His physical qualities are sprung from my imagination, but I like to think she wouldn't be too cross with me for giving her such a handsome literary partner.

Caroline died in 1990 and left her treasured home in the care of Connecticut Landmarks, which has kept it in lovely condition, just as Caroline wished. It is well worth a visit at any time, but in late May when the lilacs are blooming, you will understand why Caroline and her mother could not be away from their beloved garden for too long.

If my version of the story has inspired you to learn more about the events surrounding *Lilac Girls* and you would like to continue reading, there are many fine works of historical fiction and memoir that deal with the same topics, including *Women in the Resistance and in the Holocaust*, edited and with an introduction by Vera Laska; *The Jewish Women of Ravensbrück Concentration Camp*, by Rochelle G. Saidel; and *Ravensbrück*, by Sarah Helm.

Enjoy the journey. With any luck it will take you places you never dreamed possible.

Acknowledgments

MANY THANKS TO THOSE WHO MADE WRITING *LILAC GIRLS* such a joy:

My husband, Michael Kelly, who happily read every draft, shared my dream of telling Caroline Ferriday's story, and never doubted this day would come.

My daughter Katherine, for her supreme wisdom, her encouragement, and for being the model for Kasia's resourcefulness and intuition.

My daughter Mary, for her splendid editorial suggestions, cheerful, unflagging support, and for inspiring the character Zuzanna.

My son, Michael, for traveling with me to Poland, for discussing infinite plot variations as we drove to and from high school each day, and for his lightning in the sand.

Kara Cesare at Ballantine Bantam Dell, the most caring, talented editor a person could wish for, who understood and embraced Caroline's story like no one else.

Nina Arazoza and the whole team at Ballantine Bantam Dell for their seamless collaboration and enthusiasm: Debbie Aroff, Barbara Bachman, Susan Corcoran, Melanie DeNardo, Katie Herman, Kim Hovey, Kara Welsh, Kristin Fassler, Jess Bonet, Emma Caruso, and Paolo Pepe to name a few.

My amazing agent, Alexandra Machinist, who plucked me from

the slush pile, insisted this story needed to be told, and made it happen.

Betty Kelly Sargent for her early encouragement and expertise, and who said, "All I need is a chapter."

My sisters, Polly Simpkins for her wisdom, generosity, and unconditional love, and Sally Hatcher, a model big sister.

Alexandra Shelley, independent editor extraordinaire, for her honesty, deep knowledge of the subject, and manuscript help.

The wonderful Alicia Kubecka, Ravensbrück survivor, for her friendship and for telling me her incredible stories of loss and forgiveness.

Wanda Rosiewicz and Stanislawa Sledziejowska-Osiczko for their sweetness and love and for courageously sharing the details of their experiences as victims of the Ravensbrück sulfa experiments.

My mother, Joanne Hall, who could have had a houseful of lovely antiques but chose a houseful of children instead.

My father, William Hall, for his positivity.

My sister-in-law, the author Mary Pat Kelly, who said, "Just do it."

Alexander Neave, Benjamin Ferencz, George McCleary, and Cecile Bernard, who knew Caroline and generously shared their memories of her.

Kristin Havill, Erica Dorsett-Mathews, Marj C. Vitz, Carol McCleary, and Barbara Bradbury-Pape of Bellamy-Ferriday House and Gardens, Connecticut Landmarks, for sharing their vast knowledge and support.

My mother's dear friends Betty Cottle, Jan Van Riper, and Shirley Kennedy, who showed me how a generation of strong New England women can make the world a much better place.

The filmmaker Stacey Fitzgerald, for her friendship and for showing me the importance of mutual aid and cooperation.

Kristy Wentz, for her love and for keeping my life together.

Jamie Latiolais, for his color wizardry and insightful manuscript comments.

Dr. Janusz Tajchert and Dr. Agnieszka Fedorowicz, who welcomed me to Poland and lent me their knowledge of Ravensbrück and the sulfa experiments.

Bernard Dugaud, who shared his Frenchness and his champagne.

Barbara Oratowska, director of the Museum of Martyrdom "Under the Clock," Lublin, Poland, for her stories about Lublin and "the Rabbits," and for her dedication to caring for the remaining Ravensbrück survivors.

Anna Sachanowicz, who guided and interpreted our way through Poland, and Justyna Ndulue, who helped us in Germany.

Hanna Nowakowskicz, for her friendship and assistance.

David Marwell, director of the Museum of Jewish Heritage, for his time.

Cathy Murray, who keeps me together, body and soul.

Nancy Slonim Aronie, for her fabulous Chilmark Writing Workshop.

Natasa Lekic and Andrea Walker at New York Book Editors, for their help and encouragement.

Carol and Chuck Ganz, for their support.

Carol Ann Brown, president of the Old Bethlehem Historical Society and Museum, Bethlehem, Connecticut, for her insight into beautiful Bethlehem's past.

Jack Alexander and Chris McArdle of the Arnold Arboretum of Harvard University, for sharing their considerable lilac knowledge.

Janie Hampton, author of *How the Girl Guides Won the War*, for her research help.

Irene Tomaszewski, for her support and for co-writing the wonderful book *Code Name: Zegota: Rescuing Jews in Occupied Poland, 1942–1945*, with Tecia Werbowski.

Lilac Girls

MARTHA HALL KELLY

A
READER'S
GUIDE

A Conversation
Between Martha Hall Kelly
and Lynn Cullen

We asked Lynn Cullen, bestselling author of *Twain's End* and *Mrs. Poe*, to pose some questions to Martha Hall Kelly, author to author.

Lynn Cullen: The story of the prisoners at Ravensbrück, the only all-female concentration camp in Nazi Germany, is one that begged to be told with the insight into human behavior that only a novel can provide. Yet, more than seventy years passed before you brought this important episode in history to light in your novel, *Lilac Girls*. I strongly believe that important stories like this choose their tellers, not the other way around. Why do you think this story chose you?

Martha Hall Kelly: I do feel like something inhabited me the day I stepped into the lovely Bellamy-Ferriday House. Caroline? The Rabbits? Whoever they were, they led me on an incredible journey, through Poland, Germany and France to find the truth about this story. Perhaps all of those brave women, almost seventy years after World War II, wanted their story told.

LC: Is there one particular bit of research that drove you to write this book? Did the same trigger sustain you as you made your journey of discovery through what must have been painful territory?

MHK: I found two manuscripts in Caroline's archives, memoirs written by two of the so-called Rabbits. Caroline had paper-clipped the rejection letters from publishers to the manuscripts, as well as her apologetic notes to the women, telling them she had submitted their work to publishers and there was no interest in their stories. Seeing those rejections spurred me to write *Lilac Girls* and kept me going when I would hit a bumpy spot. It was great motivation knowing Caroline and the Rabbits wanted the world to know their story so badly.

LC: The incomprehensibly inhumane behaviors carried out in Ravensbrück represent the darkest side of the human animal. I applaud you for giving your readers an unsparing look at these atrocities but yet I'm also grateful that you juxtaposed the darkness with characters who appealed to what Abraham Lincoln called "the better angels of our nature." Was it difficult to switch back and forth during the writing?

MHK: Writing in first person, it's so easy to get immersed in the characters, good and bad. So, yes, it was a wonderful relief, after living with some of the terrible things that happened in the camp, to switch back to write about Caroline's life in New York City. Not hard, really, because I loved writing every bit of it, even the most heinous scenes, but definitely an emotional relief sometimes.

LC: Has the writing of *Lilac Girls* changed your life?

MHK: *Lilac Girls* was my first novel and introduced me to the world of writing. Now, having something I can't wait to do when I get up each morning has transformed my life in every way imaginable. It made me more confident about *everything*, more curious about the world and just a million times happier. Also, I'm a shy person but wanted to be able to speak out and stand up for things I believed in. Now, after spending so much time researching Caroline, who always did the right thing, I find myself looking for people to help and wrongs to right. It seems corny to the usually cynical me, reading this over, but it's true. Many readers write and tell me they have experienced that same urge to incite positive change after reading *Lilac Girls* and it makes me incredibly happy.

LC: Can you share anything about your next project?

MHK: I can only say it's a prequel to *Lilac Girls* and takes place during World War I. So far it has been great fun to write and I have done extensive research in Russia for it. I can't wait to share it with everyone.

*Portrait
of
Caroline
Ferriday*

*Caroline's
incredible
lilacs*

The "Rabbits" pose postwar. Polish survivors of the Ravensbruck concentration camp sulfa experiments

Lublin, Poland, hometown of the Rabbits

Ravensbrück concentration camp blocks

Interior of the two-story
Ravensbrück punishment bunker

The author meets a survivor of the experiments, Mrs. Stanislaus Sledziejowska-Osiczko, known to friends as "Stasia."

The shooting wall, on the seventieth anniversary of the liberation of Ravensbrück, at The Ravensbrück Memorial Site

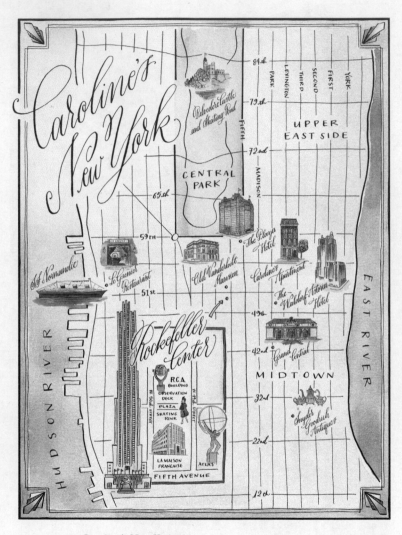

Caroline's New York

Kasia's Lublin

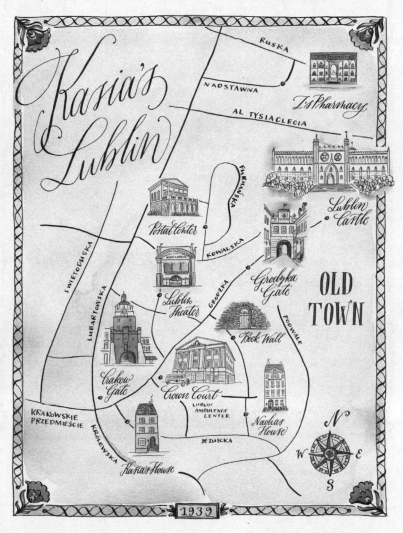

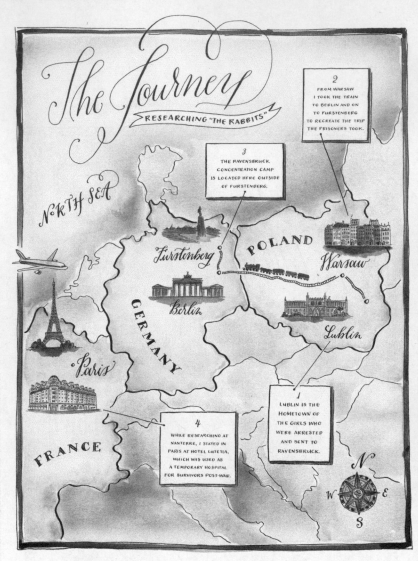

The author's journey

Questions and Topics
for Discussion

1. In what ways do you think the alternating points of view help to enrich the narrative? Was there ever a time you when you wished there was only one narrator? Why or why not?

2. The primary settings of this novel are starkly different—Caroline's glamorous New York world of benefits and cultural events, and the bleak reality of life in a concentration camp. In what ways did the contrast between these two settings affect your reading experience?

3. Caroline's relationship with Paul is complicated, taboo even. Was there ever a time when you didn't agree with a choice Caroline makes with regards to Paul? When and why?

4. As Caroline becomes more and more invested in her work with the French Families Fund, and eventually with the Rabbits, did you feel that she changes in any way? If so, how were those changes apparent through her interactions with others?

5. Throughout their time in Ravensbrück, Kasia and the other prisoners find subtle, and not so subtle, ways to demonstrate their resistance. Discuss the variety of actions they take. Which of them did you find to be most powerful? Most moving? Most effective?

6. When Kasia learns that they were hunting Rabbits, she thinks, "Just don't feel anything. If you are to live, you cannot feel." Do you agree with this statement? What do you think it says about the nature of survival? Is it relevant to any other characters in the book, not just the prisoners?

7. Did you find Herta to be a sympathetic character? Why or why not?

8. When Vilmer Hartman comes to visit Ravensbrück, he shows concern for Herta's mental state. What do you think this reveals about her character? Had you previously thought about any of the points he makes?

9. Though the Nazis made sure the German people only got their news from one media point of view, Herta's father continues to read as many newspapers as he can. How does this relate to media usage today?

10. Did you feel that Halina's ring is an important symbol in the book? How does Herta feel about the ring? Why does she keep it?

11. Throughout the novel, in and out of Ravensbrück, the characters experience harrowing, difficult situations. Is there one that you found more memorable than the others? Why do you think the author chose to include it?

12. If you had to come up with a single message or lesson to represent each of the main characters' experiences—Caroline's, Kasia's, and Herta's—what would it be and why?

13. Many of the themes explored in *Lilac Girls*—human rights, political resistance, survival—are a direct result of the historical World War II setting. How are those themes relevant to current events today?

14. *Lilac Girls* also touches on a number of interpersonal themes, including female friendship, mother-daughter relationships, love, infidelity, mental health, and more. How do these themes impact the characters' lives?

15. What do you think the author hoped her readers would take away from this reading experience?